LIMINALITY

LIMINALITY

THE ANCIENT ONES TRILOGY
BOOK II

CASSANDRA L. THOMPSON

QUILL & CROW PUBLISHING HOUSE

CLEVELAND

LIMINALITY BY CASSANDRA L. THOMPSON.
BOOK TWO OF THE ANCIENT ONES TRILOGY.
PUBLISHED BY QUILL & CROW PUBLISHING HOUSE.

Cover Design by Lauren Hellekson

Printed in the United States of America.

Cataloging-in-Publication Data is on file with the Library of Congress.

ISBN 978-1-7371049-5-7
ISBN 978-1-7371049-4-0 (ebook)

Author's Website: http://cassandralthompson.carrd.co

For

L.

FOREWORD

The Ancient Ones is a story twenty years in the making. From the initial idea at fifteen, to the moment I got the courage to finish it in my thirties, the entire process has been an incredible journey. I knew in the back of my mind, I wouldn't be able to stop with just one book, and no sooner did I finish The Ancient Ones and sent it for editing, did Lucius creep back into my mind.

I was driving through the Cleveland Metroparks, listening to Tool's new album, when I got a vision of him and Morrigan in the Underworld. I realized I'd only written a small piece of an epic story. There was an entirely different perspective that needed to be heard. I suppose you can guess whose perspective that is.

Within one year, Book Two and Three were finished, and I am so excited to give readers a completed trilogy that is exactly the type of story I have always wanted to read. I hope that if you were a fan of Book One, that Liminality will not disappoint. We begin the story right at the point where we left off, but in case you need a quick reminder, allow me to assist.

Book One tells the story of an ancient immortal named David, the last of his kind, who is in the midst of an existential crisis. The year is 1857 and David has just bought an old abandoned house called Lardone Manor, once a countryside cathedral. After a particularly long depressive slump, he heads to his favorite Limehouse pub where he meets a brash, unapologetic lady of the night who is dying of consumption. After taking him along for a taste of her self-destruction, she convinces him to tell her his story.

David reveals he was born in Ancient Gaul, the son of a Druid Elder. Julius Caesar invades their tribe, kidnapping him to be sold as a slave. On the harrowing passage home, he is comforted by a mysterious woman who protects him from harm. After a particularly gruesome arrival at the

Roman Port, he realizes she is The Morrigan, a Celtic war goddess who has decided to look after him. In the Roman forum, he finds a young slave girl named Gaia who takes him under her wing and into the forced employ of a winemaker named Eridus. She gives him his Roman name, Davius.

Eventually, Davius falls in love with her, convinced that one day he will earn enough money from his paintings to buy their freedom and get married. But strange things start to occur, including nightmares of a hideous, bloodthirsty dragon. Eventually, he meets a strange man named Lucius, who seems to be a world traveling philosopher. He hires Davius to paint for him and the two become fast friends. He is warned by the apparition of a boar that he should steer clear of Lucius, that he is not all he seems.

Davius learns Eridus wants to marry Gaia and panics. He looks to his new friend for help and finds out he is a reincarnated dark god, brought to the earth flawed, therefore becoming the world's first immortal blood drinker. Lucius wants Davius to join him, but Davius flees in terror. He returns to the villa to learn Eridus knows he's been sleeping with Gaia. He sells her off to an abusive slaveowner named Nirus and beats Davius half to death.

Davius wakes up to discover Lucius has rescued him and killed Eridus. Lucius encourages him to use his inherent Druidic power to rescue Gaia. Davius realizes he has command of the wind—he can create windstorms and channel its energy. Unfortunately, Gaia dies and Davius vows to avenge her death. He decides to become a creature like Lucius to do so.

Five years later, in Ancient Greece, the boar that once warned him returns, revealing that he is a liminal being named Libraean. He reveals more about Lucius's past, including the fact that Gaia was pregnant with Davius's child at the time of her death. Davius decides it's time to avenge her death. He decides to summon the Morrigan for help, unknowingly igniting a war between him and Lucius for her attention. She says she will help, but only if they make her one of them. Lucius doesn't think it will work, but Davius insists it will.

Davius is approached by a strange council of creatures who tell him they want him to bring back Morrigan. He meets Anubis, and they fill him with power to help him. Davius succeeds in killing Nirus and brings Morrigan to life. The problem is, she decided Nirus's wicked daughter, Delicia, would be her vessel and instead of taking her over, the two souls braid together, making her half-Delicia, half-Morrigan to become an entity called Morgana.

Jump to 15th century Wallachia. Davius (now called David) lives with

Lucius and Morgana in a Romanian castle. Lucius has stolen the identity of the Wallachian prince, Vladimir Dracula, and presides over a court of self-created *nemorti* and revenants. Tension is at an all-time high: David and Lucius are at odds, compounded by Morgana slowly losing her grip on reality and bouncing back between Delicia and the Morrigan. Delicia seems content with Lucius as her lover, but Morrigan and David have a special connection that neither one of them quite understands. She begs Lucius and David to kill her so she can be a free goddess once more, but neither one of them are willing—they love her too much.

At a feast, Lucius brings in a prisoner for entertainment, who turns out to be a hideous lycanthrope. He terrorizes the entire court, forcing David to take Morgana's blood so he can shapeshift into a wolf and stop him. Her dying wish is for him to follow the wolf to a witch named Hekate. He obeys, discovering a group of otherworldly beings called the Council (the creatures from before), who inform him they are responsible for all magical workings in the world and they need his help to stop Lucius, who is upsetting the balance on earth. He meets Dragos, one half of a pair of healer twins, and he discovers the true identity of the beast, a reincarnated Viking god who goes by the name of Danulf. He learns there is an Insurgence rising up against Lucius made of human subjects and escaped nemorti.

Eventually, Lucius's knights catch up with David and Danulf in the Carpathian Mountains as they travel to find Hekate. Lucius ties him up outside to die in the sun, but Danulf saves him at the last moment, and delivers him to Hekate, a pregnant healer/witch who holds the secrets to his past.

As she heals his wounds, she reveals that all of them—Lucius, David, Morrigan—were once part of a quartet of Egyptian gods who existed at the beginning of time, reincarnated on earth with no memories of their past lives. She reveals that Lucius and Morrigan were once husband and wife (named Set and Nephthys), but David (Osiris) slept with Morrigan, impregnating her with his sons (gods Anubis and Horus). Morrigan flees, letting her sister, Isis, raise her sons as her own in order to protect them from Set. He still manages to find out, and murders Osiris.

The sisters, Isis and Nephthys, decide to bring back Osiris from the dead. Anubis and Horus, now grown adults, assist, knowing they have to use Set's blood to revive him. The plan fails—Horus kills Set, but not before Set plucks out Horus's eye, therefore cursing his reincarnation, and

Osiris comes back wrong, biting Nephthys's neck and forcing Isis to stab him in the heart.

Nephthys and Osiris (Morrigan and David) go to the Upperrealms (heaven), Set (Lucius) is banished to Tartarus (hell) with Anubis guarding him. Isis frees her soul and puts her body and magic in an acadia tree. Horus reincarnates as Libraean.

With this new knowledge, David is ready to end Lucius for good, and freely joins the Insurgence. Anubis and Libraean contact him beforehand and Librean gives him the last bit of power so David is strong enough to defeat him. After a brutal war, which includes the deaths of Dragos, Hekate, and Danulf, and one last embrace with Morrigan in spirit form, David evokes the power of all the elements and slays Lucius, who had become the horrible creature from his dreams.

Throughout the story, David and his companion (the prostitute from the tavern) arrive and talk at Lardone Manor, but towards the end, David learns her death is coming quickly. She still wants to hear his story, and after he finishes, he is content to hold her in his arms until she passes. At the last moment, and with the help of some very ornery crows, he realizes she is the Morrigan incarnated. He runs to find Libraean, who has also been alive this whole time, living in the secret vaults underneath his cemetery. Libraean turns her into a blood drinker and they happily reunite...until there is a knock at the door. It is Danulf, surprisingly still alive, come to tell them Lucius has returned.

Hope you enjoy Book II of The Ancient Ones Trilogy, Liminality.

Dreadfully Yours,

Cassandra L. Thompson

FOR AS LONG AS HE REMEMBERED, he hated the little boy. He observed him quietly from afar, dressed in rags, grime perpetually smeared across his face, dirt trapped underneath his fingernails. He watched the boy neglect the endless array of alluring books his tutor presented each week, scowled at his untouched piano in the corner, and salivated over the painstakingly prepared lunches brought each afternoon on a silver plate. Although the boy's parents were never around, he had a full staff under his command and control, and oh, how he hated him for it.

His keeper scolded him, pulling his ear and clicking her tongue, reminding him that he was an orphan whose survival depended upon the good graces of the de Sadet family, and that hating their only son would not do him one bit of good.

So, he became clever. He hid himself so well that none of the other servants saw him as he studied the boy's every detail. He noted the way he crossed his legs, the way he grasped his quill, his languid drawl when forced to recite Latin. He learned all his lessons in secret, taking notes with bits of salvaged ink and the parchment he'd hidden behind the wall.

He kept his muscles still even as he watched the boy beat the family hounds into submission, letting his self-produced seed spill onto their wounds as they cowered beneath him. When the boy became a young man and turned that same whip on the servant girls, he forced his own hand over his mouth, lest he scream out when the terrible boy relieved himself on the poor girls as they cried.

He continued to watch until the moment the shy, raven-haired piano teacher arrived to teach him. She was older than the Marquis's son, but he looked at her in the same lustful fashion as the others he'd abused. The servant boy tried to remain detached like before, but she had been kind to him when she noticed him lurking in the shadows, ignoring his shabby clothes and rustled hair. They quickly became friends, sharing lunch together while the rest of the staff was preoccupied. She complimented his peculiar eyes, and he impressed her with his ability to recite the works of Plato and name the constellations. He looked forward to her company, a beacon of light in an existence hidden by shadow.

He continued to watch until the moment he witnessed her attack, two days after the Marquis's son turned thirteen. It happened during a lesson when she accidentally brushed up against him, causing his fleshy face to turn red with excitement. He threw the sheet music to the floor before grabbing her, twisting her arms behind her waist as he had done to the others. The servant boy silently withdrew from his hiding space between the two walls and pounced, moving so fast that not a sound was heard as he wrapped piano wire around the Marquis's son's throat, choking him until he grew limp and fell to the marble floor like a sack of potatoes.

He feared her reaction as he caught his breath, but the piano teacher merely beamed. She surprised him further by assuring him that if he would drag the body to her room, she would take care of the rest. Though his heart hammered in his chest, shocked at what he had done, he trusted her, calmed by her words and demeanor.

He looked down at the bloated, purple-faced body and knelt, gently removing its powdered wig and slipping it over his own unruly black curls. He struck a pose for the piano teacher, presenting the perfect imitation of the Marquis's son.

She lit up as she realized his intentions, offering him a playful curtsy in response. They met each other's eyes, coming to a silent agreement before he dragged the asphyxiated corpse out of the parlor while she trailed behind. From that moment on, he was no longer the servant boy hiding in the shadows, longing for greatness—he was the wealthy son of a Marquis and heir to a small fortune. She would make sure it was so.

He was only nine years old.

PART ONE

IN VARGR, IN MANI
WOLF, MOON

CHAPTER ONE

🕸 The Visitor 🕸

London, 1857
David

DAVID STARED MOUTH AGAPE AT THE MAN IN HIS DOORWAY dripping rainwater onto his floor.

"My word," Libraean murmured from behind him. "It's you."

Danulf attempted a close-lipped smile as he nervously fiddled with his hat.

"If this night reveals one more shock, I think I might finally keel over," Libraean whispered to David. He lacked his usual cap, his graying hair in disarray around the blunted horns that interrupted his hairline.

"My sentiments exactly," David agreed.

Libraean placed a hand on his shoulder. "I am headed to the vaults to fetch her some of the leftover pig's blood in my pantry. She still appears calm, but I remember the thirst of the newly transformed and I don't think we should depend on her placidity for too much longer."

David nodded, patting his hand in appreciation before the creature slipped through the doorway into the night. David turned his attention back to Dan, resuming his astoundment. "I thought you were dead—I knew it, actually. I folded your arms over your silent heart."

"Perhaps our guest would appreciate the warmth of a fire in your parlor?" Old Man Jacob appeared behind them. He'd changed out of his robe and into a formal housecoat, his snow-white hair slicked back from his large forehead, accentuating the thickness of his eyebrows. He moved quickly to lift the dampened cloak from a surprised but compliant Dan, draping it on the nearby coat rack.

"I don't think he minds the cold," David hinted.

Jacob's light eyes widened with understanding. "Are all of you vampyres, sir?"

"Let us move to the parlor." David gestured Danulf fully into his foyer, pulling the door shut behind him with an echoing clang.

Dan's eyes swept the manor as he followed Jacob, beholding the vaulted ceilings and the twin staircases that crawled up dark papered walls holding dusty black sconces. A few chandeliers glittered in the dim light, the dreary storm outside preventing the illumination that normally radiated through the stained-glass windows above. The house was drenched in shades of burgundy and ornaments of darkly stained wood, which would have given the house a stately facade had they not faded with time.

Jacob entered the parlor first to prepare a fire, regardless of the vampyre presence. The fireplace attempted to dwarf the room, a substantial structure that held its own next to the ornate furniture upholstered in silk, the crimson walls and rugs, and the ostentatious grand piano that sat, unused, in the farthest corner.

The building light offered David the opportunity to observe Dan as he sat awkwardly on the sofa, his oversized legs crossed in front of him. His movements were more graceful than David remembered, despite his bulky frame, his suit made from French silk and tailored to fit his unusual size. His current nervousness was peculiar to David, an expression he would have never attributed to the bold heathen from his memory.

"Shall I bring you...I'm not sure exactly what I should retrieve, sir," Jacob stumbled, his furrowed eyebrows betraying his perplexity.

"It's quite alright, Jacob. I'd much rather you attend to our guest upstairs. Once things begin to settle, we can discuss the terms of your employment here."

"Oh no, sir," Jacob flustered. "I'm perfectly content to remain your manservant. We do not have to adjust a thing. I will look in on the lady and leave you gentlemen in peace. Please call if you need anything." He gave a curt bow, his professionalism unaltered by the recent turn of events. As he left, David noticed he'd put on his best shoes.

The parlor was left quiet in his departure, the only sound in the room the crackles and pops of the growing fire as it gradually consumed the fresh logs. The two immortals sat across from each other in silent, mutual observation.

Danulf managed to maintain the feral prowess he once had in his eyes, their deep blue intensifying the longer he stared at David. His skin had somehow managed to grow tan and his silvery hair was free of its former ratted braids, leaving behind thick, wiry strands that swept freely across his forehead and down below his ears. Both his mustache and beard were kept low, the bulk of his tattoos concealed behind his high collar and cravat, the rich blue and grey silks of his suit boasting refinery and high class.

The observation reminded David he'd not yet changed out of the waistcoat and trousers of his own three-piece suit, which he had been wearing for several days now. He smoothed his wrinkled pants awkwardly as he finally broke the silence. "You look so different."

Dan laughed, revealing a flash of gold and silver crowns, the one thing David remembered of him that hadn't changed. "I've had to blend in for survival purposes, but rest assured, I can still behead a man with my bare hands if need be."

David chuckled, delighted the tension melted away. "I cannot believe you are still alive."

His expression turned grim. "Much has transpired since that day. Simply put, what you saw on the battlefield was real, but somehow, Dragos and I were brought back to life shortly after."

"How?"

"I'm not exactly certain," Dan admitted. "I ran into him many years later, after being trapped in my wolf state for nearly just as long."

David leaned back in his chair. "I had no idea."

"I did attempt to seek you out after my time as a mindless beast scouring the Carpathian Mountains, but there were other things distracting me." Dan's voice lowered, taking on a hint of regret. "But that is a story for another evening. I'm here to take you back with me to France, where I believe Lucius is hiding."

"You plan to leave?" A soft voice interjected from the hallway.

David turned to see his lover in the doorway, radiant with her newly endowed immortal life. The sickly lady of the night he'd met days ago had been transformed by Libraean's blood, her body the perfect home for his beloved Morrigan. She stood taller than most women, reaching just under David's nose when they embraced, lithe underneath a fresh nightgown Jacob must have found her. Her raven hair spilled down her shoulders, shocking against her pale, angular face, as it simultaneously highlighted Morrigan's azure eyes. It took everything for him to remain seated, overwhelmed by the desire to scoop her into his arms.

"This is your lover," Dan stated, rather than asked.

"Oh yes, forgive me, I'd forgotten that you never met. Danulf, this is... well, we've discovered she is the Morrigan reincarnated, but I failed to learn her mortal name." David looked at her sheepishly.

"My given name was Liliana, though I suppose it doesn't matter now."

"We have had a rather tumultuous evening," David attempted to explain.

"As much as I would love to catch up, it's urgent that we leave for France," Dan pressed.

David frowned. "How do you know that he has returned?"

Morrigan drifted towards the loveseat where David sat, settling herself next to him. The faintest hint of cedarwood wafted from her hair. "Who has returned?"

"Lucius has found his way back to Earth," David told her as he took her hand.

Morrigan did not appear surprised. On the contrary, she looked thoughtful, calmly gazing out the window before snapping her eyes back towards Dan. "Is that why I have returned?"

"All I know is that Lucius arrived on this earth in mortal form in seventeen forty to a family of aristocrats, only to be raised later by Dragos and a vampyress who calls herself Angelique. Around seventeen seventy-six, he discovered a way to switch bodies with King Louis XVI, up until the Revolution when he abandoned the ruse. He has been in hiding ever since. He is, as you may have guessed, immortal once again."

"He's been masquerading as the bloody King of France, and I haven't known?" David cried out, unable to hold back his bewilderment. "Where is the Council? Why is there no communication between creatures? How is he immortal if Libraean and I were the only blood drinkers left, besides you? Are there more of us still?"

Morrigan squeezed his hand, calming him.

"Again, I regret being unable to find you until now," Dan restated, his expression genuinely apologetic.

David leaned back in his seat, grateful for Morrigan's presence. He suddenly felt very tired, as if the series of revelations in one evening finally proved to be too much.

"We need to rest," Morrigan asserted, raising her hand as Dan tried to protest. "You have traveled many hours to reach us. I fell asleep last night a dying woman and woke up this morning a blood drinker. Libraean and Gabriel have just discovered each other after eons apart and David has not slept soundly for weeks. We can discuss this all tomorrow, refreshed."

Remarkably, Dan did not argue.

Old Man Jacob appeared in the doorway. "Forgive my interruption, sir, but did you arrive by coach?" he asked Danulf.

"I paid a coachman to deliver me here," he replied as he rose to his feet. "My effects are at a hotel in the city."

"We can put you in the southern guest room," Jacob decided. "I'm afraid the main guest room is still unkempt, but there is spare clothing in the south bedroom's wardrobe, as well as house slippers and a shaving sink."

"That would be fine, thank you." Dan nodded.

A thought suddenly occurred to David. "Where is Libraean?" he asked Jacob.

"I'm afraid he still needs time to digest all that has transpired," he explained, a touch of sadness in his voice. "He has locked himself in your study with his books."

"Please tell him that he's staying in the manor tonight. I don't feel comfortable with him alone in the vaults now that I know Lucius is back. Perhaps you should do the same. I admit I'm being overly cautious, but I'd feel better knowing we are all under one roof."

"Yes, sir." Jacob nodded. "I only need to grab a few things from my residence after I've gotten everyone settled."

"Please, Gabriel, call me David."

"Only if you continue to call me Jacob. I have not been in my other form for many years, and I've grown quite used to my human name."

"Agreed."

"I will tell him, Mr. David," Jacob said, still unwilling to drop formalities, oblivious to David's subsequent sigh. "And the lady?"

David flustered, unsure of how to respond. He attempted to answer the question and recover from his embarrassment while he tried to ignore Dan's amused expression.

"I will stay in the master bedroom," Morrigan spoke up, relieving him of his awkwardness.

"Very well," Jacob nodded. "I'll leave you two in peace, and I will show Mr…?"

"Daniel. But you can call me Dan."

"I will show Mr. Daniel to his room, then deliver Libraean the news," Jacob declared, motioning for Dan to follow him. The two men disappeared into the shadows, Dan's considerable frame towering over the short statured man as he led him down the hall.

David was alone with Morrigan at last, a sensation of relief settling across his shoulders. He faced her, taking her hands in his. "Are you feeling alright?" he asked her, gently. "Do you need blood?"

"Strangely, I feel quite sated with the animal blood Libraean brought me," she replied. "I remember you describing an insatiable thirst when one turns, but I do not seem to be suffering from it."

"It may be because he was the one to turn you," David speculated aloud. "He seems to be another sort of creature altogether, one driven more by compassion than destruction."

"In any case, I only need rest and perhaps some proper clothing in the near future." She drew his attention to her nightgown.

"I will go into town for you tomorrow," he assured her.

"Lovely." She smiled, the warmth lighting up her eyes. He barely recognized the sickly woman he'd brought home from the Eastern Tavern days before, her cheeks now flushed with radiance, her lips ripe and plump like raspberries. Save for her ghostly pale skin, Libraean's blood had improved her physicality, rather than leaving her with the sickly presentation common in the immortal.

"Are you going to show me to your room?" she asked.

Again, David was struck with an odd sort of nervousness. He'd gone from being completely alone to having a house full of creatures, he hadn't changed his clothing for days, he wasn't sure what state he'd left his bedroom, and he certainly hadn't anticipated being reunited with his aeonian inamorata. He pushed the trepidation aside, retrieving a solitary candle holder and gesturing for her to follow him. He led her up the west wing steps to the second floor, where the stained-glass windows were the most brilliant in the daytime. In the darkness, they seemed more eerie than majestic as the gruesome scenes of Jesus Christ's crucifixion picked up the flickering candlelight from his meager flame.

They traveled down a long, scantily lit corridor, dusted with cobwebs, to the end, where a door opened to a suite of rooms. Contained within the spacious master bedroom was a barely used four poster bed, mahogany desk, and a couch and loveseat arrangement around a cold, empty fireplace. An annexed room served as a private bathing area. Russet browns and evergreens furnished its entirety, dark emerald wallpaper crawling up the sides to greet stained wood ceilings etched into designs. He was grateful Jacob had ensured the room's cleanliness in his absence, the typical coat of dust that covered his furnishings removed. He'd even made up the bed with clean linens and wool blankets.

"It's lovely," Morrigan assured him, noticing his worried expression.

"I just cannot believe you are really here," David admitted. "I honestly don't know what to do."

She approached him, gently removing his grip from the candleholder and setting it on a nearby table. Then she kissed him, the aroma of fallen leaves and bonfires assaulting his senses, the familiarity of her taste rendering him lightheaded. He forced his legs to stay firmly planted as he wrapped his arms around her waist, enjoying the conflicting sensations of kissing a soul he knew and caressing a body he didn't. "Quite a different body than I remember," he murmured through kisses.

She laughed and mischievously placed his hands on her upper curves. "It suits me, though I'm not sure I shall ever get used to these."

His body responded with immediate desire. "As much as it pains me to let go of you," he said as he pulled away, his voice shaking, "I must insist on taking a bath. These past few hours have me feeling as though I've been hurdled through a windstorm."

"Speaking of such, it seems you have maintained your powers," Morrigan remarked, gesturing out the window where the storm was now tossing the trees.

"Amazing," he remarked, beholding the tempest building outside. "I have not used them in centuries."

She slipped her hand into his. "A bath might do us both well," she purred, pulling his attention back to her.

David wasted no time in preparing it, grateful temperature was not of importance to either of them, the cool water kept in jugs against the bathroom wall sufficient to fill the large porcelain tub. He lost time in her embrace, floating in and out of consciousness as they explored each other's bodies for the first time, moving from bath, to bed, to floor, to couch, to bath again. He felt immersed in an impossible dream. For so long he had pined for her, aching to be reunited, to look into her eyes and feel the softness of her skin. It was as if time no longer had meaning, measured only in the moments of breath he took in between kissing her.

At some point, his eyes had finally closed, then drifted open to behold her asleep next to him, her creamy white skin glowing in the beams of moonlight that streamed through the window. Moist, cool air drifted through the room, threatening to extinguish the dwindled fire. The storm had ended, finally satisfied.

He pulled her body closer to his as he put together his thoughts, his befuddled mind clear at last. Dan was alive and Lucius had returned. He wondered if Anubis had been deceived by him again. But how could he have achieved such a feat without the aid of Isis and her magic? When he rose to Earth the first time, becoming the immortal blood drinker Lucius, it was because of her power. Since that time, her soul had long been fragmented, the bulk of her magic taken by Morrigan when she abandoned them in Romania, returning her soul to the astral plane. How had Lucius managed to come back to earth?

David realized he'd spun his mind beyond the point of additional rest. He gently rolled Morrigan back on her side, draping one of the blankets over her before slipping out from underneath them. He found his housecoat and slippers, fumbling around the messy room for a cigarette and a match. He retrieved them both and used the tiny flame to illuminate the lamp he kept at his bedside. It immediately bathed the room in muted beige light.

The halls of the manor were quiet, its visitors appearing to be asleep. His footsteps, though soft, seemed to echo as he walked, contorted shadows following him along the walls. He'd only met the Lardone ghosts a few times since he moved into the manor, the frail daughter who died from scarlet fever and the son who'd fallen from the third floor balcony in a drunken stupor. He knew there were more lurking about, but they kept to themselves, and he wondered how they were taking the sudden influx of visitors into their home.

His eyes caught a sliver of light beneath the door of his study and he moved closer, entering to witness Libraean seated at his desk, surrounded by an alarming array of books and manuscripts piled high around him. He didn't notice David enter, continuing to rapidly scratch his quill against the paper with feverish concentration.

"Trouble sleeping?" David interrupted softly.

Libraean peered up over his glasses, the folds around his eyes pronounced with stress. He threw them off to rub his eyes. "I cannot believe any of this is really happening."

David sat down across from him, gingerly placing his lamp on the only clean spot on the desk, hoping the oil wouldn't upset any parchment. "I know what you mean," he sighed.

"Let alone Gabriel slumbering underneath the same roof as ours. Gabriel, of all creatures!"

"Did you have a chance to speak with him?" David asked him carefully. The look of surprise on Libraean's face after discovering that David's manservant was a reincarnation of his estranged former lover was enough to provoke David into approaching the topic lightly.

"Not more than a few words," Libraean replied, the tone of his voice revealing his continued hostility towards Gabriel. "I smell his humanity when he is near, and it makes it difficult for me to think clearly. I feel I'm going mad, actually, which is why I've decided to isolate and catch up on the work that soothes me."

David frowned, immediately concerned. "You are craving blood, Libraean. You haven't had the human variety for many years, but you awoke the craving when you turned Morrigan. We should go hunting."

"For humans?" Libraean was horrified.

"Well, I was referring to game, but there are humans who willingly give their blood near the end of their lives, alleviating us of any wrongdoing. I have indulged myself in such situations once or twice since we moved to London. Or, as you told me many years ago, we can sample human blood without having to kill them."

"I cannot do as you do, David. I am trying to right my wrongs, not indulge in loopholes...though I suppose that really doesn't matter now." He looked wistfully out of the darkened windowpanes before resuming his furious scribbling.

David slapped his hand down on the desk. "Libraean, you need to eat."

"Am I interrupting?" Dan's towering frame appeared in the doorway, observing their interaction with lifted eyebrows.

"Hello." David straightened his crouched position. "Are you unable to sleep as well?"

"My body would love nothing more, yet my mind will not allow it," Dan agreed. He'd donned a simple housecoat over a set of silken pajamas, the inadequate hem of his pants rising high above his shoes. It seemed the guest slippers were too small for him to even bother. Regardless, however mismatched his appearance, it did little to rob him of his intimidating presence.

"Please, come in," Libraean offered. "I must warn you, though, I am going to have real difficulty holding in all the questions I'm desperate to ask you. Especially with my books out."

Dan gave a chuckle. "I understand. I overheard someone talking about hunting. Perhaps we could have a meal before we converse? I have not fed much myself, being preoccupied with my arrival."

Libraean flinched. "I do not eat humans," he maintained.

"I have not had an English fox in quite some time." Dan shrugged.

"Should I wake Morrigan?" David wondered aloud, as he rose from his chair.

"It might be best to let her rest," Libraean suggested mildly, packing up his desk and securing the top of his ink bottle. "In fact, let's not tell Gabriel we are leaving either."

"That might be difficult if we leave out the front door," Dan pointed out.

"Oh, that shouldn't be a problem," Libraean nodded towards the elongated windows of the study, opened to the cool breeze.

David smiled at Dan. "When is the last time you've flown?"

Crisp and biting cold, the wind served as a reminder that winter approached. The late autumn woods had proven quite the hunter's arena as Dan unintentionally reminded David of the vicious creature he was, taking down two full grown bucks and an aged bear, which he promptly shared with a very pale, but still very hungry, Libraean. Although David's thoughts centered around Morrigan more than hunting, he found and enjoyed a red fox, the meal proving good for them all. They strolled back towards the manor in good spirits, and for a moment, David forgot the impending doom of Lucius's return.

They reached the manor gates and headed up the cobblestone drive to find Jacob at the front steps, dressed in his riding cloak and hat, and wringing his hands. It was hard for David to see him any differently than the wizened gentleman he'd discovered at the Agency, whom his coworkers had jokingly referred to as "Old Man," yet Libraean remembered the archangel inside and continued to grow tense each time he was around.

"Jacob, what is it?" David asked, concerned by his trepidation.

Jacob pulled off his hat, leaving his thick white hair unkempt. "She has disappeared, sir," he said anxiously. "I searched all over the house, but it appears she left shortly after you did, under my notice."

David's chest seized up in alarm. He had just found her—how could he have let her slip out of his grasp?

"Don't worry, we will find her," Dan assured him, noticing his expression and placing a sizable hand on his shoulder. "We would do best to split up. There are only a few hours left before sunrise."

"I will help," Libraean offered, fresh color in his weathered face.

The galloping of a horse rudely interrupted their plans, its hooves thundering down the narrow dirt path that led up to the manor. It came in through the gate, left carelessly ajar, and as it drew closer, David was surprised to recognize one of his own mares. The rider brought the horse to a halt and slipped easily from astride it, revealing with a swish of black skirts that, although dressed in a man's riding cloak, she was, in fact, a woman. She pulled off a man's riding cap to reveal coils of recently shorn, ebony hair that sprang up immediately once it was released.

"Morrigan," David exhaled in relief.

Beneath the billowing black cloak, she wore mismatched mourning clothes, black skirts hanging loose about her long legs without a cage to flare them, her high collared black shirt opened low and cinched together with a black corset. Black heeled boots peeked out as she walked forward.

"I would like you all to join me in the parlor," she said immediately, "and I should hope not to hear one word regarding my excursion, as I wasn't invited to partake in the boys-only hunting trip." She strode past them, but her mood was more playful than genuinely upset.

"Well, at least she's returned safe," Jacob said mildly, following her through the front door.

Gratitude washed over David, grateful that she had simply gone into town and back, and grateful she was showing glimpses of the goddess he'd once known and loved.

He looked back at Dan, noticing that a shadow of grief had passed over him. "She reminds me of someone I once knew," he explained with a forced smile, heading inside.

Jacob had already ensured all the curtains were drawn in anticipation of approaching daylight and was now hanging up the cloaks being removed all around him. Libraean instinctively moved forward to assist, then caught himself, faltering as Jacob noticed the slight and turned towards him, lifting the folded jacket from his arm with a shy smile.

"I would like you both to join us," David requested as he observed their interaction.

"Shall I grab tea?" Jacob asked, forgetting once more whose company he was in.

"We will need something a bit stronger if she wants to discuss what I think she does," Dan suggested over his shoulder as he headed into the room.

"Ah, yes, you all drink...yes," Jacob nodded. "I will grab tainted brandy."

Libraean sighed as he watched him disappear down the hall. "He does not wish to stop playing manservant, I see."

"Give him time," David said. "He is the only human among us and quite a lot has transpired since the night before last. I believe continuing his normal routine is comforting to him."

"Perhaps you're right," he sniffed. "It's none of my business, anyway."

The two entered the parlor to observe Morrigan draped across the loveseat in front of the fire, the seat she preferred when David first brought her home. Her arm was stretched along the back, one leg curled under her as she studied them all, her eyes settling on Libraean. Her face softened in wonderment. "So, you are my son?"

Libraean startled for a moment before nodding. "Yes, in another life-time... yes."

"My memories have been slowly coming back to me, and your face grows familiar," she explained as she rose to her feet. She approached him, taking both of his hands in hers. "Thank you for saving my life."

Libraean blushed. "There is no need to thank me, madame. I am quite glad you've returned home to David, though we still don't know the reason why. From what I've been told, you did leave quite definitively."

"Let us all sit," she suggested.

The group settled around the parlor, Morrigan resuming her place on the loveseat. Jacob returned with a few bottles of blood-infused brandy and drinking glasses on a tray, which he set on the low table near the couches. David motioned for him to sit.

Morrigan waited until all was still before she spoke. "As I mentioned, memories have been floating back to me in gradual pieces. From what I can recall, which was confirmed when David told me his story, I took Hekate's power with me to the Underworld after she died. That would explain the abilities I had as a mortal, being able to hear thoughts when I focused or watching my emotions pull rain from the sky." Her eyes found the window. "I can remember when I left earth the last time, jumping from the towers of our Wallachian castle to certain death, yet I cannot seem to recall what happened from that point until my mortal birth. I need to know why I've returned, when I swore to those I cared for most that I never would." Her eyes swept across the room to meet Dan's. "Maybe you can offer some assistance in these matters."

"Yes," David agreed, though her words pulled at his stomach. A part of him hoped she'd returned for him. "How is Lucius back on earth? We have not had any communication from the Otherworlds for centuries. Libraean and I were convinced we were the only two creatures left."

"That is because the Council and most of the gods are dead," Dan sighed.

"Wait," Libraean interrupted before anyone could react. He flew from the room, returning with an armful of books, parchment, quills, and several ink bottles. He dropped them all onto the neglected grand piano in the corner, sending up a cloud of dust. He pulled up a table and chair and fumbled about his supplies, setting up an impromptu writing station that he swiftly sat behind. He adjusted his glasses, smoothing out the paper before him, and dipping the quill in the ink. He stared at Dan above his frames. "Continue."

Dan cleared his throat, uncrossing his legs so he could help himself to David's box of cigarettes. The smoke from its freshly lit paper wound through the air as all eyes rested on him. "I suppose I should explain how I survived the Night War."

"No," Morrigan interrupted him with a wave of her hand. "Some of us have no idea who you are. Start from the beginning."

Dan raised his eyebrows, clearing his throat once more. "Well, then, I will start from the beginning."

CHAPTER TWO

ꕤ The History of Lycanthropy ꕤ

Scandinavian Territories, 793
Dan

H E WAS STILL YOUNG WHEN HIS FATHER RETURNED HOME, the age when a boy realizes he's no longer a child, but far from a man. He was a decent seaman and excelled in combat—more so than his mother preferred—but he was too young to be included in the raids, long voyages where groups of men would explore faraway lands to pillage for gold. He counted the days until they returned, hoping this would be the last voyage he'd witness waiting on shore.

He remembered watching the ship materialize out of the fog on an unusually cool midsummer morning. He'd shaken his younger brother awake when he heard the arrival horns, the two of them racing to the harbor barefoot and still in their bedclothes.

The raiders exuded joviality, regardless of the exhausting voyage, and his father all but leapt from the ship when he saw his sons. "I have brought you gold from faraway lands!" he exclaimed, beaming with pride as he squeezed them tight. His clothes and furs stank, coated with grime, dried blood, and sea air, but they burrowed into his chest unaffected, grateful their father had made it home.

The following evening was alive with celebration, the entire village roaring with bonfires and drenched in mead as the raiders regaled their clan with wild tales of marauding. Children ran about gaily, well past the point of slumber, wolves adding to the frenzy as they begged for scraps from the fresh slaughter. One trotted up to him, settling itself across his feet like it did for no other, allowing him to scratch between its ears.

"Ulfson." His father appeared from behind him. "Why are you not running along with your brothers and sisters?"

Annoyed that his scratching had been interrupted, the wolf sulked as it slipped away. Dan frowned. "I should be sitting with the men."

His father smiled, a twinkle in his eye. "Ah, yes. Next summer, you might be." His breath was sweet with mead.

"Not if I have a say in it," his mother negated, sneaking up beside them. She wore her best jewelry, her long blonde hair, dusted with gray, in loose braids atop her head. "Ulfson will marry first and start a family before he joins you on your voyages. He needs to learn how to be a proper man before he sets sail."

"Bah!" his father said good naturedly, taking a swig of his mead.

"Look, someone has her eye on him already," she teased, her eyes flicking towards the back of the gathering hall. She pulled his father away before he could protest, as Dan's eyes caught the woman his mother referred to.

He knew her, but he hadn't seen her since childhood, and it seemed that she'd gained a womanly shape overnight. Her light blue eyes danced as she caught his, a cascade of light blonde hair spilling down her back.

"Nanna," he whispered. His mouth had gone dry upon sight of her, and he hurried to moisten it with mead.

She approached him with a smile. "Your wolf ran off."

"The wolves belong to no one," he said, then immediately wished he hadn't, his voice a bit gruffer than he had intended.

Fortunately, she did not seem bothered by his retort. "I like to believe they are yours. You are the only one amongst the men who they listen to. You have been given the perfect name, son of wolves."

Dan hoped the firelight dancing around them did not reveal his reddening cheeks.

The low music that had been playing around them suddenly escalated in tempo and she brightened. "Will you dance with me?"

His cup and its contents sloshed to the floor as she pulled him forward, adding them to the throng of convivial bodies who now hopped and twirled around the banquet hall. Upended tables smashed to the ground, sending dishes flying, as grown men threw themselves around in uninhibited displays of mirth and merriment. He lost himself to her that night, the gods sealing their fate as they swirled happily around their brethren.

They wed on the shore at Yuletide, snowflakes catching in her icy blonde mane and the red flowers of her crown. She tasted of sweet milk and honey, her skin smooth and soft under his fingertips.

He was grateful to have lost his senses as the wolf tore through them all, but when he awakened to see her pale skin sliced to ribbons, her hair clotted with crimson, it burned an image into his mind that he would never forget. He had retched immediately, staggering backwards and nearly tripping over what lay behind him. With horror, he discovered his entire village lying slaughtered in the fresh snowfall, the nearby waters running red with their blood. He could hear wolves howling mournfully in the distance, but somewhere inside he knew it hadn't been them.

He looked down at his tattered clothes, realizing he, too, was covered in gore, his fingernails ripped and torn, his arms covered in scratches. His mouth carried the sharp taste of blood and bile, bits of wolves' fur still clinging to the pieces of cloth that hung around his trembling body.

He didn't realize he was running until he reached the edge of the cliff, the one the elders had named Dead Man's Jump, a precipice that stretched high above jagged stones jutting menacingly out of the ocean waves. Many an enemy had been tossed off the cliff, and the villagers were well versed in the tales of the ghosts who still lingered nearby.

The wolves' howling grew louder as he closed his eyes, the salty spray of water stinging his open wounds as the sea beckoned to him. He could not remember, but he knew, deep in his bones, it had been he who had killed them all. He had changed somehow, into what he was uncertain, but the way the wolves sang a somber requiem gave him an idea.

He slipped closer to the edge. Forgive me, he begged the gods, hoping for mercy in the afterlife. The shriek of a raven gave him pause. He turned, his eyes wide as he witnessed Odin, the All-Father, standing before him, the weathered skin of his face twisted into a scowl.

"Son, there is work for you here." His mouth did not open to speak, his voice instead echoing in Dan's mind. Wind whipped at his long gray hair, causing it to lash the hollow space where his eye should have been. "Do not end your life with dishonor and turn your soul away from Valhalla. Gods have shaped your bones and warrior blood runs in your veins. You will bring the wolf to heel."

Dan willed away his tears and nodded. He backed away from the cliff's edge, watching as the apparition dissipated with the wind. He sprinted back into the woods, hurtling through the trees, as far away from the corpses of his dead clan as he could muster. He stopped only to vomit when he thought of his family's blood still lingering in his mouth and stomach, imagining the stark terror that must have been in their eyes.

He didn't collapse until daybreak, falling into a cold, dreamless sleep in the frosty brush of the forest floor.

Several days passed before he stumbled upon another village, nestled in the hills near a small stream. He had grown weak with hunger, the allure of fresh food and clean water dragging him forward. He barely made it past the fence that surrounded the closest farm when he collapsed, drawing the attention of a woman who had been gathering water outside.

She brought him into her home, mystified by the extent of his wounds and dehydration, and ordered her two sons to bring her water and bread as she draped him in furs to quell his shivers. Dan was completely at her mercy, letting her care for him as he trembled, his frozen extremities warming themselves painfully back to life. He drifted in and out, nightmares of his mutilated wife and mother plaguing his subconsciousness.

Finally, he awoke in full health to find the woman's home empty. He gingerly raised himself from the sickbed, curious where she and her children had gone. He could hear the echo of voices gathered, wondering what transpired without him.

As soon as he opened the door to greet the setting sun, he was accosted by two full grown men who grabbed his arms and hauled him to the place where he'd heard the commotion. Although Dan was larger than most men, they bore impressive strength, maintaining their grasp as they dragged him into the center of town.

A large crowd had gathered, draped in furs and holding torches that fought the cold. The men pulled him to the forefront where the chief of their tribe stood waiting with an axe. Dan panicked as the realization hit him. He tried to flee, but his head spun, still weak from exposure. His captors shoved him easily to his knees, the chieftain scowling above him. His full beard shook as he spoke. "You, Ulfson of Valok, are hereby sentenced to death for the murder of your clan."

"Please," Dan begged. "I do not remember killing them—it was a wolf that lives in me!"

The mob jeered.

"Believe me!" he cried. "I went to throw myself over our cliffs once I realized what had happened, but All-Father came to me, ordering me to live!"

The crowd chuckled their disbelief. He searched their faces frantically, dismayed there was no kindness to be found, not even in the eyes of the children standing solemnly nearby.

Dan sighed in defeat, watching tiny flecks of snow turn clear as they hit the blade. Perhaps it was what he deserved, the cure to his curse. Odin would understand since it was not by his own hands. Perhaps he would allow him a place to rest in Hel. He ceased fighting against the men who held him, bowing his head to expose the nape of his neck, his ash blonde hair sweeping the ground as visions of his wife's tiny frame danced in his head.

Before the chieftain could strike, a woman pushed forward, preceded by the jangle of bracelets and charms, her hand clasped around a staff carved in symbols. "He tells the truth," she declared.

Murmurs and scoffs rolled through the horde.

"It is true," she said, walking up to the post and laying her hands on him. Her hands were warm with power, the scent of wild herbs caught in her long white hair. "He is a reincarnation of Baldr, the bright one, son of Odin, fused with the horrible soul of Fenrir, the wolf."

The crowd gasped.

The chief frowned as he crossed his arms. "If he has the son of Loki attached to his soul, it is all the more reason why he should die."

"We do not question the gods," she reminded him. "Odin spared his life, we must do the same."

"Then what are we to do?" A woman called out. "He cannot go unpunished for the murder of an entire clan!"

The *Völva* stared at him in quiet contemplation as the snow picked up around them, its frosted fingers twirling her hair. "We will bind him now and when we are finished, he will be labeled *skógarmaðr*, banished to the woods."

The mob gave their approval.

Dan's relief was fleeting, for the two men who held him now pulled his body flat across the wooden plank he was originally forced to kneel upon. They tied both his legs and arms together with rope, holding him firmly in place as the *Völva* moved closer.

"What are you doing?" Dan cried.

He heard the bleating of a calf as it was dragged forward.

"Odin," the *Völva* called as she stretched her arms up to the sky. "Accept our sacrifice as we bind your son from the cruel tricks of Loki—let our mercy bring us your good fortune!"

A man hoisted the calf high above Dan as it squirmed. The *Völva* swiftly unsheathed her knife to slice its throat, releasing a waterfall of hot blood onto him. Dan fought revulsion, struggling fruitlessly at his bounds as the scent of raw viscera choked him, reminding him of his slaughtered clan.

Dan fought to see through his shroud of fetid crimson, blinking rapidly to see a thin-lipped woman approach, carrying a bowl in one hand and bone shards in the other. She handed them to the *Völva* who now knelt beside him. The elder witch dipped a sharpened bone into the bowl and pulled it out to reveal black ink, then with a small hammer, she began to etch his skin. He howled in pain, but the men tightened their grasp.

The other woman dipped her bone and carved his skin simultaneously, dragging the point across his flesh until it pulled out his blood, both his and the calf's swirling and mixing with the ink. He gritted his teeth as he looked up at the sky, who released gentle snowflakes to kiss the wounds creating tiny pools of gore beneath him.

"This pain is nothing like what you have done to your kin," the *Völva* reminded him. "Find power in it. It is in the pain of these markings, created of blood and ash, that will prevent you from becoming the wolf for twenty-five days of the moon. When she is at her fullest, the markings will no longer hold you, and you must hide yourself away from all creatures. Do you understand?"

"Yes," Dan whispered, closing his eyes.

After several hours, the women finished, and the men released him. The crowd gathered, watching him try to upright his now doubly weakened body, his skin throbbing. They had covered him from his neck, down his arms, down his legs with runic letters and symbols he could not understand.

"You, Son of Wolves, are banished from contact with any of our tribes," the chieftain commanded. "Go, but if any one of us should look upon your face, we have the right to murder you without fear of the axe."

Dan fell off the platform, stumbling as he forced his legs to move. The woman who once nurtured him showed another bit of mercy, tossing him a thin blanket to cover his wounds. Kindness was absent from the rest of the crowd, however, who jeered as he staggered out of their territory. He limped as far away as he could manage, back into the protection of the forest. A blanket of snow had covered the ground as he withstood his mutilation and he collapsed into it now, his skin prickling from its bite. He pulled himself towards a nearby thicket for shelter, wrapping the blanket tightly around him. He thanked the gods for their mercy, wondering as he shut his eyes if he would even survive the night.

LONDON, 1857

DAN EXTINGUISHED HIS CIGARETTE, the tapping glass the only sound in the room. He kept his gaze averted as he folded his hands in front of him, visibly discomforted by the rapt attention that was still fixed upon him.

A moving quill scratched through the silence as Libraean resumed his note taking. Jacob stood to retrieve a cup of water. From the hall, the grandfather clock chimed noon, though no sunlight escaped from the heavily draped windows.

David blinked, realizing how unwavering his stare had been on the creature before him. "It's curious how similar our stories are," he remarked.

Dan broke free of his trance, looking at David with kind eyes. "Yes, I believe that's why we became such fast friends."

"I am so sorry for the pain you suffered," Jacob offered quietly as he sat back in his chair. "It does not seem fair to bear such a curse."

Morrigan withdrew from the loveseat to pour a glass of brandy, which she handed to Dan. "We can take a break if you'd like," she offered.

Dan shook his head, taking down the contents of the glass in one swallow. "There is more that needs to be told and we do not have much time."

Jacob stood again to add another log to the fire. The dry wood caught quickly, the fire casting its glow onto the troubled creature and the old, jagged tattoos his rolled-up sleeves revealed.

"David knows what follows," he continued. "In fourteen twenty, Libraean found me in the Carpathian Mountains, wandering around half-mad. I had been a traveling recluse for centuries, kept semi-mortal by the wolf inside of me. Libraean reiterated what the *Völva* had told me, that I was indeed a hybrid of reincarnated gods. He introduced me to the Council, who told me that if I aided a group of revolutionaries in Wallachia against their Imposter Prince, they would help me get rid of the wolf for good. Instead, the human part of me died, then the blood drinker in me died, and the wolf remained."

"Which brings us to the Night War," David said. "When I stumbled upon you, you were clearly dead, splayed out near Dragos's dismembered corpse."

"Yes, I can only surmise that what you saw was part of a spell. In reality, I was somehow split in two, the conscious part of me left to wander the astral plane, while the wolf escaped into the forest. In fact, I wouldn't have a human consciousness again until I met her." He reached for another cigarette.

ROMANIA, 1740

THE BLADE THAT SPILLED THE LAST OF HIS IMMORTAL BLOOD clattered beside his ear. His vision wavered until the cloudy night sky, crying frigid rain onto his face, faded to black. Yet he did not enter through the gates of Valhalla as he'd hoped, nor did he see any signs of an afterlife. Instead, it was as if he slumbered, the occasional fuzzy dream breaking through his conscious mind only to trickle away as randomly as it had come. Sensations came to him in increments, the taste of blood, the sound of screaming, the throaty exclamations of birds. But mostly, it was a confusing, quiet oblivion.

And then, one day, he was alive, staring down into the eyes of a girl. They were rimmed by furious tears, her pale, sun-splotched skin painted with crimson, her body shuddering with power as she held him in her thrall. She burned with hatred, her fury heating skin that smelled of wild apples and newborn fawn. He saw slaughtered wolves sprawled out around her, the metallic taste of offal in his mouth. *The wolf did this,* he discerned, realizing he was once again trapped in its body. *It has happened again.*

"No," said the little creature in front of him, her power buzzing around her like a swarm of angry bees, her hateful eyes the color of honey. He realized he was frozen in place, held by the spindly branches of the trees she commanded, their splintered fingers digging mercilessly into his flesh. "You do not get to absolve yourself from this. You killed my mother and my pack, and now you belong to me."

His chest stung, and he looked down to see that she had carved runes into his chest, the fur around the angry gashes matted with blood. I am so sorry, he thought helplessly.

"I do not wish to acknowledge your human side yet, for I still feel the urge to skin you alive from head to tail. Stop speaking to me and remove the pelts from the wolves you slaughtered. You may eat what good meat is left. We cannot leave such waste in the forest, and we have a long journey ahead of us." She shook his blood from her knife and sheathed it against her thigh. "I refuse to stand by and watch as you ravage my fallen family, so I will be at the creek washing their blood off my skin. I cannot find my mother's body, but if you do, leave it intact and bring it to me. She will be the only human among them."

Dan had no choice but to obey, watching her disappear behind the brown and yellow leaves. The tree branches unwound from his limbs, releasing him to the forest floor and resuming their petrified reach into the sky. He set to work retrieving the pelts for her, though he quickly found he had no appetite. He left the skinned bodies in a pile near an open patch of forest, hoping the vultures and crows would notice and enjoy the feast. He saw no murdered woman amongst the carnage, unsure if that was or was not in his favor.

As grateful as he was for the sudden arrival of consciousness, he was alarmed it happened while he was in his feral state and in broad daylight with no sign of a full moon. He wondered how long he'd been unconscious and if he would be human again soon. The woods offered no answers, although the trees that surrounded them were mainly pine and spruce, offering an aroma familiar enough that he believed he'd once been there.

He gathered the pelts over his shoulder, heading towards the creek on his hind legs.

In his absence, she'd emerged from the water and dressed in clean clothes, seeming even more childlike with her long chestnut hair and cream-colored skin clear of gore. Matured muscles rippled, however, as she flexed to tie makeshift boots up around her ankles, making it clear that she bore physical strength beyond her supernatural endowments. Her clothing was mostly fur and leather, a knife tucked in one boot, and another secured to her thigh. As she stood, she repositioned a bow behind her back, a sack of arrows at her waist.

I did not see the body of your mother, he told her carefully.

Her jaw still clenched with revulsion as she apprehended him, but her voice did not betray any emotion. "I didn't think you would," she sighed. "Perhaps she was a ghost after all."

She took the furs and set to work cleaning them in the rushing water. He noticed she'd started a small fire nearby, an appalling looking mixture heating above it. She spread out the washed pelts upside down onto the rocks and began applying the mixture to the underside of them with her hands. He picked up the scent of viscera.

"You will carry these pelts for me until we find shelter," she told him. "The early spring still brings frigid nights, and it is best to sleep covered. The furs will take a few days to prepare, but then we can sell them for supplies." She finished her task, rinsing her hands in the water and dumping the tanning mix out near the rocky bank. She then snuffed out the fire with her boot, gathering the clean metal pot into a nearby leather bag. She draped her own previously treated fur cloak over her shoulders and stood, bag in hand. "Lift me up."

The command took him aback, for he knew how frightening he looked, a massive abomination on hind legs with razor sharp teeth and exaggerated claws. Yet she showed no fear, apprehending him as a human would a common pet. He complied, careful not to slice her skin as he positioned her on his shoulders. He pulled the pelts into his arms, ignoring the accumulation of flies.

"Go forward until you see the thickest cluster of red pines, then head east," she ordered. "In four days, we will take our leave of these woods. We are going to find a man named David."

They traveled in silence, Dan carrying his little master through acres of forest. The spring season matured as the days passed, offering steadily warmer afternoons and plentiful game to eat. Each night, as the temperatures dropped, she found them shelter, rinsing and preparing the furs in the nearby water while he hunted. Her skillful navigation of the woods impressed him. He surmised she had been raised in them, much like he had been forced to as a young man. She never strayed far from the closest water source, a creek that seemed to stretch for miles. She didn't speak much, but when she did, it was neutral, curiously free from the hatred he expected. He soon found himself enjoying her company, though he wished to be free of his wolf guise. Its body was cumbersome, pulsating with the urge to destroy and furious at the inability to do so.

At dusk on the fourth day, his young master told him it was time to rest, guiding him to a cave neatly concealed behind a waterfall. She slipped off his back easily, pulling the pile of furs down after her. "Go find us some wood for the fire and kill us some meat. I would like to eat soon," she told him.

He obeyed, also famished from traveling. He hunted and ate to his own satisfaction, rinsing the leftover scraps of meat in the stream before bringing them up to her. The cave went deep behind the flowing water, offering enough space for her to start a fire without worrying about its spray. She had hung up the pelts, an array of ivory and grey fur surrounding her where she sat.

She accepted the meat from him without comment, pulling her cooking utensils out of her bag and cooking it over the fire. He curled up against the wall as she ate, watching the sun setting beyond the cascade, throwing shades of red and orange against his face. His belly full, the rushing water and crackling fire soon lulled him to sleep.

She interrupted before he could. "Since the moment I bound you to me, a man appeared inside of you. Am I wrong?"

You are not, he replied.

"And that man was not present when you killed my mother and my pack?"

I have not been conscious until the moment you bound me to you. I believed I was dead for more years than I can recall.

She peered at him, the firelight glinting in her eyes. "I will need to trade these furs with the men in a nearby camp to secure enough funds for our journey to the west. They will not take a young girl seriously, however, and I cannot keep a direwolf as a pet around other humans. I have decided the best course of action would be to bring back your human self. But know that you will be bound to me, just the same."

How can you bring me back?

"A spirit has been whispering to me since you arrived, along with the spirits of the trees, an ancient magic lying dormant for years. They have been guiding me throughout our journey and have informed me that I am the descendent of powerful witches with this ancient magic at my command. They told me that I should release your human soul from its prison, to serve and protect me as the wolf has."

Dan found himself at a loss for words.

"In order for me to restore your human self, we must meet in the astral plane. Do you know how to do that?"

I have never heard of such magic, he admitted.

"It is the place you were before I brought you back. I believe that since your wolf half was still on earth, you could not ascend to the heavenly realm, trapped in the astral plane until the moment I bound you."

How does a girl raised among the wolves know so much? Dan wondered.

"My mother taught me everything there is to know in this lifetime," she replied without hesitation. "She knew one day that I would have to survive alone without her. She spent her life preparing me for this world."

And I was the one who took her from you, he thought, haunted by remorse.

"I know your human self is not to blame," she said casually, but without a hint of forgiveness. She reached into her bag and pulled out a tiny sachet. "This will help you return to the astral plane." She took her cup and filled it with the water she had been warming over the fire, then added the sachet as one might make tea. Then she stood, moving across the cave floor to the spot where he sat. She knelt down, her delectable scent maddeningly close to him. He was grateful to be under her control, the wolf screaming at him to tear her apart. "Open," she instructed him.

He cracked open his jaws and she poured the mixture down his throat. He choked, the unfamiliar herbs bitter on his tongue.

She surprised him by taking a sip herself, following it with a bite of leftover rabbit to wash down the taste. Then she curled up next to him, pulling one of her old fur blankets over her as if she planned to sleep. The drowsiness hit him then, revealing what the drink was intended for. He tried to focus on her, but his eyelids stubbornly drooped. He heard her yawn next to him. "You will see me there," she said.

And then, he was plunged into darkness.

He awoke to the cold caress of snow. He bolted upright, realizing he sat on an icy riverbank, an old Viking ship thumping gently against the dock. The handcrafted masterpiece wore a veil of white, artfully masking its antiquity, an eerie ghost ship that time had long forgotten. He stood, surprised to discover, as he brushed the snow from his skin, that it was supple and free of ink. He was his young, human self again.

He looked up to see a doe in the distance, watching him with quiet interest. She stood amongst an oak grove, the ancient bulbous trees glittering underneath the pale sliver of moonlight that hovered in the winter sky.

"I do not even know your name," he said.

The snowy trees sighed, whispering names, Isis, Hekate, Artemis, *Diana*. The last name shook the realm, the docked ship groaning with agitation. Frightened by the noise, the doe darted off into the woods.

"Wait!" he called after her.

"I am here," a voice said next to him. She looked no different than the girl he knew on earth, rivulets of chestnut hair spilling down her shoulders, her light brown eyes wise beyond her apparent years. Her tiny frame only came up to his chest. "My mother called me Cahira."

"Hello, Cahira. My name is Danulf."

"Are you ready to come back with me?" she asked, extending a hand that was small even to his human appendages.

The abandoned ship creaked and moaned, creating, with the mournful wolf howls and wailing crows echoing in the distance, a poignant lamentation calling him home. He looked towards it, longing to join his father and brothers on the eternal seas, yearning for the gates of Valhalla.

"Odin says you are not yet ready for death," Cahira told him, as if she read his thoughts. "He speaks to me in the wolf and crow calls."

Dan looked at her sadly. "I believe you, even though their beckoning is strong," he admitted with a sigh. "I am ready."

She nodded, once again holding out her hand. As soon as his skin touched hers, they were back in the cave.

He gasped, his body overcome with tremors, similar to a newly birthed calf. He was so grateful to be freed of the wolf that he nearly cried out in relief. He ran his hands up and down his human skin, ecstatic, when he realized she stared at him from behind her fur blanket. "Thank you," he whispered, trying to curtail his emotions.

"Your accent is strange. And why is your hair grey when your face looks so young?"

He almost laughed. "The wolf part of me kept me semi-mortal. I was already a few hundred years old before I was made into a blood drinker."

"What is a blood drinker?"

"Your mother did not teach you about creatures?"

"No," she admitted. "Some things she told me would come in time, but then she died."

A pang of regret stung Dan, causing him to cast his eyes to the floor.

"Please continue," she instructed.

"Have you heard stories of the Norsemen?"

"Yes, scholars call them Vikings. I have been taught the history of our world," she said, an air of annoyance in her voice. "You came from the north, from the Scandinavian territories. Your people pillaged the European Christians for centuries before the clans dispelled. I even know the stories of your gods."

Dan blinked, impressed. He recounted the gruesome story of his past, trying not to look at her eyes as he remembered life as a skógarmaðr. "I lived that way for many long years," he said. "It ended when I met a creature named Libraean. He told me I'd be released from my torment if I helped a creature named David kill a dark god intent on destroying the human race."

The memory jolted him as he spoke, one he never forgot even though he was barely conscious, David's sorrowful voice in his ear as he knelt and bit. The pain, the thirst.

"David turned me into an immortal blood drinker to save my life," he told her. "They are creatures who live forever but must do so by consuming the essence of others. They cannot bear sunlight and have supernatural strength and speed. Being both wolf and blood drinker was not enough, however, and I was killed not long after my transformation. Well, he killed the human part of me, anyway."

Cahira was silent, digesting his words. "I was also told that I must find a creature called David. Now I understand why you were given to me."

"Given to you, eh?" Dan chuckled.

"Your most recent marking, the one etched into your chest says you belong to me."

Dan looked down, fingering the deep scar under his bright grey chest hair. "If it will save me from murdering others, then I accept it willingly."

She seemed satisfied by his response, although her stoicism did not lift. "I wonder why you are no longer a blood drinker."

"When I was alive, we had otherworldly beings that kept track of these things. Have you heard anything from them?"

She shook her head. "Only what I hear from the trees." She yawned. "It is late and we have a few more miles to travel before we reach the village. My mother warned me about men, so I will tell you now that if you move an inch further into my space, I will kill you without a second thought."

As she closed her eyes, Dan smiled to himself. "I have no doubt that you would," he said, "but you do not need to fear that sort of thing from me. I come from a time when men and women were equal, and that to harm a woman in that way was dishonorable, therefore displeasing to the gods."

"Good," she murmured sleepily. "And make sure you put on clothing in the morning."

Dan looked down to see that underneath the fur blanket she had given to him at some point in the evening, he was entirely nude. He looked up at her in surprise, but the tiny snores emitting from her lips revealed she was already fast asleep.

The next morning, he awoke to an empty cave. Their fire had dwindled down to ash, the pelts taken down from the walls and the clean furs and supplies missing. He pulled himself to his feet, noticing that clothing and a pair of boots had been laid out for him. He pulled on the trousers and shirt, both a bit tight for his liking, but he surmised it was better than running around the cold spring forest nude. The shoes also fit poorly, but he loosened the straps so they would do. He finally wrapped his fur blanket around him like a cloak, stopping to take a sip from the waterfall as he exited the cave.

She waited for him by the widest part of the creek. "Does the clothing fit?"

He nodded. "It will do, thank you."

"I stole them as I scouted the village in the wee hours of morning. Keep your furs covering them and hopefully the men won't notice."

"You went by yourself?" he asked, surprised.

"You seemed like you needed the rest," she shrugged before heading up the bank. "Please grab the bundle of furs."

He nodded, following after her. He noticed she'd left her weapons behind and wondered if she still concealed a knife in her boot. The deeper into the woods they went, the more tightly clustered evergreens overwhelmed it, the forest floor rocky and strewn with needles. "I recognize this place," he realized after some time. "We are in Transylvania."

"Yes, as I said, we have a long way to travel. Which is why we will need more supplies, perhaps even a caravan for when we exit the mountains."

A tiny settlement appeared in the distance. The houses were made of simple planks and topped with straw roofs, wood fences lining its borders. Livestock grazed nearby, new vegetation sprouting up through mud contained in carefully arranged garden plots.

Cahira took a deep breath, revealing her uncharacteristic nervousness. "You must do the talking," she said in a low voice. "Tell them whatever you must, but it is important that we sell these pelts."

Dan nodded, feeling the urge to comfort the young, tiny creature walking beside him, but thinking the better of it.

Their presence drew stares immediately as they walked into town. Most of the villagers were out of their homes, taking advantage of the mild day-time temperature to prepare for the growing season. Dan wondered how the two of them must appear to civilized humans, a heathen the size of two men, covered in blue ink with wild grey hair, walking beside a scowling woodland pixie dressed in wolf fur.

Three men finally approached them, their faces pleasant though they kept pistols at their sides. They did not appear to be Transylvanian, instead light eyed and fair haired, their heritage indiscernible to Dan. They looked out of place in a Carpathian village, and although they spoke the common tongue, their dialect was harsh, their pronunciation clumsy. "How can we help you, travelers?" one of the men asked, his nose as pointed as his facial hair.

"We have come to see about making a trade," Dan replied, gesturing to the bundle of pelts he carried on his shoulder. "My daughter and I are passing through on our way East and are in need of supplies."

The pointy nosed man nodded. "That we can. Our gathering hall is up ahead, if you'd like to warm yourselves by the fire. I will let you speak to Joduk, the man in charge of trade."

Dan nodded. He snuck a glance at Cahira, who studied the men and the village with tentative scrutiny, keeping next to him as they walked.

The men led them into a large rectangular structure overwhelmed by its straw roof like the other homes, held up by four sturdy poles and walls of rammed earth. The lingering smells of eggs and meat met them as soon as they entered, a generous fire crackling in a southern fire pit. They passed by long tables arranged in rows, drawing stares from the men seated around them, who picked at breakfast scraps and swilled ale. The conversation paused as they watched them. Dan realized for the first time that every villager they had seen thus far had been male, not a female nor child in sight.

Near the heart of the structure sat a scowling man, his stomach rounded between two stubby legs. Hatless and wearing well-made leather boots and clothes of good linen, he apprehended them coldly with stone-colored eyes.

"This man and his daughter have come to trade wolf pelts for supplies," one of their guides informed him, his strange accent worse than his pointy nosed associate's.

"Ah." The potbellied man nodded, though his eyes remained hostile. Dan wondered if they should leave. "We can offer you one horse for the lot of them."

46

Cahira's eyes widened with surprise, though she tried to conceal it. She stole a glance at Dan, silently commanding him to take the offer.

"That will do," Dan told him, though his unease remained.

The man extended a fleshy hand which Dan took, resulting in an unpleasant transfer of hog grease. Dan wiped his hand on his pant leg. "We keep our horses in the woods behind our settlement for protective purposes," the man explained. "My men will lead you out that way. You can hand over the pelts after you've received your horse."

They followed the three out of the hut and down a dirt path that led into their wooded territory. Dan was still wary, but Cahira appeared to trust them, so he tried not to give it any thought. She had scouted it beforehand, selecting the village to trade with. It was because of this, that their sudden attack caught Dan unaware.

He cried out in surprise as two of the men forced him to his knees, slamming a pistol into the back of his head before he had a chance to react. He looked up to see Cahira's horrified face, struggling as the third man held her arms behind her, a cruel looking blade pressed into the soft flesh of her throat.

"Please do not kill my daughter," Dan attempted to bargain with them. "You can have the pelts."

"We know she is not your daughter," the man holding Cahira sneered. "This child has more power than you can hope to imagine. She is a crossbreed, the spawn of the mythical creatures that reside in these mountains. We sensed it immediately when you arrived. Her sacrifice will bring us prosperity, just like the sacrifice we made that gave us this land. We took it from those who first settled here. Their bodies lie in fresh graves not far from this place, which you will soon be joining."

Dan looked helplessly at Cahira's face, now frozen in fear. It infuriated him to see her stripped of her confidence, and he found himself frantically trying to come up with a way to escape his captors without bringing her harm.

They are the same group of men who once tried to kill my mother. Her small voice surfaced in his head. I didn't recognize it at first. He met her eyes just as the man behind him pulled back the trigger.

"*Veniunt ad me lupum!*" she suddenly screeched.

The man holding her startled. Dan felt his body grow, snapping and popping as it expanded into the monstrous shell that was Fenrir. He saw the look of terror flashing in the men's eyes as he rose above them. He realized with a start that although he'd transformed, he was still in complete control.

He whipped around to confront the man who held him at gunpoint, now cowering behind the weapon he was trembling too hard to fire. Dan grabbed his arms in one hand, his legs in the other, and promptly tore him in two.

The remaining men screamed, the sound drowned out by the howling of a dozen wolves who descended upon the rest of the town, intent on its slaughter. Dan looked at Cahira, realizing she had full command of the distant canine army, vibrating with power, her pupils blackening her irises. The earth seemed to respond to her anger, quaking as the few ash trees that interrupted the surrounding evergreens pulled their roots free from the dirt, stomping forward to halt the men trying to flee the village. They whomped them with their branches, sending them flying into the stagnant trucks of pines, breaking their bones on impact. The man holding Cahira finally let her go, attempting to run. With her arms now free, she could direct her power, energy flowing from her fingertips as she halted him, lifting her former captor into the air and flinging him against a red pine, impaling him on the sharp spikes left behind from their fallen branches.

Dan was consumed by his own carnage, tearing apart the last man in his path with his teeth, when he suddenly caught a whiff of her blood. He turned to see her wavering as she stood, a crimson stain spreading across the fabric of her clothing. He raced towards her, lifting her up and flinging her onto his back. She gripped onto his fur as he took off into the woods, leaving the massacre behind them, weaving through the spruces and firs until they reached the creek they had been following. She slumped off his back as she whispered, "*Restituere*," restoring Dan to his human form before succumbing to unconsciousness.

He picked her back up in his human arms and carried her to the water, gingerly setting her down in the soft moss. She was covered in blood, making it difficult to discern the extent of her wounds, but he was certain the gash at her waist was what copiously bled. He pulled off his shirt and tore at the cloth with his teeth, creating a makeshift bandage. He lifted up the back of her shirt and wrapped the fabric around her waist, tightly pressing the wound after he'd secured it.

As he held the cloth to stop her bleeding, he noticed two appendages on her back that he hadn't seen before, two irregular stumps as if she'd once had wings. He thought of Libraean, the creature from his past, wondering if they were somehow related. His suspicions were confirmed as he laid her down and saw similar, smaller bumps on her forehead that had been hidden by her wild hair. Their assailant's words came back to him: *She is a crossbreed with more power than you can imagine.*

She stirred, interrupting his thoughts. Snow began to trickle down through the pines and lightly budded beech trees, causing her to shiver. He realized he'd have to find them shelter, for the cave they'd come from was too far away to reach in time. He scooped her back up into his arms, bundling her in his fur cloak, snow building on his bare skin.

At last, he found a deeply concave portion of the creek's edge, several fallen trees preventing water flow and providing additional shelter. He ducked inside, grateful to discover dry ground beneath the rocky overhang. Her lack of consciousness still concerned him, but the makeshift bandage remained free of blood, signaling the onset of healing. He stretched out his fur cloak to cover her completely, debating whether he should build a fire.

"You can sit by me," came a soft whisper from beneath the furs. "Your skin is very warm."

Elated that she was conscious, he obeyed, burrowing next to her and draping himself and her in their last fur. "Rest until the morning, little warrior," he told her as she drifted away once more. "I will watch over you tonight."

The next morning, he left to hunt for breakfast and when he returned, she was awake. Relief flooded over him. "Good morning," he greeted her.

She looked up at him silently, her lips dry and cracked, dark shadows around her amber eyes.

"You need to eat and drink," he told her, revealing the cooked squirrel he'd prepared and a bowl of fresh creek water.

She grabbed for the bowl, wincing as she did so. She gulped the entire thing down before speaking, her voice ragged. "We need to return to the village and take what supplies we can. I believe we killed them all. I also think I reopened my wound, so I will need to rewrap it before we go."

Dan frowned. "You cannot travel like that. You need to eat and drink for strength. I spent enough time around healers to know when someone is weak from blood loss, and I am certain all the power you invoked drained you." He set the meat in her lap and went to gather more water from the stream.

"Will you come back?" she asked weakly when he returned. She caught her vulnerable tone, clearing her throat to correct it. "You will come back," she ordered.

"Yes, I will," he promised. "If you eat, drink, and rest while I am gone."

"Fine," she agreed, leaning back against the dirt.

Dan found his way back to the village easily, following the sour smell of putrefying flesh and the swarms of flies. He realized he hadn't felt the slightest regret tearing the men apart, the synergy created when his wolf body obeyed his human mind feeling natural...as did protecting her. He wondered if his desire to do so was purely a result of her spell over him, or if it was of his own accord. He realized, as he reentered the decimated village, that he honestly didn't care. For the first time in a great many years, he had a purpose.

He stepped around the remains as he pillaged, procuring a large sack that he filled with various utensils, a canteen for water, and the wolf furs they'd left behind. He helped himself to their coins and papers, as well as a gun and a box of ammunition just in case. He set free the horses left alive, taking the remaining eggs and a miraculously spared chicken out of a blood splattered coop. He killed and defeathered it with their tools before returning to the forest, looking forward to eating more civilized meat.

He found her looking more alert, wrapped tightly in his fur as she gazed into the dwindling fire. He threw down the sack with flourish, proudly holding up the chicken meat. "I come bearing a feast!"

He was pleased to see her eyes sparkle with amusement, though her lips stayed still. He knelt to unpack the supplies and stoked the fire back to life so he could cook the chicken.

"We won't be able to stay here long," she remarked softly as he worked. "If any man did manage to escape the village, word will swiftly travel."

"Well, I am sure we have nothing to fear, for you will just kill them all," he joked, his mood still uplifted. But when she let out a tiny sob, his expression fell. "What is wrong?"

"I've never felt so weak before," she said behind gritted teeth. "How foolish of me to trust those men and their words. Even after my mother showed me the vile atrocities men are capable of. I scouted that village ahead of time and nothing about them raised my suspicions. How could I have made such a terrible mistake?"

"In your defense, I fell for it as well," Dan pointed out.

"Furthermore," she continued, ignoring his comment, "I can't explain how I knew the words that would bring the wolf out, or how I summoned all that power."

"You have more of it than I have ever seen, and I have been around plenty of powerful beings," Dan admitted, turning the meat so the underside would cook. Their creek-side nook grew warmer, filling with the aroma of roasting chicken. "Are you saying you cannot control it?"

"That is precisely what I'm saying." She pulled up her knees so that her chin could rest atop them. "My mother didn't have a chance to explain my powers to me, if she even knew I had them. They surfaced the day before she died."

Dan frowned. "What do the woodland spirits say?"

"They only guide me, telling me what to do when I'm in danger. It's as if the powers take over and my mind goes to sleep."

Dan nodded. "That was how the wolf was for me. Strangely enough, the day you brought me back was the first time that both my mind and the wolf's body existed together."

She looked surprised. "Interesting. So, it was your human mind that killed those men?"

"Yes," he replied as he removed the cooked chicken from the fire. He tore off a drumstick and handed it to her, which she accepted gratefully. "And I don't regret it, either." He tore off his own, pulling the flesh from the bone with his teeth and chewing loudly as he reflected on her words. "I wonder if I can help you control it," he finally said aloud. "As you have helped me."

She stared at him, her expression unreadable. "It happens when I feel rage," she told him in a low voice.

"That makes sense. Anyone who wields magic must raise the energy to do so."

"Surely there must be more to magic than rage," she insisted.

He peered at her, a small, crumpled being with the old, tired eyes that came with heavy responsibility. She reminded him of someone. "A long time ago," he began, "I watched a woman called Hekate channel energy from the earth to heal. Her power did not come from fear or rage, but from a place of peace. Then there was the dark god I told you about, the one that David tried to kill, who would set the world ablaze with his anger. He could control it in neural moments, but when his fury overwhelmed him, so did his power."

"How did he learn to control it?"

"I do not know that he ever did," Dan admitted. "We will have to ask

David when we find him. In fact, I am uncertain whether he even succeeded in killing the beast, though the fact that humans are still living among us hints at the answer."

"What are all those papers?" she suddenly asked, eyeing the contents of his sack.

"Ah." He threw the cleaned chicken leg into the fire and pulled the bag along with him as he sat down next to her. "I thought maybe they would be useful." He shuffled through them, squinting at a language he could not read.

"I think they're written in the language the Austrians use," she remarked, snaking an arm out of her shroud of furs. She grabbed a piece of paper and held it closer to her face. "I can speak a few languages, but that one gives me trouble."

Dan looked at her in surprise. "Your mother sounds like she was quite the intellect. Why did she raise you alone in the woods?"

Cahira ignored the question, pulling forward an aged piece larger than the rest. "This is the only one that isn't written in that language …it's a map."

Dan recognized the surrounding territories, and although the titles were written in a language he could understand, the names were different. His eyes moved to the top of the page. It was titled, *Europe, 1730.*

He jumped to his feet.

"What is it?"

"I have been dead for almost four hundred years," he realized in panic. "Which means the wolf has been alive, unrestrained for that long. Who knows what kind of damage it has done?"

"Well, it isn't in control of you anymore," she offered in a soft, kind voice.

Dan stared at her for a moment before he let out a sigh. "I suppose you are right." He slunk back down beside her, letting his shock subside. "That means David has been alive his whole time. I guess he did kill Lucius after all."

"I was told that David is the last of his kind, a group of ancient gods who died and came back to life as human beings with powers," Cahira explained. "The spirits told me this before they discovered you were also alive. They said there has been a great disturbance in the outer realms, those that exist outside our earth. The astral plane, the place where you met me when I brought you back to human form, is the only accessible world. The heavens, the underworld—all have been mysteriously locked, and they don't know why. They fear something is happening that will alter the course of life as we know it, destroying our world by upsetting the precious balance that holds it all together. David is supposedly the one who can shed light on it. That is why I seek him."

Dan considered her words. "That was what we feared when I knew David in the fifteenth century—what we fought against. I can understand the concern, especially if the spirits are the only things left that you hear. We had a Council back then who protected the realms, and a creature who kept track of all things mythical. It does not seem right that no one else has approached you."

She agreed. "I also worry for my mother. I hope her soul is at rest, but if it isn't, then it is up to me to save her, as she once saved me."

Dan did not speak, unsure if she wanted to explain further, and not wanting to push her to do so.

"I was just a baby when she found me," she chose to divulge. "In the arms of a wicked woman who wanted to steal my power. My mother killed her before she had the chance to kill me, taking me in as her own and raising me here in the woods, where I was protected from all who might harm me. She spent my whole life teaching me all that she knew so that I could survive one day without her. I owe her my life."

"Then David we shall find," Dan said firmly. He turned his eyes back to the map. "I do not even know half of these territories. My journey here was from the north, nearly a millennium ago, when the world was covered with forests. We are going to have to rely entirely on the map and your magics to get where we must go."

She slid him a look. "I don't need your navigational skills. I just need…"

He met her eyes.

She grew flustered. "I'm feeling tired now. Let me rest."

Dan rose to his feet, taking the map from her. "I trust you and your spirit guides, but I would like to study the map a little while you rest. I have just found out that it is an entirely different century than I thought it was and this might help me make sense of it."

She acquiesced, burrowing back under the furs and closing her eyes.

Dan left their creek-side dwelling, stepping out into the twilight woods. Orange light peeked through the branches as the forest abated its stirring in anticipation of nightfall. He located a freshly fallen tree trunk preserved by the crisp weather and sat beside it, flattening the map against the bark. In the upper corner, he found his homeland, now labeled the Kingdom of Norway, and traced the path he had once traveled with his finger. It glided down through the Kingdom of Sweden, across the Baltic Sea, into the

Kingdom of Poland, through Hungary and Transylvania to Wallachia. It had taken him a few months, but he hadn't even realized how long he traveled. He enjoyed roaming, almost disappointed when he reached his destination.

He recalled the night Fenrir tore free of their full moon bounds, deep in the surrounding forests of the Carpathian Mountains. He couldn't visually remember the fight with the lynx that left him near death, but he woke to two black haired children with almond colored skin who looked upon him with concern rather than fear. They visited him for weeks while he mended, bringing him food and water, and changing his bandages. He recalled Dragos as an innocent boy who helped him to his feet when he was well enough and brought him to their underground apothecary in a shadowy Wallachian village. He remembered officially meeting Hekate, the one who named him Danulf, the woman who would one day fall in love with him even though he consistently spurned her advances. He loved her in his own way, keeping watch over her even as she grew pregnant with another man's child, up until he joined her brother's fight against the deranged prince that lived in the village castle. And then, he died. Nothing remarkable ever came from aligning himself in their fight, he realized, and he died like any other Viking warrior who'd come before him.

Dan realized it had started to snow again, a substantial coat resting on his shoulders and legs. He stood, shaking both the flakes and his memories off him, and rolled up the map before moisture had a chance to ruin it.

He returned to find Cahira snoring soundly, her messy chestnut waves spilling out around her in the dirt. Though her features were delicate, with long lashes and a cherubic face, she looked completely in her element covered by the fur of wild beasts, sleeping in the warm earth.

Maybe Libraean had it all wrong when he told me to come here, he thought as he settled next to her, pulling his own fur blanket around his legs. Maybe I wasn't brought here to help them. Maybe I was brought here to protect her.

Dan woke to the sound of chirping birds and the slow drip of snow melting off the treetops. Cahira still slumbered next to him, oblivious to the sunrise. He rose, stretching the sleep from his limbs, enjoying the sun on his skin. He wondered what Libraean would think of him if he was still alive, how interested he would be to study the only creature in history to become a blood drinker and then turn back into a human.

Cahira's eyes drifted open as he pondered. She immediately checked her wound. "It's healed," she said, relieved.

"Then our journey begins." Dan gathered the pilfered items back to the sack, kicking dirt onto the embers of the extinguished fire.

She rose to her feet, wincing slightly at the effort, but pleased at her ability to stand with her feet planted firmly on the ground.

"Most of our journey is through the woods," Dan told her as he closed the sack. "I was thinking it would be best if I carry you like I did before, to make sure your wound does not open again. After we move into civilization, we can rest and find a caravan."

Cahira stared at him. "I guess studying the map really did give you your confidence back."

He felt his cheeks grow hot. "I need to believe I am in charge of things, even when I am not," he blurted out, surprised by his admission.

She gave him a sly, close-lipped smile. "As long as all it takes is foolish belief." She secured her fur around her shoulders. "*Veniunt ad me lupum.*"

Dan became the wolf once more. He found the transitions were becoming faster and far less painful. He threw the bag over his shoulder and lifted her up to sit between his shoulder blades. He glanced back at their dwelling to make sure nothing was forgotten, then headed out into the distance.

BOHEMIA, 1740

A FEW WEEKS OF TRAVELING with pleasant weather passed before a random spring snowstorm hit, the thick, obtrusive flakes making it difficult to continue forward. Dan was content to persevere, but he could feel Cahira shivering on his back, even though she was draped in every fur they owned. He knew they only had an hour or so before sunset. They had been traveling on flat ground since they'd left the mountains, and by sheer chance he noticed an isolated cabin as they crossed into Bohemia. The structure was covered in a heavy blanket of snow, with no sign of life behind its windows. He broke down the door to the gruesome discovery of two bodies in the early stages of decay, laying across the floor. The reek of putrefaction wafted out of the opened door, causing Cahira to gag. He lifted her off his shoulders and set her down, then scooped up the corpses from the floor. From the look of their clothing and lack of wounds, they appeared to be an old couple who died naturally, peaceful in the solitude of their cabin. I'm going to find a place to bury them.

Cahira nodded, shielding her nose against the odor with her cloak. "I'm going to leave the door ajar while you're gone."

He returned to the world of white, his canine limbs moving easily through the snowy terrain. Burying the dead still seemed unnatural to him, but he knew it was the modern custom and he was grateful to use their dwelling. He found a patch of woods not too far from where the cabin stood, and he set the bodies down to dig through the frozen earth. It didn't take him long to burrow and then cover them, and he headed back towards the cabin before the sun fell behind the outlying trees.

He shut the door against the howling wind. The cabin was already warm, his eyes catching a stack of leftover logs piled nearby. She had tried to clean the rot from the floors in his absence to make the smell less potent, every rug available draped over the leftover stain. He found her sitting on the ground near the fireplace, sipping from a tin cup, the smell of steeping herbs gently replacing the scent of death in the air.

She looked up at him, noticing his spine oddly bent to fit inside the confines of the cabin. "*Restituere*," she murmured, restoring him to his proper form.

He settled into it, stretching his limbs and arching his back before joining her. "What are you drinking?"

"Tea." She lifted the cup to his nose so he could smell it. "The woman left behind crushed herbs and spices, so I decided to brew them with some melted snow. There's some in the pot, if you'd like to try some. Cups are in the cupboard."

Dan rose to retrieve one, enjoying the potent aroma that filled his nose as he poured the steaming liquid into his cup. The tea felt good going down, warming a body that gradually grew colder without its insulating fur.

"I haven't heard anything from the spirits," she told him when he settled down next to her. "It's as if they've abandoned me in this strange land."

"Perhaps it is because you are on the right path and they do not need to intervene," he suggested.

"Maybe." She took another sip from her cup. "Have you ever been in love?"

Dan nearly spit out his mouthful of tea. "Why do you ask?"

Cahira's face was impassive. "I have my reasons."

Dan frowned, turning to the fire. "I do not know."

"Surely you do," she insisted. "This is the warmest my bones have been for days and I am in no hurry to leave this place. We have plenty of time for conversation."

He stayed silent until she said, "Don't make me force you to tell me your story."

Dan sighed, shifting his weight. "If you want to fill the time, then I will tell you a story of my people. Once there was a giantess called Skadi," he began, "a tall, beautiful creature with long white hair and bright blue eyes, who made her home in the snow. One day, she left her homeland to journey to Asgard, home of the gods, dressed in armor with weapons to avenge the death of her father, Thjazi, who Odin had killed in battle. When she arrived, the gods convinced her to accept reparations instead of seeking vengeance, which she reluctantly agreed to. While they discussed the best way to appease her, she ran into Odin's son, Baldr, who was described as the fairest amongst the gods. She fell in love with him, and he with her. He decided to wait until after the gods made their restitution to her before he would ask to marry her."

He took another sip of tea. "The next day, Odin took Thjazi's eyes and cast them into the night sky, where they became two stars, to honor Skadi's father. She was pleased, but still not satisfied. So, the gods decided to make her laugh. Loki, the trickster god, was the only one who succeeded, but her laugh was slight, anger still vibrating throughout her bones. Finally, Odin offered her a god to marry, one last attempt to soften her anger. The only stipulation was that she must choose only by his legs and feet alone. Thinking of Baldr, she agreed. Baldr also heard of Odin's plans and hurried to join the lineup of gods for her to choose from. She picked the fairest legs amongst them all, thinking they were his, but instead they belonged to the sea-god, Njord."

He cleared his throat. "Baldr's heart was broken, as was Skadi's, but she had to agree to Odin's terms. The two had a magnificent wedding, which Baldr did not attend, but that was the extent of their happiness. The two were horribly paired; Njord was from the warm, sandy beaches of Noatun, and Skadi lived far to the north where the snow never melts. Neither one of them was happy in each other's lands, Njord complaining of the howling wolves and the frigid air, Skadi abhorring the warmth and the calls of sea-birds echoing in the blue skies.

"Odin accepted their divorce, realizing there would be no way for either of them to be happy. But before Skadi could be reunited with Baldr, he was accidentally killed by his own brother. The two would never cross paths again."

Cahira gazed up at him, her face soft in the firelight. "Do you remember any of that life?"

"No," Dan replied, unable to meet her eyes. "Some reincarnated gods recall their past lives strongly, but I cannot. In fact, I would not have believed it, had I not transformed each full moon into Fenrir." A thought suddenly occurred to him. "I have not been keeping track of the moon. Ever since you brought me back."

"I have," she told him. "It actually hangs full tonight, but even if the clouds weren't obscuring its view, you won't turn unless I command it."

Dan smiled. "Ah, so you are my moon now."

She smiled back for only a moment before it abruptly fell, and she looked away. "So you were only in love in your past life as a god, the life you don't remember?"

Dan sighed, dismayed to have to return to the subject. "I did take a wife before I discovered what I was. I often look back on her and wonder if she was Skadi, come to find her mate, for the two shared the same pearly blonde hair and icy blue eyes. In any case, I killed her before we grew to love each other as married people do." He pulled his legs away from the increasingly warm fire. "After that, I spent my life prowling the woods. I stopped in towns briefly throughout those years. Sometimes there would be a woman who wanted to spend the night with me, but I always left before the sun rose. I refused to get close to anyone. So, to answer your question, no, I do not believe I have ever been in love, and I probably never will. When you live as long as I have, those desires no longer drive you and you become used to solitude."

Cahira looked into the flames. "I understand."

"When I finally reached Wallachia, I moved in with a pair of twins, a boy and a girl, both healers who ran a village apothecary. Those years were the longest I had ever spent in one place. Eventually, the twins grew up and it was not too long after that the sister confessed her love for me. I was not ready to love anyone at that time, and besides, she felt more like a sister to me than a lover. Eventually, she became pregnant with another man's child, a man who abandoned her. I took care of her after that, but I do not believe she ever forgave me for not loving her back." He sniffed. "Her name was Hekate, the healer I told you about."

Cahira was quiet.

"And now, it is your turn. Tell me why you wanted to know about my past."

She shrugged. "I don't know. I've been hearing strange whispers since we arrived, but nothing I can make sense of. For some reason, I keep thinking about my mother. She raised me alone, alongside a pack of wolves who were loyal to her. She was the only human who I had contact with for many years. As I told you before, she spent hours teaching me everything she knew, including the ways of other humans. My most cherished lessons were those that involved the hunt, how to survive. History, language, customs...while I did learn them, they could never keep my interest." She hugged her knees close to her chest. "Then, on the day I reached my first moon, she decided to tell me about men. She told me that I once had a grandfather, and I think he was her lover. She said he was once a cruel soul, but that he'd changed and although he was dead, her heart still carried love for him. Then she took me to a nearby camp, where I witnessed what men are capable of. I was enraged by what I saw, and my power came out of me unrestrained. I killed most of them before my mother whisked me away. It was the first time either of us had witnessed my powers. She died soon after, so I was never able to learn anything about my power from her. As I look back, I wonder if loving my grandfather weakened her, for to love a creature capable of such cruelty has to be a sign of weakness."

"Women can also be quite cruel," he pointed out.

"Love is weakness, either way. I don't ever want to be in love."

Dan considered her words. The wind wailed outside the cabin walls. "You are very strong and very independent, so there are not many men worthy of your love. But I do not think it wise to be so resolved. Look at the man and woman who died here in this cabin in each other's arms. Love can be pure and kind."

Cahira snorted. "I don't believe that for a single minute."

Dan laughed. "I suppose it is pretty unbelievable."

Cahira stood up to stretch, dropping her layers of furs. The cabin had reached a level of comfortable warmth, the fireplace glowing steadily. "Enough of this talk. We should use this time to prepare."

Dan was confused. "Prepare for what?"

"You and I will eventually reach civilization and the way we look and act, we will draw attention to ourselves. So I am going to teach you everything I've learned about how to be a proper human, so we can play the part."

"I know how to be a proper human," Dan scoffed.

She raised an eyebrow.

"Things were different back then," he said defensively.

"Come," she gestured for him to come to the table. "Sit, and we will begin your lessons."

Dan sighed but obeyed. "I think I would rather talk about love."

The snowstorm finally ended, the rays of the rising sun brilliant in the clear blue sky. Melting snow dripped off the roof as its icicles dwindled into nothingness. Cahira lifted her head from where she'd fallen asleep, face down on the table. The notes she'd written in chalk on its surface left a grey smudge on her cheek. "Is it morning already?" she yawned.

Dan chuckled, pulling on his boots. "I will go survey things while you pack up."

She nodded, stretching life back into her arms.

He exited the cabin, squinting in the blinding sunlight as it reflected off the snow. Birds sang joyfully at the passing of the storm, fluttering about the dripping tree tops. He barely made it more than a few steps when he began to profusely sweat. He attempted to ignore the sudden wave of heat and walk forward, but his head started to spin from the blinding light, his chest tightening. He rushed back to the cabin, throwing off his shirt as soon as he entered to see the pale skin around his tattoos had turned a bright shade of pink, as if he'd spent long hours in the sun.

Cahira ran up to him, visibly concerned. "What happened to you?"

"I do not know, but it is as though my skin is on fire." He shivered, his tender skin pulsating with heat.

She opened the door and stuck her head out. When she closed it, she revealed an expression deeply troubled. "It's still quite cold outside, enough that the snow remains on the ground."

The cool darkness of the cabin soothed his skin, but for the first time in a long while, he felt a pang of worry.

"We should travel today with you as the wolf," she decided. "We can stay in the woods. Maybe I'll hear the whispers again to guide us on our way. Eventually we need to find an alternative means of travel when we get closer to civilization, but we should be alright for now."

Dan agreed. He shifted into the wolf and reentered the sunlight without incident, but he couldn't shake the feeling that something was terribly wrong.

Spring resumed its hold on the land, and the farther they moved away from the mountains, the more the abrupt snowstorm seemed like a dream. The trees that surrounded them were no longer conifers, but a vast array of trees, the bright greens of spring painting their path as they moved across rolling hills. Gently burgeoning plants wound around the rock formations, as birds twittered in the skies. Although it was not home, Dan enjoyed the scenery, and though the air was unfamiliar, it was crisp and fragrant with the promise of pleasant travels.

They walked for miles in silence before she broke it, talking to him in her mind like she often did when he was the wolf. He heard the rustling of paper as she examined the map atop his shoulders. *We're nearing a stretch of land labeled the Great Bohemian Forest. Perhaps we should travel through it, to keep us away from humans. I know we planned on a more direct route, but I think we should remain concealed until we figure out what's wrong with your skin.*

Dan grunted an agreement.

He continued through the sprawling green to a grove of ancient, towering trees. Their long, spindly arms stretched overhead, intertwining with each other to create a natural patchwork ceiling. He noticed the woods were unnaturally quiet for the time of day. A chill fog lingered around the tree trunks. His footsteps crunched as he navigated around the decayed leaves and brush, but he heard what sounded like human whispers drifting through the wind.

What is this place? Dan wondered. *Can you hear what they are saying?*

Shrieks pierced the silence before she could answer. He felt Cahira being lifted off his back, and he whipped around to confront trees that had transformed into hideous renditions of women. Their peeling white bark looked like ripped flesh hanging from their narrow curves, their branches like claws. They had slits for eyes and hollow mouths filled with crooked teeth, their branches lashing out as they advanced.

He roared, snapping their arms as he searched frantically for Cahira. He couldn't see her, his eyesight obscured by the whipping branches. Finally, one of the horrid trees succeeded in hitting him from behind, the blow on the back of his neck hard enough to send him crashing to the ground. He cursed, but his frustration wasn't enough to prevent his eyes from rolling back in his head, and before long, his world went black.

He was back in the place where Cahira brought him to life, the icy tundra spilling out before him. Yet the wolf howls that had provided the melodious backdrop of that dream had been replaced by the anguished wailing of spirits floating listlessly in the wind. The sky behind them was black, interrupted by their ethereal glow and the blustery white snowfall that accompanied the realm.

He rose to his feet, intent on searching for Cahira.

Instead, he was greeted by a waif, the brisk wind picking up her tattered dress. As she moved closer, he saw that one side of her face was beautiful, with clear, pale skin, flaxen hair, and dark blue eyes, but the other was hideous and decayed. The skin on her left side was mottled, a greenish blue that surrounded an entirely coal black eye, and her tangled black hair clung desperately to her skull. The lips on her left side had rotted away, leaving a cruel grimace that exposed her teeth.

"The goddess Hel," Dan whispered in recognition, falling to his knees. "I have died."

The Norse death goddess shook her head. "I have brought you into the Middleground, the space between realms, for mine is gone. You are still alive on earth in the Birch Grove. It is a place in the Dark Forest where the souls of murdered women attack those who travel through it. They are wraiths trapped inside the birch trees."

"Niflheim is gone?"

"All of the realms have been destroyed by a creature who artfully escapes our detection."

"They have destroyed Valhalla? Folkvang?" Dan was incredulous.

"Yes, and not just the realms that belong to our people, but every realm that exists beyond earth."

"How can this be?" Dan sputtered.

"You must listen, son of Loki. The gods and goddesses are all dead, forced to be reborn as humans on earth, not knowing who they are. The dead souls we once housed in our realms have all been released, either to come back with no plan or to wander the Middleground. I am merely a projection, for I now live in a land foreign to me, a miserable place where the snow never falls. I tell you this because you are my brother and you watch over the only being with enough power to help us. Ensure the little doe makes her way to The Dragon Slayer. He stopped the Dark One once before, and he is the only one who can stop him now."

"I will protect her with my life," Dan promised.

"Rise now and take her out of these cursed woods. There are more wraiths in them than ever before, unable to find peace in the heavenly realms. I can only keep them at bay for so long; they grow restless the longer they are trapped here."

"Can you tell me where she is?"

"They gave her to Vodnik, the water *daemon*. He lurks in a swamp not far from where the Birches grow. You must understand, creatures can smell her power and she is not immortal, so they believe she is weak. They will always try to find her as long as she breathes. Take her deeper into the Dark Forest, where the evergreens grow thick and plentiful. There, you will both be safe, for the wolves will be there to help you. She has command of them all, not just you."

Dan nodded. "Thank you."

"Do not thank me, thank Anubis when you meet him." And with nothing more, she disappeared.

Dan's eyes flew open to reveal he still lay on the forest floor, his head throbbing. He was still in wolf form, the trees settled back into their natural places, no longer twisted wraiths. He jumped to his feet and ran, trying to pick up both her scent and the stench of stagnant water. Miraculously, it did not take him long to discover a bog not far from where they were attacked.

Dan surveyed the black waters for any sign of life, hackles raised and ready to attack. He heard a low grumble and turned to see a creature situated on a rotting, moss covered log. He looked like a fat, naked man with the face of a frog, his long hair and beard spoiled green, his skin a chaotic pattern of black fish scales. Where hands should have been were webbed paws, he had a fish's tail for legs, and bore eyes like smoldering coals. "Who dares come to my waters?" it croaked.

Give me the girl. She does not belong to you.

The bulbous creature chortled. "She does not belong to you either."

I am not afraid to dive in there and tear you apart, Dan warned.

"You would drown before you even came close enough to touch me," the creature mocked him. "You are not in your land, direwolf. In fact, I can make this water so hot, your eyes would melt from your sockets, your flesh food for the fish."

Although he presented a strong visage, Dan grew more anxious the longer Cahira was missing, her scent absent from the air, her thoughts silent. He was at a loss, for his power lay in his brute strength above all else. Though he speculated the creature was bluffing, he couldn't risk entering a bog that would boil him alive, lest he rob her of one of the few things in the world protecting her.

His heart hammered against his ribs, fueled by frustration. His body responded with a violent shudder, the same way as it did each time he became the wolf. He didn't have time to be confused, for his head soon filled with the screeches of carrion crows, so loud, it was as if they burrowed into his skull. He was seized by the sensation of shrinking, soon amazed to discover he was turning into a crow. He wasted no time in wondering how, immediately jumping up into the air and diving back down to peck at the vile creature's suppurating, gelatinous flesh.

It howled in pain, trying to fight him off.

Invigorated by his new power, Dan refused to relent, pulling chunks from the creature's face.

Finally, it screeched through torn and bloody lips, "Behind the rock! But she has most likely drowned by now!"

Dan left the moaning creature behind, soaring across the bog to the large rock poking out at the center, just as a tiny hand disappeared below the water's surface. He caught her finger with his claws, flapping his wings furiously until he pulled her out of the stinking muck. She gasped for breath, the rank water clinging to her skin and hair as he continued to flap, higher and higher, until she was finally free. He tightened his grip around her hand, taking her above the treetops and flying forward until he saw the throng of conifers Hel had described.

They tumbled to the forest floor together, Dan snapping back into his human form, his energy fully exhausted. He laid supine on the ground, his chest heaving for breath, struggling to scoop air into his constricted lungs.

Cahira removed the rope and rock that had been weighing her down from her ankle and rolled closer to him. Although she was weak herself, she pulled her body so that her head could rest on his chest, placing her hand on his heart. Soon he felt heat radiating from her palm into his body, restoring normalcy to his breath and refueling his aching muscles. He realized she siphoned healing energy from the earth to mend them both.

They lay quietly for several moments as the ground warmed and restored them to health. "I didn't know you could turn into a raven," Cahira softly remarked. "Though you were as white as your fur is when you are a wolf."

"Neither did I," Dan admitted, grateful to be able to finally speak. "I never knew how draining power is."

"Oh yes," Cahira lifted her head from his chest. "However, someone once taught me I could pull energy up from the earth to heal."

Dan beamed.

"Come," she said as she rose to her feet. "I need to rinse this stink out of my hair. We also should find food and shelter soon. Our supplies have been lost."

Dan bolted upright as he realized she was right. Their sack of utensils, weapons, and the map were gone. The only thing they had left was the clothing on their backs, Cahira's now sopping wet with swamp water. He cursed. "What are we going to do?"

"Survive," she shrugged, heading into the forest.

He followed after her, grateful to see a lush, winding stream up ahead. She dove in headfirst, wearing a relieved expression when her head broke through the surface. Dan tore off his shirt and dove in after her, relishing in the crisp, clear water.

They swam for a while before Cahira paused, gesturing down to her feet. "Fish," she said. "Let's build a fire."

She grabbed his shirt after she exited the water so she could leave her own to dry on the rocks. It swallowed her tiny frame as she gathered wood, bringing it quickly to flame. They let their boots dry beside it as Dan fished in his wolf form, tossing his bounty for her to descale and debone. Soon, they'd sated their appetites, just as the sun began its descent behind the trees.

He remained a wolf so his fur would keep them both warm, curling around her as she fell asleep in the scattered leaves. He was grateful to remember they did not need supplies to survive, for they both were of the woods, the wolf and his guiding moon.

SHE STOOD IN FRONT OF HIM, one hand on her hip, the other clasped around a pair of shears. "You have to let me do it."

Dan frowned, crossing his arms in front of his chest as he stared at her. Though she looked the part of a rural Frenchwoman with her long, green peasant's dress and her wild brown hair trapped in a loose braid that hung down her shoulder, her eyes were just as fierce and unwavering as they'd always been. "I do not understand why we have to go to Paris. This village has served us well for years."

She sighed with exasperation. "I told you last night, I had the first clear dream since we arrived in France, and I believe it was a true vision. The entire reason we came to this country was to find David - and we've finally been given the guidance to do so."

A sinking feeling settled in the bottom of Dan's stomach, though he knew she was right. The rest of their journey across Europe had been without further incident, traveling through the lush and magnificent forest across Switzerland and into the Kingdom of France. Although they were both long accustomed to the nomadic lifestyle, something had struck them when they found the sleepy, unsuspecting village in the southern part of the country. Since they left the Bohemian Forest, the spirit world grew quiet again, leading them to believe that whatever was responsible for destroying the realms had finally ended the last line of communication. The village seemed the perfect place to stay and wait for a sign that would guide them on. Yet nothing came, and soon days became weeks, weeks became months, months became years.

The villagers accepted them, for although the giant, rugged man with a lion's mane and his tiny, muscular wife appeared strange, they were friendly, speaking their language with furs to trade. Eventually they realized how good they were with the livestock, knowing exactly when one of their cows would give birth or when one of their horses was in pain. And so, Daniel and Cahira Pelletier established a household for the very first time in either of their lives, where they lived comfortably and undisturbed. Until now.

"You cannot blame me for wanting to stay," Dan continued to protest.

A sudden severity flashed in her eyes. "I did not leave my woods to come to a strange town and play housewife. I came here to find a creature named David to restore the realms and ensure my mother has a safe resting place in death. We may have become friends over the years, Dan, but my mission has never changed. If my dreams tell me that David is in Paris, then I will go there, with or without you."

Her words stung him, but he refused to let her know. He looked down at the pine slab floor, where one of their domesticated wolves rested by the fire. He tried not to look around the room at the home they'd built together, at the logs he'd painstakingly cut and fit for walls, the fireplace she'd built with rocks from the nearby river, or the furniture they carved together as they sat by the fire. He caught the scent of her herbs drying in the warm summer breeze, his eyes drawn to her overwhelmed bookcase, brimming with any book she could get her hands on. Her thirst for knowledge was never satisfied, and she read to him during the long winter nights, teaching him everything she learned, whether he wanted the information or not.

His mind drifted to the evening prior, when the rest of the village had retired for the night, birds offering their last calls across the plain. "It's my birthday tomorrow," she said softly, as she stared out the window, watching the setting sun.

He looked up from his dinner, surprised at her easy admission. "I hadn't realized you kept track of such things."

"Tomorrow is the first of May when the entire world is in bloom. The ancient Celts called it *La Bealtaine,* or the Feast of Beltane. It is considered the first official day of summer and was celebrated with roaring bonfires. To ensure a good season, and that their livestock would be protected from harm, the Druid elders would walk the cows through rows of fire. Then, after the pyres burned out, they would spread the ashes over the entire village. Girls made crowns of yellow flowers to wear in their hair, draping them around the necks of the cows for good luck. No greater celebration was had than on the first day of May."

"Sounds perfect," Dan offered with a small smile.

When Cahira turned, he was surprised to see that tears welled up in her eyes. "I don't even know if that's my true birthday, but that's the one my mother picked, for she always said I reminded her of spring. But it means I have been alive for twenty-four years, ten of which have been without her. I once had a purpose—to find David—and instead I am here, slowly ticking away the years until I am dead."

"Well, that's a pretty bleak way to view existence," Dan remarked.

"That is easy for you to say. You are immortal."

"Immortality is more of a curse than a blessing, Cahira," he said quietly. "The day you die, I will be alive to witness it, after witnessing you grow old, weak, and in pain, and then I will be forced to live out the rest of my days without you." He grew uncomfortably silent, realizing what he had just said aloud.

Her expression grew soft in the warm, golden sunset, before she blinked, and it resumed its hardness. "Oh, I am sure you will be fine," she dismissed. "You have lived hundreds of years without me and have only known me for ten of them." With that, she abruptly left their common room, retreating to her bedroom. Their wolf, Geri, rose up from her resting place to follow.

Dan exhaled, flopping down on his own bed, kept in the far corner of the main room, near the cool breeze of an open window. He couldn't shake his unease, beyond the sadness their conversation had evoked. It was the closest he'd ever come to admitting how much he loved her, and she had responded in the same manner she had for years whenever he got close. Now he knew how Hekate must have felt, to love someone who had no love to give in return.

The next day, as a peace offering, he brought her home a bouquet of yellow flowers. She responded by wordlessly putting them in a glass of water and grabbing the shears off the kitchen table.

"Of course I will come with you," he said as the memory faded. He raised an eyebrow at the glinting metal. "But I still do not see why I have to cut my hair."

"Because it is not the fashion in the city," she explained in exasperation. "You altered your appearance when we first arrived here, what does it matter if we shave your beard and trim your hair?"

Dan was not convinced.

She grabbed her hand mirror from her room, turning the reflective side towards him. "Would you let this man into a decent establishment?"

He looked at his image. Months of traveling had left his hair long and matted, his face covered with a full silver beard that ended at the top of his chest. The skin on his forehead and around his deep blue eyes had grown tan and leathery, its way of protecting itself in the brief moments he was forced to endure sunlight, his chest darkened from the blue ink of his tattoos. "What about the sun?" he pointed out. "If we take away my beard and hair, it will leave more skin exposed."

Cahira sighed. "Your skin has not gotten worse since you first realized the sensitivity. You can wear a hat during the day, like you do now, with a high collar and cloak to protect it. We will keep to night travel whenever possible, like we used to."

Dan growled. "Fine."

She pounced before he could change his mind, the snipping loud in his ears as his hair fell to the floor, clumps and wiry braids of bright metallic grey. He closed his eyes as she clipped his beard, so close to him that her fragrance filled his nose with the sweet smells of spring, apple blossoms and fresh morning rain.

When he opened them, she was staring at him with an expression he couldn't quite place, the tops of her cheeks a faint pink. She showed him the mirror again, and this time it reflected a stranger, a creature older than he remembered, with the same sapphire eyes, but a face that looked chiseled out of stone, with weather-beaten skin, dotted with silver scruff.

When he looked away, he saw that she had loosened her own hair, the warm brown spilling down her shoulders as she lifted a thin strand of his off the ground. Dan grew very quiet, watching as she wove them together into a braid, the tendril bright against the darkness of her own hair. Her eyes caught his. "I love you in my own way," she murmured, tucking the finished multicolored braid behind her.

Emotion caught in his throat.

She withdrew, replacing the shears in their cabinet and retrieving a broom. "We will need to take all the money we've saved and find appropriate clothing," she said, resuming her matter-of-fact tone. "What we've worn to blend in here will have us stick out in a city that cherishes fashion and refinement."

Dan groaned, thinking of nothing he'd rather do less than try to fit in with civilized humans, wearing ridiculous accessories such as stockings and wigs.

"I also plan to travel to the nearby villages to see if we can sell the farm—"

"No," Dan said firmly, rising to his feet.

"We need the money, Dan."

For the first time in many years, his anger rose. "There are other ways to make money. We are not selling this house," he snapped.

Fury tightened Cahira's mouth, setting her golden eyes ablaze. "Fine," she snapped back. "Then you will be the one to find money for us." She stormed out of their cabin, letting the door crash behind her.

It was as if Fenrir had crept up behind him, whispering in his ear, *Tear them all apart, feast on their flesh and leave.* Instead, he looked down at their hound, who sat at his feet, staring up at him.

I am not selling our home. He repeated to the domesticated wolf. She looked back at him solemnly. *Look after her for me, will you? I need to go into the woods for a few days.*

The she-wolf nodded, pushing the door open with her nose. Dan pulled on his cloak and hat, grabbing one of her shawls to wind around his neck against the sun.

The village bustled in the early summer breeze, the scent of freshly baked bread overwhelming the blacksmith's fires, women strolling the dirt paths to gather their wares for supper. He blew by them all, trying to withstand the heat of the sun though his skin screamed for darkness. They paid him no mind, used to their strange but friendly neighbor with the remarkable knack for animal husbandry. He made it to the outlying woods, sighing with relief in the shade. He unwound the scarf, the breeze hitting his bare neck, a sensation he had not felt for many years. It wasn't unpleasant, but as he reached up to touch the shorn strands of hair, he scowled in contempt.

He headed inward, not sure exactly where he was going, but relishing in the comfort the woods provided him. He knew he was a fool to think they would settle; it was a dream he hadn't even realized he had until he found her. He hadn't anticipated falling in love with her either, the lines between protectiveness and desire blurring as the years passed, as a woman's tenacity replaced a child's precociousness. He never wanted to ruin what they had, an unbreakable companionship built on trust and loyalty, but the longer they spent together, the more difficult it became to bite his tongue.

The snap of a broken stick interrupted his thoughts, freezing him in place as he listened. He scanned his surroundings, realizing he had traveled much farther out than expected, closer to the mountain range than where their village lay. A random creek had established itself in the midst of the woods, and there, his eyes caught a flash of auburn hair. He prepared to strike, but the young man who confronted him was unarmed. "Easy does it, you are in my neck of the woods, old man," he said, holding up his arms in a show of reasonableness. His homespun cotton pants and tunic showed signs of wear, revealing his peasantry, his accent thick with countryside.

"Forgive me," Dan muttered, though annoyed his musings were interrupted.

"No worries, unless you plan on telling my employer that one of his stable hands decided to take the day off to swim in the creek." He smiled up at him, good-naturedly. He was not small, but he was very thin, giving his limbs a wiry look that made his head appear too big for his body. His nose was narrow and pointed, accompanied by a slanted chin, and a bushel of bright copper hair that very poorly concealed two tiny stumps on his forehead.

Dan blinked with recognition. "You are a creature."

The young man laughed. "Well, sure if that's what you want to call it. Aren't you? A little audacious to be out here in the daylight if you ask me. I thought your kind shriveled up in the sun."

"I am not a blood drinker," Dan said hotly, growing more annoyed as the conversation continued.

"Oh, forgive me," the boy backpedaled. "My name is Henri. I didn't mean to offend you—you just smell very much like a blood drinker. We call them *les vampires*. Most folks don't realize that I'm a liminal being either. It is not exactly something I choose to divulge. In fact, my hat is around here somewhere..." He found it hanging on a nearby bush and pulled it over his curls.

Dan felt his irritation subside, replaced with curiosity. "What is a liminal being?" he asked.

The boy gave him a wide grin, which only exaggerated his pointed features. "We are the creatures that don't fit, born of other creatures that defy explanation. We aren't exactly a class either, some of us have powers, some of us are essentially mortal. The only things we share are a set of devilish horns and a pair of angelic wings, stunted at birth by earthly restrictions. I have heard stories that there are some who can still sprout wings and wear full horns popping out of their skulls, but most of us just appear as deformed humans."

Dan was stunned. "There are more of you? Are you all related?"

Henri suddenly looked nervous. "What brings you to these parts, friend? We are not far from my employer's castle and most villagers stay out of these woods. Especially since they've become overwhelmed with wolves these last few years."

Dan sighed, realizing he'd made him nervous. "Again, I apologize. I believe my companion is a liminal being. She has the same horns and stunted wings as you do, yet she keeps them carefully concealed."

Henri lit up. "I have never met another Liminal before! Only what I've been told in stories. You must let me meet her."

Dan frowned, instantly wishing he hadn't been so forthcoming. "I'm not sure that would be a good idea. She isn't exactly pleased with me at the moment. Besides, we are leaving for Paris in the next few days. If I can raise enough money for our journey, that is. That is the reason I'm wandering the woods, hoping that in the fresh air, the answers will come to me."

"Why don't you steal from the Marquis? He has more than enough gold locked away in his dungeons to miss a chunk of it."

Dan's eyes narrowed, immediately suspicious.

Henri shrugged, giving him another mischievous grin. "He's a wicked man, if the prospect of stealing offends your morals."

His words took Dan aback. He had never really considered his morals before—he was a man who simply acted. He supposed he was a good man. He'd never killed without needing to eat or protect himself, and he refused to harm a woman or a child. In fact, he often felt the urge to tear apart those who did. His life had been such a long period of survival, he hadn't much time to ponder philosophical convictions. "I never stopped to consider my morals," he admitted.

Henri chuckled. "Good. If you're headed into Paris, you'll need to be prepared for what transpires there. The Third Estate is positively brimming with animosity towards the rich and tensions are high. If you aren't stealing from and hating the Estates General, then you are one of them. I've stolen my fair share from the Marquis myself if you doubt my intentions." He brightened. "I have an idea. How about you help me, and I help you? Tonight, I will leave the servant's door to the castle unlocked for you to enter. You can take whatever you need, and I'll make sure you are unbothered."

"And in return?"

"You take me with you to Paris. I have enough of my own money saved and I'd like to start a new life there. The countryside has never been for me, neither is serving rich bastards either."

Dan faltered. "I'm not sure my companion would approve…"

Henri snorted. "You let a woman make your decisions for you? She must be one formidable dame."

"She is formidable, strong, and smart enough for me to trust her opinions," Dan said flatly, crossing his arms.

"Ah, no offense intended." Henri lifted his hands again in submission. "I was hoping that maybe as fellow creatures, we could look out for each other in this world. Especially since the realms have been closed. I know plenty of creatures in the city if you need connections."

"Do you know a man named David?" Dan quickly asked.

"Not personally, but I happen to know the right les vampires to ask."

"Then we have a deal." Dan stuck out his hand.

Henri took it with another wide grin. "Pleased to do business with you."

Dan waited until nightfall before he crept up to the castle, an over-whelming, aged structure that appeared to have been built hundreds of years prior. It boasted architectural magnificence, the type of building that had been in a family for generations. He'd heard stories of the Marquis who lived behind its walls and his three sons. They were arrogant souls that rarely visited the nearby village it once depended on in the days of feudalism, an arrangement the villagers did not seem to mind, for they were left to exist in peace. He could hear the rustling of wolves in the nearby mountains, but they sensed him and respectfully kept their distance. Dan located the entrance Henri told him about, pausing briefly to contemplate whether he was making a mistake. Cahira had not come looking for him, nor had she summoned him, as she still could do, though she chose not to. It appeared as though this was his choice alone to make. He took a deep breath, lifting the iron latch that kept the heavy wooden door shut. Miraculously, it opened.

Henri was waiting for him, holding a torch that tossed light into the shadowy corridor behind him. It was cold, dank, and still, thick cobwebs hanging from the ceilings like tapestries.

"We are in the old dungeon," he explained to Dan. "Long ago, this was the passageway prisoners walked through to their courtyard deaths. No one uses it anymore, save for those who know about it and want to escape the confines of the castle for recreation." In the shadows, Dan saw him wink.

"I didn't expect you to be here," Dan remarked.

Henri shrugged. "The more I thought about it, the more I figured you'd appreciate my assistance. And I would like to take out a bit more for myself before I leave." He gestured to his hip, where he'd secured a sack to the waistband of his trousers.

Dan was not amused. "Let's get this over with," he told him.

He followed the spritely creature down the winding hall until they came upon another ancient door bearing three heavy padlocks. He watched in amazement as Henri effortlessly picked them all with the tiny tool he retrieved from beneath his cap. When he finished, he shoved the door, which obeyed with an irritated groan.

The torchlight revealed a room swept clean of all dust and debris, an old cell transformed into a chamber of treasures. Trunks filled the better part of the room, while shelves lined the walls bearing gold and precious jewels. Henri immediately scooped a ruby necklace into his sack. He turned back to Dan to offer his now signature grin. "Well, what are you waiting for?"

Dan sighed, lumbering over to one of the trunks. He cracked it open to see it held reveal hundreds of glittering coins. Satisfied, he snapped it shut and lifted the entire trunk to rest on his shoulder.

Henri raised an eyebrow. "That's all?"

Dan grunted in reply.

"At least put some jewels in there. You're stealing enough money to buy you and your wife a nice sized residence, but it is smart in these times to have some insurance beyond the coin."

"You can steal as many jewels as you'd like," Dan told him. "I just want enough to get us established in Paris."

Henri shrugged, scooping more jewelry into his bag. "Let's go before we arouse any suspicion."

Dan followed Henri back down the hall and out the old dungeon door. The night air met them crisp and humming with summer insects. The estate was still quiet, assuring Dan that his entrance and exit went unnoticed. He didn't break stride as he re-entered the woods. "Goodbye, then," he called back, without waiting for a reply. He repositioned the trunk, preparing to sprint back to the cottage, when he realized Henri trailed behind him.

"I forgot to mention, I'm coming back with you tonight," the impish creature said. "If the Marquis discovers we've taken half his fortune, there will be hell to pay, and I want no part of it."

Dan was highly agitated but felt powerless to argue. Henri didn't seem like the type to keep quiet under distress and he didn't want to risk any unnecessary threat to their travels. He scowled, resuming his march.

"I feel a lot better knowing I'm traveling with you," Henri called, trying to keep up. "Something tells me with your kind of strength, we don't have to worry about wolves."

Dan led him into the village, past the closed stores and taverns in the center of town to the cluster of farms where their cottage was nestled. He saw a lamp aglow in the window, signaling Cahira was still awake. He opened the door to a pair of angry amber eyes, accompanied by the low guttural growling of Geri.

"What on earth is going on?" Cahira demanded as she glowered at the stranger at her door.

Dan directed his attention to his wolf first, lest Henri be ripped to pieces. "Geri, calm yourself. He is a friend."

I don't like the way he smells, she sneered, though she backed away.

"This is Henri," Dan told a seething Cahira. He carefully entered, gesturing for Henri to follow. "You can come in."

"Pleasure to meet you, mademoiselle," Henri offered shakily, taking a step forward.

"I met him in the woods. He is the stable hand at the castle," Dan explained.

"Why is he in our house? What are you carrying?"

"He is a fellow creature who knows where we can find David." Dan slammed down the trunk. It popped open to reveal its shimmering bounty.

Cahira gasped. "You stole that from the castle? It looks like a small fortune."

Henri smiled nervously. "That's because it is. I helped your husband steal it and in return, he said I could accompany you both to Paris. I know other creatures who live in the city, including one who knows the David you seek."

"You told him he could come with us?" Cahira looked to Dan, surprised.

"Yes," he sighed.

"Interesting." She searched his eyes for a moment before she shrugged. "Fine. But we must go quickly. It's only a matter of time before the Marquis discovers he has been robbed and sends a search party into the village."

"Tonight? We cannot go tonight," Dan protested. "We aren't even prepared for travel."

"You should have thought of that before you decided to rob the Marquis," Cahira shot back. She put on her cloak and pulled up the hood. Then she pulled open their weapons cabinet to retrieve her knives, sliding two into her boots before flinging her crossbow over her shoulder.

Henri looked mystified.

"My name is Cahira," she offered. "If you plan on traveling with us, you must know that we are vagabonds, creatures who have lived our lives in the woods. We move quickly and efficiently, and if you can't keep up, we will leave you behind."

Henri nodded, his eyes wide.

She tossed Dan a stack of furs. "I will prepare the horses," she told them, disappearing out the door.

Dan looked down at the trunk of coins. "Help me disperse these into bags, will you?" he asked Henri.

The two of them managed to fit the coins into three burlap sacks, which they filled and brought to the stables. Cahira had already saddled three horses and waited patiently as they divided their belongings to evenly distribute weight amongst them.

Dan hated to travel by horseback, but he greeted his horse lovingly, running his hand along its soft beige mane.

"Are we ready?" Cahira asked, devoid of emotion.

Dan searched the eyes beneath her hood, unable to find any warmth. She'd closed herself off, becoming once again the young girl standing amongst her dead family, who'd forced a direwolf to do her bidding. As if the years they'd spent together in their home meant nothing to her, their connections shattered, her emotions left behind.

Dan swallowed his own rising emotion, forcing himself to nod.

Cahira's horse abruptly sped off down the path, Henri following closely behind her.

Dan took one last look at the house, a pang of sorrow threatening his resolve. Geri stood at the door, unwilling to move.

I didn't think you'd be willing to come with us, he said sadly. *Will you watch over our home until we return?*

Of course. Be safe.

Dan felt a pang in his heart as he nodded and took off after his moon, leaving behind their dwelling to follow the only true home he'd ever known.

Her.

CHAPTER THREE

❧ The Ghost ❧

London, 1857
Libraean

L IBRAEAN SET DOWN HIS QUILL, watching the shining ink slowly dry to matte black. He had used his last piece of parchment, pages of notes stacked high around him on the makeshift desk. The scent of sunrise hung in the air, and he glanced at his pocket watch. They'd been listening for the length of an entire day and night.

He glanced up to study David's face. A frown had settled on his lips, furrowing his brow. Though other immortal beings surrounded him, his skin looked impossibly smooth in comparison, as if it had been etched out of stone. Libraean recalled a time when he once had sunspots around the bridge of his nose, a fresh-faced youth with wide, emerald eyes and perpetually unkempt auburn hair. The man before him now had not changed drastically in appearance, but his expression had grown weary, his eyes telling the stories of a hundred lifetimes. They searched now for his lover, who wore a similarly troubled expression.

Dan slumped down in his seat, swirling the last bit of brandy in his glass as he stared into oblivion. "I need to rest," the hybrid creature decided, looking up to reveal the dark shadows beneath his royal blue eyes.

David nodded. "Absolutely."

"Before I do," he said, taking a long drag from and extinguishing his cigarette, "let me tell you that we met a host of creatures in Paris, including a very young, very rich Lucius. When I left them, they were in the midst of plotting some sort of uprising that I was not included in. Cahira joined their crowd, but I could not will myself to do the same. I ended up traveling back to our village, which had been overrun by wolves. Most of the villagers escaped but many, including the Marquis and his family, died trying to fight them off. I couldn't stay in our home without her, so I took over the castle until one day, a raven appeared at my window. It told me you were here, and that I needed to find you to stop Lucius, Angelique, and their following. So here I am. But I cannot speak any more of Cahira. Not tonight, anyway." He finished his drink and stood, filling the room with his broadness and height.

David stood as well, usually taller than most men, but appearing average next to his herculean friend. "You have been more than helpful tonight, and I thank you for it."

"Yes," Morrigan echoed. "Thank you for telling us your story, Daniel."

Dan nodded and left without another word, leaving a trail of cigarette smoke behind him.

Morrigan's eyes swam with worry, as if her mind was racing behind them, connecting ideas and memories at a rapid pace. Finally, words spilled from her lips, reflecting what they all were thinking. "If the realms have been destroyed, that means if we die on Earth, we will not return to the Upperrealms. We will simply no longer be. There are no human believers left to bring us back into existence and the only thing keeping track of any reincarnations was the Records Hall I left behind in the Underworld." Her expression seized up with worry. "David, if there is no Underworld, that means Anubis has died. We have to find him."

"We will," David promised her. He turned to Libraean, addressing them both. "I guess it is settled then. We must go to France."

Libraean frowned but gave a nod of acquiescence. He noticed Jacob had dozed off at some point in the night, burrowed under a wool blanket on a couch near the fireplace. He did not stir, even with the movement around him, emitting tiny, grumbling snores.

"We should let him rest," David suggested.

"Yes," Libraean replied, the word light with his apathy. He packed up his things and retrieved one of the dwindling lamps. "I will take the upper rooms."

"Are you certain—"

"I am," Libraean interrupted firmly.

David sighed in easy defeat.

"What is the problem with the upper rooms?" Morrigan inquired, observing their exchange.

"It is where our ghosts reside," Libraean replied, too tired to explain any further. He withdrew in a similar haste as Dan, hoping no one would follow him as he headed up the east wing stairwell.

He couldn't remember a time that his body didn't feel tired, a persistent ache in his bones that grew worse with lack of sleep. His knees popped in protest as he hobbled up the stairs to the third-floor corridor, holding the railing tightly with one arm and a stack of papers in the other, taking his time up the spiral. He was too exhausted to organize his notes, but he already thought of a title for Dan's story: The History of Lycanthropy. The term was used in the ancient times by Petronius, the first to blend the Greek words for "wolf" and "man" to describe the affliction. He wasn't sure if that was the earliest source he had; he would have to check his records, which were sealed in the Lardone vaults that lay underneath the manor's cemetery.

The subject of Cahira was of particular interest to him, though he decided he would keep his thoughts to himself. She had naturally tapped into a power that had been undocumented for centuries. Although he was certain she was a liminal being like himself, he knew it wasn't the sole reason for such power. There was something more. He would need time to sit with the information, to consult his records.

He sighed in relief when he reached the top of the stairs, taking a moment to catch his breath before he opened the door, releasing the scent of musty old wood.

The third floor of Lardone Manor had two spacious bedchambers to the west, accompanied by their own staircase. The eastern set led to a single room that should have been an attic, a drab, spartan chamber with no fireplace and no windows except for a small half-moon shape near the ceiling. The bedroom held a simple bed in the corner, an unfinished pine desk against the wall, and a chamber pot. The man who sold them the house referred to it simply and uncomfortably as "the inhospitable upper rooms."

Libraean shuffled towards the desk, setting down his papers and lamp. He and David once speculated what the room had been used for, since it was noticeably set apart from the rest of the house in its deliberate lack of extravagance. Although most of the Lardone belongings remained on the property, Libraean could find no records belonging to them, save for an old deed to the house, a crudely drawn family tree that had been tucked in a book, and a binder of the Lardone Company's financial records. Any photographs, letters, or keepsakes had apparently been destroyed along with the family. Anything Libraean did know of them came from the ghost of their youngest son, Philip.

He was already seated on the bed, his dark, cheerless eyes sweeping across Libraean's hobbled form. "Oh yes, I remember you. The cripple."

"Good Morning, Philip. If you don't mind, I came here to rest."

The young ghost sighed, rising to his feet in disappointment. He paused to adjust his head back on his shoulders, his neck cracked after his fatal fall off the third-floor balcony. "Too bad," he said wistfully. "I have to tell you something of great importance."

"Oh, yes?" Libraean sighed, realizing the apparition blocked him from the bed. He took the desk chair, setting down his glasses to rub his tired eyes.

"Yes, since you have finally discovered that the afterlife has been altered."

Libraean frowned. "How do you know that?"

The ghost shrugged, the action almost knocking his head back off its shoulders. "My sister likes to eavesdrop on you all. She finds the master of the house quite handsome."

"What do you know of the predicament?"

"I can confirm what the wolf says is true. There is nothing left now but Heaven and Hell. The ancient realms that existed alongside them are now in shambles and there are no gods left to fix them. You are all earthbound, like us spirits, who have been trapped here since the space between realms was altered."

"The astral plane has been affected as well?" Libraean was taken aback.

The young boy nodded. "There are still many in our world who do not accept the God of man, though they aren't likely to admit it out loud. Souls once had the ability to choose where they rested in death, or if they'd return in a new vessel to begin life again. Now these deceased souls are stuck in limbo, either forced to spend an eternity in the overcrowded astral plane or trapped trying to find peace as an apparition on earth."

"Is that why you are here?"

He smiled sadly. "Not everyone is accepted into Heaven. Though He does not cast me to Hell as some would hope, there is no place for men like me there."

Libraean realized what he meant and was overwhelmed by emotion. "My dear boy, of course there is a place for you to rest in peace."

The boy shook his head, his sorrowful eyes like saucers. "You have written it in your own books, Mr. Libraean. Gods exist because men create them. The ancient gods have all been murdered, their realms destroyed. There are too scant believers to bring them back. There is one deity left, but the God who lives in Heaven has been altered so many times by hateful humans throughout history that He has become exactly what they wanted him to be—exclusive and condemning. It does not matter what his Son or his angels believe—the Watchers who sit with Him now will not allow any benevolence. They are the ones who make the rules. Each religious sect has its own heavenly paradise for their followers, but for those that sin, entrance is strictly forbidden."

"You are not a sin." Libraean fought against rising tears.

"I can accept being stuck on earth, but my sister would like to rest," Philip continued. "So, we have decided to help you. There is an old gypsy woman who lives near Limehouse, working under the facade of a tea and cake parlor. She is secretly a gifted medium who once performed seances at this very house for my siblings, long before you and the new master arrived. She can travel about the astral plane and perform what is called hypnosis, a tool which she uses to access memories that have been hidden away. My sister believes this will be of much use to you."

Libraean was amazed at his random benevolence. "Why thank you, young sir. And my gratitude to your sister, wherever she may be."

The boy nodded. "Please restore the realms. Stalking the earth is getting tiresome."

Before Libraean could say anything further, the figure of the young man evaporated into the air as if he'd never been there. He stared at the empty spot, mystified at what had just transpired, when he heard a sharp knock at the door.

He looked up to see David standing in the doorway, his apprehension almost palpable. "I know you do not want to be bothered, but I cannot rest knowing you're distraught."

"No, I'm glad you are here. I just had the most curious conversation with young Philip Lardone. We need to go into town."

David looked surprised. "You spoke to the ghost of Philip Lardone? He hasn't surfaced for years. We cannot go into town. The sun has just risen—it will be hours before dusk."

"We can take the carriage with Jacob as the driver," Libraean formulated a plan out loud. "By the time we get ready, travel, and arrive, it will be nightfall. The weather has been dreary enough that we can use parasols and cloaks. Or you can give us a proper windstorm, as it was revealed earlier you still can."

"Libraean, will you please pause for a moment and explain what is happening here?"

"The ghost confirmed Dan's story—there are no realms left except the ones under the dominion of the God of men. The ancient realms are irrevocably destroyed, and the astral plane is overcrowded with lost souls who have no place in Heaven nor Hell. All the ancient gods and goddesses are dead. We need to access Morrigan's memories from the time she died in Romania until now. From them, we can figure out what happened and how we can fix this mess."

David put his hands on his forearms. "Libraean, why do we need to go into town?" he repeated gently.

"Philip says there is a medium that uses a trick of the mind called hypnosis which can unlock Morrigan's repressed memories."

"Ah." David nodded. "Now I understand. Allow me to speak with her first—we both know better than to make plans in her absence. Why don't you rest for a few hours before the sun sets?"

"I'll go wake Jacob."

"Libraean, you need to rest," David insisted.

"I will have plenty of time to sleep when I am dead," Libraean muttered as he brushed past him. "There is no place for me in heaven, either."

PART TWO

AINGEAL AN BHAIS

ANGEL OF DEATH

CHAPTER FOUR

❧ The Return ❧

Morrigan

THE WIND TOSSED MORRIGAN'S HAIR AS SHE STOOD watching them prepare David's carriage for travel. It had grown back to its full length even though she'd chopped it the day before, an unsettling reminder that she was no longer a human being, but a creature frozen in time. She tucked the long waves behind her ears against the breeze, debating whether to chop it off again as soon as they left.

David hadn't slept since before she arrived, deep set circles hanging beneath anxious green eyes, his skin ashen and lined with worry, a perpetual cigarette pressed between his lips. She longed to comfort him, to be alone again in each other's arms, but she knew things must be resolved before they could have their long-awaited time together. She had helped him get dressed in suitable outing clothes, an unassuming shirt and vest with a traveling jacket that hung to his trousered knees. The dark olive fabric looked good on him, and though his hair refused to stay in place underneath his cap, he looked comfortable as an English gentleman. Of all the eras she'd known him, this one seemed to suit him best.

He had been trapped in thought as he observed Libraean and Jacob preparing the horses when he abruptly turned to her as if remembering she was there. He pulled her into his arms. Her head fit neatly in the crook of his neck, the aroma of tobacco, grass, and freshly cut hawthorn wood drifting into her nose. "Are you sure you'll be alright here alone?" he asked.

She pulled away, an eyebrow raised. "I've been known to do quite well on my own," she reminded him.

He gave her a small smile as he cradled her face with his hand, running a thumb across her cheek. "I know. But you did just die and resurrect as a vampyre and are slowly remembering the warrior goddess within. It is a lot for one to bear. My worry is logical, you should not fault me for having it."

She put her hand on his. "I do understand your apprehension, but I promise you, I will be alright. Someone needs to keep watch over the household and be here when Dan wakes."

"Ah, but still." David kissed her lips. "I do hate to leave you."

"Go," she urged, catching Jacob climbing into the coachmen's seat in the corner of her eye.

He kissed her once more, longer, before climbing next to Libraean inside the coach. Jacob gave her a gentle wave as the trio disappeared down the winding dirt road that took them out of the countryside and into the city.

Morrigan sighed. She'd agreed to their plan, yet trepidation settled in when she thought of receiving more of her memories so soon. She expected it would be a maddening ordeal for any creature to endure, and she tried to relax, allowing the visions to surface as they wished while she pieced her identity together. Her mortal life had already become distant, even though it had only been a few short days since she'd transformed, and she felt like a voyeur who watched another woman live it. Yet even as the threads of her identity ebbed and flowed, there was a deep, constant, primordial knowing that she was far older than any fleeting glimpse of life mortality offered. The ancient goddess Morrigan was gradually reclaiming existence.

The sun finally abandoned the sky, bathing the landscape in darkness. She adoringly observed the tree lines against the lingering hues of sunset, swirls of cobalt blue and black corrupting the pure radiance of day. To the east, a waxing moon grew brighter, ready to take its place as queen amongst the stars. It seemed wasteful to retire so soon on such a crisp, clear night, so she decided to explore instead.

Morrigan wandered away from the manor into the nearby graveyard, admiring the mismatched stones that jutted out from the earth. The ground was still damp from the previous day's incessant rain, and it squished between her toes as she lifted her skirts high around her thighs to save them from spoil. She headed towards the Lardone crypt, a colossal block that dominated the stones around it, made of the same imported marble as the floors of the manor foyer. Although it was obnoxiously large, it was plain, lacking the extravagance found throughout the manor, as if the being who created it was not a Lardone, but someone left behind to clean up the mess. One of the names had been left blank, while another had been scratched out to the point of illegibility. Her eyes drifted to the towering manor, wondering exactly what sort of humans once made their home there.

Her attention was drawn to the woods, where limestone tablets spilled down the hill like wounded soldiers coming home from battle. They were separate from the family plots, and as Morrigan walked through them, she surmised they either belonged to the former church congregation or to the families that once lived nearby. Hidden behind an old oak tree sat another marker that could have easily been mistaken for a family stone. It was an angel carved out of bronze, sitting on a throne and holding an extinguished torch upside down as if snuffing out life itself. Its mouth was a thin line of gratified finality. Underneath bore the inscription: The Angel of Death.

Morrigan approached it, gliding her fingers along the masterful carving, wondering what such a magnificent sculpture was doing in an old countryside graveyard, far beyond what the naked eye could see.

"Why are you not taking us home?" a small voice asked from behind her.

Morrigan startled, turning to see the apparition of a little girl aglow in the darkness. "Whatever do you mean?"

"Do you not recall?" The little girl squinted in confusion. As she grew closer, Morrigan saw the dried blood on her lips and the gauntness of her face, a child held captive by a fatal malady she never should've had to bear. What must have been glorious bouncing curls hung limply around her face as she spoke. "You used to talk to us, to guide us home."

Morrigan almost collapsed as the memory rushed back to her, memories forged eons ago in the Underworld. She smelled roses, heard the rivers of the dead. She closed her eyes, deeply moved. "My child, I am just now remembering..." But when she opened them, the girl had vanished. The bronze angel of death stared back at her with cold, blank eyes and she almost heard it whisper, Victorious.

Her experience was interrupted by the sound of an approaching horseman. She turned to observe a solitary rider navigating the twists and turns of the path that led up to the manor, his horse kicking up a muddy spray. She headed back towards the northern plot to get a better look at him. He wore the riding boots and cloak of a well-to-do gentleman, a high collar and hat concealing his face. He slowed the horse to a trot as he grew closer, stopping immediately when he noticed her. He swung long legs around the steed easily, landing on the moist earth with a gracefulness uncommon in someone so tall. "Mademoiselle, are you alright?" he called to her, his accented voice marked with concern.

She frowned as she put her hands on her hips, both annoyed that she was being bothered and suspicious of a stranger approaching David's home. It occurred to her that she could not pick up his scent, realizing it was not a human standing before her, but a creature. "I am quite fine, thank you," she replied. "I am Lady of this house. Might I ask exactly what you are doing here?"

He faltered, pulling the cap from his head respectfully, revealing shorn, wild hair that mimicked David's, though it shone like polished onyx in the moonlight. "Forgive me, madame. I am looking for a gentleman that goes by the name of David. Does he live here?"

Morrigan felt a wave of unease. She was not threatened by the stranger physically, for she knew her own strength simmering underneath its prison of flesh and dainty bones. Yet there was still so much she didn't know about David's life or the war being waged against the ancient gods. It left her feeling vulnerable, a sensation she had difficulty accepting. "Who are you?" she demanded.

"Ah, my manners seemed to have escaped me this evening," he stumbled. "My name is Aidoneus, and I was told by a mystic in France that I must sail to England to speak to a man named David. Apparently, there are curious things happening in the unseen world, things he can shed light on."

Morrigan relaxed. "Well, you are in the right place. I am David's wife, Morrigan."

"What a lovely name," he remarked as he took her hand in greeting, giving it a faint kiss.

"Our manor lies ahead, but I'm afraid David is off on errand. Would you join me for tea? Although something tells me tea is not your drink of choice."

The man beamed behind the shadows. "I should have known you'd sense I was a vampyre, as it seems you are one as well. Though, I must admit, at first, I thought you were a ghost."

"My transformation has been recent, but a vampyre I most surely am," she confirmed. "Would you mind a short walk?"

"Not at all," the stranger agreed, gently taking the reins of his horse to lead it forward. It was a beautiful animal, its hair black and gleaming like its owner's. "I happen to love late autumnal weather, right before the frost," he commented.

"As do I," Morrigan admitted, lifting her skirts once more over the mud as they headed up the hill and through the manor gates.

She led him to the stables where he tied up his horse, passing by the gatehouse to the front door. "We only have one manservant and he's with David tonight, so you'll have to make do with me," she explained as they entered. "I'm afraid I don't make a very good lady of the house."

Aidoneus chuckled at her frankness. "I think you are wonderful." The dim light of the manor finally revealed his face. He appeared youthful, but burdened by intelligence, a few lines creasing smooth pale skin against warm brown eyes. Long sideburns grazed his angular cheeks and settled onto a pronounced jawline. Morrigan was an unusual height herself, yet he still managed to be taller, not brawny like Dan, though they were dressed in similar French fashion. Dark purple lined his black wool cloak and decorated his silk cravat. The shining aubergine fabric caught the lamplight as he hung his cloak near the others before following her into the parlor.

She was grateful that Jacob had straightened things before he left and kept a low fire on. She gestured for him to sit as she stoked it, then moved towards the bottle of tainted brandy and clean glasses Jacob had arranged for later. She caught a glimpse of herself in one of the mirrors and winced, awkwardly smoothing her hair and skirts, wondering how she must appear to a gentleman born in this era. She frowned, additionally wondering how she'd managed to go from a war goddess running wild and free over the hills of Ireland, drenched in blood, to a woman stuck in an English estate, pretending to be a lady and worried over the state of her hair.

Her guest had seated himself in David's preferred chair, looking around the room with curiosity. "A dreary old house, but with such character."

Morrigan handed him a glass of sanguine liquid which he gratefully received. "It was once a church built by defiant, wealthy Catholics on Protestant land. They tried to capture the old Greek Revival tradition in its architecture."

"Ah, so you are both beautiful and intelligent," he observed as he sipped his glass. He winced slightly at the taste, setting it back down on the table.

"Has it gone bad?" she asked, grateful for an excuse not to address the compliment.

"I prefer my blood fresh and warm," he shrugged. He leaned back in his chair, studying her. "Why does it feel as though I've met you before?"

Morrigan stiffened, immediately thinking of her human past. "I have never been to France, so I wouldn't imagine we have. I only arrived in England recently, as well," she half-lied. "I am not native to this place."

"No, I didn't expect you to be. Although you speak English quite well, you seem out of place here. I'd wager you're the type of woman who needs fresh air, mountains, and seas more than finery and smog."

Morrigan was stunned into silence by his accuracy, but he didn't seem to notice, peering out the dark window instead. "Do you know when we can expect David to return?" he asked. "Though the current company is quite pleasant on its own." He smiled at her, revealing strong, ivory-white teeth.

"I'm uncertain exactly when he'll be back," she managed. "There is a problem in the unseen world, as you called it, and they went into town to speak with someone who is rumored to have answers."

"Ah, perhaps someone who can help rebuild the realms," he said hopefully.

Morrigan was taken again by surprise. "So, you know what has happened."

"Not entirely, which is why I made the long journey here," he replied, as he patted the pockets of his frock coat. He produced a slim black case lined with cigarettes rolled in dark paper. When he lit the tobacco, the air filled with an infusion of exotic spices. "How strange it is that, as of now, there is no afterlife, and should our immortality be prematurely interrupted, we would be doomed to roam with no direction, never to return again."

Morrigan stood to pour another glass of brandy for herself, a sense of unease she couldn't explain settling around her shoulders. "I can only hope that our lives do not end," she murmured, as she gazed out the window at the glowing moon.

"But perhaps it is a good thing," he suggested, taking another hit from his strange cigarette. "If there is no life after this one, then it would be repugnant to squander our fleeting time here—forcing us to live each day like it is our last."

Morrigan smiled as she made her way back to the loveseat. "A very good point," she said softly, taking a careful sip from her glass.

The fire crackling behind them suddenly grew in intensity, brightening the room.

"My word, you have the most beautiful eyes I have ever seen," he remarked, his own appearing to scintillate as he gazed at her. They didn't look brown anymore, more like the color of refined topaz, brought to life by the flames. He took another long drag from his cigarette, releasing the spiced scent back into the air.

Was it cinnamon? She wondered as it wafted to her nose, frustrated to have forgotten so many simple things. "Clove," she whispered aloud when she remembered the word.

Understanding hit her so hard that she bolted to her feet, sending her glass crashing to the floor. "Aidoneus is another name for Hades," she sputtered. "The Greek god of the Underworld, the guise he once took to avoid detection…" She realized with perfect clarity that she stared directly at none other than Lucius.

He looked confused as he stood. "Please calm down, madame, I gave you my other name because my human name is more dangerous. I was told by the mystic that I am a reincarnation of the Greek god of the Underworld, so I thought it would be a good alias."

Morrigan backed away until she reached the edge of the fireplace, reaching behind her to retrieve the poker. "I know exactly who you are."

He exhaled sharply, visibly exasperated. "I was told that David and I had a colorful past and that I should be wary, but no one warned me about you."

"I believe nothing you say," she said, gripping the poker tightly in her fist.

"Then you probably wouldn't believe me if I told you that somehow you look even more alluring when you're poised to kill someone." He smiled playfully, the light dancing in his eyes. The longer she stared into them, the more confident she was that she hadn't made a mistake. No matter what body he'd come back in, their mischievous glimmer remained.

"Tell me why you've actually returned, and I won't skewer you with this poker," she growled, surprising herself with her ferocity. It felt natural, the way her heart hammered her blood through her veins, pulsating at her throat. From outside, she heard the distant call of crows.

"I should warn you first that I'm carrying a revolver filled with silver bullets. I'm well aware that the metal can kill our kind. Secondly, I can easily raise that fire behind you so high it would devour the room in moments. But the longer I stand near you, the more I find you completely fascinating and no part of me wants to hurt you. So let us be civil, and I will answer all of your questions."

Morrigan narrowed her eyes. "You mean to convince me that you just stumbled upon me by sheer chance? That you have no idea who you really are and what you have done?"

"Please." He softened his voice. "My name is Louis de Sadet. I was imprisoned in France for murder and for inciting a riot that spurned an insurgence like no other. I escaped, and have been on the run ever since, taking on various personas until I made my way here. I was betrayed by my own kind, the ones who gave me immortal life. I believe it was they who destroyed the realms and murdered the gods, and who now seek to kill all who have reincarnated on earth so only they are left to rule. I believe they made a deal with the only god who remains incorporeal, the God of modern men."

"We were told you were masquerading as the King of France," Morrigan informed him.

"Ah, but that never occurred. While that might have been the initial plan of my associates, I rebelled against their weak attempt at garnering power. They eventually found me and ordered my death. And now I stand before you, a hunted man looking for answers."

Morrigan studied him, searching his eyes. While history implored her to proceed with caution, she couldn't ignore the sense that he was telling the truth. She didn't have time to ponder it further, however, for David suddenly flew into the room. Lucius ducked out of the way just in time, managing to come up behind her and press the barrel of his pistol against her temple. The rich aroma of cloves reached an overwhelming peak, heat radiating off his body as he held her against him.

David shook with anger, squalls of wind pummeling through the windows, sending the room into a flurry. Libraean stumbled through the door after him, his eyes widening as he took in the scene before him. He ran to shut the windows, trying to fight wind that shrieked in rebellion.

"You must be David," Lucius said dryly. "I was just telling your wife that I have no idea who you think I am, but that I came to you for help."

"As you press a gun to her head?" David snorted.

"You all seem extremely unreasonable, and I have to protect myself," he huffed.

Morrigan felt as if she'd lived through this exact moment a hundred times before, the room shifting and bending to reveal castles, temples, battlegrounds, all pointless backdrops showcasing a war that always was, and always would be. She saw herself between it always, both the conduit and the calming waters, her image always changing but her expression staying the same. She felt Lucius's heart thumping against her back, fighting against the fiery emotion he kept caged within. Its beat kept time with hers and in that moment, she knew he had no intention of harming her, and she knew what needed to be done. In a quick, fluid movement, she snatched the gun away, aiming it directly at David.

He stared at her in disbelief.

"David, stop the wind," she commanded.

He realized what she was doing and took a deep breath and relaxed, the windstorm ceasing its agitation. Libraean sighed with relief as he fell back from the windows.

Morrigan backed away as she alternated her aim between the two of them. Lucius stood in equal surprise, watching her curiously with his arms up in a gesture of submission.

"Nothing will be solved this way," she explained. "Lucius does not remember our past and has come to us as another creature who needs our help."

"And you believe him?" David sputtered incredulously between the deep heaving breaths keeping his adrenaline at bay.

"No," she admitted, "but we cannot be certain. We know the memories come when and if they choose to."

"So, what will we do with him until then?" Libraean spoke up, worry tightening his words.

"Put him in the vaults," Dan's booming voice interrupted the exchange as he strode through the doorway. He was in the process of pulling his shirt over his head, revealing acres of tattooed runes, his hair disheveled as if he'd just been woken up from a deep slumber.

"Wait just a minute—" Lucius began to protest.

"You will be fine," David snapped at him. "The vaults have been turned into a residence with ample space and provisions. If you are who you claim you are, then you won't mind if we proceed with caution."

Lucius scowled. "This is obscene." He hadn't moved from his position, but every candle that surrounded them in the parlor suddenly burst to life.

Morrigan turned to aim the weapon directly at Lucius but realized she didn't need to. As soon as the candle flames rose in intensity, they were promptly extinguished with a wave of Libraean's hand. All eyes turned to him. "You say you do not remember who you are, so let me inform you that as your first creation, I share the same endowments as you," Libraean told Lucius. Although his stature was stooped and his skin weathered, a glimmer of strength shone behind his eyes, warm light hovering around him. "My manipulation of fire may not be as strong as yours, but when combined with a ravenous wolf, an ancient weather god, and a warrior goddess, we will win this battle. It is best that you come quietly. Besides," he added, "it is my dwelling they're putting you in, and while I hate the idea of you in my home, you will be perfectly comfortable there."

"Fine," Lucius sighed in defeat. "What a grand mistake coming here was."

Dan looked at David. "I will go with them."

"Nonsense, I can go—"

"No," Morrigan interjected. "You and he should remain separated until we can figure this out."

"I can manage him," Dan assured David.

He sighed, and reluctantly agreed.

Lucius's eyes flitted back to Morrigan. "I suppose this means I won't be getting my pistol back."

She lowered it, answering only with a raised eyebrow.

"Regardless of circumstance, it was lovely to meet you," he said brazenly, without any regard for who stood in the room. "I do anticipate our next meeting."

Morrigan did not reply, keeping careful watch as Dan led him out of the room, Libraean shuffling after them.

As soon as the door closed, David flew to her, holding her tightly for a moment without speaking. She could feel his body trembling against her. "I knew I shouldn't have left you," he finally said.

Morrigan slipped out from his embrace. "I am able to take care of myself, David," she reminded him. She set the pistol down on the table to make her point.

He didn't smile, his eyes still wrought with trepidation. It appeared as though they'd sunken into their surrounding shadows, shades that seemed to grow darker as the nights passed. His skin had lost its luster, the black blood that ran through his veins so vivid beneath it that it gave him a grey and sickly pallor. He licked at cracked, parched lips.

"David, you need to sleep," she told him gently.

"How can I? There is so much going on, so much that I must do…"

She reached up to brush away a rusted gold curl from his forehead. "What will it take for me to get you to rest?"

He didn't answer, just pulled her back against his chest. His heart felt weak against hers.

"Did you find the medium?" she asked.

"Yes. She agreed to help us, though I had to ensure that her time was well compensated for."

She led him to the loveseat, where remnants of her shattered glass sparkled amongst the floorboards. She scooped them into her hand before tossing them into the fireplace. "So she will be able to access my memories?" she asked as she dusted her hands off on her skirts.

David nodded. "If you still consent to it, she says that she can. I'm not sure I feel entirely comfortable with her, so it will be up to you to decide."

Morrigan considered his words. "I don't think I can bear knowing that Anubis is out there somewhere, vulnerable. Or any of the gods we once knew… Lugh, Ogma, the ones from our time in Ireland."

"My word, I'd completely forgotten about them."

"If there is any way to discover clues as to what has happened, then it is my duty to try whatever I can."

David gave her a weak smile as he rested his hand at her knee. "You still have a choice, love."

"My choice is made."

David nodded, leaning back as he rubbed the space between his eyes. "Now please explain to me why Lucius is underneath my cemetery?"

"Apparently, he has been betrayed by the ones who turned him into a vampyre, meaning there are more creatures out there than we thought. He believes it is they who destroyed the realms, that they are aligned somehow with the God of men."

"You know what he says cannot be trusted," he reminded her.

Morrigan sighed. "I know, but I once saw right through him and I'd like to think that ability has never left me. I believe he is being truthful. But perhaps my memories could shed light on that mystery as well."

She caught the scent of humans, turning to see Jacob in the doorway, accompanied by a woman seasoned with age. She stood shorter than Jacob and frail, her hair hanging full, free, and blinding white against skin that had spent long hours in the sun. Her ruffled blouse was loose, her skirts long, beaded jewelry hanging from her neck. The memory of her sister's spawn, Hekate, sprang forward in her mind, as did the vision of her skirts darkening with moisture, her eyes wide, as the child inside of her let her know it was time to come out.

The crone's colorless eyes bored into Morrigan's. "Are you the one?"

Morrigan moved closer. "Yes."

The woman studied her for only a moment before she shook her head. "I cannot do what you ask of me," she told David.

His eyes resumed their frantic worry. "Whatever do you mean?" he protested.

"That," she pointed a gnarled finger at Morrigan, "is not a human, but the most ancient power that exists in this world—the one who created us all. There is nothing I can do for her that she cannot do herself. Even if I tried, I would be risking my very life."

"Woman," Morrigan suddenly asserted. "I am bound by the same rules of earthly life as any other being. I have no more power here than you, for it has been dispersed over many millennia."

"Great sorrows befall those who upset the balance between worlds," she argued. "Aiding Lilith would show I have chosen a side."

Morrigan blinked, the sound of her very first name tugging at a long dormant piece of her soul. "I intend on preserving the balance," she told her.

"Then why are you here with him?" the woman demanded, pointing at David.

"Because I do not remember. I need your help, just as I needed the help of my sister. You say there is no greater power than mine, yet you forget there were two of us who created this world, not one. Heka's power runs through your veins—stronger than that of our ancestors, I might add—for I released more into the world with my death centuries ago."

The old woman peered at her quietly for a few more moments, then nodded. "I will help you, but I choose no side."

"Thank you," David said, relieved.

Morrigan noticed Dan and Libraean had rejoined them, standing transfixed in quiet observation. Libraean held stacks of fresh parchment in his arms and Dan had fully dressed. Although he was the only one amongst them who had rested, his deep blue eyes were somber, his expression weary.

"What will you need?" David asked, surveying the parlor.

"All windows must be shut, all the curtains drawn," the crone instructed. "She and I must sit across from one another at a table. The rest of you may attend, but no sound is to be made amongst you."

"Perhaps the library would be better suited to our needs," Jacob suggested, catching David's eyes.

"Good idea." He nodded, leading the entourage across the long hall beneath the twin stairwells into an echoing chamber, dark and cold with neglect.

Morrigan quickly learned what Jacob meant, for as soon as the gas lamps were lit and the fire rose, she saw the large oval table sitting at the crux of the windowless room, surrounded by ample chairs. Towering bookcases lined every inch of the walls, crammed with hundreds of bound leather books with no space left on the shelves. The room dripped with masculinity, its edges hard, decorated in rustic earth tones accented by gold. A handsome mahogany desk was situated near the fireplace, the chair behind it tall and upholstered with leather. The way the books rose to the edge of the domed ceilings reminded her of a place she couldn't recall, the look of it strangely familiar. She wondered why David hadn't opened the room to them until now.

"It reminds me too much of Lucius," he said softly, as if he'd read her mind.

The men scattered around the room to meet the medium's demands, leaving Morrigan and the crone alone to stare at each other. A thud reverberated through the room as Libraean dropped his books and parchment on the desk.

"Thank you," Morrigan said to the mage before her in a quiet voice. "For agreeing to help me."

"Do not thank me yet," she warned. "You might not like what I uncover."

I appreciate you just the same, Morrigan said in her thoughts, hoping the woman was also connected to the channel used by animals to communicate.

Are you certain you want me to do this? The crone reiterated, confirming Morrigan's suspicions she was a reincarnated goddess, one that could speak to beasts.

What can't you say amongst them? Morrigan asked her as she began building a layer in her mind so David could not hear them.

You were dead during the burnings but hear me when I tell you there is no place for those who worship the earth and revere the matriarch. There is a war brewing beyond the eyes of mankind—the gods against the goddesses.

Morrigan scoffed. *That cannot be true.*

Look around you, Lilith. You wear a corset around your waist, but do you know why? Have you not heard the cries of your daughters while you spent your years floating listlessly amongst us? The humans have abandoned the religions of old and those that refuse to are eventually murdered. Why would the spirit world be any different?

I was told that both the gods and the goddesses were killed, Morrigan argued.

The old gods were killed because they honor and respect you, the crone insisted. Look how the humans behave! The Egyptian gods have been twisted into symbols of evil, the reason they call my people "gypsies" and why they have persecuted us for centuries. Lilith now represents pure evil, seductress of the first man and eventual consort to the Devil, the name they gave their dark god. The Celtic gods have been turned into nothing more than fairies and leprechauns, the Norse gods, heathens wiped from history, the African goddesses, evil, the first Americans, savages—every religion that venerates our precious earth and the women that create life upon it has been warped and twisted into detestable pillars of wickedness. Gods cannot exist without their worshippers and humans all worship the great punishing God of man who lives beyond the zenith in the sky.

Then that is all the more reason that I must do this, Morrigan asserted.

Yes, but there will be a price, Lilith. And that price is that Osiris will turn against you.

Morrigan was stunned. *David? I do not believe that for a moment.*

I am Cassandra reincarnated, the prophetess of doom, cursed by the god Apollo to give true predictions that no one believes. You deciding to ignore my words now does not make them any less true.

"Are you ready?" David's voice gently broke in.

Morrigan looked around to see them all seated around the table, save for Libraean at the desk, a cigarette already smoldering between Dan's fingers. They had draped the table with an old tablecloth, Jacob scattering the various crystals and charms from the medium's bag atop it. Morrigan saw a ball of polished quartz at the crux of the table, recognizing it as a tool of divination, used for centuries. David squeezed her hand reassuringly. She searched his eyes as she squeezed it back, finding love in them, as always.

The medium took her seat, gesturing for her to follow suit. "The room must be dark, save for a few candles," she told them.

Libraean waved his hand, dimming the fireplace to flickering embers. The library was once again plunged into soothing darkness.

"Where are we going?" she asked Morrigan, her eyes like glass behind the folds of her skin.

"After I died in the Wallachian Kingdom, the year fourteen sixty-four," Morrigan replied quietly.

"Do you remember the moment you died?"

"Yes."

"Think back to that moment. Stare into the ball until you can see yourself there."

She began to tap her fingernails rhythmically against the table as Morrigan searched the glass. After a few moments, she could smell the river and the piney aroma of evergreens, interrupted by the sourness of spilled blood. She could see vampyres tearing each other apart in the war waging below her, heard their screams and growls. She saw Lucius and David standing frozen in front of her in the castle, wearing masks of horror as she edged closer to the window. She saw Delicia's body smashed against the rocks, surrounded by crows, watching them lift her soul into the air.

"Take us there." The medium's voice was far away now, her tapping fingernails echoing in Morrigan's mind, like the beat of an ancient drum. She gradually slipped into subconsciousness, her nose filling with the scent of extinguished fires and the curious bite of cloves.

CHAPTER FIVE

🎋 The Underworld 🎋

Morrigan

MORRIGAN AWOKE WITH A START. Darkness surrounded her, but she could not hear the familiar sound of the wailing dead and the rushing waterfalls that funneled into their accompanying rivers, the macabre melody that marked her presence in the Underworld. She surmised she was still there, but things felt more solid to her than they had felt in years, the floor that she lifted herself off of firm under her bare feet. She walked forward and hit a stone wall, and her breath caught in her throat. She was trapped.

For longer than she could remember, she drifted quietly throughout the many hollows of the Underworld, her presence undetected. Only the dead who wandered aimlessly down its corridors could see her, and soon she found herself counseling the lost souls and the wounded mothers, the suicides and the frightened children, guiding them to the spaces where their souls could rest in peace. She worked alone, for long ago Anubis and she decided it was best that even he could not find her, lest David or Lucius catch wind of her whereabouts. It proved bittersweet, for she finally had the opportunity to know her son better, but neither one of them was willing to risk the potential trouble it could cause.

Resuming a less intensive version of her work as a death goddess proved good for her, and Morrigan fell easily back into the role. She tried not to pine for Earth, choosing instead to remember the pain she caused there and her firm resolution never to return. Her soul ached for him of course, the one she loved, but she hated to indulge in the longing, distracting herself instead with the affairs of wayward souls. It was a life she could accept, one that was meaningful and good, until this very moment, when she awoke to imprisonment.

The room flooded with light, confirming her suspicions. Her prison was three walls of impenetrable stone, the fourth, a wall of cast iron bars. A bed was pushed into the corner next to a table that held a trio of candles. Torches burned brightly against the ashen stone walls, their glow revealing her solid form, the one she remembered most fondly, tattooed arms, bare stomach, and tunic cut into two. She reached up to graze short hair, chopped just the way she liked it, and adorned by a thin crown of avian bones. She was Morrigan again.

"Ah, you're awake."

Morrigan threw herself at the bars with a snarl. "You," she growled. "Let me out of here or I will tear off your limbs."

Lucius sighed from where he stood, far enough away that her arms wouldn't reach. He had chosen to appear to her as a cross between the Egyptian god Set and the vampyre Lucius, shirtless, his narrow white chest adorned by a thick obsidian collar in the old style, his wrists in gold cuffs. His jet-black hair spilled around his shoulders in waves, his ochre eyes glittering in the torchlight. "This is why I imprisoned you. I couldn't trust that you wouldn't attempt to harm me or run."

"Why shouldn't I harm you?" Morrigan cried. "After all that you have done. I told you both I did not wish to be found and your solution is this—to imprison me?"

"Please, Morrigan, just hear me," he pleaded. "I have had a long time to ponder my actions and have nothing but the deepest regret for what I became on Earth. I want to make it up to you."

"By locking me in a cage?" she sputtered. "Why are you not bound to Tartarus? Where is Anubis?"

"Your son is the one who let me out," he replied calmly. "He and I have grown civil over time. One day, he decided I'd paid enough for my transgressions and allowed me to have my own realm in the Underworld, provided I never attempt to find you."

Morrigan narrowed her eyes. "So you deceived him."

"Well, unintentionally, yes," he admitted. "But I did so for your own safety."

"My safety," she snorted. "And you expect me to believe that Anubis has forgiven you for mutilating his twin?"

"It's true, though I'm not sure I'll ever forgive myself." He looked away, as if struggling to be forthright. "I was incensed when I discovered you all planned to sacrifice my life for Osiris's, and I acted out of sheer fury. However, I may have plucked his eye out to keep him out of the afterlife, but I never knew the act would curse him to a disfigured reincarnation, no matter what anyone has told you. Anubis knows the truth of what happened, which is another reason he decided Tartarus was no longer a place for me. It is a realm for the vilest of creatures, not those who see the error in their ways. Besides, it's now being ruled over by some insignificant brute the humans created, who appears as a cross between the Greek god Pan and some caricatured daemon. Apparently, he is supposed to be the archnemesis of the Christian God, but no one could ever figure out exactly who or what he actually is—half the attributes were already given to me. He is a pointless being who ended up following me around during my stay like an unwanted apprentice, irritating me with his primitive questions. I was glad to be rid of him."

"Enough," Morrigan cut him off in frustration. "Tell me, why am I here?"

Lucius suddenly looked nervous. "Not long after David sent me back to Tartarus, I stumbled upon a woman down there who looked and behaved like Delicia, like you, when you were Morgana…" A far-away look crossed over his face before he blinked it away. "I thought it was you for a moment, though I was confused why you took on that form. It turns out she was an imposter, an old chaos goddess who calls herself Discordia."

She realized what he implied. "You must be joking."

"You think I would do this to you if the situation was not severe? She has already killed several dark goddesses searching for you. I could not love her the way she wanted me to, Morrigan. If anyone could understand that, it would be you."

"I do not believe anything you say," Morrigan sniffed, though her grip relaxed on the bars.

Lucius noticed, edging closer to her, though he remained hesitant. "I promise you—Discordia hunts you now, believing you are the reason I left Tartarus and why I could not give her what she wanted. That is the only reason I searched for you, so I could make sure you were safe."

"As endearing as you wish to sound," she said flatly, "I know the true reason you want me here is because if she does succeed in killing me, my soul would find itself back to earth to reunite with David."

Lucius did not attempt to lie, only shrugged with a sheepish grin. "Bitter rivalries seldom die."

Morrigan sighed, placing her hands on her hips as she studied him. "If you cage me too long, I will grow mad," she warned.

"I know, I just wanted to speak to you without you…overreacting."

"I do not overreact," she growled.

Lucius raised an eyebrow.

She threw up her hands in exasperation. "Set, let me out."

Lucius sighed and flicked his wrist. All around her, the prison disappeared. They were in a palace, the one he'd once built when he orchestrated the grand facade that was Hades, the Greek god of the Underworld. It was a beautiful, towering structure that appeared to be carved entirely out of deep blue and black marbled stone. Its color highlighted the paleness of his skin and the poisonous warmth of his eyes. "Please stay here, at least until Anubis can find the rogue murderous goddess."

"I would pull her teeth out," Morrigan insisted, her temper building, annoyed to be treated like a weak fawn rather than the fierce she-wolf she was.

"Give me a few days," Lucius begged her. "What are a few when we are down here for eternity? Besides, I have something to show you, something I have been working on that I think you will love."

Morrigan eyed him suspiciously.

"Morrigan, please trust me for once," he pleaded, gesturing for her to follow.

"Never," she replied lightly as she strode past him, following the direction of his arm.

The palace dissolved into a swirl of black clouds, dissipating to reveal a rocky path surrounded by low water on both sides. Morrigan couldn't help but be intrigued, steadily following the path laid out for her as he trailed behind, until they reached a door made of tree branches and bones.

He flicked his hand to open it, like he had done to remove her prison, revealing the most magnificent landscape she had ever seen. It was a combination of all her favorite places, seeming to span for miles, with rolling hills, acres of woods, and running streams stretching out before her. She could smell the damp earth and the crisp leaves, feel the wind in her air. It felt like earth—like home.

"I cannot believe you did this," she murmured, genuinely amazed. "How is it possible?"

"I was once the architect of the Underworld," he reminded her. "I never lost the ability to create and bend the realm. It was how I was able to create Hades's Palace, how I was able to fool Anubis into believing I was a Greek god."

"It's beautiful," she admitted, watching white, fluffy clouds drift away from the sun.

"I want you to know that I have changed," Lucius said softly from behind her. "I regret the things I have done, including how I neglected you when we lived here together so many eons ago."

Although entranced by the nearest babbling brook and the bands of trees oscillating in the wind, Morrigan was still hesitant. She relaxed ever so slightly, however, as he slowly slipped his arms around her waist, his voice in her ear. "You have always been restless and free, the qualities I most cherished in you. I was so concerned with my own affairs that I didn't think to worry that you wanted someone else, that I did not satisfy you anymore."

Morrigan was quiet. She watched as a crow swooped down from the sky to land in a patch of grass, stomping the ground for a moment before pecking the dirt in search of grubs.

"I shouldn't have been upset that you fell for my brother," Lucius continued. "We are of the same spirit, he and I, and he loved you in a way I was incapable of doing. I know my actions are inexcusable, but I have always envied him. Envy is a tricky feeling, one that can rot you from the inside out if you allow it. I kept it at bay for much of our existence but losing you to him was what finally unleashed the dragon from inside of me."

"I seem to continuously have that effect on you," she teased, distracted by the crow now stalking the riverbed.

Lucius gave a soft chuckle, his breath warm on her ear. "It is only natural that I died in Wallachia a true monster, a reflection of what I had become. I have many regrets about the latter portion of my earthly life. Enough to spend years in reflection."

The crow was joined by a second one, this one a bit larger than the first, who respectfully kept its distance as it foraged nearby.

"You kept me caged in that life, too. In another woman's body," she murmured.

"That was mostly your idea, and David's," he reminded her. "I was the one who tried to convince you both against it. Had I remembered who you really were, I would have found a better way than fusing you to some unworthy vessel. But once you were there, alive for me to be near and to hold…I couldn't bear to let you go. I became desperate."

Morrigan grew quiet again, watching the corvid pair share a meal together, existing comfortably in each other's space. "You loved my sister," she said in a low voice, hating how pathetic her final excuse sounded, as if she was nothing more than a jealous child.

Lucius turned her around roughly to face him, his gold eyes blazing with emotion. "I have always and forever loved only you," he said between gritted teeth, his fingers digging into her arms.

The crows began to squawk loudly behind them, but Morrigan could not see them. His intensity captured her, taking the breath from her lungs. She struggled to pull back her emotions, finally succeeding with a sharp, "Let me go."

He released her, also realizing that he had temporarily lost himself. His gaze moved away, settling in the distant trees. "If you wish to stay, this place is yours," he told her. "I will not bother you as long as you are here, but if you need anything, the palace lies beyond the river. That is where I will be."

He disappeared without looking back, leaving her to the magical, artfully constructed world that mirrored what she'd left behind. The grass felt cool and comforting under her feet, the wind tossed her hair. She sighed, deciding to give it a few days.

Two days, no longer.

The pair of crows drew her attention back to them as they soared above her, flying away into the distance, side by side.

She wasn't sure how much time had transpired since she'd first arrived, but she knew it was longer than she anticipated. The solitude was deliciously soothing, and she spent it hiking the acres of woodland, swimming in the creeks, or traveling the skies with her birds. Some days she ran, enjoying the ache in her legs and cold air in her lungs, discovering that the realm built for her was seemingly endless. The sensation of being physical, grounded in a body with mud between her toes and cold water on her skin was exactly what she needed.

Each night, she built herself a fire and fell asleep under the stars, tracing them with her finger as she mouthed the constellations David had once taught her. She missed him still—always—but the longer she spent in the dark realms, the less painful his absence became. Sometimes she would smile as she imagined him happy, wherever he was, and other times she grew so angry she'd pummel her fists into the ground until her skin tore, the cuts growing bloody and raw. Sometimes she thought of Lucius, which brought its own conflicting emotions. As of late, it was a quick fury that would eventually cool into an appreciation for the world he'd created just for her.

It was dusk when she finally decided to visit him, calling down to one of the crows. "Can you take me to him?" she asked. It replied with a clanging squawk, darting towards the river. She followed its direction and dove in, the waters pulling her down until she landed on polished stone floors. Creek water came along with her, rolling down her skin as she stood up in front of him, his eyes wide in surprise.

He wore billowing black robes, opened at the chest, his wrists and hands free of jewels, save for a simple chain that hung from his neck, the obsidian jewel at the end barely visible above the folds of fabric. His arms held stacks of leather-bound books. "You came," he said in open wonderment. "Do you need a towel?" he added.

She suddenly wondered if she'd made the wrong choice, the way his eyes moved across her wet, barely clad frame. "I was beginning to grow bored," she explained flippantly, grabbing a nearby blanket to drape around her.

"I imagined you would. I'm surprised you stayed down here as long as you have."

Morrigan sighed as she squeezed the moisture from her waves. "I do long for earth, so it was a nice distraction."

"Come, let me put these away," he gestured for her to follow him down the hall into his library. It towered over them both, a duplicate version of his beloved Library of Alexandria, one of the greatest libraries to have ever existed before it was prematurely destroyed. This version held rows upon rows of heavy volumes instead of scrolls, stretching as high as the eye could see. She recognized it from their old Egyptian palace, the familiarity of it pulling forward memories of the long hours they'd both spent there. She could see him perched over his desk in ruminative vexation, brightening when she'd come into the room.

"It's nice to see you reading again," she commented. He'd fallen away from his favorite pastime in Wallachia, focused more on conquest than simple pleasures.

"It does pass the time," he said lightly as he began to place the books back into their proper places. "The longer I exist, the more humanity produces. It still astonishes me the way their minds continue to evolve. No matter how long a period of philosophical stagnation, one lone rebel publishes something that awakens the masses. It's fascinating, really."

A colossal fireplace roared white flames at the center of the room, drawing attention to the large furry creature curled up next to it. It lifted not one head to greet her, but three, its six glowing eyes studying her as she moved.

"Cerberus, it's Persephone's sister, Nephthys," he warned him as he reached up to push a stubborn book back on the shelf. "She is always welcome here."

Hearing the goddess of spring's name reminded Morrigan of the past, when Lucius had risen from Tartarus under the guise of Hades, with her sister, Isis, masquerading as his queen. She grew quiet, her mouth settling into a frown.

"Is everything alright?" Lucius asked, as he looked over his shoulder.

Morrigan realized she had wandered over to the beast during her reflection and began absently running her fingers through its wiry black fur, much to his enjoyment. "Oh, yes," she murmured. "Cerberus remembers me from long before you brought him here, when you first created him as your companion in Duat. You loved creating animals and creatures back then."

"You do remember!" Lucius delighted. "You preferred being the goddess Morrigan for so long, I thought you'd forgotten your life as Nephthys. It seems he remembers you, too."

The three headed dog, once the notoriously terrifying guardian of the Greek Underworld, curled itself back up by the fire like a common canine pet, content from her affection, and drifted back into a peaceful slumber.

"Being down here does remind me of my life before," she admitted. "I suppose there are parts of it I do miss, parts I'd long forgotten."

Lucius brightened. "Do you remember our Egyptian palace when we first came to live down here?"

Morrigan paused to think. "I remember this library clearly, but specifics are still hazy."

"I can reconstruct it if you'd like. It has been dormant for a long time, but I'm confident I can bring it back."

Morrigan hesitated. "Actually, I came here to tell you, it is time for me to leave this place, to resume my solitary work. It was good for me… it kept me busy."

He deflated, the corners of his mouth falling as quickly as they had risen. "I understand."

She waited for him to begin his verbose appeal, but he surprised her by quietly turning back to his shelves.

"That's all?" she blurted out. "No waging a crusade to convince me to stay?"

He turned back to face her, surprising her again, this time with the sadness that dimmed his eyes. "What do you want from me?"

Morrigan was taken aback by the question, finding herself unable to answer it.

"Of course, I want you to stay," he finally said with a sigh. "But I know better than to try to convince you. I have heard nothing from Anubis regarding Discordia, and I believe we would have heard something by now if the situation hadn't been resolved." He replaced the final book on its shelf.

He turned to face her, suddenly struck with an idea that brought the smile back to his lips. "Why not dine with me once before you go? I can put together the old courtyard. I actually intended on doing it at some point and this would give me the perfect excuse."

She considered it. "Alright," she said, "but then I wish to go back to being a shapeless spirit with no physicality, no feelings, nothing. Just as I was before."

He peered at her. "Is that really what you want?"

"It is what I deserve," she murmured before she could help herself, hoping her voice was low enough as she turned away that he hadn't heard.

She watched the last sunset in her private world, admiring how its glow painted the clouds a radiant shade of carmine. She knew she would miss it, but she'd long accepted that when it came to her life, all good things came to an end. She took one last deep breath of clean, fresh air, sighing as she followed the new path he'd laid out for her to reach the palace by foot.

As soon as she walked through the towering black doors and into the foyer, she noticed the dress that had been set out for her. She was mystified to discover it was the exact one she once prefered in her past, a long black tunic with a plunging neckline that wrapped tightly around her waist and swept the floor as she walked. Her old jewelry was laid out neatly next to it, handmade Egyptian pieces of lapis lazuli and quartz, set in bright silver instead of the typically preferred royal gold, a preference she had developed over time in the Underworld. She once explained to him that it was because it reminded her of the moon.

Again, she found herself appreciating his thoughtfulness, slipping on the costume of her former self. Her eyes caught her reflection in the mirrors that lined the hall, giving her pause. She wore the clothes and jewels of Nephthys with Morrigan's tattoos and muscles, a seamless blend of the goddesses she personified. She had never seen the two pieces of herself together, surprised by their synergy.

She couldn't help but smile as her eyes settled on a nearby glass vase brimming with white roses. Once her favorite flowers, their petals were strewn down the hall, beckoning her to follow. She entered the long atrium that ended with Hades's throne, following the flowers down the hall lined with wide mouthed basins holding either radiant white fire or murky sapphire water in an alternating pattern. The path ended with a cracked chamber door, the aroma of food escaping from behind it.

She pushed it open and gasped, for in an instant, everything came rushing back to her.

Their palace above ground, where they stayed on occasion with Isis and Osiris, was a grandiose structure that stretched a mile long and a mile across, home to exotic gardens, a menagerie of animals, and exquisite fountains and pools. In the Underworld, Set and Nephthys created a replica altered to fit their own tastes. He was the architect, but she was the designer, the two of them piecing together a monochrome world of jet black and shimmering white, from the statues of obsidian jackals to the columnea ornamented with skulls.

It sat high on the rocks, surrounded by water that separated it from the rest of the Underworld, including the rivers that delivered souls to their respective afterlives. Set obeyed her every wish and command without reservation, even when she requested an enormous library that would keep track of the souls and their reincarnations, so she could make sure everyone was cared for.

Morrigan smiled at the recollection. He'd even remembered one of her favorite places in the palace. She called it her Thinking Pond, an oval pool filled with lotus blossoms that danced lazily on the surface. She loved it for its soothing water, often finding herself lost in thought for hours at its side with her feet submerged. He'd also brought back a variation of the indoor courtyard that once housed it, except now it was overwhelmed by hundreds of rose bushes, all white, and the stone tables that surrounded them holding nothing but vases teeming with the ivory petaled flowers.

He stood before the pool, his eyes hopeful and his skin flushed with trepidation. He was wearing his best black robes, his hair neatly combed away from his face, accentuating his narrow face and high cheekbones. He licked his lips anxiously. "You look exquisite," he managed.

"You scattered the walkway with rose petals," Morrigan pointed at the floor. "Are you trying to seduce me?"

Lucius let out a nervous laugh. "Perhaps. Or maybe I knew you'd enjoy the slow recollection of your former home."

He gestured her to the white marble table he had arranged near the pond, draped in black silk with more roses arranged at the center. He'd laid the table with small plates of figs, dates, and pomegranates, a few slices of bread, and a carafe of wine. She smiled as she picked up a ripe pomegranate. "And to think, this fruit is actually my favorite."

"Humans do mix up our stories. I suppose it is in our nature to confuse them," Lucius shrugged. "Does this suit you?" he asked, referring to the arrangement.

"Very much so," she nodded. She took her place, studying the fruit in her hand. "I have not eaten a pomegranate in quite some time." She split its rind apart with a crack, staining her fingers and lips maroon as she pulled a few seeds into her mouth with her teeth.

Lucius tried not to stare at her as she licked her lips, retrieving a date for himself and taking a bite. He grimaced slightly, setting it back on his plate. "I never did gain much of an appetite back since my days as a blood drinker."

Morrigan slipped another few seeds between her lips. "Do you miss that life?"

Lucius looked thoughtful. "Yes and no. I was young and hostile as Set, bent on destruction and revenge. I did love you, and eventually, I did begin to appreciate our work down here, but there was always a fire burning inside me, aching to be released. I felt like I was left behind as the world above us flourished, and I became blinded by my determination to be a part of it." He paused to pour them both a glass of wine, and she noted it was the blend of white she once preferred.

"When I was first resurrected as Lucius," he continued, "I forgot so much of who I was that I felt free, reborn to a life of endless possibilities. Memories would float back to me on occasion, but I was like a fresh piece of stone, ready to be carved. Yet, even then, I felt that same burning desire for something I could not name. I assumed physical destruction would sate the inner hunger - I was a blood drinker after all—but eventually, even that grew dull. I realized it was my mind that needed to be stimulated, and once I discovered this about myself, I embarked on a quest for knowledge, conversing with humans, traveling the globe, discovering new lands and ideas - only to return to the same land years later to witness it completely transformed with even newer ideas. I was still a bloodthirsty immortal, of course, but in those days, the days before the first millennia, I was content. I was happy, even. So yes, to answer your question, I do miss those days."

"What changed?" Morrigan asked innocently.

"You."

Morrigan sighed. "Why must you always blame me?"

Lucius chuckled. "Why do you always rise to the defense? I'm not blaming you—I am answering your question. What changed was you came back into my life, and I fell in love with you, again, only to have you fall in love with David, again, without any of us knowing we were repeating the same damned mistakes we'd made before. Having you around made me feel like Set again, though at the time, I didn't realize nor understand it. Morgana was vicious and deranged, bringing out that dormant side of me. I felt close to her in our fleeting moments of battle camaraderie, so I sought out more wars, created more chaos. Over time, I became less interested in the minds of men as I was in power. And then, at some point in time, I snapped. Probably around the time I found you and David cavorting in the river." He looked away, taking another sip from his glass. "Again, I am not blaming you, Nephthys, I am simply answering your questions."

"Morrigan," she corrected him, an unintentional sharpness in her tone.

"Oh yes, the entire persona you concocted with a bunch of Druids to escape me and run off with him," he deadpanned. "How could I have forgotten?"

Morrigan scowled. "I knew we could not dine together without discord."

His jaw tightened. "Maybe you are right."

Morrigan looked up at the mirror above them, watching as tiny white fish wove around the floating blossoms in the sapphire pond below.

He interrupted her musing with a sigh. "I just want to know why."

She could feel him staring at her, but she didn't want to meet his eyes. "Because he was kind," she said softly.

Lucius snorted. "I can be kind."

"No, back then, you weren't," she insisted, finally meeting his fiery irises. "You viewed the management of souls as a daunting task, one to coldly speed through so you could focus on your wars. You created a labyrinth of trials for them to go through simply to rest or reincarnate. I heard the way the humans spoke of you—they feared you and our realm. They began to fear me even though I worked alongside them." She sighed. "Eventually, I started to believe that perhaps I really was the dark side to Isis's blinding white light, like you'd become next to Osiris. But I didn't want that—I wanted to be good, to be kind. I suppose his love for me proved that I was."

"You shouldn't need someone else to prove your worthiness," he quietly pointed out.

Morrigan looked away, taking a quick sip of her wine. "Yes, I know that now. I was very young back then."

"Well, in any case, you could have told me how you felt."

"When?" She felt a flash of irritation. "When were you around to talk to?"

"I was here, Morrigan. You were the one who was always running. You hated the feeling of being trapped in one place—you still do. And further-more, you love fighting battles just as much as I did—do you really expect me to believe that me going off to manage wars was one of the reasons you ran to David?"

"You never took me with you!" she argued, anger starting to rise. "You went your way and I went mine."

He surprised her by not matching her frustration, staring instead at his hands in silence, as if acknowledging she was right. It held for a moment while she gradually deflated.

"I do not know why I did what I did, the true reason I fell for him," she said finally in a voice barely above a whisper. "It just happened. But you cannot ask me to regret it. That would mean I regret bearing my sons and they are the only decision I ever made right."

Lucius turned his entire body away from her, the opening of the oldest, deepest wound he bore, the one that she had caused him, sending him eas-ily into despair. "Those were supposed to be my sons," his voice trembled.

Morrigan saw his grief-stricken face reflected in the water, threatening to melt away the brick of icy anger that held her together. "I did not know Osiris and I could create life that way," she told him, trying to stay cold as emotion seized her. "I would have never done that on purpose. When I realized I carried his sons, I was terrified that if you found out, you would kill them."

Lucius whipped around to face her, an inferno behind his eyes. "I would never have harmed your children!" he cried incredulously as he pounded both fists on the table, causing the dishes to clatter. "I would have raised them with you! We could have been with them—both of us! I knew that was something I could never give you, but don't you dare believe for a moment that I never wanted it. Of course, I would have preferred it to play out differently, but we were given an opportunity to have what we both secretly desired, and instead, you chose to give them away and flee."

Morrigan felt tears crawl up into the corners of her eyes, her turn to have her old wounds painfully resurface. "How was I to know you would have accepted them?" she whispered. "You hated Osiris—I had to protect them."

"But I loved you. No matter what you thought about me back then, I never stopped." Lucius's rage subsided the longer he stared at her. "You left and I had no idea why. I just wish… I wish you would have told me. You broke the last bit of goodness I had left in me."

It was Morrigan's turn to cast her eyes down in silence.

Lucius rose up from the table. "I need to be free of this place. There are too many memories here."

"I think that would be wise," she agreed softly, as she stood.

Lucius waved his hand and they were back at Hades's palace, a fire steadily roaring behind his throne. He positioned himself as close to it as he was able, visibly comforted by its intensity and warmth.

Morrigan gazed at the great tapered doors that exited out of the palace. Her feet seemed unable to move towards them, though her mind told her she should go.

"You can leave," Lucius assured her. "Forgive me for ruining our meal."

"We needed to speak plainly." Morrigan looked down at her maroon stained fingertips. "We still do."

Lucius turned towards her, a dark silhouette against the radiant fire. "What more do you want to know?"

Morrigan broke into a pace, her robes swishing around her bare feet. "I am going to ask you this once more," she said as she started slowly up the steps where he stood. "Did you love my sister?"

"No," he replied firmly, meeting her eyes. "Not like I love you. Isis and I fell into each other's arms once out of hurt, jealousy, and confusion, but nothing came from that moment except that I unintentionally received some of her power. She became a dear friend to me over the years, here when no one else was. She visited me while I was trapped down here, her presence offering a bit of solace - but that was the extent of our interactions."

"Yet you still managed to impregnate her."

"That was a plot hatched out of desperation," Lucius insisted. "Our interactions were never about romantic love."

"You cannot expect me to believe that."

"You are confusing lovers, Morrigan. David was the one who fell in love with another woman, not me," Lucius shot back.

Morrigan promptly punched him in the nose.

He shook off the blow before grabbing her by the arms. "You know what I say is true. That was the reason you left us both in Wallachia. You hated him for falling in love with another woman, for not loving you like he once did."

Tears rose up in her eyes, her face flushed by an overwhelming mix of pain and fury. "No, you are wrong. He didn't remember me when he took another lover and besides, I've long forgiven him. I left you and him on Earth because I needed to be gone—for both of your own good."

"You are a liar." He released her wrists, taking a step back.

"How very hypocritical coming from you," she sneered. "I shouldn't be here. I am taking my leave of this place, something I should have done long ago."

"As you wish. Return to the one who does not deserve you." He waved his hand dismissively as he turned back towards the fire.

But again, she couldn't leave. Her eyes instead caught the churning pool of black liquid situated at the foot of his throne. "I want to know more about that mortal girl he loved. Was that one of your plans?"

His eyes were honest but curious as he crossed his arms before him. "No," he asserted. "I was afraid Isis would never be freed from her prison, like she so desperately wanted. I was only trying to speed up the process by pulling her out of the tree prematurely with the Druids. Believe me when I say that I sincerely regret both my impatience and failure."

Morrigan looked at him blankly. "What are you talking about?"

His eyes widened. "You don't know?"

"Know what?" Morrigan's temper started to climb.

"That the slave girl David fell in love with was a piece of Isis, the human part of her without magic."

"Explain."

"Isis hid after my initial creation, and when I found out she'd resumed her place in the Acadia because she was afraid to die, I wanted to bring her back and make her an immortal like me. I tried, but all that came out of the tree was a human girl. I found out, long after her death, that she was actually a piece of Isis's soul. I assumed you had been told as well."

Morrigan was stunned for a moment before her face turned resolute. "Let me see them," she said suddenly. "In your scrying pool."

Lucius shook his head. "Absolutely not. I might not be pleased with you at this moment, but I will not let you do that to yourself."

"Set, please."

"No."

He turned to retreat from the main hall, but she swiftly blocked him, taking his hand in both of hers and cradling it to her chest as she looked into his eyes. "Please. I need to know."

His resolve melted and he threw up his hands in exasperation. "You are the most frustrating of creatures!" He stormed towards the throne with her on his heels and sat, grabbing her by the waist and pulling her onto his lap. The waves immediately stilled at their presence, letting them gaze into the glassy, premonitory water. "Give her the answer she seeks," Lucius commanded the pool.

The waters shifted and swirled until she saw him, the young human Davius, walking barefoot in the dirt under the Italian sun. She watched scenes of his life roll by, of his days as a slave boy in a winemaker's villa, his quiet moments with his first love. She watched as they laughed and chased each other through the vineyards, Davius skipping after his strawberry blonde nymph, making love to her finally in his chambers, and teaching her the names of the constellations before kissing her passionately under the stars.

The same way he'd once taught Morrigan the stars in Ireland, tracing them with his finger.

She blinked, numb, as she slowly rose to her feet. "I've seen enough."

Lucius looked up at her, concerned. "What did you see?" he asked carefully.

Morrigan suddenly felt very cold, as if her body had been submerged in a frozen lake. "He really did love her," she whispered.

"Oh, Morrigan…"

"Their souls found each other through time. He saw me after she died, he knew who I was, and yet, he didn't remember me. You were the one who saw through me—even though your memories were not clear at the time, you knew instantly that you loved me."

Thunder crashed outside the palace as she spoke, immediately followed by a barrage of heavy rain that hammered angrily at the palace roof. The vases of water that lined the walkway to the throne suddenly burst from their confines in violent geysers, raining black water onto the marble below.

Lucius realized what was happening. He jumped to his feet. "Morrigan, you are both a Celtic war and water goddess, and goddess of the dead—you have the power to shape and destroy this realm," he warned her.

"How could I have been so foolish?" she said disgustedly, not hearing him. "So many decisions I have made based upon a lie." The ceiling above them grew heavy, bending with the pressure of rapidly accumulating water, threatening to give way.

"Morrigan, he was only a boy when he fell in love with her," Lucius reminded her quickly. "He loved you as a man, as an immortal. He eventually remembered who you were."

"No, not until my niece—one of your daughters—told him," she spat. Without warning, her clenched fists sprung open, pulling the water down from above.

Lucius leapt forward from where he stood, catching the rush of water and throwing it back into the air. He sealed the roof with a wave of his hand before whipping around and tackling her to the ground. He pinned down her arms as she struggled against him.

"This is your fault—yours!" she cried. "You could have just left her be—they would never have met had it not been for you!" She wrestled her arms free so she could pound him with her fists.

Lucius did not argue with her, letting her thrash and hit him, wincing only when she split his lip. Finally, she stopped, giving in to the tears that began to stream down her cheeks, as the funnels of water that had risen around them fell back into their basins. "I hate you," she whispered.

Lucius melted with sadness. "I know you do," he said as he wiped away a trickle of blood from his mouth.

She growled with frustration as she grabbed a fistful of his hair, pulling his surprised face towards hers and kissing him roughly. The old familiar taste of smoke and cloves filled her mouth, disarming her instantly, the memory of knowing him intimately comforting to her, alleviating her pain.

Lucius broke away in shock.

"I don't really hate you," she admitted softly, finding herself lost in his swirling gold eyes.

Her words jolted him into action, and he pounced, his mouth hot on hers as he ripped apart the fabric of her clothes, his body firm and inviting as they fit as seamlessly together as they always had. The way his knowing hands explored her skin with untempered hunger set her insides ablaze, provoking her to kiss him deeper, faster, angrier.

Finally, she managed to kick him off of her, sending him crashing into the flaming vases which spilled, setting the surrounding fabric that hung from the columns on fire. Oblivious to the destruction, she lunged forward and mounted him, tearing away his clothes as she resumed their ferocious kisses. She ground herself against him until he could not bear it any longer and he grabbed her hair, pulling her off him so he could resume his position on top of her. He knew exactly how to move to please her, reminding her that he could overpower her, tear her apart at any moment, but instead, he chose to submit to her, the notion driving her mad with unbridled desire.

She raked her fingernails across his skin as he thrust himself inside her, still pulling at his hair and struggling until he rolled back over. She hopped astride him once more, kissing and biting at his lips until they both hit the point of greatest pleasure. The palace seemed to shudder with their climax, the flames that roared around them growing stronger before they fizzled out in a puff of ashen smoke.

They fell away from each other, breathless.

After a few moments, he turned his head towards her. "Will you stay with me now?" he asked with a sideways smile.

"Take me to your bed," she replied.

Morrigan sighed as she closed the book in front of her, replacing the quill in its holder. Her hands were stained with ink, a telltale sign that she'd spent hours at her desk, correcting and updating her records.

The Records Hall was blissfully quiet, its endless volumes looming high above her head. They held the histories of every reincarnation she had ever overseen, an extensive catalogue of names, dates, and events. Many souls preferred to remain in their respective heavenly realms, but many still chose to repeat the life cycle on earth, and each time this occurred, a new record was made. She'd left the Hall a self-sustaining entity that carried on in her absence, yet she swore she heard it sigh with relief the moment she returned to maintain it.

She leaned back in her chair and stretched the knots from her shoulders as she watched the books organize and reshelve themselves to accommodate her new entries. She started to get up when she sensed his presence behind her.

He swooped down to set a cup of spiced tea on her desk, grazing her forehead with a kiss. "You have been here for hours."

"There was much that needed to be done," she explained as she stifled a yawn. She took a careful sip from her cup, savoring the taste of cardamom and clove.

"Shall we retire to bed?" Lucius attempted to sound casual but when she looked up at him, she caught a salacious glint in his eye.

"Not quite yet," she replied with an amused smile. She rose from her desk, blowing out the sputtering stubs of candles which dwindled down to the last bit of wick. "I want fresh air."

Morrigan wasn't sure how long it had been since she'd decided to make the Underworld her home again, but at the beginning, Lucius opened up his palace to accompany sprawling night gardens and pools that led out to the earthy realm he'd created for her. They strolled through it together nightly, basking in the glow of the brilliant moon and starlit sky. Lucius enjoyed the prospect immensely when she first suggested it, for it reminded him of his days as an earthbound blood drinker.

Tonight, she noticed that he added the chill of autumn to the realm, knowing how she adored the crunch of leaves beneath her feet and the hint of sweet decay in the air. She shivered as the breeze hit her bare skin and he immediately responded by draping a cloak over her narrow shoulders. She smiled to herself, touched by the gesture.

He seemed so different now, but she couldn't determine which one of them had changed. He was still the same obstinate, long-winded intellectual prone to bouts of narcissism, but he was calmer, more considerate, as if he'd matured after long years of introspection. Yet his love for her was just as passionate as always, and she could tell it took great pains for him to give her space and patiently await her company.

She recalled their third or fourth night together, when he discovered her sitting upright next to him as he slept, staring out the window at the moonless, drab backdrop of the rocky Underworld.

"What are you longing for now?"

She smiled sadly, tucking her legs up under her chin. "The moon."

"Come," he said immediately, throwing off the black silk blankets to reveal his pale skin and the taut, shapely muscle that defined his tall, thin frame. He pulled on his robe, tossing her another.

"Where are we going?" she asked, draping the soft fabric around her equally nude body.

He snapped his fingers to light a nearby candle, using it to guide them down the winding stairs from the master bedroom, through the vast, echoing halls to the door of her earth realm. As soon as the fresh air greeted them, he waved his arms like the conductor of an unseen choir, darkening the radiant sky until it turned black, interrupted only by a slice of silver moon and hundreds of dazzling stars. He added the low hum of crickets and the croon of tree frogs, finishing by giving the wind a gentle moisture, much like the humidity after an autumn rain.

Morrigan sighed happily, enjoying the fragrant woods he'd captured so well.

He turned towards her, unkempt hair around his shoulders, his eyes bright in the darkness. "Is that better?"

She slid her arms around his waist, her head resting neatly underneath his chin. "Yes, thank you."

"Would you…" he began before trailing off.

She pulled away to look at him. "Speak."

He looked hesitant, as if trying to find the right words. "Would you tell me about your life as Morrigan? I know you as my wife Nephthys, and I knew you as Morgana, but there is another piece to you I've never known."

Morrigan looked away as a wave of sadness washed over her. She had barely thought of David since she'd chosen to remain there, his memory pulling at her heart. "I feel as though I am all of them evolved into one," she replied as she drifted away from him, the hem of his oversized robes sopping up the wetness of the grass. "The Morrigan was birthed in the minds of the Celtic people who yearned for someone to protect them in battle," she explained, beckoning him to follow. "Their women longed for a goddess to defend their honor and guide their fallen. I fit the role perfectly—a death goddess obsessed with the physicality of earth, the dirt, the blood, the rain. I needed to be a part of it, not drifting above or below it."

"And you brought David with you."

"The humans wanted an entire pantheon and a fatherly god to watch over them. At that time, I'd spent years in the Otherrealms with him, so naturally I had him join me. Back then, I couldn't imagine life without him."

Lucius was quiet.

"We lived out our new lives until the Christians came and the Celts dissipated over so many lands, they were no longer a unified tribe bound by a common religion. We returned to the Upperrealms, only to discover you'd escaped Tartarus. We assumed you'd manipulated my sister to help you do so. I wanted your head - I petitioned every god and goddess I could think of to help me enact my revenge. Yet you had ensured that no one could return to earth without your permission. The only way we could go back there was to die a godly death. So, I killed him."

"It was you?" Lucius was shocked.

"Yes," she said wistfully. "We both decided he should be the one to die, then after he was reincarnated, he would find a way to bring me there with him. I thought the act of it, and the long years I'd have to spend without him, would be my undoing. What I learned, however, was how blissful and freeing solitude could be. Without either of you around, I was free to do as I pleased. I found solace in that."

"What did you do?"

"I continued to serve my people when called," she replied. "I spent time roaming the lands as various creatures. I fell asleep next to bonfires, swam miles in the rivers, ran through forests, and climbed up mountains. Until you both summoned me to Ancient Greece."

"That's it then," Lucius deduced. "The key to your happiness, what led you to create the Morrigan, is that you wished to be free."

Morrigan met his eyes. "Yes, I believe so. And you have always struggled to possess me. Perhaps that is why I could never stay."

Lucius fell silent as he pondered. From the distant woods, an owl added its throaty hoot to the chorus of night sounds.

"I do struggle," he finally admitted. "I want you to be mine, to stay here with me. But more than that, I want to change, to be the type of god you do not want to leave behind. I would rather love you on your terms than lose you forever."

She was touched by his seeming earnestness but gave him a playful smile. "For a moment there, I almost believed you."

He grinned, grabbing her roughly by the waist so that her hips pressed up against him. "Show me. Show me what Morrigan would do."

Together they hunted through the woods, swam together in the rivers, explored the mountains, made love in puddles of mud. They laid in the cold grass, and she snuggled up against his perpetually heated skin as she showed him how to stargaze. Although her heart broke as she looked up into the celestial heavens without David, she began to heal it by teaching Lucius the constellations, tracing them with her finger.

"Ah yes, I've gazed upon them many times during my travels, as we sailed the seas," Lucius surprised her, recalling his time on earth. "They are clearest in the earliest hours of morning, and they change, depending on what part of the world one is in." He waved his hand, moving the constellations of stars across the sky to reveal more, as one would turn the page of a book. He pointed to the constellation Scorpius. "I do not doubt that you've heard of how the humans look to the stars to tell their fortunes, but those in the Western world believe that a person's qualities can be gathered simply by the placement of the sun and the moon right at the time they are born."

"Were we ever born?" Morrigan wondered. "Do you remember?"

"No," Lucius admitted. "I cannot recall the time we came to be, nor can I remember creating the heavens with David. Honestly, my first memory was looking into your eyes."

"Stop," she purred.

"I have always thought of you as being ruled by Scorpio," he continued, "the artfully dangerous protector who lay in wait until the perfect moment to strike and murder Orion, the man who had threatened to kill all of earth's creatures. Calculating, vengeful, but protective, with a deep pool of emotions that not many can even hope to dip into."

"Is that what you think of me?" she murmured, touched, despite herself.

"I have loved you for eternity. It has given me plenty of time to gather an opinion."

Morrigan thought for a moment. "All those attributes could be given to you, as well. Though your pride is your weakness, your anger, your downfall."

"Guess you have had time to think about me too," he smiled.

"Not often," she teased.

He sat up in frustration.

"No, no, I only jest." She grabbed his arm to pull him back down. He settled back into the grass next to her, his eyes following hers back to the heavens. "You are like the lion," she whispered. "Alive with the radiant fires of passion and determination, grandiose and adventurous, with an everlasting loyalty to those you choose to love."

Lucius rolled over to look at her, pain troubling his eyes as they explored her face. "I don't deserve you," he said softly as he ran his fingers through the waves of her ebony hair.

She soothed his worries with a kiss and found she could not recall exactly when she'd stopped. The memory drifted away from her as they walked the winding paths in comfortable silence. Finally, she spoke. "As I was cleaning up some of my older records today, I found myself wondering why Anubis hasn't contacted us. It feels as though I've been down here for quite a while—he must know by now that I'm here."

"Being the sole Guardian of the Underworld is not a simple task," Lucius speculated. "Especially with all the new religions and realms to contend with. He could easily be consumed with his work."

As the centuries passed, the Ancient World and its religions were gradually forgotten. Humans no longer expected to see the jackal-headed Anubis when they died, prepared for him to weigh their hearts to determine how they would spend their afterlife. So, he evolved, becoming the conductor of souls, appearing to them however they needed to see him, as he worked with other gods, angels, and ancestors to deliver the deceased to their respective heavenly realms. It was an exhausting, constant job, but Anubis performed it with patient, artful mastery.

"I suppose you are right," Morrigan sighed, "but I was hoping to eventually see him."

Lucius looked thoughtful. "It isn't like him not to visit you, though. Perhaps he is worried that you are upset with him for helping me find you."

"He was the one who told you where I was?" she exclaimed in surprise. "He would do right to fear me. Does no man among me honestly respect my wishes?"

"We were trying to protect you," Lucius reminded her.

"Although you both know quite well that I do not need to be protected," she said wryly. "What did end up happening with that situation?"

"I honestly don't know," Lucius replied. "I have to admit, I've been rather distracted lately." He gave her a wolfish grin and reached out to grab her.

She darted out of the way, playfully running ahead of him. He caught up with her just as they were interrupted by resounding squawks of crows. Morrigan felt a pull upwards towards earth, a sensation she had not felt for many years. "I am being summoned," she told an equally surprised Lucius. "It has been so long— I thought humans had forgotten about me."

His face darkened. "Do you think it is David?"

"I don't believe so…" The familiar tugging at her body grew stronger, the crows screeching with impatience. They blackened the skies as they circled, waiting for her to join them.

She turned to look at Lucius, his distraught expression softening his features. She realized that even if it was David who summoned her, she wasn't ready to go.

Lucius grabbed her hands in desperation, her figure beginning to dissipate as it was pulled from the dark realm. "Please come back," he pleaded with worry in his eyes.

She cupped her hands around his face as she pushed her lips against his. "I will," she promised.

And then he was gone, and her senses were completely snuffed out.

PART THREE

EXCORNARE

SCORNED

CHAPTER SIX

The Hunters

London, 1857
David

DAVID ROSE FROM WHERE HE SAT. "I believe I've heard quite enough," he said quietly.

Morrigan's eyes gradually opened as she came back to the physical realm, her eyes sweeping over the room she'd left, pulling reality back to her.

He turned, unable to look her in the eye.

"David…"

He didn't turn around. "Please don't."

He was out of the manor in moments, the late October wind prematurely bitter as it kicked up the dead leaves that scattered the rusting grass. He tore through their swirling piles with no real direction, needing to be freed of them all.

He reached the city on foot, the escalating wind absolving it of its daily smog as it howled angrily through the creaks and crevices of the tightly packed buildings. Travelers pulled their cloaks tighter against its chill as a few wayward hats found their way across the street. Many retreated indoors, for the pubs and theatres were still open for patronage, their dim lights glowing through sooty windows, beckoning chilled citizens into their warmth.

He was glad to be left alone on the street, knowing how strange he must look dressed in his house clothes, hatless, and on foot. He slipped down an alley, skillfully navigating its turns until he reached the barricaded door of his favorite opium den. He pushed through it, the owner blinking in surprise before recognizing him. "Come, come, shut the door, the air is too cold."

He obeyed, the suffocating haze of opium smoke resuming its hold on the room.

"The usual, sir?" she asked politely, although her eyes briefly scanned over his shabby appearance. He could hear her thoughts, clucking sounds of disapproval in Chinese.

"No. I wish to be well supplied, but regardless of that, I do not want to be disturbed by anyone." He placed several banknotes into her open palm.

"Of course, sir," she nodded, trying to temper her excitement at the overpayment.

The quiet back room greeted him with its familiar sordid appeal, though he had to wrest away the recent memory of his once nameless companion, the withering woman who would be reborn as his lover. He closed his eyes, trying not to picture her adoring gaze as he held her, the way her blue eyes managed to sparkle the same throughout their many lifetimes. Did they sparkle for him?

He wasted no time in anesthetizing, letting the murky brown smoke carry him to blissful intoxication, a blurry world where he was unable to discern reality from dream. He had no idea how long he occupied the dank back room, floating in and out of oblivion, only that the owner came in periodically to refill his spirits and tar as the hours—days ticked by.

No one ever asked him to leave, gratefully accepting the handfuls of coins and bills he continued to throw their way, lighting his bowl when his hands grew too heavy and setting the pipe nearby when he slipped into unconsciousness. He dreamt of Gaia and of Morrigan and handfuls of children, some blonde and green eyed, some with crow wings. He saw Lucius's grinning face as he held him under water, drowning him as his eyes glowed red fire. He sailed through the endless skies amongst the clouds, heard Gaia's sweet voice calling to him from the heavens.

And then, one day, the owner stood in the doorway, a deep frown creasing her face. "It has been too many days, sir. Your money has run out."

"Nonsense, I have more," David slurred. He absently wondered how much time had passed as he searched his pockets, surprised to find his money had indeed run out. His vision was still blurred from intoxication, a dull ache settling between his eyes as he looked her way. Then he smelled her, heard the blood rush through her veins. Hunger awoke inside him, an edacious beast that had gone long unsatisfied.

He lunged before she had a chance to scream, holding her tightly against him as he sank his teeth into her neck. The hot, sticky blood poured from her veins like a fountain of nectar, reviving his senses. His eyes rolled back in pleasure, drinking greedily and without remorse before her thoughts came rushing to him. He saw the long journey across the sea that had taken her mother and father away by sickness, the determined look on her face when she realized she'd be raising her brothers and sisters, her brief and failed experiment as a whore, and the clever way she'd come into proprietorship. It shook him from his stupor and his sanity returned. He threw her away from him with a gasp, frantic as he checked to make sure she still lived. He found a pulse, offering him a sliver of relief before it was replaced by shame, and he tore out of the den as fast as he could.

He realized his supernatural speed was not up to par, the days of pumping poison into his body leaving him weak and disoriented. He paused in an alley to catch his breath, attempting to steady his legs and slow his racing heartbeat while fighting the euphoria drinking human blood caused.

"Stay right where you are, blood drinker."

David looked up to see the tip of an arrow pointed inches from his face, the glinting metal tip revealing it had been dipped in silver. "Please," he pleaded, sluggishly. "I don't mean any harm. I have had quite a rough few days…"

The woman behind the arrow laughed at him, the sound echoing throughout the dead alleyway. The light from the streetlamps barely reached where they stood, but he could see the faint outline of her hair, curly and wild like the mane of a lion. "I'm sure you have," she said wryly. "Did you not just attempt to murder the owner of the Dragon Den? I'm not surprised, but to murder someone in their own establishment with witnesses present seems absolutely foolish."

"Please, I do not want a fight," David managed. He struggled to stand, his lack of nourishment and excessive intake of opium arguing against it.

"Who said anything about a fight?" she snorted. The more she spoke, she revealed an accent he could not place, one strangely familiar to him. "Our situation appears simple to me. I let go of my arrow, it pierces your heart, you die."

David sighed. "I am much older than any blood drinker you've ever known. It will take more than a silver tipped arrow to kill me."

She took a step forward, a ray of amber lamplight bringing her face into view. She appeared quite young, but her fierce brown eyes told a different tale, and the arm that held her bow string was muscular under the rolled sleeves of her linen shirt. She wore a man's trousers and riding boots, and her cloak was presumably also a man's, draped over a high collared blouse open at the neck and gathered by a handmade vest instead of a corset. He could not hear her thoughts, which let on that she was either a creature or a spellcaster. At that moment, he honestly could not tell which. "What is your name?" she asked.

"David."

She looked surprised. "Fortune smiles down upon you this night, for it seems you are the one I have been searching for. However, I have long learned not to trust a blood drinker as far as I might throw one, so you'll be coming with me."

David didn't even have time to flinch before he was shot with a net that barbed him with silver spikes. He groaned, reminded of the first time he'd been captured that way, knowing it meant he was now incapacitated beyond self-sufficiency.

She secured her crossbow and retrieved her fallen hat, putting it on her head before wrapping her arms around him. David struggled to breathe through the pain, focusing instead on her voice as she whispered ancient words he'd long forgotten, smoke thickening around them until it blacked out his senses.

When the smog cleared, they were no longer in the alleyway, but an isolated, windowless cabin, far from the city hum. She released him from the net, and he fell to the ground, the lingering burn of caustic metal adding to the dull ache of opium withdrawal. She let him be, satisfied he was too weak to cause her trouble, and went to stoke the fire.

David heard a low growl nearby, but she shushed the wolf situated in the corner with a low cluck of her tongue.

"Be warned, she will not hesitate to rip you apart if you make so much as one move to harm me," she informed him, glancing over her shoulder before resuming her task.

David looked around as the fire brought light into the room, noting the full collection of furs—from bear to fox to wolf—draped over wooden furnishings that appeared to have been made from local trees. Herbs and plants hung from the ceilings, while weaponry and bottles cluttered the tables. The casual way she stored healing herbs amongst tools of murder reminded him of Hekate and Dragos, the apothecary twins of Romania. He didn't speak, waiting patiently on the floor for her to address him. Though he frequently killed animals without much exertion, he knew that in his present weakened state, fighting either her or her wolf would present him with some difficulty.

She finally turned to study him, hands on her hips. Her face was round but defined by the apples of her cheeks, her lips full and her eyebrows pointed. Her hair was a deep brown that pulled gold flakes from her fawn-colored eyes, her skin freckled by frequent sun. "I am inclined to believe you are who you say you are," she began. "But I have been fooled by shapeshifters before. It makes it difficult when I cannot hear their thoughts."

"You are telepathic as well?"

"I have many abilities," she said shortly. "But there is only one way I will be able to discover if you truly are who you say you are."

David smiled weakly. "My blood?"

"Yes. Willingly or not, I require your blood."

David lifted his sleeve. "Would you like to do the honors?"

She searched his eyes, then threw him a knife that had been laying on a table nearby. It was followed by a metal bowl that hit the ground with a clang. "Don't worry. If you really are David, I'll make sure you get nourishment afterwards."

David winced as he carved into his arm, black blood splattering the bowl she'd provided for him. As it drained, his body buckled in defiance, a painful reminder of his lack of rest and sustenance.

She snatched the bowl and lifted it to her lips. Her eyes never left his as she drank it, his own vision wavering as he watched her consume every last drop. Her eyes rolled back as she listened to his blood song, centuries of memories trickling into her consciousness. Just when David thought he could hold out no longer, she dropped the bowl, which landed into the ground with a sharp clang as her eyes refocused. She wiped her lips, her teeth stained as if she'd eaten charcoal.

"My apologies, David," she offered mildly. She grabbed a bottle and tossed it his way, giving a nod to her wolf. It abruptly rose from its resting place and headed out into the night.

David fumbled with the cork, shaky hands lifting the bottle to his lips. The blood was cold and aged, but he swallowed it down gratefully.

"I'm sorry it's not very good. I've sent my wolf to bring us a fresh hare." She seemed a bit drowsy herself, both from the rush of his memories and the lingering opium. She slumped down onto the chair nearest to the fire, her long curls fanning out along the gray fur draped over it. "You knew Jesus?" David nodded.

"How can you bear being so old, seeing so many things?" she asked.

David considered her question as he choked down the rest of the bottle. "I forget a lot," he replied. "My memories float back when they need to."

She nodded. "My name is Cahira."

"Pleased to meet you," David responded, before his mind connected the dots. "Wait…"

Her wolf interrupted, bursting through the door along with a squall of cold autumn wind. It threw a still alive hare at David, which he tore into immediately. The warm, fresh blood revived him at once, but he did not pause until the poor creature was drained completely. "Thank you," he gasped, feeling his strength return.

Cahira nodded, taking the rabbit from him, and moving toward the table. She pulled a tiny axe out of the drawer, swiftly severing the animal's head and tossing it to her wolf before removing the skin to spit the meat.

David was amazed to have discovered the woman from Dan's tale, but decided not to tell her, curious to see what information she might have, and not wanting to turn her off from telling it.

"I am semimortal myself, but I do not survive on blood," she explained as she went to the fireplace to cook the meat.

David found himself finally able to rise, the wolf keeping a watchful eye on him as he lifted himself from the floor. "May I sit?" he asked.

She nodded.

He took the chair opposite where she cooked, its fox fur soft against his skin. The light from the fireplace brought attention to his stained clothing and the dirt that had collected under his fingernails. He winced as he remembered the reason behind his filth.

Fortunately, she interrupted his morbid contemplation. "I've been looking for you for quite some time, as I was told you are the original daemon hunter."

"Is that what you are? A daemon hunter?"

"I am what I am," she shrugged. "I was once connected to the spirit realms, but not since they've been abolished."

"So you've heard."

"Yes," she sighed.

"Do you know what caused all this to happen? Or what can fix it?"

Cahira brought her provisions with her, settling in the nearby chair. "It's funny, I've been searching a lifetime to ask you precisely the same thing. But not too long ago, I was finally contacted by an anthropomorphic jackal who called himself Anubis, who told me that I must find you and the rest of the Ancient Ones and bring them with me to Africa, where he lives."

David's eyes widened. "That is my son. So he has reincarnated ... is he safe?"

"Your son?" Cahira looked equally surprised. "How strange," she remarked. "Unfortunately, I don't know about his well-being, only that he wants you to join him. It took strong magic for him to contact me, since the realms are gone, and the astral plane is overflowing. I'm assuming he wouldn't have gone to the trouble if it wasn't imperative."

"Africa," David murmured, taking it in. "Where life began."

"I plan to sail there in two days from now when my ship is ready, regardless of your decision. But I would hope you and your following will join me."

"Yes, of course," David replied, though he frowned as he thought of returning home.

"Don't worry, we don't have to leave yet."

David blushed. "I'm not used to having to shield my thoughts from others."

Cahira laughed. "You must have done it naturally at first. It's a bit more difficult when they're linked to emotion."

"Have you always been telepathic?"

"I have quite a few natural powers, including the ability to communicate on the lines the animals use. That's all telepathy is really, humans have just separated themselves from it over the years. Your thoughts are quiet, but your emotions are loud."

"Fascinating."

"In fact, I have a few more things to tell you before we leave, if you have the time to listen."

Morrigan's face appeared in David's mind, the vision like a knife to his stomach. "Yes, please," he replied. "I have plenty of time."

"Then I will start at the beginning."

SHE GREW UP A CHILD OF THE WOODS, a wolf cub and the daughter of a ghost. She knew no other life than the one where she ran with the pack, watching as they stalked their prey, finding shelter during the snowstorms. She slept in caves under furs, ate berries and rabbits, and bathed in the rivers that melted in the spring. When she was old enough, her mother explained that her life was far from normal, and shared stories of civilized women who wore gowns and drank from crystal glasses, teaching her their ways as she carved into rock and scribbled with chalk on the cave wall.

She hated the lessons, though they passed the long winter nights, for she did not understand why she had to learn their customs and strange language. But her mother insisted, warning her that one day, she might be forced to hide amongst them. Cahira preferred the ones that included tracking animals in the woods, learning how to build a fire that could withstand frigid nights, and which plants she could eat after a fruitless hunt and which plants were poisonous. Hunting was by far her favorite endeavor, but it came with the warning that although she ran with wolves, she must always keep a weapon on her, lest she one day be caught unaware. Her mother showed her how to construct a bow and arrow, practicing with her until she could hit her mark every time. Shooting felt natural, as if the bow was simply an extension of her arm.

"Never stray too far away from a water source," her mother would say, "and if you are ever lost, stay still and listen for the crows. They always linger by wolves and will shriek when there is danger."

Cahira believed her mother was a ghost because there were days she couldn't feel her, even though she snuggled next to her under the furs. She looked like an otherworldly being, her face beautiful and fierce like she was carved out of stone, and she knew everything about the earth as if she was the one who created it. She loved her mother completely, even though she knew she wasn't the one who birthed her. Cahira had nightmares about the woman who did. They revealed her birth mother was a witch who meant to eat her before her true mother saved her, killing the witch and escaping with her in the night. Each time the nightmares came, her mother sang her back to sleep with songs in another language, songs of another time.

Cahira lived happy and free for many years, until her hair reached her waist and buds appeared on her chest. Her mother waited until her blood came before she revealed it was time for the most important lesson of all.

"Today we are going to learn about men."

It was daybreak, the wolves were snoring peacefully around them, still sated by their evening meal. The long winter had ended, and the woods swarmed with creatures, their chatter reverberating throughout the forest from the moment the sun peeked its head over the horizon. Her mother had already draped herself in furs, covering all but her forearms and calves. Underneath, she wore a plain tunic dress. She strapped knives to her thighs, securing her crossbow and arrows behind her.

"Men?" Cahira rose to follow suit.

"Yes, men. Do you remember what I told you about how civilized humans behave?"

"Of course. You said women like me are often married to men, who act as their husbands, providing them with money and giving them children. How could I forget such a dreadful notion?" Cahira shuddered at the memory.

"There are some men who are not monsters, who are kind and caring. But there are many men, civilized or not, who are dangerous."

She snorted. "I am not afraid of anything."

"Cahira," her mother sighed. "No one is safe from death, not even the gods. A warrior does not only have to be strong, but she must be wise. She can never forget that one day, she will die."

Not me, Cahira thought defiantly.

The air that greeted them was cool but not foreboding, sprouts burgeoning between the fallen leaves, signaling the end of winter. Cahira was glad. She'd grown tired of being covered in furs and wearing boots, longing to run naked and free. She wondered how much bigger her breasts would grow, and if they mirrored her mother's, how tight she would have to bind them.

Her mother walked ahead, strangely absent of her usual vigor.

"What is wrong?"

Her mother paused. "Thinking of men has caused me to miss your grandfather."

"You've never spoken of your parents before."

Her mother looked surprised. "Oh no, not my parents. I mean your real grandfather."

Cahira's eyes widened. "You knew him?"

Her mother nodded as she continued to walk ahead. "Yes, but he has long since passed."

Cahira ran to catch up to her.

Her mother continued, "He is one of the reasons I've chosen to protect and raise you, not only because I loved you instantly, but because I once loved him."

Cahira reflected on her words. "So, you once fell in love with a man … and that's your way of telling me not all men are bad."

Her mother gave her a warm smile. "You never cease to amaze me with your intelligence, a leanbh. That was exactly what I was hoping you'd see."

Cahira blushed, for her mother hadn't used the term of endearment since she was a young girl.

"However," her mother continued, "your grandfather was a cruel soul for many years before he changed his ways. Men might seem kind, but you can never forget what they are capable of. You must always be one step ahead of them—physically and intellectually."

She nodded, alarmed by the severity in her mother's eyes.

Suddenly, she heard the crack of twigs, signaling an animal nearby. They both froze, listening to the sounds the woods revealed. Cahira spotted the buck not far from where they stood, watching them with hesitant black eyes. She heard his breath, his heartbeat steadily rising with trepidation. She moved to slowly draw an arrow from her bag to set in her bow, but she heard her mother's voice loud in her mind: *No, we must hide and watch.*

She ducked down beside her in the bushes just as she heard a loud crack, a sound so loud, it seemed to shake the entire forest. The buck fell to the ground, bright red blood sputtering from a hole that appeared in his side. It kicked up its feet in terror and protest, struggling as three humans approached it. They wore full linen shirts and pants, their cloaks lined with fur. They carried long metal objects with them, which Cahira recognized as muskets from her lessons. They laughed, one gleeful as he cried out in one of the languages her mother taught her, "I got him!"

They let the buck struggle in agony as they congratulated each other on the kill. Cahira was furious, not understanding why they couldn't put the poor creature out of its misery. They seemed to gain pleasure from its pain. She hated men already. After what seemed like an eternity, the scrawny one sliced its throat, covering it with a tarp to carry back to their camp.

Her mother waited until they'd disappeared far enough into the trees before explaining, "Civilized men use guns to kill prey. Your bow is quicker and just as deadly, for you can draw and shoot yours before they've loaded their bullets. However, if you ever find yourself staring at the end of one of their guns, surrender until you can find another way."

Cahira nodded, her insides still hot from witnessing the disrespect shown towards the majestic woodland creature.

"There's more," her mother sighed. "Follow me."

They reached their camp, where a few other men had started a cooking fire. A caravan was parked nearby, several horses grazing in the nearby grass. A very large man with fat fingers dragged the deer through the dirt to the place he'd prepared to skin and eviscerate it for consumption.

Her mother gestured her into a heavy thicket which artfully concealed them from onlookers yet provided a full view of the men. Cahira could hear their pointless conversation, slurred, jumbled mutterings as they drank from metal cups, eagerly awaiting their meal. At least they are going to eat the poor beast, she thought dryly.

Her mother began to quietly remove her weapons, setting them in the grass beside her. She lifted off her fur cloak and loosened the ties of her hair. It fell like a waterfall down her back.

"What are you doing?" Cahira whispered.

Her mother knelt, taking her face into her hands so it was inches from hers, her eyes burning brightly. "Listen to me, Cahira, for I have never led you astray. You must stay here quietly while I approach these men as a woman lost in the woods. You must witness their reactions, allowing things to unfold as they may. This is simply another lesson that is important for you to learn. While there are good men in this world—wonderful, kind men—there are many who cannot handle what life has given them. These men choose to abuse women and children, those they are convinced are weak, so that they can feel powerful. To these men, a strong, capable woman is the biggest threat of all. Watch and learn, Cahira. Do not intervene, no matter how frightened you may become. I am strong enough to handle them."

Her words produced an anxious nausea in Cahira's stomach, but before she could protest, her mother kissed her firmly on the forehead and ducked out of their thicket.

She watched the men stumble to their feet as her mother approached them wearing fake tears. "Please help me," she pleaded, in a high, shaking voice unlike her own. "I am so lost, and I cannot find my way back."

"Well, you certainly can stay here with us," said the larger man with a grin, grease dripping from his chin, gore from the buck still on his fingers.

Cahira did not know how long their interaction lasted, nor when she finally snapped—whether it was when one of them grabbed her mother by the waist or when the other laughed at her helpless cries—but it felt as if an otherworldly being had taken over her body, forcing it to act and move in accordance to its will. She felt nothing but the exhilaration that rage often brings, burning with energy as she stood, watching the carnage unfold in front of her. The bear proved unrelenting, tearing the flesh of the heavy man to ribbons, his blood and fat spilling onto the forest floor. The lynx, just as vicious, took the thin man's arm as her prize. Their screams echoed throughout the woods, reverberating against the tall pines above who watched them, indifferent to their agonies. The stench of blood rose thick and metallic in the air.

She felt her mother whisk her away, running through the woods at an impossible speed, cradling her as if she was a young child again. The beat of her mother's heart soothed her, pouring water on the flames that had taken her over. Cahira burst into tears before they reached the cave, their pack awaiting with visible agitation.

They fell onto the bed of furs. "Oh, forgive me, child, I had no idea." Her mother gasped for breath. "I was not in danger, my sweet girl—I only wanted to show you something that cannot be taught in words."

Cahira's entire body trembled, too upset to reply.

Her mother pulled her onto her lap, stroking her hair as she hushed her, murmuring in her ear, "You are safe, my little warrior. We are safe here. Just breathe." The wolves settled around them, watching them closely. "We will talk when the sun rises. Rest."

Cahira suddenly felt very tired, the presence of her family soothing her with their warmth, quieting her tremors. She drifted off to her mother's gentle singing and the snoring of beasts as they journeyed along with her into the land of slumber.

Surprisingly, the dreams that followed were not nightmares of human men, but something entirely different. Her eyes drifted open to see a creature standing before her, a creature so beautiful it appeared genderless, with golden curls and radiant silver eyes. Ivory wings sprouted from behind its back, its robes an iridescent white. It appeared to shimmer as it smiled down at her, filling the cave with unnatural light. Though amazed by its beauty, she noticed her pack no longer surrounded her, her mother also missing. A jolt of panic caused her to spring up, and she scrambled for the knife she kept beneath her sleeping furs.

"Do not be afraid, child," the being told her, its voice high and melodious like the calls of songbirds. "I have only come to deliver you a message."

"Me?" she said, confused. She decided the creature was a male, but he seemed kind, the antithesis of the human males she'd seen at the camp.

"You are a child with great power, power that has been lying dormant inside you. It is the reason why your mother protects you so fiercely. You are the last of an ancient lineage of gods and goddesses."

"Where is my mother now?" Cahira asked worriedly.

"We stand now in a place between the worlds," the being explained. "She is safe in the earthly realm, fast asleep beside you in your home."

Cahira exhaled in relief. "What is your message?"

"There are realms beyond Earth, beyond this astral plane where we currently speak. They are the kingdoms of the gods, places where departed souls rest. You must warn the gods trapped on Earth in mortal form that they are being threatened."

Cahira frowned. "I don't understand. There are gods trapped on Earth as mortals? Why must I be the one to warn them? Why can't you?"

The being looked sad. "These earthbound gods are hidden, protected by magic barriers I cannot push through. But you can."

"But I don't have any power," she started to insist, but the memory of the slaughtered men surfaced as soon as the words left her lips. Although it was a brown bear and lynx who physically tore the wretched humans to bits, she knew deep down they were obeying her unconscious commands.

"My visit is only meant to be brief, and I cannot tell you everything I know," the being said quickly. "Find the creature who goes by the name of David and warn him. We believe he lives in a place the humans call the Kingdom of France. Help him, before it is too late." A look of fear suddenly crossed over his face. "I must go, child. Let all your journeys be safe and blessed." With that, his form dissipated like dandelion seeds in the wind.

Cahira jolted awake. Her mother slept soundly next to her, just as the creature had promised. The cave was completely dark, their fire cold, wolves snoring soundly around her. That was when she heard it—a howl so deep and ferocious it seemed to shake the mountains, a sound no earthly creature could conjure. The hair along her arms and neck rose as the wolves that surrounded her leapt to their feet in alarm, heading towards the mouth of the cave, hackles raised. Her mother bolted upright, feeling for her daughter in the darkness.

"I am here," Cahira said, surprised at how her voice shook. "What is that sound?"

The wolves growled, a fight breaking out at the entrance of their safehold. Cahira's heartbeat climbed to her ears.

"Cahira, listen to me," her mother said, as she felt her way through the shadows for weapons. "No matter what you hear, do not come out of this cave. I cannot turn into a wolf since I am still bound to you, but I will try to fight off this creature the best I can."

"What do you mean? What is happening?"

The sounds of struggle soon devolved into the frightened yelps of a dying pack, accompanied by the horrible sounds of tearing flesh. Her heart raced, pulling tears from her eyes. "Please don't go," she begged her mother.

She scooped Cahira into her arms, giving her a firm kiss on her forehead. "Know that I love you and I will one day find you again. I promise."

Cahira screamed, but her mother flew out of the cave, confronting the unearthly creature head on. She tried to follow, but the cave instantly filled with dozens of ravens, blocking her way forward. She screeched with frustration, batting at their sleek bodies and tiny claws, but it was of no avail—apparently her mother had the ability to command all beasts, not just wolves.

Finally, after what seemed like an eternity, the birds fell away, just in time for her to witness her mother taking her last breath. The vision of her mother's broken and bloodied body stirred the tempest inside of her once again, though this time, she remained conscious as her body shook and filled with energy that was not hers. She saw the creature ahead, a grotesque exaggeration of a wolf with snarling lips and fangs that dripped with the blood of her fallen pack—her mother's blood. Its fur was silver, its eyes as black as its terrorizing claws.

It advanced towards her but hesitated, alarmed by the way the Earth began to tremble. The woods filled with an awful, high pitched screech as tree roots popped out of the dirt like snakes.

Cahira stared coldly at the wolf as the trees obeyed her, slamming down around him so he could not escape, twisting their roots around his arms and legs. He howled in fury as he was lifted and immobilized, splayed out in front of her like a helpless animal about to be slaughtered.

A voice whispered in her ear, a woman who sounded like her mother but much older. "Make him your protector. Carve the runes in his chest and he will submit to you eternally."

Cahira pulled her knife from her thigh and walked up to the frantic wolf. Every part of her conscious mind wanted to slice its throat, but the power humming in her blood instructed otherwise. She dug the knife in its chest as it roared, spraying her with the blood from its jowls. She took her time despite his howling protestations, calmly carving symbols she had never learned into his flesh, ones that seemed distantly familiar. An arrow pointed upwards, *tiwaz*, meaning justice. Another like the end of the arrow, pointed down, *algiz*, protection.

The wolf quieted in gradual submission as she stood back to admire the jagged symbols pouring blood onto the earth, darkening its silver fur with crimson. Words sprang from her lips, a language she did not recognize, "By the powers of the gods, the ancient ones, whose blood runs in my veins, you belong to me now, creature, until your last dying breath."

The power that rushed out of her knocked her to the ground with its intensity. She jumped back on her feet as she gasped for breath, her mind attempting to comprehend what had just occurred. She saw the bodies of her wolf clan lying dead around her and thought of her mother's last breath. She apprehended the creature before her, who now stared back at her with sad, submissive eyes. She blinked, realizing there was a human inside.

English Countryside, 1857
David

"THE DIREWOLF PROTECTED ME THROUGHOUT MY JOURNEY," Cahira said, "even after I freed the man trapped inside him, restoring him to his former self. He watched over me after that for many years. Incredible as it seems, I eventually forgave him when I realized the wolf and the man were separate parts, and that he was not in control of the beast who tore my pack apart." She grew quiet, staring into the fire.

David had clasped his hands in front of him, staring between her and her wolf, whose eyes hadn't left him the entire evening. He felt daybreak crawling closer, and did not wish to be thrown into it, but he couldn't hold back any longer. "Cahira, I must tell you something that I am afraid you may not want to hear."

Cahira turned towards him, lifting a single eyebrow in a way that reminded him of Morrigan.

He swallowed. "I know Dan, the direwolf you speak of. He found me several days ago and he's still at my home. We have a history together."

"He is here? In London?" she sputtered. "How can that be?" She leapt up from where she had been sitting, causing her wolf to rise to its feet.

David watched it carefully from the corner of his eye. "I wish I could tell you more, but his reappearance in my life was just as surprising to me. He was hunting a dark god named Lucius, believing he was the cause of these events, but Lucius appeared at my doorstep as well, pleading his innocence."

Cahira's expression remained mystified as she slumped back into her seat. "And you believe him?"

David sighed, resting his head in his hands for a moment, running his fingers through his hair. "I do not know what to believe," he admitted as he looked up. "We had just begun to unlock the memories of a reincarnated goddess in the hope she would uncover the truth, but I left before the task could be completed."

"Why?"

David sighed again, closing his eyes. "Because she broke my heart."

Cahira snorted rudely. "How very human of you."

He gave her a sad smile. "Human weakness has plagued me for many, many years."

She rose from her chair and pulled open the door. Squalls of wind pummeled through it, sending the hanging herbs into disarray. She lifted her hand up and instantly, it stopped.

David's eyes widened in surprise. "How did you do that?"

She shut the door firmly before turning towards him. "Your blood gave me some of your power. Magic is passed through energy exchange, whether it was the way the original heka transferred through the trees, or in the way it is passed through the vital essence of a living being. Love is the same sort of energy, and to love another means to give them your power, rendering you weak. There is nothing remarkable about love, nor sex for that matter. It is the most efficient way to siphon energy out of a being and rob them of their power."

David found himself at a loss for words.

Cahira chuckled, resuming her seat. "Here I thought you would be the one teaching me. Tell me, did you love only this woman or were there others before her?"

David frowned. "It was not the same."

She laughed again, the sound crackling like the nearby fire. "Did she ever love another?"

David looked down at the ground, craving the hazy euphoric cave he'd just crawled out of. He took a deep breath. "I did not think so, until I heard her memories. We existed long before this time, and I fell in love with her while she was married to my brother. Their marriage had been forced, as was mine, and she convinced me she had never loved him. Not like she loved me, anyway. She left him, and we went on to live together for many years. Yet during our most recent separation, they have seemed to have found each other again... found their love again."

Cahira did not laugh this time, sympathy softening her eyes. "See," she said gently. "She weakened you."

"She wasn't the first to do so either," David mumbled, searching his pockets for a cigarette. "Do you have anything to drink?" he asked.

Cahira went to her cupboards, retrieving an aged bottle. "Homemade wine, a gift from a friend. I can add blood to it, if you'd like."

David nodded gratefully. He noticed her pet wolf had finally decided he was not a threat and succumbed to snoring by the fire. He found half a smoke in the crease of his front shirt pocket. "Do you mind?"

"Not at all," she said over her shoulder as she prepared his drink.

David leaned into the fire to light it, settling back down in his seat. "Dan told us about the time you spent together," he told her. "He never explained how you both ended up separated, but the way he spoke of you revealed how much he loved you."

Cahira set the bottle down a bit harder than necessary. "No. He was my companion because I forced it to be, not because he cared. And even so," she growled as she retrieved another bottle, dripping the coagulated liquid into a glass, "I made a vow never to lie with a man, let alone love one. I am not the type of woman that does well with settling down." She swirled the blood and wine together before handing him the concoction. "Dan knows this."

"Perhaps you have the right idea," David admitted. He took a long swallow, ignoring the bite in his stomach.

Cahira sighed, leaning up against her desk and crossing her arms. "I came to this city to kill *daemons* and to enlighten the living gods to the dire situation they are in. A total of three of such gods are currently in your home, but neither of us want to go there."

"Not in the slightest."

"Then let us sleep on it. I'm sure you could use true rest after your intoxicated sabbatical, and I could use it myself. As you may have guessed, I am not nocturnal by nature. Unfortunately, all I can offer you is the couch."

David finished his drink. "I have gotten some of my best rest in ancient crypts. A couch will be just fine."

"Keep the fire going if you'd like, there is plenty of wood. Dan always preferred it cold, but I thought it was because his blood ran so hot. I've since learned that other vampires prefer it as well." She clicked her tongue at her wolf, who rose to join her as she headed to her room. "Rest easy, Dragon Slayer. We have plenty of dreadful emotions to face in the near future."

CHAPTER SEVEN

❧ The Messenger ❧

London, 1857
David

LIBRAEAN PLACED HIS QUILL BACK IN ITS CASE and rose from behind the desk where he'd been quietly sitting, determined to go after David. Although she had been brought back to full consciousness, Morrigan's face was an expressionless mask, as if she were still lost in the mire of memory. As he stood, however, her eyes clamped onto his. "Don't go after him," she pleaded.

Libraean snorted incredulously. "I cannot just allow him to put himself in danger. Were you not the one who originally tasked me with his wellbeing?"

Morrigan rose from her chair, her black skirts settling around her ankles. "He must go when things become too much for him. We must let him."

Libraean's anger rose. "I have been looking after him for centuries—who are you to tell me how best to handle him?"

Jacob quickly placed himself between them. His shortness seemed more pronounced next to the statuesque vampyre he tried to block. "Libraean, please," he pleaded.

But the kind gray eyes that radiated from his weathered skin only sought to enrage Libraean, a fury he had not felt for centuries dismantling his usual composed demeanor. "You would do best not to speak to me," he snapped. A gust of volatile wind unsettled the parchment stacked on the desk as his wings involuntarily unfurled behind him.

Jacob's lip quivered and he flew from the room without another word.

Daniel jumped to his feet, but the crone raised her hand to intercede. "The hour is late and has brought to life many emotions thought dead," she said in a low, crackling voice. "We must let things settle how they may."

Libraean took a deep breath, suddenly ashamed of how he spoke to Morrigan, though his opinion on the matter remained firm. The light that usually danced in her sky-blue eyes had gone out as she stared ahead, waiting for him to finish. "Please forgive me," he whispered, feeling his temper, and wings, slowly deflate.

"Always," she replied with earnestness, though she was unable to break free of the murky sadness that now swam around her.

"It is time for me to retire," the medium said, pulling herself to her feet. "My work here is done."

Dan made a sound of bewilderment. "We cannot stop now—we have only received the beginning of her memories before David interrupted us. We must continue on."

"That is not how these things work," she asserted. "She must rest."

Libraean pulled off his cap, aware the action exposed the stumps of his retracted horns. "My apologies to you, as well, madam," he said to her. "Can I offer you a room here tonight?"

"I must attend to my other affairs," she replied, her expression dry. "I will be waiting at the tea and cake parlor if the master returns."

Libraean sighed, disappointed but understanding.

"I will see she returns home safe," Dan offered.

"Nonsense," the old woman negated as she made her way out of the room. "My driver has been waiting outside your gates to collect me. Good evening to you all." And with nothing more, she exited the room, her deliberate footsteps disappearing down the hall.

Dan threw up his hands in frustration, storming out in the opposite direction, leaving the two of them behind.

Morrigan was quiet, her eyes drawn to the last gasps and pops of the dying fire. A moment of empathy swelled in Libraean's chest, for deep inside, he could feel the unique connection to the woman who birthed his soul, although his loyalty to David held firm. "I think I will retire to the parlor," she murmured, relieving him of his conflicted feelings. "You should see to Gabriel."

The room was left uncomfortably quiet as the last creature left, Libraean observing his parchment strewn haphazardly across the floor. He could hear the wind howling outside, letting him know that David hadn't strayed too far. Although he was not pleased with her at the moment, Morrigan was right—he knew better than to follow David when he was this upset. But that did not mean he had to like it.

He sighed, bending down to pick up his papers and groaning with the exertion it required. He didn't bother to reorganize the pages before he stacked them, putting them back in their leather binder and wrapping it with string. He shoved it into the top drawer, assuming it would be best to keep it close at hand. He had in his possession now so many different stories, so many histories, it was becoming overwhelming, the pages severely unkempt. He'd have to reorder and bind them into books after everything had settled. If they settled.

A low growl expelled from his stomach, interrupting his cleaning efforts. He had once been able to exist on real food, such as meat and eggs, with only a bit of blood now and again. But it seemed as though turning Morrigan and sampling the essence of living creatures had awakened a craving that demanded nothing else. He sighed once more, shuffling about the room to put the last of the low burning lamps to sleep.

The manor greeted him quiet and dark, just as he liked it, and he found his way easily to the sparingly used kitchens of the manor. They once served as the living area of the priests who served the cathedral before its abandonment, and were refurbished by the Lardones, who attempted to modernize them, but couldn't do much with the size and Spartan design. The kitchen itself boasted a large cast iron stove to serve dozens, and a long preparation counter with cabinets on the opposite side. A round table, tiny by comparison, was situated in the corner for the servants to take turns eating. Beyond that, was a narrow preparation room with another long table at its center, lined with additional cabinets brimming with unused dishes, and a tiny, annexed room devoted entirely to their washing. It was in this tiny room that David stored his reserves, bottles of blood kept chilled in wash sinks filled with ice. An unused wine cellar lay underneath it, a narrow wood ladder leading down to what was once a fully stocked collection. Libraean grabbed one of the bottles from the wash sink, hobbling back to the kitchen to place a pot of water inside the stove. He lit the fire below, waiting patiently at the table for it to boil, hoping to warm it and retire to bed without notice.

Coincidentally defiant of his wishes, Jacob appeared in the doorway. "Oh," he said, startled. "Do you want me to leave? I came down to make myself tea."

Libraean sighed. He was exhausted, his bones ached for rest and his stomach demanded sustenance. He had no fight left in him. "I've got water on—you may as well wait for some for yourself."

Jacob nodded, slipping in. He opened one of the cabinets to produce two china teacups painted with delicate flowers, and a metal tin. He pulled down a matching teapot, scooping into it a few spoonfuls of herbs from the tin. From where he sat, Libraean could smell dried chamomile and lavender.

Jacob's body looked completely different than the lithe angel he remembered, shorter and a bit stockier, tightly clipped white hair replacing the glowing mane of gold, his gray eyes set deep in a mess of wrinkled skin. Yet his mannerisms were the same, his poise graceful, the way his hands moved almost artistically as he did something as simple as brew tea. It let Libraean know that inside his aged prison of flesh, he was still the ancient creature he'd once known… had once loved.

"Before Mr. Lucius arrived, I was sure you'd find a way to head back to the vaults," Jacob commented lightly. "I've never known this house to have so many visitors."

Libraean huffed. "Visitors without the master of the house in attendance."

"Ms. Morrigan is right, he will return," Jacob assured him.

"I understand they are lovers, but that does not negate the fact that I have been the one looking after him for centuries in her absence." Libraean felt his cheeks grow hot. "I might have been his son in our ancient past, but in this life, I've cared for him like he was mine. I cannot shake the feeling that we should be out there looking for him."

"I think I might understand a little of what you mean," Jacob said, not unpleasantly.

"Forgive me," Libraean caught himself. "I know you have lived with him, caring for him as well."

Jacob gingerly took a seat across from him. "How curious to live forever," he changed the subject. "How do you manage? You are, in essence, the oldest one among us."

Libraean frowned, peeking in the stove to check the pot of water. "We are graced with forgetfulness, which I think serves us well. Much like childhood might seem like a fleeting dream to an aged man—he can remember bits, but it is so far from where he is today that it doesn't seem real. It is like that for us. I can remember the ancient times if I focus on them, but mostly, memories just surface at their own discretion. Some things have been forgotten forever. Some things stay, even though I wish I could forget them." He stood as the water began to boil.

"No, no, let me," Jacob insisted. He went to the counter, adding a bit of the bubbling water to the tea kettle before placing the entire bottle of blood into what remained in the pot. He draped them both with towels as they sat. "No wonder you cherish your histories so much. You are preserving the world's memories."

Libraean nodded, almost smiling.

"I remember my life as an angel like it was a dream," Jacob said softly, his back turned. "I've only lived one human life, here, as Jacob, and that's all I vividly recall. Except for you, of course. I remember everything about you."

Libraean waited for a flare up in anger, but it did not come. He looked down at his gnarled hands. He'd become so used to the weathered flesh and surfacing veins, he could hardly remember them any different. "I thought I would enjoy growing older. It was my gift for working with the Council." He added wryly, "They did not go back on their promise."

Jacob turned to face him. "Neither did we."

Libraean scoffed. "I have a crooked spine and a set of hooves to prove quite the contrary."

"You abandoned me before I could fix it!" Jacob sputtered in an uncharacteristic display of emotion.

"I don't have time for this." Libraean rose to his feet, prepared to storm out of the kitchen.

"Sit down, old man, your blood is ready," Jacob ordered, unruffled by his words.

Libraean huffed indignantly but sat, watching Jacob swirl the bottle around to make sure it was evenly heated before pouring the contents into a teacup. He strained warm tea into his own cup, then carried both to the table. "Careful, it's hot."

Libraean did not reply, sipping the blood. He was surprised how efficiently Jacob had warmed it. It tasted fresh on his tongue.

Jacob smiled, reading his expression. "I have been Mr. David's manservant for enough years to have figured it out. He thinks I never knew, but of course I did."

Libraean stared at him. "How long have you been in this house?"

"Oh, since you two moved here," he replied. "The Lord Jesus was very kind to me after my departure, sending word once he discovered where you were. I positioned myself where Mr. David would find me, hoping he would see fit to hire me into his employ. Luckily, fate intervened." He gave a small smile as he took a sip from his cup. "You never had interest in the manor, so I never ran into you. At times, I wanted to visit, but I was afraid, so I learned to be content knowing you were safe. That was most important to me."

A few moments passed between them as they sipped their respective beverages, giving Libraean time to study him. Although Jacob was aged, his eyes and cheeks were positively flushed with life, quite a different look than the other creatures in the manor. Libraean narrowed his eyes before finally asking, "Why did you lie to me, Gabriel?"

Jacob set his cup down before looking him straight in the eye. "Will you listen to me without storming off?"

"I'll try," Libraean replied honestly.

Jacob sat back in his chair. "I don't recall the exact moment of my creation, but angels are born exactly how they appear to the human eye, like young men. We do not have to piece together our world from infancy like humans. We just know. And in this knowing is our history, the story of how God created an army of angels—his sons—to defeat the fallen ones who sought to replace mankind, and how one day, his beloved Lucifer betrayed him and started the Great War. God defeated him with the help of my oldest brother, Michael, casting him down into Hell, where soon all the human sinners would go."

"Except we call it Tartarus."

Jacob nodded. "Each religion has its own story. I was given mine as factual. I knew no different. I was born much later than my brothers, and my job was to deliver messages to those God wished to speak to. It was only later that my brothers and I began to hunt Mr. Lucius's *daemons*. Again, it was under false pretenses. We thought that the banished angel Lucifer had created such creatures as an affront to Him for casting him out of Heaven. It was during my time on earth amongst the humans, the *daemons*, and the creatures, that I realized there was a Great War happening, just not exactly what I thought."

He straightened in his chair. "When I saw you, I thought you were just another daemon, until I realized you intended to take your own life. Angels can see things humans cannot—although you were a blood drinker and marked by your differences, I saw through to your soul. I knew you were meant for better things in the world than death. The story I told you back then was not the story told to me—it was the one that I believed to be true, gathered by what I had seen around me. If I had known you were actually Horus reincarnated, born of the first god and goddess who ever existed, I would have told you."

"I don't understand how you didn't know. You spoke to God directly," Libraean argued. "You and your brothers are archangels—history hails you as being imperative in your service to Him."

Jacob sighed. "As I said, I knew nothing else, for God kept us isolated from all other deities and creatures. I have heard that many other gods do the same. It is my personal belief that humanity has suffered because of it. You are well-learned enough to know the atrocities mankind has displayed in the name of religion. My Lord Jesus, however, was different. He thought all mankind benefited from spirituality in whatever form it took. Eventually, we spoke only to him as God became more distant and fragmented as humans evolved and the religions changed. He is now protected by the Watchers, a new group of angels who act as a deciding council in His Name. Had they found out what I intended to do, they would have forbidden me to contact the girl on threat of banishment. It was Jesus who urged me to tell her what I knew secretly, even though he knew I'd have to face repercussions."

"The girl? What girl? What did you know?"

"After you left the Kingdom, there were so many times I wanted to visit you, to contact you while you lived out your life estranged from us, the life of a hermit. But when you found the Council, and later found Mr. David, you seemed content. I was prepared to leave you in peace. Then I discovered there was strife amongst the other deities." He crossed his fingers on the table.

"An unknown god found a way to siphon enough power that they could destroy the realms and the gods," he explained. "Our God wanted no part of it and all that mattered to the Watchers was that this god could not harm our realm. But although our position was passive, it didn't seem right to let it happen. I knew part of your family still lived in the Underworld, and that you and David would be affected by the destruction of realms. I had to warn you somehow." He looked away. "I approached Jesus and told him of what I'd discovered, and he told me there was a child born with ancient power, who lived on earth. He warned me that if I chose to intervene and warn her, that I could be cast into Hell, but if I only told her bits of information, I would lose my wings, but he could protect me from further punishment. And so, a decision was made. My wings were taken, and I was remade into a human being. I had no idea who I really was until much later in my mortal life when I began to dream of my history. Unfortunately, I couldn't find you nor Mr. David until well after my skin wrinkled and my hair turned white."

Libraean was speechless.

Jacob took a sip of tea. "So much time had passed since then, I assumed the threat was either gone or the girl had warned you in time to fix things. But now we know that wasn't the case because, as you may have guessed, that girl is Miss Cahira. And now that more has been revealed, I believe what I overheard was true—that for the last hundred years, a rogue god has been murdering the other gods and destroying their realms. It would explain why Ms. Morrigan and Mr. Lucius are here at the same time—perhaps they even died together."

"We must tell the others." Libraean stood up quickly.

"Ms. Morrigan must finish her tale." Jacob stopped him. "My information is nothing without her to fill in the details. She holds the exact memory of her godly death."

Libraean sat back down. "Yet, she rests."

Jacob yawned. "We should do the same."

"Humans," Libraean sniffed, though a hint of a smile crept through.

"Oh, come now, your age is not far off from mine—we grow tired, regardless of supernatural capabilities," Jacob said playfully.

"It seems wrong not to tell the others."

"Mr. David is not here," Jacob pointed out. "Our medium has left us and our mistress rests. There is nothing for us to do immediately."

Libraean sighed, pulling himself back up to his feet. "I still don't forgive you."

"I didn't expect you would."

"I'm still quite upset."

"I understand."

"Would you like to retire to my room tonight?"

"Of course." Jacob nodded. He put out the stove, leaving the dishes behind, and followed him down the hall.

CHAPTER EIGHT

🦂 The Galère 🦂

London, 1857
David

DAVID AWOKE TO THE KIND OF SWELTERING HEAT that could only come from the sun. He sprang to his feet in a panic until he realized its light did not burn him, his skin unbroken under its rays. He looked down at his feet to observe parched earth, the staggered flora revealing he was standing in the midst of a desert. He blinked as the arid wind blew clouds of dust around him. He was dreaming of Egypt.

"Close, but not quite."

He whipped around to behold an onyx jackal standing before him on its hind legs, a rippled arm gripping a golden staff. "Anubis," he said in disbelief. "I thought the astral plane was closed. How are you here?"

"I am a direct projection into your mind," the former guardian of the Underworld explained. "We are in a place close to the astral plane, but just outside it, so we are not disturbed by the swarms of souls trapped in its boundaries. I am surrounded by souls who practice death magic—they are the ones who helped me to finally reach you."

David nodded. "It is good to see you again. Though I wish it was under better terms."

Anubis smiled, offering a glimpse of his fangs. "Always. Unfortunately, we do not have much time for pleasantries."

"Understood."

"I've wanted to reach out to you, but you've been veiled by magic that has prevented any of us from finding you for years. Mother was the only one who could, lighting the way for the wolf and the witch to find you."

"So, everyone arriving at my doorstep was not a happy coincidence."

"No, it was not. And now that the European Ancients have come together, it is time for us all to reunite, for it is the only way we stand a chance against that which threatens our existence. Unfortunately, the affairs of humans are keeping me trapped in this land, forcing me to ask you all to come to me."

"Africa."

Anubis looked relieved. "Good, so the witch did receive my message. There are several other gods who have reincarnated here—Thoth, the Norse goddess Hel, and the African god Xevioso. Yet it is the original six—Osiris, Set, Nephthys, Isis, Horus and I who must be together."

David felt a chill crawl up his spine like he did every time his ancient name was used. "But Isis has long since passed," he pointed out.

"Ah, but her power is alive in the witch Cahira."

"How can that be?" David wondered aloud. "I thought Isis's bloodline ended with Hekate's death, the last of the heka taken by Morrigan."

"I believe the answers that you seek lie in the minds of others," Anubis suggested.

"And what about Danulf?" David asked.

"The wolf is an ally, and he will gladly go wherever the witch goes."

"Then we shall journey to you," David decided. "Have you discovered who threatens us?"

Anubis suddenly glanced behind him as if his ears picked up a noise David could not hear. "Believe me when I tell you, once we are all united, the answers will come. Even Lucius can be an asset to us if we allow him to be. I must leave you now, David. The powers holding me here are growing weaker."

The god did not lie, his bold apparition slowly fading into the desert winds.

"We will see you soon," David promised. "Take care until then."

And then he woke, his vision focusing to see Cahira in her cabin, leaning against a table as she peered at him from across the room. The fireplace roared nearby, the aroma of fresh pine in the air. In its brilliance, her eyes seemed more gold than brown. "I didn't realize vampires dream," she commented, taking a bite of stew.

David sat up groggily, running a hand through his hair. "I don't know about all of them, but I certainly do."

"Interesting. You look better than you did last night," she offered. She set down her plate, wiping her hands on her trousers. "It occurred to me," she continued, "that Dan was only able to tell you half the story, since we parted in France."

"He told us how you cast a spell on him in Transylvania, and your journey throughout Europe to France. He stopped when you left your village in the province of Auvergne to go to Paris to find...well, me."

Her eyebrow raised. "So, he told you nothing of Paris?"

"Only that he found a young Lucius there."

She sighed. "Are you hungry?" she asked.

David shook his head.

"Well, please let me know. We may be here awhile." She sighed, grabbed her plate, and tossed the scraps into the fire.

CAHIRA
PARIS, 1751

DUSK SETTLED AROUND THE PARLOR OF THE MANSION, casting a pink hue onto the polished, white marble floors. Dan stood next to her, visibly uncomfortable in the fine clothes she'd stitched for him, his high collar and the long, ruffled sleeves of his shirt obscuring his tattoos from view. She'd blushed despite herself when she'd first seen him in his latest guise, the tightness of the new clothing exaggerating his brawn, while his shorn hair and cropped beard revealed the appealing ruggedness of his face. She had swallowed, reminding herself who he was—and who she had chosen to be—and pushed any intrusive thoughts out of her mind as soon as they filtered in.

"Are you two married?" asked the woman seated on the loveseat as she fluttered a delicate fan. Her entire ensemble projected exaggerated elegance, from her powdered wig to her billowing pink dress, to the daintiness of her high heeled shoes, adorned with delicate bows.

"No," Cahira replied quickly.

"How wonderful," the woman purred, scanning the length of Dan's body with her eyes.

"Henri told us that you know a man named David," Cahira interrupted, trying not to reveal her annoyance.

She smiled. "Straight to business, eh? I like that quality in a woman." She leaned over to ring a tiny bell with the tips of her fingers. A trim butler appeared instantly in the doorway. "Please tell my brother and Henri they are needed in the parlor," she instructed before turning back to face them. "My name is Angelique Delaroux and if you haven't noticed by now, I am *un vampire*, as I believe you are becoming, Monsieur Daniel."

Dan grunted, but Cahira could tell he was surprised by her attention to detail. Neither of them had spoken the words aloud, but as he slowly started keeping nighttime hours and barely touched his food unless it was raw, they both realized what was happening. Somehow, for reasons they could not explain, he was being restored to the creature he was right before he died.

"And you, my sweet mademoiselle, have been whispered about for decades. She who commands the earth and its power." The vampiress smiled once more, her pink lips sliding across her pearly teeth.

Cahira was speechless, feeling vulnerable as the exposing words hung in the air.

Angelique rose to her feet. She was as short as Cahira and very slight, her eyes a radiant blue that reminded her of her mother's. Wisps of dark hair peeked out from the hairline of her wig, grazing smooth, porcelain skin that didn't need the heavy power and rogue it had been dusted with. The closer she drew in, Cahira could see black blood running through her veins, the slight edge to her teeth when her lips lifted around them. She smelled strongly of powder and roses. "My, aren't you a delicious little creature," she murmured as she apprehended Cahira more closely.

Her gaze moved back to Dan, and she studied his face with squinted eyes. She frowned. "I must tell you something before I introduce you to my brother," she told them, devoid of her playful smirk. "Just as all of us true vampires are reincarnated gods, so is he. You met him before, long ago, in a distant land far away from here. You need to understand that he was acting upon the orders of his human sister, one who was twisted by her own intentions. He has aligned himself with me and *mon Galère*, and he will not present you with a problem."

Cahira watched Dan's face harden, and felt the steady climb of his heart rate, even from where she stood. *Please*, she begged him silently. *Remember why we are here.*

The door opened, revealing the impish Henri and a tall immortal with eyes like coal. He was dressed like a French noble in a handsome pastel coat with a flowing shirt, the stockings tucked into his boots as crisp and white as his wig, but his skin told an entirely different story. It looked as if it was poorly stitched together, jagged crimson lines creating a jigsaw puzzle of flesh. He limped as he walked, as if his limbs had also been sloppily pieced together, his mouth a thin, angry line.

"*Prohibere,*" she whispered before Dan could lunge.

The gruesomely patched blood drinker scowled in his direction, but did not speak, positioning himself beside his sister. Henri flopped down on one of the floral couches behind them, throwing his legs casually on a nearby table.

"Are we going to have a problem?" Angelique asked Dan as she searched his eyes.

Though his jaw was clenched so tightly together his teeth creaked, he shook his head no.

"Wonderful," Angelique delighted. "Cahira, this is my brother, Ares, though Dan remembers him as Dragos, a creature he thought he'd killed in the medieval times. Though I can assure you both, he is now on my side."

"And what side is that, exactly?" Cahira frowned, crossing her arms in front of her. The longer they stood in the pompous room, dripping with flamboyant carvings in theatrical motifs, the more she yearned to flee from the dreadful city and back to the fresh, clean woods. Perhaps they had made a mistake after all.

"Henri says you know all of what has occurred. The realms have been destroyed, for reasons no one knows. My brother, Henri, and several friends of mine, have created la galère in response—a band of undesirable creatures who seek to establish immortality and reclaim our power on earth with no need for any other realms."

"I was told a rogue god is the one responsible for their destruction," Cahira told her.

"On the contrary," Angelique replied. "Humans are the ones who destroyed our realms the moment they decided to worship a new, exclusive God and murdered those who believed differently. Yet if we creatures bind together with mutual intention, we do not have to depend on humans to survive. We can live here, forever, undisturbed amongst them."

"Well, I am not immortal. I still care about the reestablishment of the realms."

"Oh, my sweet girl," Angelique laughed, the sound much like her tiny bell. "You are a Liminal, which means you are a creature. Like our Henri."

"I'm semimortal," he boasted proudly from where he sat. "All I needed was to drink a bit of our siress's blood to make it so. I'm not technically a vampire, but I will live just as long."

Cahira's eyes widened.

Unfreeze me, Cahira. Dan's voice was acid in her mind.

Do not kill them yet, she warned him. *I am interested in what they have to say.*

I will not kill them.

"*Persevero,*" she said, under her breath.

"Blood drinkers can be killed," Dan immediately said. "There is no way to ensure that you will live forever."

"And he speaks!" Angelique said joyfully, turning her attention back to Dan. "We have no need to fear the sun nor the silver bullet, for our numbers are rising and we protect our own. The blood that runs in our veins stems from Ares, our Fount, for he was created by the father of vampires, the dark god Lucius. It will take a lot to kill us...if anyone ever tried."

"So, Henri was not simply a stable boy, but a recruit to bring us here," Dan said flatly.

Henri gave him a shrug accompanied by a sheepish grin.

"Forgive me," Angelique said sweetly. "Once we'd caught wind that two powerful creatures entered our lands, we had to investigate."

"We came to this place searching for David," Dan interjected before she had a chance to continue. Cahira noticed his eyes had not left Ares, who continued to glower in their direction. "We would like to speak to him."

"Absolutely," Angelique assured him. "But it may take some time to retrieve him. I will send word immediately, but until then, I am extending an invitation for you both to stay in my home. I am certain you want to be here when he arrives."

Dan sighed but gave Cahira a weary nod.

"Yes, thank you," Cahira replied.

"Wonderful. Dinner will be served at seven, but if Monsieur Daniel is feeling peckish, we have chilled blood in all of the guest rooms. My butler, Jacques, will be more than happy to warm it for you. You're free to come and go as you wish, or we can bring you a fresh human to dine on."

Cahira suddenly felt uneasy, Angelique's words reminding her that she was surrounded by predators.

Dan shook his head. "That won't be necessary."

"The offer stands, regardless. Would you prefer to sleep in separate rooms or together?" she asked, her voice resuming its playful tone.

"Together," Dan determined before Cahira could ask for two.

Angelique's eyes sparkled, openly enjoying their uneasiness. "I have a suite available that I think you'll both be happy with. Jacques? Take them to the Spring Room."

The butler re-entered, offering Cahira a better look at him. She realized he was less trim than he was gaunt, his cheeks hollow and grey, the whites of his eyes a milky yellow. "This way, please," he said curtly, gesturing them down the hall.

Their footsteps echoed as they walked down the corridor, cavernous but cluttered by fine art, sculptures, and flowers arranged in overflowing vases. The high ceilings were drenched in pastels depicting cherubs dancing in the clouds, the imitation frescoes surrounded by molded stucco and intricate carvings. The entire mansion kept the same theme throughout—monumental ceilings, pastel colors, white marble, and gilded bronze, exuding wealth and prestige at every turn. Cahira hated it.

The butler led them to a set of rooms at the end of the hallway, opening the door and gesturing them inside with an exaggerated bow. "Dinner is at seven," he repeated, before slipping back out.

Dan slammed the door shut. "We need to leave here immediately," he said, his expression grim.

"I'm not exactly comfortable here either," Cahira said as her eyes swept the room. The guest suite was less grandiose than the rest of the household but was still designed with elegance in mind. It consisted of two bedrooms, one with a sitting area near the fireplace and the other tucked away next to an indoor bathroom, both rooms done in spring greens and yellows, adorned with pale lacquered wood.

"No, beyond the accommodations." Dan was uncharacteristically agitated, which was beginning to make her nervous. "Dragos is the blood drinker who left me for dead in Wallachia, four hundred years ago. I am the one that dismembered him. And that butler is what we used to call a *nemorti*, a human that is turned by immortal blood, but without the strength to bear it like a reincarnated god can. Lucius created them in Wallachia to serve him because they are weak and easy to control. We killed them all back then—if they exist, it is because she is making them. Just like she stitched together and reanimated Dragos. Perhaps she even reanimated me as the wolf. In fact, she strikes me as the female version of Lucius—the resemblance is uncanny."

Cahira frowned. "Remind me again why this Lucius is so detestable?"

Dan threw up his hands. "Do you hear what I am telling you? Lucius wanted to create a world of blood drinkers, submissive creatures that would serve him. The earth needs balance to function, it cannot be filled with otherworldly predators intent on spreading destruction. That's why I was recruited to help stop him."

"And you think Angelique has the same idea?"

He genuflected to be at her level, grabbing both her arms as his dark blue eyes bored into hers. Panic had seized his expression and brought a dryness to his lips. "Cahira, they admitted to tricking us with Henri. Then it just so happens you had a dream summoning us here. How do we know that wasn't part of the attempt to bring us here? I don't see David anywhere, in fact, the David I remember would have no part of something like this."

Cahira shrugged him off. "I know what I dreamt, Dan. You are acting uncharacteristically irrational," she warned him. "I understand your concerns, but what does it matter to us what she does? We came here to find David and resolve the trouble with the realms. Even if he isn't here, perhaps we can still wrest valuable information out of these creatures. I'm not convinced she knows absolutely nothing like she claims."

Dan stood, throwing his hands up atop his head in frustration, gathering fistfuls of silver hair. "We need to leave, Cahira," he insisted.

She felt her cheeks grow hot. "I appreciate your concern, but I am not going anywhere. You're going to have to trust me that everything will be alright."

"Like the time you convinced me that the villagers were safe to trade with?" Dan's words dripped with derision.

"I was a child then," she snarled, her anger beginning to rise.

"You would have died had it not been for me, and I will be damned if I let it happen again," he snapped.

Cahira quivered with fury, grateful they were behind stone walls in the midst of a concrete jungle. Nevertheless, the nearby city birds began to squawk loudly outside, attracted to her rising power. She could hear them circling the mansion. "You have no choice but to obey me," she reminded him cruelly.

But what surfaced in his eyes was not anger, but a look of hurt that overwhelmed the oceans of dark, watery blue. "Yes, after years of companionship, of authentic friendship and loyalty, you still keep me as your pet."

Cahira deflated, but he had already turned to leave, shutting the bedroom door firmly behind him. She could not bear another moment in the room. As soon as she rounded the corner in the hallway, she collided with Angelique. "Is everything alright, mon cherie?" she asked her. "I noticed the birds."

"Yes," Cahira muttered, irritated by the confrontation.

"Not a lover's spat, I hope," Angelique continued, ignoring her tone.

"He is not my lover," she maintained.

"Ah, I see," the vampiress nodded. "Why don't you accompany me while I prepare for dinner? Although we have become a house filled with creatures, only two of them are female and they keep to themselves. I grew up around sisters and find myself longing for the company of women."

Cahira hadn't realized she led her forward until after they'd reached her chambers and she gestured her inside. Angelique's rooms were precisely what Cahira would have imagined, featuring the same extravagant architecture as the rest of the house with painted stucco ornaments in the shapes of angels and flowers, blinding white against the shades of pink used in each neighboring fresco. Pink satin covered every piece of furniture, including the rugs that bore pink floral motifs.

Several meager looking servant women stood in attendance. Cahira watched their eyes flicker as they smelled her humanity, one swallowing as if her mouth had filled with anticipatory saliva.

Angelique must have noticed as well, for she said loudly, "You may leave us. She is a fellow creature, and I will not risk one of your instincts getting the better of you."

The female *nemorti* obeyed, bowing their heads as they drifted out of the room.

"We will just have to dress ourselves," Angelique declared, heading to her monumental wardrobe. She opened it to reveal hundreds of dresses in variant fabrics and colors. She considered her assortment for a moment before pulling out a marigold-colored gown, accented with bows. "This would be perfect with your eyes."

Cahira recoiled immediately. "While I appreciate your generosity, I do not require any charity," she said, suddenly wondering how she had let herself become trapped in the room of a French debutante.

Angelique laughed. "This is not charity, but a gift to a friend—a sign of good will. I know you both do not feel comfortable trusting me, as you did just meet me. I know I can appear quite grandiloquent, but I have learned an appreciation for the finer things in life. I was born a poor servant woman's daughter, rising to the noble class through my own guile. I don't even have a husband. Well, yet." She smiled to herself before remembering that she was in the midst of a conversation. "I may not be a warrior like you, but do not be deceived—I am a formidable woman, myself."

Cahira was intrigued despite herself.

Angelique changed the subject. "You look quite lovely the way you are, I just enjoy having someone to fawn over. I lost my mother when I was quite young."

A tiny pinprick poked Cahira's heart. "As did I," she admitted softly.

Angelique met her eyes. "Motherless orphans are forced to grow into maturity far more quickly than we should have to." She came closer to Cahira, pressing the dress up against her. "Sometimes it's nice to let your guard down and enjoy the finer things life has to offer."

"I suppose," Cahira sighed.

"You can dress behind the wall over there while I find an outfit for myself. You'll need my help lacing you up."

Cahira quietly groaned, grabbing the silk dress and lacy stays before disappearing behind the faux decorative wall near Angelique's bathroom.

"So, what can I do to convince you to join our collective?" her high-pitched voice continued to chatter over the rustling of fabric. "How can I help you see that immortal life on earth is far better suited for us than existing in other realms?"

"I am a human—or a liminal being, as you call it," Cahira reminded her from behind the wall. "Not a goddess. I am earth bound until death, where I suppose I will end up wandering the astral plane like the other poor souls with nowhere to go." She pulled on her stays, already uncomfortable with the narrow fit. She suddenly yearned for the days of roaming the woods, half nude and barefoot.

Angelique's face appeared around the corner, startling her. It held a look of pure wonderment, her sky-blue eyes sparkling. "Do you not know?" she breathed. She wore only her stays, the tops of her ample breasts soft without a corset, catching the curls of her naturally dark hair.

"Know what?"

"You are a reincarnated goddess!" Angelique sputtered. "You are Artemis, the Greek goddess of the hunt, the wolves, and the moon, known as Diana to the Romans. The mere fact that you are both a Liminal and a goddess endowed with powers ensures your longevity. But if you did want to be truly immortal like your lover, you would only have to drink a little of my blood. Do not doubt for one minute that you are one of us."

Cahira was too stunned to correct her again about Dan. "A goddess?"

"Of course!" Angelique laughed. "I would know, I am a Greek goddess myself. Our souls would have been returned to Mount Olympus, along with my brother, Ares, when we died. It was a perfectly dreadful realm ruled by childish men. I'm glad it's no longer our destination."

"Which goddess?" Cahira asked, unable to contain her curiosity.

"Aphrodite, the goddess of love," Angelique said proudly.

Cahira frowned, thinking back to her books. She recalled a thin volume she'd acquired through a traveling book salesman, one that told stories of the Greek Gods of Olympus. "I thought Ares was the lover of Aphrodite."

Angelique's mouth twitched. "My, for a girl raised in the forest, you do not lack intelligence."

"My mother taught me everything she knew about this world, the rest I discovered on my own," she shrugged. "Tell me, how do you know so much about me, yet I know nothing of you?"

"I have powers of my own, *ma chérie*," Angelique replied coyly. "Now you know you are a goddess, and you can easily be immortal. What reason do you have not to join us? Is it morality? Because if that is so, you have nothing to fret over. Gods make their own rules." She spun her around, tightening her stays with her unnatural strength.

"It's because my mother is dead," Cahira managed, as she gasped for breath through the binding clothing. "She deserves to rest."

Angelique spun her back around. "But how do you know she has not already come back? That there isn't a child out there, holding the soul of your mother, waiting to be found?"

Cahira had no answer, surprised by the thought.

Angelique pulled the gown she'd selected for her over her head, settling the fabric around her waist and adjusting her sleeves. Finally, she stood back, admiring her creation. "You fill this dress out much better than I can, though your stunted wings show in the back. But I think I may have a solution for that. In any case, you look simply ravishing. Your lover will not know what to think." She clasped her hands together in excitement.

Cahira did not respond, her thoughts consumed by their conversation. If she was truly a goddess, which would explain the intensity of her power, then it could mean her mother was a goddess as well. Perhaps that was why she seemed noncorporeal at times, how she could command animals just as Cahira learned to.

Before long, they were both fully dressed, Cahira's breasts shoved high above her low neckline, her waist painfully cinched above ridiculous ballooned skirts that made walking difficult. She'd put her foot down when it came to wearing a wig, allowing Angelique to lift and pin the top layer of her hair into place, the rest falling freely down her back. If Angelique had noticed the braid holding a lock of Dan's hair, she didn't comment, spritzing her with stiflingly aromatic rose water and dabbing waxy red paint on her lips. Only when she seemed fully satisfied did she allow her to leave, guiding her to the dining room as Cahira struggled to maintain a comfortable stride.

"There is someone I would like you to meet," she whispered excitedly in her ear.

As they entered, a woman with raw umber skin and striking eyes rose from her seat at the table, unfolding to reveal a statuesque build and hair in coils so tight they seemed to spring from her smooth, unlined forehead.

"This is Sandrine, one of my closest associates," Angelique introduced her. "She is a reincarnate of the Greek goddess Medusa."

"Goddess? The Greek myths say she was Gorgon, a monster," Cahira blurted out before she could help herself. She winced, making a mental note to pause before saying exactly what she thought.

Fortunately, the woman smiled, bringing warmth into her hazel eyes.

"She is very much a goddess, her story distorted by the men who write our histories," Angelique explained, her voice flavored with disdain.

"Forgive me," Cahira stammered. "I hope I didn't offend you."

"Not in the least," Sandrine offered, though her expression resumed its impassivity.

Angelique guided Cahira to the chair across from Sandrine, not far from her seat at the head of the table. "I thought we could speak a bit before the men join us," she explained.

Cahira tried to sit as smoothly as the other two women but found herself struggling with her skirts. She managed, her thoughts suddenly drifting to Dan. Although she was becoming increasingly intrigued by her current company, she wished he was nearby. She wondered how he'd been able to keep himself away from her for so long, assuming he was probably still angry with her. Disagreements were something they'd rarely been faced with, being amongst civilized humans so much different than their lives in the forest. Living in the woods had created a mutual dependence upon each other for survival, seeds that grew into trust and companionship. But what they built had no place in this new, stifling world that demanded titles, forced pleasantries, and uncomfortably starchy clothing. They were beginning to fall apart at the seams.

Several male waiters appeared around them, interrupting her thoughts. They held bottles of bubbling spirits which they poured mechanically into the three women's glasses. Cahira noticed they looked even more emaciated than the typical *nemorti* Angelique surrounded herself with, bearing dull, empty eyes that made them seem mindless. She looked away, uncomfortable by their presence. Her gaze settled back on Sandrine, whose own thoughts appeared to be wandering. She didn't acknowledge the waiter who poured her drink, staring off into the distance as they retreated from the room.

Angelique noticed Cahira's stare. "Although there are mostly men in *La Galère*, we are hoping to recruit more powerful females into our family. Sandrine, why don't you tell Cahira the true story of Medusa? Apparently, she is a student of mythology."

Sandrine folded her hands in front of her, leaving her bubbling glass untouched. Her unwavering stare rested on Cahira, her eyes a mosaic of different shades of green, flecked with sparkling gold. "The myth that has been written around Medusa," she began, "claims that I was raped by the Greek god Poseidon in a temple that belonged to Athena and in response, she turned me into a Gorgon, a monster with venomous snakes for hair. One look into my eyes would turn a man into stone. In reality, Poseidon was my lover and Athena was one of my dearest friends. It did not take a man's rape to give me my power—the ability to turn creatures into stone was a gift that I inherited, not a curse. Snakes are my power source. I am sure you understand this, since you are the girl who controls the wolves."

Cahira nodded, finding herself moved by their commonality.

"I must say I envy you both for your ability to commune with beasts," Angelique commented, taking a dainty sip of her glass. "My powers are not nearly as impressive. But I am grateful for them, regardless."

"Oh?" Cahira imitated her hostess, discovering the beverage was tart and tickled her nose and tongue, but not as unpleasantly as she expected.

"I am a psychic," Angelique explained. "I hear and see spirits as clear as you see me before you. I can also see through to a soul, which is how I can tell which humans house reincarnated gods and goddesses, even before they do."

Cahira bit her tongue, wanting to ask her a question, but afraid of knowing the truth.

Angelique sensed it immediately. "Speak, Cahira. You are among friends here."

"Can you see my mother?"

Her face grew somber. "If I tell you what I know, it may cause you pain."

"I can handle much more than you know," Cahira said quietly.

Angelique leaned over to take her hand, ignoring Cahira's instinctive flinch. "Your mother has already been reincarnated, for she does not exist in the astral realm where the spirits live. But I cannot tell you where or who she is. What I can tell you is that your mother raised another girl long before she met you, a young girl seeking refuge from the bondage she was forced into, who sits a grown woman across from you now."

Cahira locked eyes with Sandrine as emotion rose in her throat. "Is this true?"

Sandrine looked back solemnly. "I believe it is. My mother left me under the care of Angelique right around the time you were born, explaining that she was bound by duty to protect the last bearer of earth magic. I didn't piece things together until we heard word that you arrived in France."

Cahira found herself incapable of pulling her eyes away from Sandrine, even as the men entered, Dan breathless as if he'd been searching to find her. "Are you alright?" he asked her worriedly as he rushed to where she sat.

"Ye - yes," she stammered, still distracted by the revelation. "Sit down," she hissed when she realized he was causing a scene. She rose to her feet to push him down into the seat beside her.

His jaw dropped. "What are you wearing?"

She blushed, remembering her ridiculous ensemble. "Angelique dressed me."

"You don't even look like yourself."

"Dan, sit down," she repeated, pushing him into his chair. Mercifully, the others were not paying attention to them as they settled into their respective places. Though they were already well enough acquainted with one another for light conversation, the room had taken on a tone Cahira could not place. She noted the horrific looking Ares in attendance, as well as the spritely Henri, and another creature she hadn't met before. He hobbled forward on a polished cane, wearing a powdered wig that stood out against sepia toned skin similar to Sandrine's. As he inched closer, she could see tiny smallpox scars across his face, his fingers laden with silver rings, and his fingernails unusually long and curved. He barely glanced her way, but Henri offered her a pleasant flash of his teeth before taking the seat between her and Angelique.

Angelique waited until they all seated themselves before tapping her glass daintily with her spoon, commanding their attention. "Good evening, guests," she said in her singsong voice. "I would like to introduce you to Cahira and Daniel Pelletier. Cahira is Artemis reincarnated, a Liminal, and a naturally powerful witch. Monsieur Daniel has Norse roots I believe, something to do with wolves?" He offered no further information, but she kept speaking regardless, her apathy revealing how irrelevant he was to her. "You have already met Ares, Henri, and Sandrine," she said to Cahira, "But this is Lesplaies," she gestured to the pock-marked man who finally noticed her. "He is a special guest who has come to us all the way from Africa, the god responsible for the European plagues."

He simply smiled, a silver tooth catching the light from the gaudy overhead chandelier. Cahira heard the faint buzzing of mosquitoes in her ear as he stared at her. "Pleased to meet you," she said awkwardly, unsettled by his grin.

"Is David planning on joining us?" Dan interrupted darkly.

"I have sent for him," Angelique replied, unaffected by his insinuation. "I will make you both aware of his presence immediately when he arrives. Now, there is another one of ours who is not in attendance, but he is still quite young and combative, with little self-control. We have great plans for him in the future, hoping he will be our next king."

"We plan to replace him with the heir apparent's son when he comes of age," Henri whispered to her.

Cahira snuck a glance at Dan whose mouth had turned into a thin, angry line. His eyes were fixated on Ares, who had not made a sound from the moment he arrived. "So, Dragos, does any of this remind you of the old days?" he asked. "A blood drinking imposter on the throne, ruling over the humans?"

Ares remained silent, though his eyes smoldered with hatred from inside their prison of sewn together skin.

"Do you even speak, or do you simply glower?"

Angelique cleared her throat. "No, he does not speak," she replied for him, her patience wearing thin. "His voice box was destroyed when his head was...removed."

Dan continued to glare at the creature across from him. "You mean when I took an axe to his neck."

Ares twitched.

"Oh, yes, in the Principality of Wallachia," Angelique said lightly, taking a sip of her drink. "My brother has told me quite a few things about your time there. Apparently, he was under the thrall of a woman named Hekate, who claimed to be his sister, until her untimely death at the hands of your friend, David."

Cahira turned to look at Dan.

"I do not know what you speak of, but that sounds nothing like him," Dan replied, hotly. "I had little time to observe my surroundings, as I was busy fighting Dragos to the death."

"Oh, yes," Angelique continued undeterred. "She was definitely murdered. I'm surprised you aren't affected by hearing the details of her death, I heard she was pregnant with your child."

All eyes turned to Dan, whose face was now white with rage. He did not negate her words, causing a small knife to twist in the pit of Cahira's stomach. She took another sip of the bubbly drink, wondering when dinner would be served.

On cue, the emaciated waiters appeared, pulling the attention of the dinner party away from the building quarrel.

"You know that is not true," Dan hissed in her ear. "I don't know how much longer I can take this."

"Please, just give it time," she whispered back. She glanced up to witness the unexpected arrival of humans into the room, shuffling nervously behind the waiters. They seemed peculiar, all very thin with sallow skin covered in heavy layers of makeup. They were dressed like shabby versions of nobility, their clothing tattered and frayed, wearing bands of cloth around their necks and wrists instead of jewels.

She watched as a young man with pink rouge and a black beauty mark approached Angelique, rolling up one of his sleeves and unwinding a grimy piece of cloth from around his wrist. She gasped as she saw the barely healed wound, which he reopened himself and positioned over Angelique's glass. The dark, syrupy liquid poured into it, releasing the metallic tang of blood into the air as Cahira struggled to hide her revulsion. She subconsciously grabbed Dan's leg under the table, trying to stabilize herself with his energy as she stared ahead in quiet horror.

The dinner guests carried on as if nothing unusual transpired, a woman positioning her wrist over Ares's glass in similar fashion as another approached Sandrine. The frail woman carefully unwound the wrapping from around her neck as she sat on Sandrine's lap, pushing the clotted bite marks on her neck close to her lips. Cahira almost cried out as Sandrine bit, watching the human woman shut her eyes as if overwhelmed by the conflicting sensations of pain and pleasure.

"Don't let it bother you," Henri said cheerfully from beside her. "After they eat, they bring out some raw meat and wine for me, since I don't have the urge to drink blood like a true immortal. I'm sure they will bring out some human food for you, too."

Cahira forced a tight smile.

Another woman came around the bend to approach Dan, younger than the rest, with a slight build and a cascade of flaxen hair. She smiled shyly at him as she drew in closer, a lace choker wound around her pale neck.

Suddenly, the earth beneath them began to tremble, the place settings rattling as a few pieces of silverware hit the floor.

Surprised, Angelique turned towards Cahira as she steadied her glass. "Cahira, whatever is the matter?" The dinner guests all stared her way, as they also attempted to stop their vibrating dishes. "Are we bothering you? These humans come here of their own will, and we pay them handsomely for their service."

Dan bolted up from the table, pulling Cahira up from her seat. "She hasn't been feeling well since we arrived here," he told them quickly. "You're going to have to excuse us."

Angelique began to protest, but something about Dan's eyes and the unsteady ground silenced her. Dan guided Cahira out of the dining room and back to their suite, holding her tightly against him as the earth, and the objects around them, gradually settled.

"I am going to say this again—we need to leave. Immediately," Dan said as soon as he shut the door.

Cahira fell into one of the couches, her body shuddering from the sharp rise and fall of her power. She tried to push away the image of the bloodletting and repulsion that came over her, putting her head in her hands. She had been raised in the woods, had killed and skinned her own meat, witnessed predators tear apart their prey without mercy, but there was something about their feeding that did not seem right, its unnaturalness unnerving. Was this how deer felt when they stumbled upon a long picked over carcass? "I'm fine, Dan," she insisted wearily as she lifted her head. "I was just not prepared to see that."

"You almost unleashed every tree surrounding this estate onto a group of dining blood drinkers," Dan deadpanned. "You are not fine."

"I am," she maintained as she stood. The unsettling sensation had passed, her power grounding itself back into the earth. "And I am staying here. That woman, Sandrine, was raised by my mother before she left to find me in the woods."

Dan was shocked. "How do you know?"

"Angelique told me. She is a reincarnated goddess with psychic gifts."

Dan sighed, unaccepting of her answer. He attempted to soften his voice as he pleaded, "Cahira, this is wrong, all of it. Beyond their dining preferences, this Angelique has both nemorti and revenants amongst her. Did you see the mindless waiters that look like walking death? It's because they are mindless, able to be controlled and manipulated. This is exactly like the Wallachia I left four hundred years ago under the rule of Lucius, the one we all fought to change."

"Yes, but this is not Wallachia," she insisted, growing frustrated with his unreasonableness. "Angelique does not want to take over the world by creating vampires, she simply wants to live a peaceful life on earth without fear of dying."

"By replacing the King of France with an immortal? That sounds pretty damned power hungry to me."

"If you are trying to protect the supernatural creatures on earth, it makes sense that you should maintain a leader who is sympathetic," Cahira argued.

"How can you be so blind?" Dan said helplessly. He began to pace about the room, distraught.

A part of her wanted to comfort him, but the other part stayed furious at his inability to hear her.

"What about our quest to find David?" he tried again. "I never told you this, but the goddess Hel visited me in a dream, telling me that it's my job to bring you to him. That the fate of the realms depends on it."

"Dan, we have found other creatures, creatures who are like me. What does it matter if the realms are restored? Angelique has assured me that my mother has already been reborn. A link to her exists here, in this very house. I want to stay," she repeated. "There is nothing else out there for me."

His demeanor was now unrecognizable, his calm blue eyes now raging storms, his skin flushed with emotion. "What about the home we left behind? Our life together?"

"What life?" she cried, exasperated. "I made you my slave! You followed me everywhere I chose to take us because you had to."

"I love you," he said simply, finally, after years of unspoken adoration. Yet the words she had secretly wanted to hear for so long did nothing to soften her resolve. Instead, they enraged her.

"You do not love me," she sneered, fighting back the furious tears that threatened to surface. "You are here because you are bound to me."

"You do not know what I think and feel," he growled, taking a step towards her.

"Don't come any closer," she warned him.

"Or what?"

She knew the power was there because her rage had called it to be so, and she slammed her hands into his chest, right over the spot where she'd branded him. She locked him in the power swirling around her before he had a chance to jump away. It took over, as it always had, humming throughout her body, causing every inch of her to vibrate with its unrelenting intensity. She stared directly into his eyes as she once again spoke words that came from another time, another place, words that were not hers, "By the powers of the ancients, whose blood runs through my veins, I release you from your servitude. You are no longer bound to me, no longer mine to control. You are free."

The power released her, sending her to her knees as the earth around them quieted, the wolf finally freed of its bounds and crumpling, defeated, on the ground. He stared up at her, shocked and dismayed.

Cahira finally felt tears pour down her cheeks, her emotions momentarily freed from their prison. "There," she whispered. "You don't have to love me anymore."

Before he could respond, she flew from the room, down the theatrical hallway to Angelique's room, where she pounded on the door. She was grateful to learn dinner had ended and Angelique was there to answer.

The vampiress tightened her silken robe as she searched Cahira's face. "What has happened?"

"I need another room," Cahira said shakily.

Angelique pulled her inside. "You can stay here tonight. My chambers have an annexed room with an unused bed. You can stay as long as you'd like, and I will make sure no one disturbs you."

Cahira was too drained to thank her, following listlessly to the spare bedroom and falling onto the four-poster bed without bothering to remove her bulky gown.

Angelique sat at her side, gently stroking her hair with her fingers. "Men are monsters, my dear," she murmured.

Cahira closed her eyes, thinking it would be only for a moment, but she drifted off to her hair twisting in a vampire's fingers, falling into a deep and dreamless slumber.

She had no idea how long she'd slept, but she was faintly aware of bodies moving around her in the dark, mainly Angelique, who she picked out by her telltale rose-water fragrance. When her eyes finally opened, it was to the outline of sunshine peeking out around heavily drawn curtains. She sat up quickly, realizing she was famished. Her eyes caught a tray set out next to her, holding a platter of cooked eggs and a sweet pastry, as well as a teapot and cup. The aroma of fresh coffee drifted into her nose.

She lunged for the food, the sweet and savory flavors pulling her into full consciousness. Although she felt refreshed, and the warm air through the cracked window was pleasant, the events of the night before came back to stir her insides. She closed her eyes, trying to push the image of Dan's stricken face out of her mind, but it was to no avail. She threw off her covers, learning that at some point, Angelique had removed her gown and replaced it with silken bedclothes. A matching robe waited for her near the bedside. She pulled it around her petite but muscular frame, searching the rooms for Angelique, who was nowhere to be found. She went to the door and pulled it open to reveal Sandrine standing behind it.

The statuesque vampire startled before offering her a light smile. "You're finally up."

Cahira was instantly nervous. "Yes, where is Angelique?"

"She is away on business," Sandrine explained. "I have been tasked with your wellbeing in her absence."

"How long have I been asleep?" she asked, still unable to shake her uneasy feeling. "Where is the man I came here with?" She searched Sandrine's bright hazel eyes, hoping to find some comforting familiarity in them, but she could not.

"Angelique took him along with her to David's house," Sandrine explained.

"They left me behind?" Cahira cried out incredulously, preparing to go after them.

Sandrine put out her arm to stop her. "There is no need to rush," she said, gentle but firm. "I was tasked with bringing you to them as soon as you woke. From what I remember about being human, you need to eat to gather your strength back. The platter near your bedside is fresh, brought only moments before you opened the door. Eat, then dress for traveling. Comb your hair. I will be right here when you are finished."

There was something about her tone that caused Cahira to acquiesce easily. Perhaps the striking, majestic stranger was indeed raised by her mother. She shut the door behind her, heading back towards the platter. Though they had cooled, she wolfed down the rest of the eggs and pastry, enjoying the sweet flakiness of the dough as she washed it down with the strong, tepid coffee. She pulled off her bedclothes, searching Angelique's wardrobe for something suitable to wear. She settled on a robin's egg colored riding habit and boots, twisting her unruly hair into its signature braid. She flew out the door to find Sandrine waiting patiently behind the door. "I'm ready."

Sandrine bent to retrieve Cahira's traveling bag, which she had packed for her earlier.

Cahira nodded her thanks as she followed her down the steps. She was struck by the gracefulness of her movement; where Dan had been bulky and lumbering at her side, Sandrine was just as tall, but poised like a dancer. She barely ruffled the fabric of the riding outfit she wore, a deep maroon that brought out the cool tones of her skin.

"We are headed towards the residence of a young marquis named Louis," Sandrine explained as they entered the foyer. Several nemorti stood in wait, one handing her a parasol that matched her outfit. She slipped on a pair of tinted glasses that obscured her eyes from view. "Some of us can walk about in daylight with protection, but I'm especially fortunate to have skin that can naturally bear it," she explained. "Nevertheless, it's always hard on the eyes. Angelique insisted you come as soon as you woke, regardless of the time of day, so I have to take a few precautions."

"I do appreciate it," Cahira offered.

The sky was clear and bright as they moved from Angelique's *hôtel particulier* to the open carriage waiting for them. Cahira was surprised at how green the entrance court was in the daylight. It amused her how civilized nobility kept their greenery clipped and perfectly manicured, every aspect of their lives, from their groomed horses to their flat driveways, controlled. The skies, however, remained untouchable and she stalled for a moment to drink in the light fluffy clouds and watch the sea birds that ventured over from the not-too-distant Seine River.

Sandrine gave her a close-lipped smile when she entered the carriage. "I do miss the sunshine," she remarked.

"How long have you been a, um, a..." Cahira fumbled for a moment.

"A vampire?"

"Yes," Cahira said as the horses began to move forward. The windows were covered, but she could still smell the summer breeze. How terrible it must be to be one of them, she thought to herself, shackled forever to the night. Her stomach turned as she thought of Dan.

"For several years now," Sandrine replied. "Enough to become used to it. I came here against my will, as many of my people did, with the intention of being sold into slavery. Yet a priest joined us on our journey. He served the god you met at dinner, Shakpana, the god of disease and insanity. He brought smallpox along with him. Many died on the voyage before we even reached shore, including the traders. I was miraculously untouched. When we arrived on shore, the French burned the ship, but I had long snuck out. Our mother found me wandering the streets, an eight-year-old child, homeless, vulnerable, and starving to death. She rescued me, taking me to her home in the country. Her mother, our grandmother, was a governess who had inherited a great sum of money and decided to raise her away from the city in a distant cottage. It was there that our mother raised me the same way, with as fine an education as any noble man, but with the unique knowledge of the earth and her secrets."

Sandrine folded her hands on her lap. "One day, Mother fell ill, and I went to town alone to fetch a doctor. I was met with scorn, the townspeople openly suspicious of a young African woman claiming to be a freed slave. The police attempted to apprehend me, but I ran, finding myself in a squalid part of town. It was there that another man tried to attack me, but I stabbed him in the neck with my hairpin before he could succeed. Unfortunately, he had wounded me enough that I was bleeding out faster than I could flee. I ended up laying helplessly in the mud, awaiting death, when Angelique found me and gave me immortal life. She brought me back to my mother, explaining what had occurred, including the revelation that I was a goddess. She offered our mother the same gift, but she refused, even though she was moved by Angelique's intentions to protect and venerate creatures and wanting to help our cause. It was decided that I would stay behind with Angelique while my mother went out to rescue you, a child who was born of power and birthed by a daemon. She was supposed to return, but she never did."

Cahira sat back in her seat, absorbing the information. It sounded unbelievable, but then, all of it did. "Do you remember your life as a goddess?"

"Oh, yes. As soon as I was reborn a vampire, Angelique helped me uncover the buried memories lying within. I can now recall my time spent as a desert goddess, she who ruled over the slithering creatures. Poseidon loved me for many years before I finally let him into my bed. I had taken a vow never to lie with a man until the day I realized it is not women who risk losing power from the act, but men. It cripples them, for they can be controlled that way."

"I see," Cahira murmured.

Enough time had passed for Cahira to assume they were out of the city, her theory confirmed by the sudden twitter of robins. She peeked out the curtain to see another vast estate, one that managed to be larger than Angelique's town house, an isolated palace against a hilly landscape, speckled with trees. The sight of woods soothed her soul, and she sucked in the fresh, clean air. She exhaled with relief, grateful to be closer to normality.

The horses came to a stop, jolting her back into the carriage seat. Sandrine smiled. "We are here."

Several servants holding parasols greeted them, opening the carriage doors and hurrying them through the shadowy walkway they'd created before shuffling them through the arched doorway. The chateau was just as pompous as Angelique's *hotel particulier*, but older, recalling the architecture of great medieval castles. It was free of gaudy pastel paintings, relying instead on masculine shapes and woodwork to display its magnificence, the walls a natural beige against deep chestnut arches. Though the curtains were drawn around them, the sweet countryside air managed to trickle through, casting flickers of sunlight across a cavernous front room. It was quiet, the nocturnal household apparently at rest.

Cahira sensed Dan nearby, though his thoughts were quiet. She turned to comment to Sandrine, when a woman appeared in the doorway.

Cahira took a step back, immediately recognizing a threat.

"Why did you bring her here?" the woman scowled at Sandrine. Her eyes were as black as her hair, piled on her head in a single braid that accentuated the hard angles of her face. She wore the clothing of a warrior in blatant defiance of gender, a long sword sheathed at her waist. Her scowling lips were blood red, as if she'd bitten her tongue and licked them.

"It was upon Angelique's request," Sandrine replied coldly. "Is she available?"

"She's asleep with the young master," the woman matched her pitch. "If you are here, then I'll take my leave. Tell her to fetch me when it's time."

She strode past them, stopping to sniff Cahira. Every hair on Cahira's body raised as she prepared to strike back. Yet the strange woman only laughed.

"This one is as pure as they come," she derided Sandrine. "Have fun with that." With nothing more, she flew out the door, right into the sunshine.

"My apologies," Sandrine offered. "Kali serves as Louis's bodyguard when we are all away. She isn't a very forthcoming goddess by nature."

Cahira watched the front doors close. "She is not a vampire?"

"She refuses to turn," Sandrine explained, "but she drinks vampire blood and eats the flesh of humans. It makes her one of the most dangerous creatures among us. Stay far away from her."

Cahira nodded, trying not to put a visual to the idea of human consumption.

"We visit the chateau often," Sandrine continued, "therefore, our rooms have long been designated. You can share mine tonight until we can make other arrangements."

"I would like to find Dan," Cahira murmured, her eyes sweeping the clusters of rooms and winding halls.

"Of course." Sandrine released the servants from their positions and guided her down the corridor that led to her room. The room smelled strongly of lilies, the woodwork still dark, but the bedspread and furnishings a soft sable green, bringing out the shades of jade in her eyes. She set her traveling bag and parasol down on one of the couches. "Your bed is around the corner when you return. I think I will rest a bit while you attend to your companion."

"Yes, thank you." Cahira nodded, her anxiety rising. She slipped out of the room without another word, relying on her senses to guide her through the labyrinth of halls. Soon, she picked up his telltale aroma of evergreens in the winter woods, could almost hear the slow drum of his heartbeat and feel the warmth of his skin. It occurred to her, as she wound around a corner, that as angry as she had been, it didn't feel right being away from him. They would have to work things out. She could tell she was getting closer, which should have brought her relief, but she couldn't shake the foreboding feeling that wrapped its fingers around her shoulders. She sped up her pace, following a long line of doors until she reached the end.

She turned the handle on the last door.

Dan was already standing near the doorway in anticipation, shirtless, revealing the scores of blue inks scrawled over each plane and curve of his muscle. His face twisted in confusion, his light hair rumpled as if he'd just risen from slumber.

Cahira was relieved to see him but noticed something out of the corner of her eye. A woman behind him, naked, staring at her in surprise from underneath the covers of the bed.

In an instant, all became clear.

"Cahira, wait—" Dan said in panic, but she flew from the room as fast as she could.

She burst down the door to Sandrine's room. "Keep him away from me!" she pleaded.

Sandrine's expression immediately darkened, her eyes shifting from their lovely serpentine to coal black as she jumped up to assist. Cahira watched in amazement as dozens of snakes burst from her skull, immediately hissing with indignation. Dan barely had time to make a sound before she turned him to stone, his expression frozen in a painful grimace.

Cahira fell to her knees, her stomach seizing up in knots. "Is he dead?" she stammered, as she fought the sway of the room.

"No," Sandrine sighed as she was restored to her normal visage. Her eyes softened as her natural hair bounced back, free of its reptilian projections. "If he was a true human, perhaps, but we have an antidote that can heal vampires from any affliction. We will have Henri take him back to your village with it. Then it will be your decision what becomes of him."

Cahira nodded. She sat all the way down and pulled up her legs, burying her face in her knees while she tried to steady her pulse.

Sandrine crouched down beside her. "My dear child, did you love him?" she asked in a gentle voice.

"I don't know...but for a while I believed he loved me."

"I am so sorry," she offered with genuine emotion, placing a comforting hand on her shoulder. "Sometimes a man takes another woman to his bed, but it is no fault of ours."

Cahira's head snapped up, anger replacing her brief moment of sorrow. "He is free to do as he wants. I have released him from his servitude to me."

"So that is why you were together." Sandrine suddenly understood. "He was another beast you controlled."

"Well, yes," she admitted. "Though I suppose a part of me hoped his loyalty to me was genuine, evolved into something more."

Sandrine sighed, looking back at the man frozen in place by stone. Around the bend, Angelique finally appeared. "What has happened?" she demanded.

Sandrine rose from the floor. "We arrived a few moments ago and were told you were indisposed with Louis. I showed Cahira our lodgings, but she sensed Dan was near and went looking for him. She discovered him in bed with one of the servant girls."

Angelique let out a small gasp. "He and Louis were up late last night, drinking heavily. I did not think to keep an eye on him…"

"It is fine," Cahira insisted as she stood. "He is his own person, free to make his own choices. I have not been myself since we arrived in this city and discovering him in that way proved to be one surprise too many."

"Of course," Angelique cooed, draping her arm around her. She reeked of perfume, but it was different, a woodsy sort of smell that reminded her of the woods in the peak of autumn. Her hair was also natural, dark curls pinned behind her head. "You just woke from a long-needed rest, anyone can understand that." She draped another arm around her, pulling her into an embrace. The feel of her cold, dead skin gave Cahira the urge to recoil, but she forced herself to stay still. "I am so sorry, ma cherie, I told you men are monsters. They do not realize how easy they are to control and manipulate, for they think only with the organ that lies between their legs. I will have that maid removed from this household at once."

"And I will tell Henri to remove the petrified creature," Sandrine told Angelique.

"Yes, thank you. And tell Louis to get rid of the courtesan maids," she added haughtily. "There are ladies here."

Sandrine withdrew, closing the door on the only true friend Cahira ever had. The click proved resolute, as if signifying the end of a chapter in her life. It was oddly comforting, as if she was finally given an answer to the confusion his presence had been causing her. Dan and Cahira were no more.

"What is this place?" Cahira asked, eager to change the subject.

Angelique brightened. "This is the home of Louis de Sadet, the young man I told you about, who we are preparing to be king. I wanted you to meet him too, but your companion demanded we leave to see him and David immediately. He didn't want to wait for you to wake. I had to make my daily visit regardless, so I decided to take him with me, allowing you to rest."

Cahira frowned. It didn't sound like Dan, but she had just released him from her control. She honestly had no idea the type of man he was freed from bondage, and it was wrong she kept him tied to her as long as she had. A small part of her had hoped that nothing would change, that somehow, he'd still want to be near her. Apparently, that was not the case. She hated herself for feeling so broken with disappointment, hated herself for not heeding her mother's warning—she had allowed herself to become weak.

"Perhaps you should rest a moment before the introductions," Angelique suggested, breaking through her thoughts.

"The last thing I need is rest," Cahira insisted.

Sandrine reentered the room, giving Angelique a nod. "It is handled."

"There, see?" Angelique gave Cahira a warm smile. "No need to worry about him any longer. I will go rouse our Louis. We shall meet in the sitting room, say within the hour?"

"That would be fine," Sandrine answered for them both. She waited until the vampiress exited before folding her hands in front of her, gazing at Cahira with gentle eyes. "What do you need, Cahira?" she asked.

"I want to be outside."

"There is a door on the southern side of the house that leads into a courtyard," she told her.

Cahira moved forward to rest a hand on her shoulder, though the intimate gesture startled her. "Thank you," she said.

Sandrine nodded, the look of surprise remaining on her face as Cahira withdrew. She followed the long hall into the foyer, heading towards the back of the house, past the servants' quarters, and into an indoor garden. As lovely as the collection of fountains and flora were, she marched straight through it to the back door, which she pushed open with vigor. A burst of sunlight promptly assaulted her eyes as its warmth simultaneously soothed her skin. She waited for her pupils to adjust, scooping in breathfuls of clean, sweet air. Birds warbled while butterflies flitted around the flowers, both bringing their color into the courtyard, a few of the birds pausing to bathe in the marble baths.

It occurred to her that every creature residing in the chateau was a vampire, and none of them could stop her if she decided to run. She envisioned it, pulling off her stiff boots and dreadful clothing and dashing into the woods, free at last. There would be no one to worry about, no one to argue with, an autonomous existence without discord.

She sighed. As enticing the notion, it was not yet time. She was far too curious to abort the mission so soon. While she wanted so badly to believe the story Sandrine was selling her, for she did genuinely admire her, things fit a bit too perfectly for her liking. She wanted to be sure both she and Angelique were who and what they claimed to be.

She found a stone bench behind a table and sat. She took out a stub of pencil and folded paper from the pocket of her dress, items she carried as religiously as the pocketknife jammed in her boot. She flattened the paper out on the stone table and began to take notes, the graphite smudging her fingers.

She was twenty-five years old, which meant she had been born in the year seventeen twenty-six. According to her mother, she had discovered her in infancy and raised her until she was thirteen, meaning she died in the year seventeen forty, the year she met Dan. Her mother still appeared to be a young woman when she died. According to Sandrine's story, their mother found her as an eight-year-old child and raised her to the age she was frozen in time as—at least thirty, if not older. Even if her mother was an adolescent when she found Sandrine, it would mean that she was in her time of croneage when Dan's wolf ended her life. Either her mother was not human, or it was a lie.

She set down her pencil.

Miraculously, she picked up whispers floating in the breeze. She paused, realizing they were familiar, the voices she once heard in her homeland. Trust yourself.

She closed her eyes.

The sunlight seemed to grow brighter above her, as if all the clouds had moved away, the sounds of the nearby woods intensifying as she felt the presence of her ancestors, the spirits of the trees. They surrounded her, reminding her of her power, their power.

It was in that moment that Cahira realized that her entire life, she had been attached to someone: first to her mother, as children generally are, then to Dan, who helped guide her through life. Now she was a full-grown woman, yet she had never stood alone. It wasn't for lack of capability—it was simply fear. For as much as she quietly longed for moments of solitude, she was afraid of what it would really be like.

Yet as the sun smiled down upon her, the trees filling her lungs with their breath, she remembered that no matter where or when she was, the spirits were always there. She was never truly alone, for she was guided by forces as old as the earth itself. She only needed to remember her own strength, and they were there.

Sudden indiscernible whispers in the distance confirmed it.

She stood up from her seat, flushed with new resolve. It was time for her to sort through this mess and find David. Alone.

She re-entered the chateau to see Sandrine waiting for her. "Did you find what you were looking for?" she asked.

"Yes," Cahira said. "Give me one moment and I will meet you in the sitting room."

Sandrine looked as if she wanted to say more, but her lips did not move as she stepped aside to let her pass.

Cahira hurried back to their room, opening her traveling bag. She was grateful to discover that Sandrine had not only packed her clothes but had the foresight to include her collection of knives. She slipped one into her boot, strapping another around her thigh. The leather and metal felt good against her skin, restorative. She recalled the times she'd used them to cut through the flesh of both animals and men. She longed for her bow and arrow but knew the knives would have to suffice. She took a deep, settling breath. She was ready.

She navigated her way to the sitting room, realizing the enormous estates she kept finding herself in were more like the woods than she originally thought—once you navigated one, they were essentially all the same. She boldly entered the room as its already gathered occupants startled at her appearance.

Angelique blinked. "Cahira."

She scanned the room, taking note of Henri, Sandrine, Ares, and Lesplaies, with the addition of a boy, not more than ten years old. She was surprised to discover he was human, the way he carried himself and dressed giving the illusion that he was older than he appeared, an ascot settled around the neck of his frilled dress shirt, his coat long over his breeches.

"Who are you?" he demanded. She was shocked by the intensity of his eyes, a golden shade similar to hers, but that seemed to burn with ancient secrets. His hair was pitch black, thick and wild, though there had been care taken to slick it back into submission.

"Louis, this is Cahira, the woman I was telling you about," Angelique explained, her voice light and airy, like a songbird. Cahira noticed she had kept her hair natural, the darkness of her curls bringing out her bright blue eyes. Cahira had a sudden sensation that they were not real, but she reminded herself that she wasn't there to explore impossibilities, only to observe and reflect at a later time.

"Pleased to meet you," she offered the boy. It seemed strange that he was permitted to carry on with drink and whores, making her briefly wonder where his parents were.

"Our young Marquis is the head of this house, orphaned long ago. Ares and I look after him," Angelique explained.

Cahira suddenly wondered how much of her thoughts the vampiress could hear. She pulled power up from the ground slowly, like a tree pulls water from the ground, creating an unseen shield around her mind.

Louis stood up from his seat, already quite tall for his age, and ambled up to where she stood. He studied her, his darting eyes giving the impression that his mind was working at miraculous speed. "Do not let my age fool you," he told her, coldly. "I have killed more men than you have."

"Louis," Angelique floated up to him, resting her hand on his arm in an eerily maternal fashion. Cahira noticed she was still missing her stifling rose water perfume, replaced by an earthy aroma that clung to her powder blue gown. "Cahira is one of us, part of the family we are building."

Louis did not respond, pulling himself away so he could sit behind the stained wood desk. He folded his hands. "Is she here to help make me king?" he asked, as he continued to study her.

"Well, I haven't been told much about the plan," Cahira broke in lightly, taking an empty seat amongst the cluster of creatures, some already sitting while others stood. Her ears picked up the buzzing of mosquitoes once more, catching Lesplaies staring at her with coal black eyes, his mouth an amused line dancing across his pox-scarred face.

"That makes two of us," Louis muttered with an eyeroll, leaning back in his seat and crossing his arms.

The room's seating was arranged like a horseshoe around the fireplace, save for a single chair with its back against the flames. Angelique directed an obstinate Louis into it, settling herself on its arm after he was seated. "It is a simple plan," she explained. "We will be switching Louis with whatever son ends up in line for the throne after our current king."

Cahira stared at her in disbelief. "How exactly do you plan on doing that? Certainly there are people around him who would notice if his appearance has changed."

Angelique merely smiled. "Do not fret yourself over the details, my dear. Every angle has been thought of, not only by me, but our Louis happens to be quite the child prodigy." She beamed down at him, though he still looked incredibly bored, refusing to look back her way. "He is also an extremely skilled actor."

Louis met Cahira's eyes with icy indifference. "I murdered the true son of the Marquis and took his place. His own father and mother were none the wiser. Humans are deeply stupid animals, gullible enough to believe anything you sell them. Rare is the man who thinks to question, to contemplate, to rebel."

"I thought you were a human," Cahira pointed out.

"I am a god," the boy corrected her. "The reincarnation of Hades, king of the Underworld. And on my twentieth birthday, I will become an immortal, like all of you."

"I am not immortal," Cahira corrected him.

Louis frowned, the movement furrowing his brow. "Then why do you smell as if you've been drinking our blood?"

"Let us move on from this conversation and discuss the matter at hand," Angelique quickly interrupted. "I call the quarterly meeting of the Galère to order."

Cahira and Louis continued to stare at each other as the others settled in their places.

"Lesplaies, I believe you have the floor," Angelique nodded his way, adjusting her skirts as she crossed one leg over the other.

"I bring to the table the proposition that I be allowed to return to Africa, before the Switch occurs, for there is business there that I must attend to," the man grumbled in a heavy accent.

Angelique frowned. "You are needed here."

"We still have many years before the boy is ready, enough time for me to travel to my homeland and back," he insisted. "My followers have dwindled, yet the slave trade still thrives. I must go back and continue my work, bringing disease to those who harm Africa's children."

Angelique sighed, visibly displeased. "While you have my sympathies, you made a vow to be a part of our collective in return for the immortality I granted you. What is to say that if I release you from your duties here that you will even bother to come back? Your position here is imperative to our cause. I cannot risk losing you."

"What if I take Sandrine with me, to ensure that I return?" he suggested.

"Absolutely not!" Angelique jumped up from the arm of Louis's chair, who watched the exchange with detached amusement.

"Sandrine speaks for herself," Sandrine reminded her in a low voice. "Might I remind you, Angelique, that we are not your slaves, but your equals."

Angelique's lips turned into a thin, flat line, rage flushing her pale cheeks.

Sandrine turned towards the old, scarred god seated across from her. "Lesplaies, no part of me wishes to return to the people that sold me to be imprisoned in a strange land. I trust in our collective, in Angelique's vision. She has proven to be a solid, capable leader."

"Very well," he shrugged. His dark gaze shifted towards Cahira. "What about the new one?"

The buzzing in Cahira's ears reached a fever pitch, causing her skin to crawl. Although struck with the desire to itch her limbs, she forced herself to remain still, imagining a hawk swooping down to eat the detestable insects. All at once, the noise stopped, Lesplaies turning away from her. She swore she saw a look of disappointment cross over his face.

"Cahira is a human," Angelique negated his suggestion. "We cannot ensure that she wouldn't be harmed throughout the voyage. In fact, not one of the Galère is expendable."

"Then perhaps you should agree to my voyage and trust that I will return." Angelique glowered at him. "Louis? What do you think?"

Louis had been studying them all with interest, holding his jaw in his hand. "I think you should let him go," he decided. "He makes the human girl uncomfortable."

It was Cahira's turn to be surprised.

Angelique threw up her hands in defeat. "Then it is settled. Lesplaies, you may take your leave of us. But I do hope you remember the vow you made. I am not one who forgives betrayal."

Lesplaies removed his hat, upsetting his ratty grey wig, and gave her a curt bow.

Angelique was unmoved. "If there is nothing more, our meeting is adjourned," she told the rest of them. The creatures rose and obediently disbanded without much commotion. Cahira remained seated, as did Louis.

"How did you know that Lesplaies made me uncomfortable?" she asked him.

"I can just tell," Louis shrugged.

Angelique stood, putting her hands on her hips. "He is important to our cause, Louis. I cannot believe you are allowing him to leave."

"He will return," Louis said flatly. "So, how long are you planning on staying in my home this time?"

"Not long, *mon prince*," Angelique cooed, swooping back down to his chair to pat his hand. She looked at Cahira. "I have a few things to discuss with him alone, if you don't mind. I trust that you can see yourself back to your room?"

Cahira nodded, grateful to leave them. She found Sandrine standing in the hall as if waiting for her. As soon as the door to their room closed, she put a finger to her lips to hush her, transforming into the snake-haired creature. Cahira took a step back in alarm, but soon realized she could look at her without turning to stone

Only men, Cahira, Sandrine's voice echoed in her mind.

Why do you choose to speak in this way? Cahira asked her, confused.

Angelique can read minds, yet she cannot hear the line of communication used by beasts, the one we speak on now, she replied.

Cahira folded her arms. *So things are how I suspected. She is not what she seems.*

No, she is not, Sandrine confirmed, her snakes twisting around each other in a tranquil dance as she spoke.

Is that how you knew that I'd stumbled upon Dan in bed with another woman, because it was a set up?

Yes.

And the story you told me about my mother, was that also a lie? You said that you were only eight years old when she found you, but the dates do not match up. My mother died young.

Sandrine smiled, revealing a pair of snake's fangs situated on top of her teeth. *I was hoping that you'd catch that.*

So, tell me. What is the meaning of all this?

Angelique is nothing more than another power-hungry goddess, invested in her own agenda, she began. *She wants to make that boy a king so that she may one day be Queen of France. We are all pawns in her game, all bringing something to the table that she can exploit. She is interested in you because of your power.*

Does she know more about the realms than she lets on? Cahira asked. *Does she even know a creature named David?*

She does not know David, or we would have met him long before she brought you here. I do believe she knows more about the destruction of realms than she lets on, but I have been kept strategically in the dark.

Then I must take my leave of you all, Cahira informed her. *My entire reason for coming here was to find a vampire named David and restore the realms. Instead, I have been brought here under false pretenses.*

Sandrine stopped her. *Please wait until I have told you everything,* she asked, suddenly looking uncomfortable. *Cahira, she has been slipping you bits of her blood in everything you have eaten and drank since you arrived. It is her way of controlling creatures that are not turned. Eventually, she planned on using Louis to do the final deed, hoping that if he drank your blood, he would become infused with some of your power—power she can then use herself.*

Cahira felt her stomach turn. She pulled out the knife from her boot in one fluid motion, aiming it directly at Sandrine. *Do not get any ideas yourself,* she warned.

You do not have to worry about me, Sandrine assured her. *I do not care about siphoning earth power from a young mage. What I care about is returning to my homeland where I am needed. There is more to my tale than I have let on. The great god Anubis lives there as a constant beacon of hope for my people, murdering corrupt kings and continuously ruining any attempt of human trafficking that he can. I must go back to ensure his safety. Lesplaies and I have been planning this trip together, though his intentions are a bit more malicious than mine. We knew Angelique would not want to let me go, but we had to try. Now we must leave against her wishes and hopefully under her detection.*

Let me help you. Cahira offered.

You forgive me for deceiving you? Although her beautiful facade was twisted into leathery scales with slitted pupils and fangs, Cahira could see behind it, feeling the sincerity in her words.

Of course. A thought struck her. *Does this mean that I am now immortal?*

You are no longer human, Cahira. You will live much, much longer than the average human lifespan, for if a Liminal drinks a vampire's blood, it strengthens them without them ever needing to drink from the living. However, if a vampire manages to drain all of your blood and fills you up with theirs, then you will become one of us, an immortal blood drinker. Right now, you are semimortal, like Henri.

Cahira was stunned. She would no longer be forced to die a human's death. She was free to live on earth, as long as it would have her. And Dan would not have to watch her die, she thought before she could help it, her entire being suddenly yearning for him. She forced herself to think of the woman in his bed, remembering the pain she felt. Even if it was just a ruse, he weakened her. *If I am not human, then I can come with you to Africa. Perhaps there I will finally find David.*

Sandrine smiled again. *I would love to have you join us. But there is more that I must tell you. The creatures you have met are but a small number, we are the ones who were once gods and goddesses. Yet Angelique is not just turning any gods, but those that create havoc amongst mankind - myself, the god of smallpox, the god of war. She never revealed to you who Henri is; he is not only a Liminal, but a Norse chaos god called Loki.*

Cahira's breath caught in her throat, recognizing the name of the god responsible for cursing Dan, the one who had been tasked with returning him to their village. She jumped to go after them, but Sandrine stopped her. *Before you go, I must also inform you that Louis is not a reincarnation of Hades, but of a dark Egyptian god named Set, who once lived in this land as Lucius, the first vampire on earth. He is a powerful chaos god, who she intends to use to resume havoc on mankind.*

Cahira's heart rate began to climb. Dan had been right all along.

She is also turning humans at an alarming rate through Ares, who hunts fervently each night. In turn, these vampires are creating their own broods, fledgling, ignorant vampires who have no idea what or who they are, only that they want to feed. She has brought back daemons and abominable creatures once eradicated from the consciousness of men. She has no desire to exist peacefully amongst the humans, she wants to rule over them, creating chaos however she can.

Cahira gripped her knife tightly in her hand.

I tell you this, Sandrine continued, *because I believe you can be the one to stop it. Find David, wherever he may be, and tell him Lucius has risen. He was the only one able to stop him before. I will trap Lesplaies in Africa. Angelique has already used him once to unleash a deadly plague on humanity and is planning to do so again. He needs to be stopped. I will also contact Anubis, who I believe will be helpful in the matters of the realms. Perhaps he can tell us what is truly happening, for he was once Guardian over the netherrealms. I will hopefully return with good news.*

Cahira nodded, surprising Sandrine by taking both her scaly hands in hers without fear. *Thank you for telling me this. You have been a brief, but true friend.*

Sandrine's reptilian eyes swam with emotion. *Go to your wolf before she realizes you are gone.*

Cahira flew to the window, pulling back the curtain to the setting sun. She closed her eyes, calling to the earth spirits who had revealed themselves earlier, the ancestors who lived before her. A gust of summer wind hit her face, their whispers resuming their intensity as if she'd never left the courtyard. She imagined home, the village they'd left behind. She thought of Dan, painfully immobilized in stone. *Take me to him,* she commanded.

And she was flying, transformed into a golden hawk, its wings taking her high above the treetops. She reached the village within hours, swooping down to land in a dusty field. She was immediately confused by its lack of crops, the houses empty and neglected. She headed on foot towards their old home, nearly tripping over a half-eaten severed head rudely left in the middle of the road. She gagged, throwing her hand over her mouth as she gingerly inspected it, recognizing pieces of Henri's pointed chin and reddish hair amongst the maggots. She hurried past the gruesome pulp toward their old cabin, throwing open the door as soon as she arrived.

Relief flooded over her as she discovered her wolf, Geri, who bolted upright, happy to see her.

"Is he here?" Cahira asked her nervously.

He is alive, but he has left this place.

Cahira exhaled, inspecting the cabin. It had been ransacked, the tables and chairs upended, her books thrown around the room, her bottles shattered. "They will be coming for me soon—I cannot stay here. Will you join me?"

Where you go, I go.

Cahira smiled, though a dull ache had settled in her stomach. She refused to give it any power, turning to march back out the door with Geri at her heels. Any lingering feelings of sorrow and regret left as soon as she entered her forest, and she inhaled the sweet fragrant woods, grateful to return.

PART FOUR

L'Amoureux

THE LOVERS

CHAPTER NINE

❦ THE FIRE ❦

LONDON, 1857
DAN

DAN SAT NEAR THE DEAD FIREPLACE, listening to tiny bits of wind protest as they found themselves trapped in its flue. He'd kept his room entirely dark as he awaited true nightfall, the temperature frigid without a fire to raise it. The windstorm that had descended upon southern England had shown no sign of letting up, now mixed with a hint of snowy rain. It left droplets along the tall windows of the southern guest room, capturing random fallen leaves swept up and thrown at the glass.

His chest still burned where she'd marked him, the way it always did when he thought of her. Although much had transpired since he abruptly ended his recollection, he had trouble thinking of anything else. He realized he'd been gripping the arms of his chair for hours, his knuckles white. He slowly flexed life back into them, listening to the crack of old, weary, but immortal bones. He wondered if David ever sat in the same room, longing for his lost lover, staring at the same empty fireplace, his mind wrought with sorrow and regret. It seemed so, the drabness of the room the perfect setting for despondency, with its plain grey wallpaper stretched across flat walls that lacked any architectural flair. The only thing of note in the entire room was the fireplace he now stared at, the stones carved and etched by hand, the craftsman relying only on the beauty of the medium without adding embellishments.

From the corner of his eye, he caught an opaque bottle next to an upturned glass, set far on the other side of the room near the bathroom. He rose out of his chair to inspect its contents. It was a bottle of aged scotch, a thin layer of dust settled around it from lack of use. He left the glass, tipping the bottle to pour the old liquor down his throat, ignoring his stomach's protestations that he offered it something other than its preferred liquid nourishment. He sat back down with a belly of fire, tipping the bottle once more.

Though the sun had been steadily hidden by clouds since he arrived, he could sense that night had officially descended. It had been six days since the medium pulled memories from Morrigan and David had left, six days far too many. He was going after him, despite any objection, but he figured a bit of drunkenness beforehand wouldn't hurt.

There was a sudden knock at the door.

"Come in," he said gruffly as he polished off the bottle.

The manservant slipped in first, shivering immediately in the draftiness of the room, followed surprisingly by Libraean. Dan marveled at him as he walked in, realizing his spine had been straightened, a pair of standard shoes where his misshapen boots had been. Their body language revealed that their animosity had melted away, replaced by a certain air that surrounded them both. Dan smelled traces of the human hanging on the creature like old cologne, provoking a playful smile. "Patched things up, have we?"

Jacob smiled shyly, but Libraean blushed, quickly dismissing the comment. "We come with a proposition for you."

"You do, eh?" Dan studied them in the dim light. "Shall I light a fire so the human doesn't catch cold?"

"I appreciate the gesture, but we will be brief," Jacob replied, though he wrapped his housecoat around him a bit tighter, slipping his hands underneath his folded arms.

"Morrigan has not emerged from her room since David left and shows no signs of vitality. Jacob has brought her blood routinely over the past week and she barely acknowledges his presence. We made sure our medium was compensated for her services, but we fear the longer we wait, the less likely she will be to help us again."

"I plan to go after David tonight."

"You see, I am not alone in my opinion." Libraean glared at Jacob.

Jacob sighed. "I understand that retrieving David makes the most sense to both of you, but it is not his memories we must unlock. It's hers."

Dan frowned. "What makes you think she's going to speak while he's away?"

Libraean suddenly appeared uncomfortable. "That is why we are here. There might be another way to encourage her compliance."

Dan realized what he meant. "Absolutely not, no, you cannot—"

"Mr. Daniel, please," Jacob pleaded as he drew in closer, his grey eyes desperate. "This might be our only option."

Libraean chimed in. "He has no memory of his former self, nor has he been on earth long enough to grow mad. We were right to proceed with caution at first, but he has proven that he poses no threat to us," he pointed out.

"Do you hear yourself?" Dan sputtered. "I must be drunk."

"I am not suggesting we should trust him completely. This is the soul who once pulled out my eye," Libraean reminded him. "But his sway on her is just as strong as David's—you heard her memories yourself."

Dan scowled. "Do what you must, but I want no part of this. Retrieve me only when you have her sitting in the parlor with the medium. Then I will give it one more day and if nothing is resolved, I am going after him."

"Absolutely," Jacob agreed quickly.

"Is there more scotch in this house?" Dan asked him.

"In the kitchen wing, there is an opening in the washroom floor that leads to the cellars. There is no more wine left, but I discovered several bottles of spirits stashed down there while I was cleaning."

"Then that is where I will be," Dan decided, breezing past them. He was in no mood to see Lucius, nor the young blood drinker that currently housed his soul.

"Actually," Jacob stopped him, "we were hoping you could help us. As the only human amongst you, I was thinking it would be best if I steer clear of those who regularly drink human blood."

Dan groaned, knowing he was right. "I am going to need a lot more scotch for this."

Jacob brightened. He ducked into the bathroom, coming back with a bottle dustier than the first. "When David moved in, there were bottles hidden all over the house. Apparently one of the Lardone sons was a slave to the drink. I left many of them where they were."

Dan took it from him gratefully, then turned towards Libraean. "Lead the way."

"I will be in the guest room if you need me," Jacob said, giving Libraean's arm a gentle squeeze before disappearing into the folds of the house.

"Follow me," Libraean sighed, apparently just as dismayed about the idea as Dan was.

The wind that greeted them was bitter, Libraean pulling up the collar of his coat as he strode forward. Dan did not flinch, still preferring the cold above all else, watching the copper leaves and bits of ice swirl around him as he led him forward into the graveyard.

Dan still did not understand the humans' preference for burying the dead. To him, it seemed unnatural. The ornate stones that marked each plot were beautiful in their own right, but it seemed a pretentious, wasteful practice just to mark the place where a corpse returned to the dirt from which it was made. The Lardone crypt was a perfect example of this exorbitance, for even though it was built of simple marble, its enormous size amongst the plain slate stones surrounding it seemed crass and obtrusive.

Libraean removed a large set of ancient, rusted keys from his pocket, jiggling them in an equally aged lock until it clicked open. He struggled to push open the heavy door, which Dan moved forward to assist him with.

The inside of the crypt was choked by spiderwebs, the soft pitter-patter of mice whispering faintly above. There were four closed sarcophagi holding the thickest layers of dust, the clean fifth one opened just a crack. Libraean completed the task, letting the slab fall away to reveal the staircase that led below.

Lucius did not appear surprised to see them as they walked through the door to the main vault, only raising a dark eyebrow. He was comfortably sprawled out on one of Libraean's couches, the bookcases that surrounded him completely emptied, Libraean's books strewn all around him in various stages of completion. Empty bottles of blood and wine cluttered every spare surface, the scent of burnt tobacco lingering in the air.

Dan felt Libraean's temperature rise as he surveyed the mess in his room. "You helped yourself to my pipe?" he sputtered.

"Amongst other things," Lucius responded dismissively. "You've arrived just in time for the best part." He began to quote from the book opened up in his lap, "'What he lacks in decency, he makes up for in appearance, with the strong intelligence found only in the utterly mad.'"

Libraean reddened, the color teaching the tips of his ears. "I did not give you permission to read that," he snapped, advancing to retrieve it.

Lucius laughed, tossing the book his way before he could. "Sounds as if you still fancy me after all," he teased. "You should hear what he's written of you, Danulf. It's on the shelf over there, titled, The History of Lycanthropy."

"That book is not yet finished! I have more pages to add."

Dan felt his patience growing thin, the numbing reprieve the scotch had provided beginning to dwindle. "Enough," he said. "This is not why we are here."

Lucius sighed, crossing his long slender legs before him. "What now? You've decided to relocate me to another prison? Kill me?"

"No," Libraean replied as he began to scuttle around the room, closing and reshelving the unkempt books. "We need a favor from you."

Lucius laughed again, and though he had the voice of a different man, the sound bellowed, just as it always had. "That is truly something, coming from those who hold me captive. You look good, by the way, old man, without the hunchback."

Dan growled at Libraean. "I told you this was a waste of time."

"Oh, calm yourself, Wolf Man, where else do you have to be?"

Dan grabbed him by the shirt, hoisting him up above him. "You may not remember the vile creature you once were, but I do. I will snap your neck in an instant and not think twice about it."

Lucius simply grinned as he hung in his grasp, his amber eyes dancing with amusement.

"Daniel, please," Libraean said, grabbing at his arm. "We need him right now."

Dan begrudgingly released him to the ground. Lucius straightened his shirt and smoothed his vest, unaffected by his display of aggression.

"Lucius," Libraean began.

"My name is actually Louis," he corrected him. "Though the more I read about your friend, the more I don't mind the association."

Libraean sighed. "Louis, we are in a predicament. We know you do not remember your life before this one, but we creatures come from realms beyond this one."

"Yes, I have been told," he sighed. "And anything I was unsure of, I found in your painfully long-winded records."

Libraean's lips flattened. "Well, our realms have been destroyed and more gods have been rebirthed in this time period than ever before, including you, who was supposed to be banished to the lowest depths of Tartarus, and the Morrigan, who swore she'd never return. A medium offered us her services to help unearth Morrigan's memories, for we hoped it would help us figure out what is happening. The memories she unearthed were, ah, troublesome," Libraean struggled to explain, his cheeks reddening. "They have caused a disturbance among us, especially for Morrigan."

Lucius's defiant demeanor suddenly melted. "The beautiful raven-haired woman? What happened to her?"

As Dan observed his sharp shift in temperament, he suddenly realized that Libraean and Jacob were right—their plan might actually work.

"David left as a result of what we uncovered, and she's been despondent ever since," Libraean explained. "She has not left her room in six days, and she barely eats."

Lucius frowned. "What do you propose?"

Libraean sighed, removing his glasses with one hand to rub his eyes with the other. "I cannot believe I am saying these words, but we want you to check in on her."

"Oh." Lucius blinked. "Well, of course I will. Though the last time I saw her, she was determined to kill me."

"I don't think you'll have to worry about that now," Libraean assured him, replacing his spectacles.

"Well, in any case, her fiery temperament is intriguing." Lucius adjusted his cravat and ran his fingers through his shorn black hair. "How do I look?" he asked Dan, with another arrogant grin.

Dan scowled, deciding that he definitely needed more scotch. Somehow Lucius proved just as detestable to him now as he was before, and he didn't even know him beyond association. He pulled Libraean to the side. "Are you certain we can trust him?"

"No," Libraean sighed, "but if anyone can handle Lucius in any form he takes, it's Morrigan."

A gust of wind met them as they exited the vaults. "The winds seem unusually strong," Lucius remarked.

"The weather has been like this since he left," Libraean said mildly, prying open the great manor doors. Jacob's absence added to the eerie silence of the cavernous foyer, the dusty sconces that surrounded them dim.

Dan turned to Libraean. "I have assisted in delivering the fiend. Now if you don't mind, I will be in the kitchen cellar until this situation has been resolved."

Libraean nodded before gesturing Lucius to the hall behind the west wing stairwell. "She is in the parlor where you spoke with her before."

Dan shook his head as he maneuvered his way down the dark back halls towards the kitchen. He hoped for all their sakes that they hadn't made a mistake.

Morrigan

ORRIGAN STOOD AT THE WINDOW, watching the howling storm toss the trees in the distant woods. The old house creaked and groaned in vexation as the wind rudely threw anything it could find at its windows and walls. The woods were almost entirely barren, the last remnants of brown leaves swirling around the cemetery below. A distant intuition suddenly whispered that tonight was Samhain, the Celtic celebration of the night between the autumn equinox and winter solstice, the night she'd first made love to David, centuries ago.

She closed her eyes against pain so strong it seemed to rot her from the inside, a suffocating, overwhelming sorrow that demanded her submission. She had obeyed at its onslaught, refusing to leave the parlor when she realized that her clearest memories were there, of David and her sitting near its fireplace as she lay dying, telling her the tale of their forbidden love affair. Even if her memories hadn't returned, she had fallen for him then, entranced by the careful way he pronounced each word, as if he fought a hundred different accents to mimic the proper English tongue. She admired the way his forest-colored eyes would dim as he recalled moments of tragedy, then burst into a vivid green as he spoke of the mysterious goddess he called the Morrigan.

She tried to picture where he was now, hoping that wherever he'd retreated over the past few days offered him solace. She wondered if she'd made a mistake falling for Lucius's charms in the Underworld, if she was unable to see things for what they really were. It was maddening to know she'd existed eons before this lifetime, done things she couldn't even remember. She had to trust the decisions she'd made in her recent past were sound, even though every part of her present being ached to be reunited with David.

Tonight, she decided to retrieve her old diadem of corvid bones from the top of his bookcase, remarkably well preserved for its age, and put it on, trying to recall every moment lost. It worked, visions of him and her swept up in battle dancing dreamily in her distant mind as she stared out into the dying autumnal forest.

The door opened behind her, but she did not turn, assuming it was Jacob bringing her a fresh bottle of blood. He was such a kind soul amid the deadly creatures who had overtaken the house, she wondered why he'd chosen to remain amongst them.

"Why so solemn?"

She whipped around, for the voice that spoke was not Jacob's.

Lucius stood in the doorway, his long frame leaning against the wood as he examined her with his arms crossed. She blanched at the sight of him. "You shouldn't be here," she said, lifting the diadem away from her head.

"Why are you taking that off? It looked lovely on you. As if you were some exotic priestess from a distant land." He smiled as he sauntered into the room.

"You need to leave," she repeated, her voice forceful even as she delicately replaced the diadem in its box. She looked back up at him with a scowl, placing her hands on her hips. "I understand that you do not remember me but believe me when I tell you I can tear a man's spine from his body, even without a weapon."

His smile didn't falter, blatantly unconcerned by her words. "Oh, I believe you," he said. "I witnessed that side of you quite vividly. And normally, I would respect your wishes to be left alone, however, I'm not here for my own pleasure, rather, sent on business."

Morrigan's recently unearthed memories made his true appearance clear in her mind, and she briefly marveled at how similar his new body was to the god she'd once known. He was still pale, tall, and thin, with cheeks that hollowed and mischievous golden eyes. This creature was more youthful, with wavy, cropped black hair and long sideburns that grazed the cut of his jaw. She could smell him from where she stood, the aroma of extinguished bonfires spiced by cloves overwhelming her senses. "I don't think you understand how important it is that you leave. We have history, you and I."

"Is that right?" His lips danced with amusement as he walked right up to where she stood, seating himself right on top of David's desk. His movement knocked over the quill box as loose sheets of parchment crunched beneath him. "I cannot begin to imagine what kind of history would exist between you and I that would make you want me to leave so badly." His words were softened by his accent, the syllables ending in a gentle purr.

Morrigan growled in frustration, the windstorm outside bringing with it a smattering of rain. Crows screeched in the distance.

Without flinching, Lucius snapped his fingers and the dwindling flames in the fireplace roared to life with such intensity, they nearly escaped their confines of stone. "Two can play at that game," he teased.

Morrigan crossed her arms. "For someone who doesn't remember who I am, you certainly spar with me just the same."

He waved his hand, so the flames quieted. "And that brings me to why I am here. The wolf and the halfling are concerned with your wellbeing and have tasked me to pull you out of your melancholy. Apparently, they'd like to tap back into that lovely mind of yours."

Morrigan frowned. "Nothing good can come from my memories. They did not serve their intended purpose and now my lover has abandoned me. I cannot stand to be in this house another minute, let alone go through that again."

"Excellent," Lucius stood, clapping his hands together. "I feel similarly in sentiment. Let us take our leave of this drafty old place."

"I cannot go with you," Morrigan sputtered, horrified at the thought. "You are the cause of my problems."

Lucius shrugged. "Then allow me to be your solution."

She barely had time to register his movement before he darted forward, tumbling out the parlor window. She raced to the edge, looking down to see him smiling back up at her. "Why do you look so surprised?" he laughed. "You mean to tell me that you've never used our abilities before?"

Not to be outdone, nor admit to him that she hadn't, she jumped down to join him, landing on the moist earth with a soft thud. She stood, surprised at how easily her body had just moved. She looked back up at the window, realizing she'd jumped down two stories as if it was nothing.

"Ah, my dear, you have much to learn. Come, I have something to show you," he extended his hand out to her.

She realized, much later, when they'd reached the heart of the city, that she hadn't even hesitated to take it.

Though the wind was still strong as they headed out of the countryside, it did not deter their travel, and soon they reached a manor larger than David's, a proper, sprawling estate that boasted over twenty rooms. Each one was fully illuminated by gaslight, humans bustling about from one corner to the other, apparently in the midst of frantic preparation. Lucius snuck her past the servants and coachmen that lingered at the front gates, pulling her towards the back of the house and up to the master suite windows where he gestured for her to look in.

"What are we doing here?" Morrigan whispered, noticing a woman seated at her vanity, the lamplight sparkling along the mirrored glass and gilded paint.

He leaned in next to her, so close she could feel his alluring warmth. "I observed them for some time before I found David's manor. She looks just like you, doesn't she? Not as beautiful, of course, but the resemblance is uncanny."

Morrigan watched the woman apply powder to her nose as her handmaid lifted and pinned up her black curls. She saw a flash of blue eyes in the mirror. "Yes, but why am I looking at her?"

"Her husband looks much like I do."

Morrigan pieced together what he implied. "I cannot kill a human, Lucius," she said in open consternation.

He stared at her, surprised. "You've never drank a human's blood before?"

Morrigan was silent.

"My word, how could they have turned you, but not shown you our way of life?" He shook his head in disbelief. "I suppose I will be the one to teach you then. You will take the lovely madame and I will take her husband. We won't kill them, only draw enough blood that they fall unconscious. It whets the appetite without having to worry about unnecessary clean up."

Morrigan began to involuntarily salivate as her mind considered the proposal. "Then what?"

"Then you will find your favorite outfit of hers and put it on." He didn't leave an opportunity for further questions, slipping in through the window and silencing the maid before she had a chance to shriek. Morrigan followed him, her instincts overwhelming as they begged her to give in to her building hunger.

The woman at the mirror saw her and started to scream, but Morrigan clasped her hand over her mouth to prevent it, pulling her head to the side and plunging her teeth into the soft flesh of her neck. She was accosted by a sensation that surpassed anything she'd ever felt in her mortal life, an insurmountable level of pleasure, the sweet blood running down her chin as she sucked harder, suddenly frantic for more. It was so fresh and warm, she could not understand why she'd been kept from it, animal's blood paling in comparison. She found herself getting lost in its thrall, the weakening heart of her victim a rhythmic melody lulling her into dreamy sedation.

She felt Lucius's gentle hand. "It pains me to stop you, but I must," he whispered.

Morrigan took a deep breath to collect herself, licking the last of it from her lips. Lucius's eyes fixed on her mouth as she did so, struggling to pull them away. But he managed, taking the unconscious body out of her arms and carrying her to the loveseat, where he draped her next to the maid. "Find your dress," he instructed. "And do not forget your mask. I will return in just a moment."

Unable to temper the exhilaration that now seized her, Morrigan flew to the wardrobe. On the bed lay clean stays which she wrapped around her with haste, and when she looked up, she noticed a rich crimson gown hanging nearby, pieced together with fine silk. She was delighted to discover it fit her perfectly, matching the delicate ruby earrings left on the vanity. She was grateful her hair had grown long with neglect, enabling her to pin it up into the current fashion. It occurred to her that it had been eons since she cared for frivolity or finery, satisfied with mud and war paint, yet somehow, she'd become completely entranced by the present moment, the fresh human blood singing in her veins.

Lucius walked in, fully dressed in a sharp three-piece suit with a corresponding black masquerade mask. He wiped the leftover blood on his lips with the back of his hand as he openly admired her. "My word, you are absolutely stunning."

Morrigan turned so he wouldn't see her flattered expression. "You must do up these buttons for me," she said.

He wordlessly obeyed, the scent of him, freshly revived with human blood, causing her to sway as his fingers crawled up her back from the base of her spine. She focused instead on her surroundings, the colors vivid even in the low lighting, every one of her senses heightened to the fullest. Why did David keep this from me? She wondered.

"Do not forget your mask," Lucius reminded her as he finished, grabbing her hand once she did so. "Tonight, we are Lord and Lady Montgomery."

She laughed as he whisked her through the strange hallways and down the steps into the carriage that awaited them. Both fully dressed and masked, the coachmen and manservant did not even realize that the two creatures they helped into the ornate carriage were not their actual employers. The butler helped her settle next to Lucius into the plush velvet seats, handing him a cane. "Take care, sir and madame," he said, bowing deeply, as the coachman seated above them stirred the horses to trot.

After they pulled out of the driveway, Morrigan realized her heart hammered in her chest. "They were completely fooled."

Lucius laughed, his amber eyes dancing behind his mask. "Greychild," he called up to the coachman, raising his voice to imitate the perfect English accent. "We need to make one stop before the masquerade ball—please take us to the corner of White's Row."

"How do you know his name?" Morrigan whispered.

"I told you, I studied them before I arrived here. Imitation is sort of a hobby of mine, if you will."

"The East End place, sir?" the coachman clarified.

"Yes, and do hurry," Lucius replied.

He expedited the horses to a proper gallop, Morrigan's eyes drifting out the window as the foggy city came into view. A sudden, unwelcome memory of riding in David's carriage came to her.

As if he sensed it, Lucius grasped her hand in both of his. "Although I cannot recall our mysterious history together," he said softly, "I must say that I am quite pleased to be in your company."

Morrigan admired the way his lips glided over his teeth, the way he ended his words with the slightest hint of a devilish smirk. "I am quite pleased to be out of that dreadful house," she redirected the conversation. "Though, the air isn't as fresh in this town as I prefer."

Lucius laughed good-naturedly. "Well in a moment, the stink won't bother you as much."

"It seems so strange to me that this was once my home," she murmured as the familiar buildings and chimney stacks came into view. "It's like a strange dream to be back with new eyes."

They ventured deeper into the bowels of the foggy city, the lingering charcoal cloud of factory smoke blurring out the streetlamps as the carriage wheels splashed through the puddled rainwater. Morrigan realized the wind had died, the air dank with fumes from the polluted river. She hoped the lack of churning squalls meant David had found some semblance of peace.

The carriage stopped at a street crossing, free from the sounds of city bustle. The coachman held open the door as they exited, his eyes flitting back and forth nervously as he watched for thieves. Lucius pulled her down a sordid alleyway without hesitation, stepping around the pools of rainwater and waste before stopping at an iron door. He knocked three times in even pressure, provoking a brawny man with a ragged cap and sailors' tattoos to open it and hurry them inside.

"*Bakkheia*," Lucius said to him. The man nodded and stepped aside, revealing the narrow staircase behind him. Lucius guided her down the steps until they reached a door with a worn handle that he subsequently turned.

The opened door revealed an underground club brimming with gentlemen and ladies, all in masks, but wearing warped versions of formal attire, made with black leather, lace, and silk. The men wore suit coats over bare chests, the women in plunging necklines with slit skirts that revealed stockingless legs. Exotic cigar smoke hung thick in the air, high collar prostitutes grinding their pelvises against grinning patrons and patronesses, who either drank stout glasses of scotch or sipped champagne from crystal flues. The entire room was accented in gold, sparkling chandeliers battling the smoke to sparkle in the gaslight.

"What is this place?"

"One of the best kept secrets in London, hidden in a place where no respectable man nor woman would dare venture," Lucius replied as he led her through the press of bodies, too immersed in their various forms of hedonism to pay them any mind. "They call it Bacchus's Den."

The man behind the bar wore a masquerade mask with the addition of an exaggerated nose, his chest completely bare except for a bow tie tight around his neck. Wiry chestnut hair covered his chest in patches. "Good evening, Lord Montgomery," he greeted them as he dried the inside of a glass with a towel. "Would you and the lady like the usual room and company tonight?"

"We would like to mingle a bit first," Lucius replied, reprising his high-pitched accent even as he pronounced a series of French words. "We would like *deux fées vertes* served at our table."

The bartender nodded, and before Morrigan could question him, Lucius led her to an upholstered couch behind a table set far against the wall with a sheer veil drawn for privacy. He removed the placard that had reserved it for them and opened up the gold-plated cigarette box next to it. He lit a cigarette off a nearby candle, offering her one with a raised eyebrow.

She took it, fingering the rolled tobacco between her fingers. "I lost my taste for them after I changed," she commented.

Lucius took a smooth drag, crossing his long legs on the table as he settled back into the cushions. "What was your life before? When you were a human. You said this was your home."

"I was a whore," she said simply, laying the cigarette down. "Dying of consumption."

His eyes met hers. "I was low born, a destitute orphan taken in by a woman who served at the home of a Marquis."

"You speak so well," she remarked.

"As do you," he pointed out.

"My mother taught me many things about the world, including how to speak so that men might listen," she explained softly, her deceased mortal mother such a distant memory to her now that she could barely picture her face. "It served me well after I was orphaned and forced into unseemly work, and for a long time, I attracted high class men with large pockets to pick."

Lucius looked delighted. "I was self-taught, but under the same notion. I realized quite young that in order to rise out of the filth, one must be a master at playing the game."

"Precisely." She smiled.

"Do you remember anything from your past life, the one before you were human?" he asked. "The do-gooding fellows told me they tried to unlock your memories."

Morrigan cleared her throat as she looked down. The room buzzed with conversation, laughter, and the sound of tinkling glasses, but her thumping heart seemed louder. "Before that, I was told the story of who I was by David—"

"You trust his version of things?" he interrupted, looking at her askance.

"And faint memories surface at their own will," she continued as if she hadn't heard him. "I remember bits and pieces of the ancient past. My human memories were the strongest at first, until the medium hypnotized me, bringing to light what happened right before I was reborn here. Now those seem to be the clearest of them all."

"Interesting," Lucius remarked as he took a last inhale from his cigarette, smashing the crackling paper into the nearby ashtray. In the distance, laughter rumbled and sang. "What are they memories of?"

Thankfully, the waiter appeared before she had to respond. He brought with him two glasses of bright emerald liquid, each with two small decorative spoons laid across, both holding a cube of sugar. He poured water from a bottle over the sugar, one at a time, until it began to melt, turning the liquid into a milky shade of green. Then he nodded curtly and disappeared into the background.

"What on earth is this?" Morrigan asked, curious as the aroma of anise and wormwood bit her nose.

"In France, it is called *La Fee Verte*, or the Green Fairy," Lucius explained. He removed the empty spoon to give the drink a stir before taking the glass in his hand. He spun the neck between his fingers as he spoke. "They claim it is no ordinary spirit, but an elixir meant to illuminate the mind."

Morrigan stared at the swirling green liquid in her glass. "Perhaps my mind has reached enough illumination."

Lucius laughed. "Nonsense. Drink with me and let the night carry us where it may." He lifted the glass in a toast.

Morrigan sighed, removing the spoon, and lifting her glass to clink against his. The drink burned her stomach on its descent, a painful reminder that her body preferred blood above all else. Yet the discomfort subsided quickly, the taste of licorice lingering on her tongue as she gazed at a stranger whose soul once belonged to a man she loved. She could almost see him again, his eyes laughing behind their double facade. She mused over how strange their lives were, how she'd begun her life as one person, but at any moment, she could be someone else. She closed her eyes. Lilith, Nephthys, Morrigan, Liliana, who was she today? ... which man did she love today?

Lucius realized she was drifting away. He interrupted her thoughts with the snap of his fingers, beckoning to the bartender to bring two more of the viridescent drinks. "I have no memories of my lives before this one," he said, resuming their earlier conversation, "though I have always felt a restlessness that I cannot seem to put into words. Sometimes I feel as though life is marred by frivolity and devoid of substance, the humans living it dreadfully vapid."

Morrigan sipped her drink, her mouth flooded once more with tangy licorice. "You have always been restless. It is your nature."

He gazed at her. "What more do you remember of me? Were we very close?"

Morrigan realized she'd once again painted herself into a difficult corner. She bit the inside of her lip, looking down as she traced the edge of her glass.

He grinned and swallowed down the last of his drink. "I have to admit,

I am thoroughly enjoying how uncomfortable I make you, especially since I have no idea why."

Morrigan sighed. "Oh yes, that quality has never changed about you either."

"Splendid." He rose from the table. "Let us go, a ball awaits. Perhaps I will be able to wrest the reason out of you at some point tonight."

"Never," she replied with a smile as she took his hand once more.

The masquerade the Montgomerys planned to attend was held at another outrageously large estate, this one mimicking the architecture of a French chateau. The entire courtyard was illuminated with lanterns, a glowing oasis in the autumnal darkness. She almost laughed at the absurdity of it, that she, a warrior goddess thrust into the body of a prostitute turned immortal, was now waltzing unabashedly into an exclusive ball intended for London's elite, with the soul whom she'd spent eons trying to escape from on her arm.

The servants who greeted them at the door recognized both the carriage and driver, none the wiser to their true identities as they helped them inside. Morrigan was immediately grateful they fed beforehand, the smell of so many humans in such close proximity nearly making her swoon with hunger.

"Not quite yet," Lucius whispered in her ear as he pulled her closer.

The ballroom was colossal, a vulgar display of wealth, dozens of sparkling chandeliers lining the vaulted ceilings of sculpted plaster. The floor gleamed bright white marble, interrupted by the swirling satin trains of ballroom dresses whose mistresses dripped with extravagant diamonds and pearls. Champagne was served in fine crystal atop gold platters, a full orchestra conducting the opulent scene.

"What do you think?" Lucius asked as he guided her through the swell of bodies towards a neglected corner in the back.

"It's far too bright in here," she sniffed, to which he roared with laughter.

He removed a glass of bubbling champagne from a nearby waiter's tray, swallowing it down and turning back to her, all in one graceful swoop. "You must dance with me," he declared. "I am far too drunk on fine spirits and your intoxicating scent not to dance."

Before she could protest, he pulled her onto the dance floor, at ease amongst the crowd. She, however, was completely out of her element. Although she had perfected her accent and poise to service high class gentlemen, she never could master the art of dance. No matter how hard she tried, her body would instinctively recoil at their touch. Lucius must have sensed it, or noticed the uneasiness in her eyes, for he pulled her tighter against him, guiding her along the way. She felt her body relax against his, the unusual warmth that seemed to radiate from his skin comforting to her, melting away her tension.

A jolt of memory hit her suddenly, in a palace that was darker, saturated with the smell of death. Romania. Lucius bursting through the door, covered in chain mail armor which he threw off with gusto. "We've won," he said breathlessly, his body smeared with blood and grime, jumping into their bed to ravage her with his affections.

The modern Lucius began to twirl her faster as she buried her head into the top of his chest. The dancing couples around them seemed to fade away, temporal apparitions that did not matter, the two of them the only beings in the room. His heart kept time with hers as another memory came, a vision of him standing in a field of fallen men, black tears threatening to spill from his eyes. Billows of gray fog snaked around them in the crisp air. "I will never understand why you keep doing this to me," he cried, his fists clenched in fury. Scotland.

The memories roared past her now with blinding speed, the wars, the adventures, the quarrels, visions of David sitting sullenly in his chambers, smiling when he looked up to see her, Lucius as a prince, exploring her body as they lay next to the fireplace, his eyes filled with adoration and lust.

Finally, a location she could not place, another realm perhaps, filled with hellfire and ash, as he shielded her from an onslaught of flames intent to destroy her with his own body, wrapping his bruised arms around her. *"Shh, it will be over soon…"*

The dance stopped, and her knees buckled. He caught her, guiding her towards a table and helping her sit. "What is it?" he asked, alarm in his voice.

"I don't want to be here anymore," she whispered.

"I'll summon the carriage. Rest here." He squeezed her hand before marching back towards the main entrance.

Morrigan took a deep breath, forcing her mind to be still. The last memory unnerved her, a foreign vision that she could only surmise came from her most recent time in the Underworld. She realized there was more that needed to be unearthed, that she must continue to dig through her unconscious mind. As her senses returned, her mind flitted to David, wondering if and when he planned to return. She now understood why she'd chosen to leave them both; the love she felt seemed eternally split between two. No matter what she did, no matter how hard she tried not to, she continuously caused them both pain.

She rose up from her chair, sweeping her hands down the crimson waves of her dress with fresh determination. This was not the time to indulge in matters of the heart that never resolve. It was time to dig back into her memories, restore the realms, and find Anubis. It was time to retrieve David.

"Excuse me, miss, do I know you from somewhere?"

A man dressed in a gaudy three-piece suit stood in front of her, eyeing her suspiciously from behind his pointed white mask. A stiff auburn mustache crawled across his lip.

Annoyed to be reminded that there were others in the room, she tried to temper her reply. But he didn't let her speak, growing too close to her, a willowy socialite frowning on his arm. "I never forget a face."

Suddenly she stiffened, for the old memories of her mortal life poked through, her days as Liliana the prostitute, watching one of her fellow whores laughing gaily in the man's presence only to return the next day with fresh bruises and a broken rib.

"Yes, I do know you." The man squinted in wonderment as he edged even closer, his breath like spoiled meat. Morrigan's anger rose, a dormant part of her rumbling to life, pulled upwards from her bowels by her rapidly ascending heartbeat. She envisioned taking one of the nearby knives and jamming it upwards into his chin.

"Yes, you are the whore from Eastern Tavern!" he laughed as the lady on his arm clucked her tongue with derision. She accompanied the sound with an eye roll, fanning herself faster with her delicate lace fan. A crowd gathered around them, curious about the commotion.

"However did you manage to screw your way up the social ladder?" He continued his loud defamation. "The last time I saw you, you were dying of the pox. Although, I did hear you were trying to convince men it was consumption—but everyone knows whores do not die of such noble diseases."

Murmurs of disgust trickled across the room.

Morrigan felt as if at any moment she would explode, tearing the flesh off the bones of England's upper class. She swallowed, trying to maintain control as she edged away from the drunken man. "You've made a terrible mistake," she said.

"You've even changed your accent!" the man roared with laughter. "How curious! Where is your companion this evening—I simply must ask him how he managed to get duped by you. He must be a parvenu, I am certain." He began scanning the room.

Just as Morrigan felt as though she could not hold in her rage any longer, Lucius reappeared, coming up from behind her. She could feel the heat coming off him like a freshly lit stove, wondering what he'd heard of their interaction.

"Well hello, old boy, pleased to make your acquaintance," the man called out as the crowd shifted their attention onto Lucius. "Do tell us why your date this evening is a diseased whore from the slums of East End?"

Morrigan barely had time to react before Lucius had him by the throat, lifting him effortlessly into the air with one hand. The crowd froze in shock until the glass the man had been holding crashed to the floor. Then the room burst into an uproar, the shrieks of ladies bringing the orchestral music to an abrupt halt. Morrigan watched as Lucius set the men around him ablaze with a flick of his fingers, the entire ballroom exploding into a frenzy of agonized wails and terrified screams. The silk curtains caught all around them as the burning bodies tore about the room, flames rapidly curling up to the ceiling like impenetrable walls of fire. They licked the ceiling in rapacious fever, sending smoldering plaster and pieces of chandelier to the ground.

The man Lucius held turned purple, his eyes bulging grotesquely from his sockets as he gasped for air, futilely scratching at Lucius's clenched fist.

"Lucius, we must leave!" Morrigan cried over the pandemonium. She tried to grab his arm, but his skin had become scalding to the touch. She looked up to see that his expression had gone blank, his pupils eclipsing his irises into an absolute black. The world around her began to crumble, the elegant ballroom reduced to a merciless inferno. "Let him down or we will burn in here with him!"

Yet he didn't listen, the man unwilling to give in to his inevitable death, still struggling against him. Suddenly she realized that Lucius was immobilized by his fury, trapped in the intensity of his power. She let out a roar of frustration, ripping the leg from an overturned chair and throwing the pointed end so that it lodged itself neatly in the man's skull. Shocked, Lucius finally dropped him, turning to reveal an expression of panic. His hands shook as he held them up, each of his fingers ablaze, two pyres that gave no hint of dying.

Morrigan grabbed him, gritting her teeth against the pain, and flew them both out through the caved-in ceiling, delivering them from the bowels of the fiery disaster. She hadn't realized she'd sprouted the wings of a crow until they reached the nadir of evening sky and she pulled torrents of cold rain down along with them. She heard hysterical mortals escaping in their carriages as she landed on the soil. The water drenched them, Lucius's hands finally releasing tendrils of extinguished smoke. She pulled him onto her lap, cradling him in her arms as he heaved for breath, the rhythmic tapping of cool rain calming them both.

"This," she whispered, as sorrow replaced her dwindling adrenaline. "This is our history together."

He did not respond, but she felt an arm reach up and curl itself around her.

From the distance, two riders appeared on horseback, but Morrigan did not have to see to know who they were. David did not speak, his face obscured by the pouring rain as he lifted the weakened Lucius out of her lap and onto his horse.

"Come on, love, let's get out of this rain," said a broad figure who could only be Dan, taking her gently by the hand and lifting her up onto his own steed.

Thunder cracked in the sky as they retreated, four broken creatures riding in the storm.

Dan opened the door for her when they arrived at David's manor, gesturing inside. The sound of dripping water echoed through the halls of the dark, empty house. "Perhaps we should change out of our wet clothes and reconvene in the parlor," he suggested.

"I've had my fill of that bloody parlor," she said with a slight shiver.

Dan shrugged. "Three floors and two wings in this blasted house, I'm sure we can manage to find somewhere else."

"When will they be returning?" she asked.

Dan sighed, running his fingers through his damp silver waves. "I was instructed to keep you out of it—" His towering frame blocked her as she immediately tried to exit. "Hear me first. David asked that I keep you here so they could talk. They are in the vaults, where no wind nor fire can be easily summoned."

Morrigan scoffed. "They will kill each other!"

"Libraean is nearby, just in case. Perhaps they need to fight things out."

Morrigan chewed at the inside of her lip. "I don't like this. You seem like a perfectly fine man, but you trapping me here makes me want to gouge out both of your eyes."

Dan couldn't help but chuckle. "David warned me as much. But I told him that I would explain to you that you are helping keep me here, just as much as I am you. I just found out that Cahira is in a cabin outside of London and it's taking every part of my being not to go find her."

"She's here?" Morrigan said in surprise.

"I don't want to talk about it," Dan muttered, heading up to his room. "I'll meet you in the kitchen. There's alcohol in the kitchen."

Morrigan sighed, dragging the waterlogged skirts of another woman's dress up the stairwell past the guest room she'd been reborn in.

On her first night, Jacob had brought her to the room of the eldest Lardone daughter, where she headed now, a room that spared little pomposity even with the dust strewn across the gaudy fireplace and ivory furniture, its floral wallpaper yellowed with time. He had directed her towards the full wardrobe that had been left behind so she could change from her tattered, bloodied clothes and, although the dresses fit, she had found no appeal in the frills and stiff, gaudy material. Unfortunately, now she had no choice, for the outfit she'd absconded from the stores downtown had been left behind during her escapade with Lucius.

She tore off Mrs. Montgomery's scarlet gown and jewels as soon as she entered, standing in her damp chemise as she rifled once more through the clothing, the frigid manor raising the fine hairs on her skin.

"I do have a mourning dress in there somewhere, since you snub your nose at all the beautiful gowns I had imported from France. I hope you know they were high fashion while I was alive."

Morrigan beheld the eldest daughter standing near the window, her face wrinkled with annoyance. It was very narrow and pointed, and though she might have been lovely in her youth, her skin was splotched purple, her eyes rimmed in red.

"I was poisoned," she explained, noticing Morrigan's expression. "Not long after I murdered my brother for being an abomination. Hence why there are only two black dresses. I did not survive much longer after his death."

Morrigan sighed, her fingers finding the dress Francesca Lardone suggested, pulling it from the wardrobe. It was scandalously low cut for a mourning gown, accented with black lace. "Thank you," she offered.

"I should not be helping you," the ghost huffed. "Since you have abandoned the dead."

Morrigan turned towards her as she began removing the pins from her hair. "I abandoned no one, I was ousted from the Underworld and none of us know why."

"Is that right?" Francesca said dryly. "Well, those of us who haven't been allowed into Heaven are just waiting around while you're off galivanting around town with some handsome Frenchman."

Morrigan scowled. "I have no sympathy for someone who murdered her own brother out of spite."

Francesca sighed, rolling her eyes. "You make a terrible goddess. I hope the clothes give you hives." With that, she faded into the wallpaper.

Morrigan pulled the macabre dress up around her body, satisfied by the way the dark, starchless fabric fell around her bare legs. She decided to stay barefoot, heading back down the stairs to the kitchen, her hair flowing behind her, wild and free.

It was already illuminated by lamps, Dan sitting at the servant's table with a half empty bottle of scotch in his hand, a short glass on the table across from him. "Glad you decided not to flee. I wasn't looking forward to David's wrath when he found out."

Morrigan slipped into the opposite chair.

"Well, you sure clean up nicely," Dan commented, approving of her attire.

"Careful," she said lightly, as she filled the glass halfway with scotch. "I have enough trouble with men as it is."

Dan chuckled. "It was only a friendly compliment," he assured her. "I love exactly one woman, one who just so happens to want nothing to do with me."

"So, if Cahira is back," Morrigan thought aloud, "does that mean David was the one who found her?"

"Yep." Dan took a swig of the bottle.

Morrigan frowned. "Do you think she is what kept him away for so long?"

"I don't know."

"Do you think they…"

"I don't know."

Morrigan quietly emptied her glass.

They sat in silence for a moment before Dan finally spoke up. "I honestly don't believe he was with her the entire time. Though we did have to fight to smooth things out." He turned his head to reveal a bruised cheek in the process of healing.

"I see," Morrigan said softly.

Dan attempted to change the subject. "So how does a Celtic war goddess like yourself stay sane, forced to remain stagnant behind four walls? I also grew up in the woods and find myself longing to be in them when I've been playing civilian for too long."

Morrigan smiled sadly. "I do not feel much like myself in this life. When they brought me back in the ancient days, I was Morrigan—in constant opposition with Delicia—but unequivocally Morrigan. In this form, I am all of them. The human Liliana, the death goddess Nephthys, sprinkled with glimpses of the Morrigan. It hasn't been easy to reconcile all these different identities. I guess that is what keeps me patient. That and I'm worried for Anubis. I believe we can retrieve him better together than alone."

"Your son," Dan remembered.

Morrigan nodded. "I didn't get a chance to raise either of my children, but Anubis was the closest to me. My second son, Horus, now lives his life as Libraean, and David and he have their own special bond."

Dan took another swig of scotch, offering her more, which she politely declined. "I never had any children myself," he said. "At first I was too afraid to, but then I was turned into a blood drinker, forever taking the choice away from me."

"I'm sorry," Morrigan offered with genuine empathy. "And I appreciate you trying to distract me from my worry, although I cannot pretend that I'm not anxious. They should be done conversing by now."

"If there was a problem, I'm sure Libraean would be rushing down here to tell us," Dan assured her. "Or there would be a tornado tearing through the English countryside."

"True," Morrigan agreed, but was still unable to shake her apprehension. Finally, she heard a rustling in the hall.

She flew into the foyer, startling Jacob so badly that he dropped his tray, shattering the glasses it held. She stared at the pieces for a moment, realizing it was the third time she'd observed glass breaking. "Forgive me," she murmured, kneeling to help pick them up.

"Do not worry, Madame," Jacob said. "Things move slow for me, even slower around all of you fast paced creatures. I have not grown accustomed to it yet." He winced as he sliced his finger on one of the shards. A bead of red blood came to the surface, freezing Morrigan in place. All of a sudden, her nose could smell nothing else but its delectable scent, the craving to taste it overwhelming her, blurring out all other senses.

"Jacob, call Dan..." she managed, rising slowly up from where she stood.

Jacob caught the look in her eyes and began to back away. The smell of his rising fear enticed her further, her body now arguing with her conscious mind, trying to convince her that she could take just one little taste, that he wouldn't mind…

Dan grabbed her arms behind her just as she snapped. "Run into the back rooms and lock the door!" he shouted at Jacob, who abandoned his tray and hurried to comply.

The sensation of being manhandled incensed an already agitated Morrigan, who bent to free her arms and whip around to kick Dan square in his chest, sending the giant creature sailing into an already smashed up wall.

He scowled, jumping back up from where he landed, his eyes narrowed and jaw tight. The sight of him standing before her with hackles raised filled Morrigan with exhilaration, faced with someone who loved combat as much as she did, bringing her dormant warrior to life.

"As much as I love a good fight, doll," he growled, his hands in balled fists. "I have no fight with you. However, I cannot have you killing one of ours."

Morrigan frantically nodded, aware that her instincts had taken over, scooping deep breaths into her lungs as she'd seen David do, trying to quiet her aggression.

"You fed from humans when you were with Lucius, didn't you?"

"Yes," Morrigan gasped, her face still flushed, her lips quivering. She could hear thunder rolling above, rain picking up around them.

Dan relaxed slightly. "Okay, then that is why. Morrigan, listen to me— you need to hunt. Outside this manor are woods filled with perfectly satisfying creatures. Eat one."

Morrigan bobbed her head.

"But please, don't bother the brothers. Come right back here when you're done."

She didn't reply, flying out the front door at full speed and into the pouring rain. Her limbs sang joyfully at the exertion, instantly invigorated by the chilled air that filled her lungs and the freezing rain that drenched her hair. The night creatures greeted her as she entered their domain, her bare feet working to keep her balanced as she jumped and dove across the muddy forest floor at building speed. Bats flew from the trees, waking up the slumbering crows who cawed out their hellos.

The slumbering stag had no time to register her presence before she pounced, sinking her teeth into its neck with such fervor that his blood sprayed up in her face and ran down her chin. It wasn't like the orgasmic throes drinking from humans gave her, but its warmth soothed her inner beast. She drank until there was nothing left, gently setting down the corpse as she whispered her gratitude. The crows that gathered around her cooed their thanks as well, circling in happy anticipation of a fresh, hearty meal.

She walked back to the manor at a leisurely pace, letting her heightened senses absorb the beauty of the night around her. The rain had stopped by the time she exited the forest, the cloudless sky boasting the brilliance of the full quarter moon, lighting her path. Her eyes flickered towards the graveyard, trying to honor her promise to Dan. She focused instead on the fluttering bats above her, the snakes crawling nearby in the dirt, and the random hooting of owls as she made her way back through the manor gates.

The doors opened for her when she arrived, revealing both Libraean and Dan waiting for her in the foyer. David stood at the forefront, his hand on the door.

CHAPTER TEN

❧ The End ❧

London, 1857
David

DAVID THREW LUCIUS INTO THE VAULT, slamming the door behind
them. He slid across the concrete floor without a fight, still weakened
from the chaos of the masquerade ball. He instead stared up at the ceiling,
crossing his fingers on his chest. "So did you bring me here to kill me?"

Libraean had left only two lamps behind, lest Lucius gain enough
strength to manipulate the fire they held. He convinced David to allow
him to wait in the Lardone crypt, just in case. It was simply a precaution,
he'd explained, since David insisted the conversation between them needed
to be had alone. David had agreed, though he assured Libraean that his
intervention wouldn't be necessary.

David slumped down in Librean's old, weathered chair, lighting a cigarette. He was exhausted, the little rest he had at Cahira's cabin mildly
rejuvenating at best. "I do not want to kill you. Yet."

"Ah," Lucius said, unimpressed. "So, what then? Do you want me to
apologize for taking your paramour out after you left her here, worried for
days on end? Ask your friend upstairs, for it was his idea, not mine."

"Are you still pretending that you remember nothing?" David sighed.

Lucius leaned up onto his elbows. It was strange to see him look so
young, for long ago, David was the fledgling immortal next to his ancient
sire. His skin was unnaturally smooth around his amber eyes, eyes that

still smoldered with the same intensity they always had, a testament to the notion that whatever shell a soul found itself in, its eyes would always remain the same. His jet-black hair was short, but in waves as unkempt as David's own rebellious locks. The face was different, a bit fuller in the cheeks than before, but his perpetually annoyed expression remained the same. "As much as I'd like to be the great mastermind that you all paint me out to be, memories of my former life have only come back to me as of this night, with her."

David's heart gave a hard thud against his chest, but he took a deep breath, quieting the flash of anger that his words provoked. "I need to know if you've destroyed the realms," he swiftly changed the subject.

"Destroyed the realms? Why on earth would I do that?"

"Oh, I don't know, perhaps so you can finally kill me for good and live on Earth with Morrigan. Or a myriad of other foolish reasons. I can't even begin to imagine why you do the things you do, but it always seems to involve being with her and getting rid of me."

Lucius snorted. "And I'm supposed to be the narcissistic one." He nodded towards David's opened case of cigarettes. "Let me have one of those."

David tossed him the lit one he'd been holding, knowing better than to throw him a book of matches.

Lucius took a long inhale, studying David as he lit another one for himself. "I only remember being with her, in flashes. Everything else I've learned from your lumpy librarian friend's records. How you fucked my wife, then conspired with the sons that should have been mine to kill me, sent me to the lowest depths of what is now called Hell, spent a lifetime cavorting with that same wife in disguise, and even then, even after I unknowingly gave you immortal life with more power than you could imagine, you once again took my wife away from me and killed me. Yet everyone seems to look to you as some sort of savior, while I'm the one that they fear." He shook his head in disbelief.

David flew out of his chair to Libraean's bookcase, grabbing the biggest volume from the top shelf and dropping it down into his lap. "Did you read about how you and I were once friends? How you slowly grew mad over time, growing to hate humans, hating life itself, until you became bent on self-destruction? How you decided to take the human race down with you? How you impaled humans on spikes around a castle you built on the blood and bones of innocent men?"

Lucius scowled. "No man is innocent." He tossed the book away from him, a few of the pages flying out as it moved. One drifted to the ground, revealing a charcoal sketch of Vlad Dracula, Lucius's maniacal eyes staring out from beneath his turban.

David fell back into the chair, resting his head in his hands for a moment before looking up to stare directly at him. "Do you remember what happened after Wallachia, when you and she died? Your time with her in the Underworld?"

"No," Lucius asserted. "I told you, only flashes have been coming back to me, of when we were younger. You know, they seem to be most clear when I'm around her, perhaps you should tell her to come down here and spend time with me?"

David growled. "If you think I'm going to allow that, then you are a fool."

"My," Lucius took a last hit from his cigarette, sniffing it out on the ground. "Who's the possessive one now? Careful, she hates that quality in a lover."

David jumped up from his chair again, taking all the energy he could muster not to attack him.

Lucius merely laughed. "I really do enjoy how much I rile all of you up."

David stomped over to another bookcase, this one topped by a closed cabinet. He threw it open, pilfering through an assortment of items before his hands found one. He pulled out a tarnished goblet, an artifact centuries old.

Lucius's eyes widened.

"Do you remember this?" David held it up. "Libraean went back to the castle after he pulled me to safety, gathering whatever he could before it crumbled into the river. He found a few items, including this and Morrigan's diadem. I've saved them all this time."

Lucius was quiet.

"You may think I'm against you, that I hate you, but I've forgiven many of your misdeeds. Whether either one of us wants to admit it, we are brothers. I was by your side for centuries as we traveled the globe, I fought in all of your wars. I remained in the shadows while you and Morgana carried on your warped love affair—for eons! It wasn't until you decided to leave me to die in the sun that I turned on you."

Lucius snorted. "You weren't in the shadows when you came onto her in the rivers of Ireland, nor at our castle when you drained the last bit of her life to save your own skin."

"Ah," David sat back in his chair. "You do remember."

Lucius was dumbfounded at first, before he burst into a grin filled with genuine admiration. "Well played. But I already told you—the memories are coming to me now after our evening together. I still don't recall my time with her in the Underworld. You can play mind games with me all you like, but I won't be able to give you anything more than that."

David sighed. "Then we are going to have to dive deeper into her mind, although the thought of uncovering more of your time together makes me sick."

"What did you uncover so far?" he asked, curiously.

"That is for her to tell you, if she wishes," David said. "The point is, our realms are gone. Human souls are now trapped in the space between life and death, the lucky ones ascending to Heaven. We are no exception. There is no more reincarnation. If we die in this world, we are dead forever."

Lucius scoffed. "Has anyone considered the humans? Can't they bring gods to life with their intentions, therefore able to recreate our realms?"

David shook his head bitterly. "This world is overtaken by new religion, you know this. No one worships the old gods anymore. We are but a footnote in books of ancient myth."

"Then what are you proposing we do?" Lucius asked flatly.

"I met a woman who has been journeying across the world, collecting all the reincarnated gods in the hopes that if we all come together, we can find a solution. She says that some are already gone, without ever learning who they truly were, and that she wants to make contact with the rest. She intends on traveling to Africa to meet Anubis."

"And I suppose you will be accompanying her?"

"I am," David confirmed. "And I'm hoping the rest of my friends will join me."

"Which means I'll be left behind," Lucius sighed as he examined the old goblet in his hand. "Do you plan on keeping me down here as a prisoner until you return?"

"No," David sighed, turning to leave. "But it is up to Morrigan to decide."

He didn't give Lucius a chance to comment further, slamming shut the vault door and heading up the stairwell. Libraean looked up from the book he'd been perusing as he sat on one of the other sarcophagi in the crypt. He looked at him over the rim of his glasses. "Well?"

"I didn't kill him," David told him shortly as he headed towards the door.

"David, wait," Libraean hurried forward to stop him. "I have been your friend for centuries and I know when you are being driven by your emotions. Can we please talk?"

David sighed, though he briefly admired how bright Libraean's dead eye had become, glowing like his skin. His straightened spine also offered him a new height, nearly eye level with him as he spoke. "What do you want me to say? I'm exhausted, Libraean. I am utterly mentally and emotionally exhausted."

Libraean rested his hand on his shoulder, gazing at him with knowing eyes. "I know. Were you chasing the dragon again?"

David's mouth twitched. He thought of the poor owner of the opium den, making a mental note to make amends to her when everything had settled. "Perhaps."

"Well," Libraean turned to gather his things. "At least you rested. These last few days have been difficult, no one blames you for wanting to escape. We were alone for a great many years."

"I almost wish it was that way again," David admitted softly.

"Did you manage to wrest anything out of Lucius?" Libraean asked as they both reentered the frosty November evening.

David noticed Morrigan had ended her rainstorm, the moon high and bright in the sky. He almost groaned when he remembered he would soon have to face her. "Lucius truly cannot recall their time in the Underworld," he replied. "Morrigan seems to be the only one who can help us."

He pulled open the door to reveal Dan standing near Jacob, who appeared visibly shaken. The floor was strewn with fragments of broken china, the scent of herbal tea in the air. Libraean rushed over to him, gathering him into his arms.

"What happened?" David asked Dan. "Where is Morrigan?" Before he had a chance to respond, David smelled her and rushed back to the door, pulling it open to reveal her standing like a dark pillar against the bright evening sky.

She stood barefoot in a billowing black gown, her lips stained crimson, her exposed white shoulders and neck crusted with blood that was not hers. Her hair and skirts fluttered in the wind, the image reminding him of the moment she'd taken her own life, many years ago. The sudden memory threatened to release the emotions he painstakingly held in, and he stepped aside to let her enter.

"I needed to kill something," she explained to him before he asked, shooting a grateful look towards Dan, who nodded in an unspoken reply. She turned towards Jacob. "Please forgive me."

Though the old man still appeared rattled, he shook his head stubbornly.

"You do not have to apologize to me, madame. I was told to stay in the southern suite, and I didn't listen. It is I who should be apologizing for presenting you with temptation. Which, I might add, I am very grateful you thwarted."

"Now that we are all gathered here, there is something I must tell you all," David began. "We need to leave London immediately. It is only a matter of time before rumors spread about what happened at the Caraway Estate, and attention is directed towards the strange folks living in the old Lardone Manor, who only come out after nightfall.

"But there are other reasons. Anubis has reincarnated in Africa, in the Kingdom of Dahomey to be exact, where he leads a resistance against their king to abolish slavery amongst their people. He finally succeeded in contacting me through psychic means after years of attempting to do so. It appears he is joined by several other incarnated gods and goddesses, yet the Kingdom itself is in turmoil and he isn't sure how long it will be before they kill him. As far as our war, he has ideas on how to restore the realms, but he believes we all need to be together to do so, all the Ancient Ones."

"You, Libraean, Lucius, and I," Morrigan said quietly.

"Yes," David tried to meet her eyes, but found he could not. He struggled to keep emotion out of his voice. "This means Lucius would come with us, but only if you allow it."

"How could you suggest such a thing?" Libraean protested, speaking for them all.

"There is not one among us with a more turbulent relationship than he and I," David pointed out. "But I trust Anubis, for he has always shown me the way."

"What about my sister?" Morrigan asked, maintaining her low tone. "She was one of us but has long since been scattered to the wind."

"Cahira," Dan interrupted. "Cahira holds the earth's power. She is stronger than Hekate was, arguably as strong as your sister."

Morrigan blinked. "How can that be?"

He shrugged. "I only know what I witnessed of her. You heard my tale and what she is capable of, I doubt her powers have waned much since then."

"Anubis contacted her, as well," David informed them. "She intends on sailing there herself, with or without us, but she agrees to wait, pending our decision."

"She is willing to travel with us?" Dan repeated in disbelief. "Does she know that I am with you?"

"Yes, she knows," David told him. "Although you are not an original in the same sense as the rest of us, she and I agreed that we would only benefit from having you accompany us on our travels. Anubis, as well."

"Well, I think we all know my vote." Dan shrugged as his lips turned up into a half grin, the first genuinely pleasant expression to cross his face since he had arrived.

"I am not leaving Gabriel," Libraean spoke up from beside him. Jacob beamed, bashfully lowering his eyes.

"He is part of our family, yes, but do you think it wise to have him around so many blood drinkers?" David asked them both gently.

"Family," Morrigan echoed to no one in particular, her gaze moving up to the stained-glass windows.

"I will make sure he is unharmed," Libraean insisted. "He will be my responsibility. The only one I truly worry about is Lucius, but if we can keep them on opposite sides of the boat, I see no reason to worry. I also think it would be good to have another human on board. He can assist us in daylight matters if necessary."

David nodded. "So, we are all in agreement regarding Lucius?" he asked, his eyes flickering towards Morrigan.

"I am not his keeper," she reminded him. "He makes up his own mind."

Libraean shuffled forward, pulling Jacob along with him. "We will meet you in the parlor," he said, shooting a look towards Dan, who abruptly followed.

The foyer plunged into silence, broken only by the house creaking in the wind as the two stared at each other. He couldn't read her face, but her sky-blue eyes swam with unspoken anguish.

"So, you didn't kill him after all," she commented.

"How could I?"

"You left me here."

"Forgive me. My heart has been shattered. I'm not certain what I'm supposed to do."

She looked down at the ground as she hugged herself. "I'm uncertain myself. It seems as though we are trapped in an impossible situation." Her eyes lifted to meet his. "I do know that in this life, I love you. But I suppose I love him, too."

"I know." David looked away. "Let us place our focus on things that can be solved. Do you agree that he should come with us?"

"I do, though I witnessed tonight the untethered rage we once saw in him in Wallachia, when the madness took him," she said. "I think we can both agree that Lucius does not fare well on the earthly plane. However, he is young in this life, and we may have a few years before he gives us trouble."

"Us?"

Morrigan was quiet.

"You're right," he sighed. "But believe me when I tell you, I might have been the one to kill him, but the only time he is tempered is when you are around. You are the only one who can control him, though it pains me that you must bear such a burden."

"You are not wrong," she murmured sadly.

"You deserve so much more from life than soothing a wild beast," he whispered, hating himself for still loving her, his body instinctively edging closer to hers.

He saw black tears bead at the corners of her eyes, though she bit the inside of her lip so they would not spill. "Do I?" she whispered. "I created this mess for myself. My sister never needed to be loved, but I did. My entire existence has been an endless pursuit of it. But when I was alone in the Underworld, after I decided to leave you both, I was truly at peace. For years. I realized that though I am Morrigan, the warrior goddess, I am first and foremost, Lilith, the protector, and Nephthys, queen of the dead. It was after I accepted this that he found me. Though it sounds incredulous, and we have no idea who he is now, the dark god Lucius has changed for the better. And although I cannot bear it in this present moment, down in the Underworld, I knew without a shadow of doubt that I belonged there with him. I was taken out of there against my wishes." Tears now poured down her cheeks, clean lines of inky obsidian.

David felt as if his chest caved in. "I am not going to stand by again in silence, watching you two together," he said between gritted teeth. "We will journey to Africa, and we will restore the realms, but then I am done with this life. I was alone for hundreds of years, believing you were also alone and content, only to discover you were content living with him. I refuse to spend any more of my life pining over a woman who I doubt has ever truly loved me to begin with!"

Suddenly, every stained-glass window shattered around them, allowing the inclement wind to tumble in. David leapt forward to cover her with his body as shards of colored glass stabbed his back and arms.

A vision struck him of Morrigan as he remembered her, slight and tattooed, frozen in place by unseen forces, her face twisted in an expression of anguish. An inferno raged around her, rocks crumbling down from above. Lucius, horrifically injured, his leathery black dragon wings ripped out of his human back and broken, using all his energy to hurl himself towards her, shielding her with his body before flames consumed them both.

It jolted him so hard that he fell away from her, his mind humming with shock.

"David—David!"

Her voice sounded far away, and he realized he wasn't just physically falling from her, but falling into the sweet, dark pool of unconsciousness, the manor crumbling around him, disappearing as he plummeted, until nothing was left, and he was gone.

PART FIVE

CHAOS

CHAPTER ELEVEN

🕸 The Daemons 🕸

London, 1857
David

THE CRASH STARTLED THE THREE OF THEM AS THEY STOOD IN WAIT, summoning them back into the foyer. They arrived to see Morrigan standing with her back against them, her long raven dress rippling in the squalls of wind that funneled through its broken windows. She turned, revealing an unconscious David in her arms, dried black tears in streaks down her face. Tiny shards of glass glittered in their skin and hair.

Jacob gasped. "Is he dead?"

"No," Libraean murmured, pushing past him. "This has happened before." He put his hand on David's chest as he examined him, brushing flakes of glass from his temple. "His body has finally forced him to rest. He is still alive, but he is no longer with us." He met Morrigan's eyes. "It could take days or weeks before he returns."

Morrigan nodded calmly, as if his words confirmed what she already suspected. "Then we will let him. Libraean and Jacob, I will need you to follow me and tend to David. Keep yourselves to the southern guest room. Dan, please fetch Cahira and tell her we will go with her to Africa."

"And you?" Dan asked with a frown, putting his hands on his hips.

Morrigan began to carry David up the stairs. "I am going to the vaults to free Lucius."

Dan sighed. "I was afraid you'd say that." He grabbed his cloak and headed out the door.

The winds were starting to die down, but the air stayed bitter, the way he liked it. He inhaled deeply, catching its moisture on his tongue. He would walk tonight, he decided, for although he was in a hurry, he wanted time to think, and David had kindly lent him a pair of boots that could handle the mud. He stomped through it now, the smell of spilled animal blood still tainting the woods, Morrigan's telltale scent drifting after it, winding through the trees. He wasn't as nervous as he assumed he would be, wondering if Cahira expected him to retrieve her.

He recalled the moment David appeared at the house searching for Morrigan. Dan was already well past the point of inebriation, three empty bottles of scotch littered around him on the parlor floor. Visions of Cahira and their last parting had been swimming relentlessly in his mind, the feel of her in his arms, the smell of her hair as it ran over his chest, her soft human skin gliding across his. It was everything he had ever imagined and more, finally able to express his devotion to her, hearing the words said back to him, the words he'd always wanted to hear. He'd lost himself in the moment, and although they had been trapped in a concrete world in a stranger's house, they were free and wild together in each other's embrace. It was the best moment of his existence, and once he realized it had all been a cruel trick, it had shattered him to his core.

He couldn't drown it out, even after a hundred years of trying to ignore its dull, persistent ache. Remembering her, speaking her name out loud to the others had brought it all back as if she'd only just opened the door to see him and the shapeshifting daemoness sent to ruin their bond.

It was during this painful, drunken recollection that David burst through the door. He was out of breath, his face appearing gaunter than before, his green eyes wild. And then he smelled her, her ambrosial aroma of apples and spring blossoms hanging on David as if they just parted. Dan had lunged at him without explanation, sending him to the floor.

David had been surprised, but he fought back, deceptively strong for his average height and medium build. Dan could not think straight, drunkenly throwing around his fists until David lifted him up and sent him crashing into the hallway, where the force of his body slamming into the wall crumbled the plaster. He sat there dazed, staring at him. "How?" he managed.

"That's what I came to tell you," David said as he heaved for breath, blood trickling from his nose. "I found her in London. She's still alive—she's semimortal."

Dan felt a sob rise in his chest. "How is that possible?"

David straightened, tucking his shirt back into his trousers. "Can we talk before you charge me again?"

"Forgive me. I'm drunk and you smell like her," Dan muttered, his head spinning.

David sighed, stepping around the ruins of plaster and split wood, extending an arm to help him out of the rubble. He guided Dan to the parlor, where he fell onto the couch, nearly toppling it over with his weight.

David fell into the opposite one, lighting himself a cigarette and tossing Dan another. "Finding out that the love of my life spent our time apart in the Underworld with her ex-husband, my horrible brother, was a little too much for me to bear. I found myself in an opium den trying to anesthetize the pain until I ran out of money. Cahira found me strung out in an alley. Apparently, she has been slaying daemons ever since she left Paris, after discovering Angelique was not who she seemed."

"I tried to warn her," Dan sighed.

"Well, now she is more than aware. Angelique has been hunting her ever since, obsessed after her plans to obtain her power failed."

Dan tried to stand. "I must go to her."

David stopped him. "She is still angered by what transpired between you, but she is willing to look past it so that we all might work together. She has told me some interesting things about her experience which I will share as soon as we are all together."

Libraean suddenly burst into the room. "David!" he said with relief, wrapping his arms around him. "I am so glad to see you're safe and sound."

David looked confused. "You're different."

Jacob came up behind him, and David slowly pieced together what had occurred. "Oh." He blinked once before his face erupted into a smile. "It's good to see you looking so well," he told Libraean, resting his hand on his shoulder.

"And the same with you," Libraean lied, placing his hand on his face as a father might lovingly examine his child.

"I hate to interrupt," Dan interjected. "But are you going to tell him, or should I?"

David's face fell. "Tell me what?"

Librean looked nervous, and he took a step back. He pushed his glasses up on his nose, anxiously licking his lips. "Morrigan fell into a deep melancholy the moment you left. She remained that way for the full week you were absent, and we were unable to get her to do much more than sip the blood we brought up to her. We had no idea when you would be back…"

"What have you done?" David said in a low voice, his expression grave.

"We thought we were doing the right thing," Jacob timidly inserted.

"We thought we could convince her to continue the process of revealing her memories. So, we asked Lucius for his help—"

"*You did what?*" David roared.

"I told them it was a bad idea," Dan muttered in the background as he watched the scene unfolding before him. David's kind, tired face had taken on a look of rage similar to that of his brother's.

Libraean began to speak more quickly as he argued his case. "After what she revealed in her memories, I thought he could be a good ally for us. We wanted to do our part to save the realms."

"Where are they now?" David demanded.

Jacob kept strategically positioned behind Libraean as he wrung his hands. "We cannot find them, sir. They've left the manor."

David swore, storming out of the room.

"I am sure they will return soon," Libraean called as he followed after him. "She loves you, David, I am sure there is nothing to worry about…"

David spun around. "It is not because of jealousy, Libraean, though of course I hate when she is away from me. It is because they are a banefully destructive pair whenever they are together. You might not remember the wars and mayhem that preceded Romania, but I do."

Libraean deflated as David marched away from him to grab his cloak. "Come on, Dan," he called over his shoulder. Dan grabbed his own cloak and promptly followed.

The memory faded as he pushed through the thickest part of the woods, his ears picking up the rustle of nocturnal beasts. He wondered what David's reaction would be once he found out that she planned on freeing Lucius from the vaults and taking him along with them to Africa, all in his absence. He sighed, determining it was none of his business, that the only thing he needed to worry about was how to repair things with Cahira.

He struggled to pick up her scent, but as he drew closer to the city, the stench of the polluted river overpowered all else. David had described her cabin as being right before the country turns into the city, nestled within a full patch of oak trees. He couldn't see anything of the sort and with no smells to guide him, it was becoming a fruitless endeavor. He took a seat on a stump flattened by wear, deciding to wait for inspiration.

The stars above shone their brightest, the wee hours of morning giving them a spectacular brilliance that streamed down through the trees. It reminded him of the night he was petrified in stone, carried to their home in Auvergne and left to die. Henri hadn't anticipated that the full moon had also peaked in intensity. The spell that had bound his canine soul had been restored after Cahira released him from hers, and as soon as the light of the pregnant moon hit the stone, Fenrir raged himself free, rocks falling away from his enormous body like pebbles. He sped after Henri, blocking the carriage with his body. The horses came to a crashing halt, jumping and neighing with fear. I'm not here for you, he told them. Stay still and you can go back alive.

Henri jumped down from the driver's seat with his arms up in defense, an unassuming grin plastered across his narrow face. "Aw, come now, son, the boss wanted you gone. We cannot control you now since the fool you're attached to got stronger."

Dan suddenly realized that he was staring at the reincarnated version of Loki, the chaos god responsible for killing him and attaching his bestial child to Dan's soul. He tried not to react as he quietly shook with rage.

"We can try to separate you again," he continued to explain, "but then we'd have to kill the forest witch. She's the one who brought Baldr back." It occurred to Dan that Loki had no idea he was conscious behind the canine visage. "But the boss has plans for her, so I'll see what she says. Why don't you just hang here for a bit?" he suggested. "Look around you. The wolves have overrun this town, forcing the Marquis and his brood out. The castle is abandoned, why don't you take it for yourself? Lay low for a while?"

Dan looked around him, realizing the entire village had indeed been deserted. Doors had been left open, garbage strewn about the empty streets. There was no sign of life, no livestock nor greenery, only trace decomposition lingering nearby.

"I'm going to get going, son," Henri continued, backing towards the carriage. "It was great to see you again."

Dan thrust out his hand, grabbing the front of his shirt with his claws. The halfling's eyes grew wide, realizing he wasn't going to be able to talk his way out of his situation. Dan was in no mood to prolong his agony, exhausted after his emotional day, so he used his other hand to grab Henri's head, decapitating him before he had a chance to scream. Blood sprayed up into his face from the torn neck into his eyes, which he wiped clean with his fur after tossing the head into the road. A standard wolf came creeping around the corner of one of the buildings, sniffing around the severed head. It's yours, just make sure there is nothing left, he told it, to which, it nodded gratefully. He removed an arm from the headless corpse, tossing it into the carriage as a message, and slammed the door.

Take this back to your mistress, he instructed the horses, which sped off with equal gratitude.

He headed back towards his old cabin, realizing he was hungry. He soon discovered he couldn't fit through the front door, but when he opened it regardless, he was pleased to see that Geri was still there waiting.

I see you all have taken over the village, he greeted her.

Many humans were driven out by the Marquis, searching for his gold. He lost all reason after his mate died and his sons left. We made a meal of him and the rest of his pack of humans. No one comes here anymore.

Is there anything left to eat? he asked her.

No one goes into the castle except the birds and the critters. You might find something there.

Do you want to join me?

No. I want to wait for the leader.

Her words stung, for he knew she meant Cahira. He thanked her and left, moving through the ransacked village to the castle.

The doors were unlocked, dried leaves, dust, and cobwebs affirming its abandonment. Geri was right, a few stray animals had made their homes inside and it didn't take long for him to hunt down something to eat. He sensed the approaching sunrise as he meandered about the castle, wondering if he should rest there. He no longer had to worry about shackling himself against the rampant instincts of Fenrir since his consciousness had been returned, but he knew he'd still need a place to hide each time the moon rose, a place large enough to house his gigantic form without attracting any outside attention. He looked around him at the ashen stone and frayed furniture. It would do.

The sound of rustling leaves interrupted his reverie. Dan paused to hone his ears to the sound, unable to discern exactly what created the noise. It was as if a thousand tiny creatures had started to scuttle around the forest floor, but he could smell nothing. He squinted into the darkness, finally seeing the outline of a lone cabin ahead. He hurried towards it as the sound intensified and he slammed the door shut behind him.

The cabin was cold and dark, the faintest smell of apple lingering amongst dried herbs, burnt wood, and musky furs. His tense muscles relaxed at the familiarity of the room, soothing a restlessness that had plagued him for years. It was short lived, however, for the stirring in the woods grew louder, accompanied by the presence of something much larger. He peered out the window to investigate.

The ground had come alive with what looked like thousands of crawling insects, creating a rippling current that steadily grew closer. He groaned, dismayed that his journey was being interrupted, but grateful that Cahira had left behind a few of her weapons, including a long sword hanging right on the wall, its blade made with silver.

He opened the door to reveal waves of spiders crawling towards him. He jumped onto the roof of the cabin, putting him eye level with the creature who was controlling the tiny beast—a woman who floated through the air, her once lovely face rendered hideous by spider fangs protruding out from where her mouth should have been, six spindly arms wiggling above a pair of distorted legs. *You are both a vampyre and a wolf, yet you feed on one of my daughters?* she sneered before he had a chance to speak.

I have had nothing but raccoon blood and scotch in my stomach for over a week. You have made a mistake.

The creature hissed, the spiders obediently halting their forward advance. *I am Jorogumo, she who protects her daughters in this land. I have been summoned to exact vengeance upon the gluttonous wretch who nearly killed one of mine.*

Dan frowned. *There are several blood drinkers in this land, but the only one who freely kills humans has been locked away. Are you certain it was one of ours?*

She was quiet for a moment as she gently bobbed in the sky, listening to her spiders. *They say it was the vampyre with the copper hair, the one they call the Dragon Slayer.*

Dan groaned, finally piecing together where David had been. *Well, he is unconscious,* he informed her. *Is there anything I can do to resolve this?*

The spider woman smiled, the movement making her look all the more hideous. If he lies still, the easier it will be to kill him.

He is protected right now by three very strong gods, Dan warned her, *including one who can incinerate your entire army with a sweep of his hand. You can try it, if you'd like, or you can heed my warning and let me make restitution in his absence. Is the woman dead?*

The creature stared blankly at him, apparently never confronted with such a predicament before. *She is nearly gone,* she finally replied. *If you fix her, the retribution will be satisfied.*

Dan sighed, lowering his sword as he considered his options. He thought of Cahira heading towards the manor, his entire being longing to be reunited with her. Yet he didn't want to risk more strife befalling them by allowing David's transgressions to go ignored. *Take me to her and I will see what I can do.*

We exist only to serve our daughter, she negated. *You can find her in the eastern part of the city, in a den by the docks.* With that, the arachnids and their mother retreated, leaving the forest as still as when they'd greeted it.

Dan jumped off the roof, returning Cahira's sword where he'd found it. He ran into the city at supernatural speed, slowing only as the ground turned from dirt into cobblestones. He darted between the alleyways so fast that he stayed unnoticed by the humans, combing the brick buildings and wood storefronts with his eyes for anything that could reveal the dying woman's whereabouts. He paused when he saw the last row of buildings near the docks, clear of factory smog but saturated with the metallic smell of freshly butchered meat and river fumes. Limehouse, the district closest to the docks.

He noted a few storefronts marked by Chinese characters, colorful lanterns hanging around the tenements above them. His eyes swept over the buildings until he caught an unassuming door, artfully masked by shadows, next to a window sooted into obscurity and covered in cobwebs. He pushed it open, revealing an opium den that appeared to cater to the upper class, but with the same dingy atmosphere as the rest of such establishments.

The woman at the door breathed in sharply when she saw him. "Take me to the sick woman," he told her before she questioned him. "The Jorogumo sent me."

She hushed him, nervously glancing at the languid patrons sprawled out on the floor behind her. Several women materialized, helping her usher him quickly into the backrooms. They wore costumes made of red silk, wearing harsh makeup that exaggerated their features.

They hurried him into the farthest room beyond an oversized curtain where he saw an older woman lying flat on the ground on a makeshift bed of pillows and blankets. Her pallor was bloodless, skin hanging slackly off her skull. Strong herbs seasoned the air, a crowd of young Chinese women sitting around her in various stages of prayer.

One of them stood, a woman of Eastern descent but different from the rest, her mouth pressed into an angry line. Her hair was straight and jet black, hanging past her waist, not pinned up like the others. She also lacked a matching costume, wearing a modern maroon dress webbed with black lace. "I told it to kill you," she said in clear, unwavering English.

"I am not the vampyre you seek, but I am here to make restitution for him," Dan explained.

The woman snorted. "How do you propose to do that?"

Dan crouched down to observe the bite on the woman's neck, crimson spider veins radiating from the puncture marks, poisoning her blood. The two open wounds no longer bled, but did not heal either, no matter how much ointment had been applied to them. She was almost gone. "I can take her to a healer I know, or I can turn her into a creature like I am," he offered.

The women erupted into scornful banter, none of which he could understand.

The English-speaking woman put her hands on her hips. "I am a healer, skilled in both Chinese and Japanese herbalism, and I could not help her. What makes you think your healer can?"

"She has power unlike anything I have ever seen, and I have lived for centuries," Dan said truthfully. "She has innate knowledge of the unseen world."

"Then bring her here."

"This woman has an hour left at most," he pointed out. "The healer I speak of is a human, she will not be able to travel here in time to save her."

The woman's cheeks grew hot, anger flashing in her dark eyes. "I will carry her then, along with you."

"It would be better if I carried her alone. I can move at speeds that you cannot."

The women clustered around their matron jumped away as six legs thrust rudely out from the speaking woman's waist, ripping the seams of her dress. She hissed, her mouth prying open to reveal arachnid fangs. You were saying?

Dan gave a curt nod. "Right this way."

Morrigan

MORRIGAN STOMPED THROUGH THE MUD TO THE CEMETERY, holding her skirts at her waist. She was greeted by dozens of apparitions listlessly drifting across the yard, illuminating the paths between the stones. They were aloof at her presence as she navigated her way towards the Lardone crypt, grateful to discover it had been left unlocked. She bounded down the narrow stone steps to the first vault door, where she summoned every ounce of strength she possessed to kick it open.

He sat in Libraean's chair reading, one of his long legs bent so that his ankle rested on the other knee. He wore the remnants of Mr. Montgomery's three-piece suit, a dark patterned vest over a black shirt opened at the throat. He looked up to see who was at the door, openly amazed to see her. "He let you come down?"

"No one has to let me do anything," she reminded him.

"Why are you covered in blood?"

"I was hungry."

He smiled, turning back a few pages in the book he had been perusing, the cover of which was labeled "The Morrigan" in Libraean's handwriting. He began to read aloud: "*While God created Adam, who was alone, He said, 'It is not good for man to be alone'. He also created a woman, from the earth, as He had created Adam himself, and called her Lilith. Adam and Lilith immediately began to fight. She said, 'I will not lie below,' and he said, 'I will not lie beneath you, but only on top. For you are fit only to be in the bottom position, while I am to be the superior one.' Lilith responded, 'We are equal to each other inasmuch as we were both created from the earth.' But they would not listen to one another. When Lilith saw this, she pronounced the Ineffable Name and flew away into the air. Adam stood in prayer before his Creator: 'Sovereign of the universe!' he said, 'the woman you gave me has run away.' At once, the Holy One, blessed be He, sent these three angels to bring her back.*

"*Said the Holy One to Adam, 'If she agrees to come back, what is made is good. If not, she must permit one hundred of her children to die every day.' The angels left God and pursued Lilith, whom they overtook in the midst of the sea, in the mighty waters wherein the Egyptians were destined to drown. They told her God's word, but she did not wish to return. The angels said, 'We shall drown you in the sea.'*

"'Leave me!' she said. 'I was created only to cause sickness to infants. If the infant is male, I have dominion over him for eight days after his birth, and if female, for twenty days.'

"When the angels heard Lilith's words, they insisted she go back. But she swore to them by the name of the living and eternal God: 'Whenever I see you or your names or your forms in an amulet, I will have no power over that infant.' She also agreed to have one hundred of her children die every day. Accordingly, every day one hundred daemons perish, and for the same reason, we write the angels' names on the amulets of young children. When Lilith sees their names, she remembers her oath, and the child recovers." He closed the book, meeting her with soulful eyes. "This is what they reduced you to. The Mother of us all."

"One of the mothers," she corrected him softly. "In the beginning, my sister created, and I protected."

"You love children. You are a goddess, not some mortal's companion to have sex with."

Morrigan sighed. "Why are you bringing this up?"

"They speak little of the Morrigan—the scant verses dedicated to her have her seducing pointless mortals for selfish gain. Nephthys is barely mentioned in Egyptian myth, overshadowed entirely by her sister, Isis. Do you realize they have written you out of history?"

"I have more important things to worry about than the opinions of men."

"Do you?" Lucius rose from his seat, sliding the book back on the shelf where he'd found it. "You all have given me plenty of time down here to read and think, and since we parted, my thoughts have been entirely dedicated to you. Not only the poignant remembrance of my love for you, but of who you are and your existence throughout time." He turned towards her. "Men want to forget you, to wipe the goddess out of the mouths of those who revere her. Earth is dominated by men who wish to exert power over any creature they can—it is the reason why they own slaves, why they abuse women and children. Is it not possible that their warped minds have created a deity that wants you gone? That they want your eradication, to wipe the goddess from the earth she created?"

Morrigan blinked. "The mystic who uncovered my memories told me the same thing," she whispered. "She says the war is not gods against gods, but one against goddesses. Against me."

Lucius frowned. "Tell David I am convinced that those who have destroyed our realms and murdered the gods are doing exactly what the humans did on earth—annihilating any competition so only their warped, exclusive patriarchy remains. I cannot do much while I'm down here, but at least I can give you that."

Morrigan found the inside of her lip. "That is actually why I've come to see you. David has fallen into a deep slumber, something that apparently happens when his body demands rest. Libraean said it could take days or weeks for him to recover." She removed herself from the path of the doorway. "I have come here to release you."

Lucius froze for a moment in surprise, but jarred himself out of it to follow her, leaving his effects behind. As soon as they reached the open air, she grabbed his hand, pulling him down the hill, away from the graveyard. "Where are we going?" he asked.

She waited until they reached the edge of the surrounding forest before she spun around to face him. The manor loomed in the distance, the waxing moon hovering above it. "Before he went still, David told me he was planning an excursion to Africa where Anubis has reincarnated. He believes that if we are all reunited, then we are better suited to solve things...and I would like you to join us."

"You want me to come?" he repeated in surprise, his lips sliding upwards.

"Of course," she said lightly. "You are part of the original four, are you not?"

"Then why are we out here by the woods?"

Morrigan took a deep, steadying breath. "I need you to see my memories, the ones recalled from the time I was in the Underworld...when I was with you. I need your mind to help fill in the blank spots where I cannot see."

"And how do you propose we do that?"

She met his eyes with calm resolve, though her heartbeat began to climb. Gray clouds gathered above them in response, casting a heavy veil over the moon and stars. She turned her head to the side slowly, exposing the soft part of her neck.

His eyebrows lifted as he realized what she implied. "You trust me?" he whispered.

"Yes," she murmured, closing her eyes.

He didn't hesitate, pulling her into his arms against his heated body, filling her nose with his spicy scent as his fingers caught the waves of her hair. A part of her hated herself for melting against him so easily, knowing David was nearby, but when he pressed his lips against her throat, kissing her softly, he lit dormant parts of her on fire, passion jolting her to life. The sky responded with a clap of thunder, obediently releasing its rain onto them. She felt herself grow limp as his teeth pushed into her skin, finding the vein that housed her tainted blood and pulling its contents into his mouth. Her eyes rolled back into her head as the memories resurfaced, filling her consciousness as they entered his, until all she could see was the stars he'd created for her in the Underworld covering every inch of sky.

Then he kissed her lips, pulling her out of her swoon, the taste of her blood in both their mouths. She heard thunder and lightning crashing all around them, could smell the trees that had caught fire, rebelling against the rain, but found she could not break free of him, the taste of metal and smoke filling her mouth, accented by cloves.

Finally, she pulled away to see black tears had collected in his eyes. "You forgave me," he said softly.

"And you forgave me," she said in a voice she could barely recognize. He held her for a moment longer, one hand on her back, the other holding her hands against his chest, until her strength returned, and she could stand.

"Thank you for showing me," he said as he gently released her. He looked away, his expression both pained and contemplative.

"I thought you should know what I know," she murmured in explanation, the wounds on her neck slowly closing.

He looked up at the enkindled tree nearest to them. "I understand much has transpired since that time, that we have both lived separate human lives and that you found David again. I understand that we can't simply resume where we left off." The flames reflected in his eyes as he gazed at her. "But I will earn you again, maybe not now, but one day."

She gave him a weak smile. "I don't imagine you'll ever be content leaving me be."

"Let's go inside," he suggested, slipping his fingers back through hers. Though the rain had stopped, the water had pulled his curls down around his face, lengthening them, reminding her of his true appearance. "I'm convinced now more than ever that my theory is correct. We would do well to be reunited with the others, because if it is who I think is responsible for this mayhem, we will need our combined power to stop it."

Morrigan nodded, hurrying alongside him to the manor.

Something in the air had shifted since the rain subsided, a low fog snaking through the trees. From the corner of her eye, Morrigan noticed that the spirits who haunted the lonely cemetery had disappeared.

Lucius abruptly paused in his tracks. "Something is here."

The ground trembled beneath them, and he quickly pulled her back through the cemetery into the Lardone crypt and to the vault. He located one of Libraean's towering cabinets and wrenched it open to reveal hundreds of artifacts collected over time.

"What is out there?" she asked as he rummaged through it.

"I don't know, but I want to be prepared," he muttered, throwing open another cabinet. This one contained ancient weaponry, some that Morrigan recognized from Wallachia. He retrieved a sword, tarnished with age, but still bright where it had been dipped in silver.

Above them, the Earth's tremors increased as if a vast army had descended upon them. Lucius offered her the sword, but she brushed past him, selecting an old spear that had been shoved towards the back. She doubted it once belonged to her, but it felt good in her hands, tiny whispers of who she once was surrounding her as she swung it around with ease.

Lucius beamed at her. "I know we haven't battled yet in these bodies, but I think we can manage."

Morrigan responded by ripping off her bottom layer of skirts and hurrying back up the stairs, anticipatory adrenaline coursing through her veins. Lucius darted after her, the two greeted by exactly what they had assumed—an army of daemons heading straight towards the manor from the woods. The obscene, lumpy creatures appeared to be made of stone, pulling themselves clumsily through the wet earth. Red, gooey tendons held together the rocks that formed their bodies, and they were armed with swords, maces, and lances, all glinting in the moonlight.

Morrigan looked up to see crows had gathered above them, awaiting her command. She smiled, grateful to know they were still with her. Her gaze moved back to survey their numbers, estimating it to be in the hundreds. It would be tiresome, especially since she just lost so much blood, but she surmised they could sweep through them within an hour or so. She wished she could warn Libraean, who was alone with Jacob and the unconscious David in the manor. Suddenly she remembered he had once been a shape-shifter, one who could take on the guise of a wild boar. *Libraean, we are being attacked by daemons. I am with Lucius, and we will hold them off, but make sure Jacob and David are safe.*

It took a moment before she heard his gentle reply echoing in her mind. *I hadn't realized we could speak this way. I will protect them with my life—be safe.*

Morrigan braced herself as the horde drew in, ready for them. Or so she thought before she noticed what came from behind.

It towered over the treetops, a massive, lumbering beast that appeared more like a detached mountain moving forward than an animated being. It let out a horrific, unearthly clamor that shook the Earth with its sound. As it grew closer, it revealed three arms with taloned fingers and three giant legs that pushed its jagged shape forwards. The same fleshy material held its boulders together, hundreds of horrible eyeballs rolling in its neckless head.

Lucius groaned. "Someone has summoned Asag from the depths of Tartarus."

"Who is that?"

"An ancient *daemon* from Sumer, a creature made of flesh and rock who commands his own army of stone," Lucius sighed. "He'll align himself with whoever feeds him a few scraps of human flesh. He is mine to take down."

The smaller *daemons* finally reached the place where they stood, the stench of sulfur now overwhelming, pulling bile up into Morrigan's throat. It offered more fuel to her fight, wanting to get rid of them as quickly as possible. "Well, we shall see who gets there first," she teased him in response and, without letting him reply, catapulted into the mob.

She ducked and twisted around them as she steadily skewered them with her spear, severing the binding cords that held them together. She was pleased to learn that although her new body was larger, it was just as limber, with an added strength and height that proved her advantage. She tore through them, invoking the inner storm that screamed at her to destroy, to kill. Her crows dove in to assist, filling the yard with their screeching as they tore out the creatures' bulging eyes, rendering them helpless until she could catch up. Soon she was covered in mud, rain, and daemon blood, her body singing with euphoria as she watched the creatures surrounding her reduced to rubble.

She paused to catch her breath, sneaking a peek at Lucius. He seemed to have no trouble recalling his inner warrior, slashing through creature after creature with his sword, dismembering them with ease. She realized he was beating her in their playful competition, inching closer and closer to the giant *daemon*, who moved steadily towards David's manor. She took to the skies, momentarily startled to observe a seemingly endless horde of daemons materializing out of the shadows. She screeched at Lucius, letting him know she was heading towards their king, hoping to blind it before it could get any further.

The rest of her swarm followed suit, the revolting stench hitting its peak as she flew up to it. The crows dove at the giant *daemon*'s eyes as it opened its huge, stinking mouth to protest. A few fell victims to its teeth as it chomped down, deciding the best way to fight them was to crush their tiny bodies in its jaws. The crows began to retreat, rising higher in the sky as the mountainous fiend resumed its persistent plod forward.

Morrigan began to worry, wondering how they would be able to stop both the swarming minions and their grotesque master, when suddenly she heard a noise she had not heard in eons. She flew upwards to join her flock, looking down to see the rock creatures devoured in a torrent of flames. Above them, a great black dragon took to the skies, fanning the fire with its leathery skeletal wings. *I gave him some of my power with my blood,* she realized. *He can now shapeshift.*

She watched Lucius release his fire onto Asag, the *daemon* king screaming in agony as its trio of arms swung fruitless swords in his direction. From the woods, they were suddenly joined by packs of wolves, who promptly tore the remaining creatures apart until all that was left was the two gigantic beasts locked together in battle.

Morrigan flew back down to aim at its eyes with her beak, skillfully darting out of the way before it had a chance to chomp down on her. The dragon fire finally succeeded in dismantling one of its legs, the *daemon* furious at its sudden incapacitation. The dragon soared higher into the skies. Morrigan flew out of the way and perched on the roof, watching as the giant black creature reached the apex of sky and dove down in a form that rivaled an osprey, letting out a torrential stream of fire. It melted every eyeball out of the *daemon*'s sockets, the boulders that created its form finally collapsing. The ground shook with the impact, the wolves retreating as giant rocks crashed to the ground.

Morrigan waited until she knew the *daemon* was completely dead and Lucius was safely back on the ground before she flew down and landed, tumbling back into her human form as she opened the clouds to rain. It drenched the scorched land, officially putting the battle to rest. Elation coursed through her veins as she ran towards Lucius, who had also shifted back into human form, bewildered at the magic he'd just invoked. She surprised him further by jumping into his arms, wrapping her legs around his waist, and planting a kiss firmly on his lips. It quickly escalated in passion, the two still exhilarated from the fight.

"Hope I'm not interrupting anything."

Lucius released her as they both apprehended a woman standing before them. She was short but not petite, masculine attire revealing a stacked, muscular physique. She held a crossbow, her long curls drenched with rain.

"Cahira." Morrigan recognized the woman from Dan's tale.

She nodded, breathless from her own fight. "Nice to meet you," she called over the rain. "We should go inside. I don't think that will be the last of the creatures Angelique sends my way." She looked at Lucius with a raised eyebrow. "Glad to see you've joined the better side."

"Hello," he said with a nod.

"You know each other?"

"It's a long story," he replied. "We met long ago, when I was still a child."

"Wasn't Daniel on his way to retrieve you?" Morrigan asked her.

"I sensed he was drawing close, but the *daemons* were approaching faster. I left before he could reach me. Although I see that you clearly didn't need my help."

"You sent the wolves ahead of you," Morrigan realized.

"Yes. I also released my scent into the air for the first time in centuries so Dan could find me—however he is not the only creature that hunts me, and we might have more company soon."

"We should get inside," Morrigan echoed her earlier suggestion.

They hurried across the slippery terrain through the front door of David's home. The foyer that greeted them was still in shambles, splintered glass glinting in the muted lamplight, a gentle breeze trickling in through the open spaces left in the window's absence. Lucius surveyed the damage with a raised eyebrow, but he didn't say a word.

Cahira seemed unimpressed by the derelict manor, studying Morrigan and Lucius instead. She wrinkled her nose. "Are you all so incredibly tall?"

Libraean suddenly appeared from the parlor hall and in an uncharacteristic display of emotion, hugged Morrigan as soon as he saw her. She blinked, thrown off by the gesture. "Forgive me for my anger towards you," he said. "You have saved us all. I must trust that no matter what happens, your heart is pure."

Morrigan felt her cheeks get hot. "I did have a bit of help." She gestured towards Lucius.

"Ah, but I would still be trapped in the vaults if not for you," he reminded her.

"Libraean, this is Cahira," Morrigan swiftly changed the subject.

The elderly creature looked her way, his overall expression shifting from heartfelt gratitude to stark disbelief. "You are a liminal being."

It was Cahira's turn to look surprised. "How did you know?"

Libraean smiled, his clear blue eye twinkling. "I happen to be the first one to have ever graced this earth. Which means you were born of creatures. I have never met another like me, only read of their existence." His gaze moved behind her. "Where is Dan?"

"I left before he could catch up to me."

"Then he should be here soon." Libraean's eyes flitted towards Lucius, picking up a bit of rueful contempt during their journey.

"How is he?" Morrigan asked.

Libraean sighed. "The same."

Morrigan turned towards Cahira. She had a familiar look about her, youth eternally frozen on her round, unlined face, but with eyes that told a different tale. They looked eerily similar to the man who stood next to her, a warm yellow brown that looked like honey. She seemed weary, even as her chestnut curls resumed their buoyancy as they dried, an attribute that only furthered her youthful visage. "David is unconscious," she informed her. "We are uncertain when he will wake."

"What do you mean—he just left my house!" Cahira blurted out.

"David is the oldest creature among us, second only to me, and he has not been right for several years now," Libraean explained gently. "It is my personal theory that he has lived in one body for far too long. While I am aging, inching closer towards a peaceful death, he remains frozen in time. It is my thought that this requires a considerable amount of energy to maintain. He is susceptible to spells of melancholy when he does not rest, and once he has fallen, he does not revive easily. Once, he lay dormant for a fortnight, another, he was gone for an entire month. It is something that I have had to accept, as did his manservant, Jacob."

Cahira was incredulous. "So, the creature we are supposed to depend on to save the realms is taking a nap?"

Lucius stifled a chuckle.

"Enough." The forceful echo of Morrigan's voice silenced them all. "We cannot possibly fathom what existing for millennia does to a soul forced to live in a solitary vessel. I once grew quite mad, myself, and I'd only been alive a few centuries. We are going to do the best we can with this situation, for it now falls upon us to make decisions in his absence. Let us move to the library and wait for Daniel to return."

Cahira sighed loudly but followed them into the room opposite the parlor.

Libraean shuffled towards the gilded fireplace, but Lucius beat him to it, bringing firelight into the room with a wave of his hand. As Cahira approached the heat to revive her cold limbs, Lucius looked around in unabashed wonderment, observing the endless volumes of books whose cabinets stretched to the ceiling. He ran his fingers along their spines, his mouth moving ever so slightly as he read their titles. Morrigan smiled despite herself, grateful to see the old familiar trait still reflected in him.

After a few moments, Cahira withdrew from the fireplace, her hair and clothing reasonably dry. For a moment, she looked equally as impressed at the array of books stacked around them, but returned her focus to the flames, flopping down on one of the leather upholstered chairs as she crossed her arms.

Morrigan settled down across from her, undeterred by her hostility. "David told us of your plans before he fell ill. We all agreed to join you on your excursion to Africa. Are you willing to discuss your travel plans with me or would you prefer to wait for Dan to arrive?"

Cahira sat upright. "I do not need to wait for anyone."

"Hm, she reminds me of someone I know," Lucius muttered behind a smile, settling down next to Morrigan.

His close proximity threw her off for a moment, even though the adrenaline she'd invoked during their battle dwindled and her rational sense returned. He managed to stir up things inside her, and she had to force her attention to remain centered on the pressing matters at hand, rather than hone in on his alluring scent, even more potent from the rain. "Do you have a ship that can take us there?" she asked Cahira.

"I have one docked at the eastern port," she replied, "though it is not a luxurious mode of transportation by any means. It brought my companion and I over from France, but I'm not convinced it could withstand a month-long journey overseas."

"Companion?"

They were interrupted by a loud commotion coming from the hallway. Dan burst through the door, an unconscious human in his arms. They all jumped up from their seats in alarm.

From behind him appeared another woman with long, straight black hair swaying behind her, with eyes so dark they looked as if they shared an equal shade. Power drifted around her like the webbing of the spider, invisible to the naked eye, but vivid to Morrigan. She was a goddess.

Cahira recognized her immediately. "What is the meaning of this, Jori?" she demanded.

When the woman spoke, Morrigan could hear the distinction of a hundred tiny voices creating one low chord that could pass for a human's voice. "They summoned me and there was little I could do. I am still bound by their magics when I am nearby. If this vampyre doesn't save this woman's life, I have to kill one of them to satisfy the call."

"Like hell you will," Lucius muttered, provoking a nudge from Morrigan. The action helped her realize how close she'd moved towards him, and she took a step in the opposite direction.

"I can fix her," Cahira caught Dan's eyes. They lingered for a moment before he set her down on the floor. She knelt down to examine her wound, pulling a small vial of liquid from her boot. She uncorked it with her teeth, dotting its contents onto the open punctures and replacing the vial, putting one hand on the ground and another over her neck.

Morrigan felt a shift in the air as the scent of jasmine and lilies drifted in the wind. The small hairs on her skin lifted, an ancient presence she had long been separated from filling the room. Lucius whispered exactly what she was thinking, "Isis."

Cahira stood, her earlier animosity absent, replaced by a serenity that set her skin aglow. "There," she said softly. The sores on the woman's neck had disappeared, life pulling back into her cheeks.

Jori knelt down to examine the woman, who was still dazed, but clearly revived. "It has been resolved," she said with a curt nod. She looked up at Cahira. "I will take her back to her family. Keep your jiangshis in line." The room filled with the hissing of insects as a mound of spiders rose up around the goddess and her priestess, only to fall away and scuttle back into the shadows.

"I thought the Jorogumo was Japanese," Lucius commented absently.

Cahira looked his way. "You are correct. Jori was born of Chinese parents, yet her reincarnated soul is the Japanese Jorogumo. She is not a *daemon*, but a deity, much like the hundreds of other vilified goddesses in history."

"Ah," Lucius nodded. "Quite a common theme as of late."

Dan cleared his throat loudly. His eyes had not left Cahira since he'd walked in, even after all that had transpired. Morrigan was hit with a wave of sympathy for him, knowing how badly he'd yearned for their time to reconcile.

Libreaen, who had been silently observing the scene before him, broke in. "Perhaps we should give you both a moment?"

Cahira quickly shook her head. "That won't be necessary. I am willing to push past our history so we can work together," she said, keeping her eyes averted from his general direction.

"Let us sit," Morrigan suggested, not wanting to prolong his discomfort, nor waste any more time. "We need to resume talk of our travels."

"Then allow me to swiftly interject," said Lucius as he took his chair. "Cahira remembers me when I was a young boy in the midst of being groomed by a group of immortals to eventually swap places with the most recent heir to the French throne. As you can probably guess, I was not up for being controlled, even with the promise of power. I ran away before they could make the switch, but I took their fortune with me. When their leader, Angelique, still managed to make herself Queen, I helped rile up the humans to chop off her head. She managed to escape the guillotine at the last moment, but that is a very long story for another day. My point being, the fortune I stole was vast, and with it, I purchased a new identity and now own several businesses under the name Victor Regis.

"As a young man, I spent long hours in the salons, engaging in conversations regarding everything from religion to abolition. It was during this time I decided to purchase several trading ships under the nom de plume for the purpose of transporting palm oil out of the Kingdom of Dahomey once the humans finally ceased their despicable slave trade. One of my ships is quite large, intended to be used for the transport of both goods and passengers. Though the idea has been around for some time, it is the first of its kind to see completion, built specifically for me."

"I see you never lost your flair for extravagance," Libraean commented mildly.

"So, you are proposing that we sail to France to retrieve it, where Angelique and her entire entourage is located?" Cahira snorted.

Morrigan put up her hand to pause the conversation. "I am going to need to know more about this Angelique."

Cahira met her eyes. "When Dan and I arrived in Paris in 1751, we thought we would discover David, but instead we met Angelique, the leader of a group of questionable gods in human form. She claimed to be Aphrodite incarnate and she had turned all of them into vampires, waiting until Louis—ah, I mean Lucius—became of age to turn him and place him on the French throne. I realized she was a vile, self-serving creature before she had the chance to turn me. I fled from her stronghold, and she has been pursuing me and my power ever since."

Morrigan turned to Lucius with a raised eyebrow. "How did you manage to be deceived by her, he who is rarely deceived?"

Lucius frowned in an uncharacteristic display of shame and regret. "I was a child, Morrigan. She knew exactly what to say, how to smell, what to do."

"She looked like you," Cahira offered.

"Oh," Morrigan felt heat rise in her cheeks.

"She could shapeshift," Dan added. "She deceived me as well."

Cahira's lips tightened, her face suddenly colorless. She leaned back into her seat, withdrawing herself from the conversation.

"I started to sense that things were not what they seemed not too much longer after I met Cahira," Lucius continued. "My instincts were eventually confirmed, but I decided to wait until she turned me into an immortal before I ruined her plans."

"Yet she is still alive and is still pursuing Cahira," Morrigan pointed out. "And apparently she is pursuing us as well since she sent an army of daemons to our door."

"Alone, she is nothing, but she has amassed quite a following of misplaced daemons and unsavory gods who look to her as if she is some kind of savior," Lucius told her.

Morrigan could feel her eyes narrowing. "I need to speak to you - alone."

"Of course," he stammered, rising to his feet.

Morrigan turned to Cahira. "You said your ship is docked at Limehouse? And we would be able to take it down the river, across the ocean to France?"

"Yes," Cahira assured her. "She is a good, safe ship. As soon as you give the word, I will make sure she's ready to sail."

"Then let us all prepare for travel during the daylight. We'll take Cahira's boat to France, retrieve Lucius's ship, and sail from there to Africa. If we do run into this Angelique, we will take care of it. Cahira, we will be ready by nightfall."

She nodded, rising to her feet. "I will have everything in order by the time you arrive."

Dan blocked her path as she started to leave. "Let me help you," he offered.

She scowled. "I'm not ready to speak with you yet. There is too much work to be done."

"Then we will not speak."

"It is daylight."

"Morrigan," Dan called, without breaking eye contact, nor moving out of the way. "Can you ensure cloudy skies, light rain?"

She stifled a smile. "I can."

Dan gave Cahira a satisfied smile. She rolled her eyes as she strode out.

"I will see you at nightfall," Dan told the rest of them as he followed after her.

"What of David?" Libraean asked Morrigan after they'd left.

"He is coming with us," she decided. "We will come up with a plan to transport him after I have spoken to Lucius."

Libraean nodded, heading back up the stairs to retrieve Jacob. Morrigan and Lucius were left alone in the capacious library, pulling memories of the Underworld to the front of her mind.

"Well?" He crossed his arms.

Morrigan studied his face. "There is more to this story that you are telling me, I can feel it."

His lips turned up into a mischievous grin. "Do I detect jealousy?"

Morrigan whipped around to snatch a letter opener from the desk, chucking it through the air at his head. He ducked out of the way so that it only grazed his earlobe. "Do not test my patience," she warned, as it skewered the wall with a sharp thud.

Lucius put up his hands in defense. "Please stop trying to kill me."

"Then cease your insufferable head games."

"I told you, Angelique found me when I was very young, a confused, angry child of nine. She was able to get into my head immediately. She appeared to me first as a young girl with dark hair and blue eyes, smelling of autumn leaves and fresh rain. Then she would appear to me in a matronly form, smelling of rosewater—the exact perfume worn by the elderly woman who adopted me. She knew exactly what she was doing, grooming me to become who she wanted me to be. I figured it out long after I became immortal, when I began remembering bits of my past."

Morrigan simmered with fury, imagining some creature manipulating him as a child, but she managed to keep it at bay. "So she knew your true nature and that I was your wife. That means she knows me. I do not believe for one moment that she is simply the Greek goddess of love. This goes much deeper than that."

"I agree, but we are not going to know anything for sure until we reach Anubis."

"No, we cannot wait that long," Morrigan murmured. "After we board Cahira's ship, we are going to access my memories, the ones that are missing from my time in the Underworld with you."

"How will you do that without a medium?"

"Cahira," she said simply, turning to leave.

Lucius grabbed her around the waist as she brushed past, his warmth coming through her dress. She swallowed as he pulled her into his eyes. "When did I lose you again?" he asked her softly.

"Let us resolve this first," she said. "Then perhaps we can resolve us."

He nodded in understanding, though he wore a wistful expression as he slowly released her.

CHAPTER TWELVE

❧ The Boat ❧

London, 1857
Dan

D AN HURRIED ACROSS A YARD NOW COVERED BY JAGGED ROCKS, beyond the plots of gravestones towards the edge of the woods. She had brought with her a pack of at least a dozen wolves, who now stalked the boundaries of David's manor. They nodded to him as he passed. He caught the flounce of chestnut hair just as she disappeared into the thong of trees.

"Cahira, wait!" he called, but he was instead met with a giant gray wolf.

He braced for attack, but as soon as he met its dark eyes, he realized it was none other than his old wolf, Geri. She accepted his hug as he scratched at her scruff, amazed that she still lived. How? he asked.

Some things I do not know. I had to protect the leader.

Dan stood but continued to stare adoringly at his old friend. She'd aged over time, her hair matted and white, but her vigor remained. Thank you for watching over her.

It's your turn now. I will watch over the others.

Dan nodded, letting her run off to join the other wolves before he invoked his supernatural speed. He was next to Cahira instantly, grabbing the crook of her arm.

She whipped around with a sharp blow to his chest, knocking him away from her. "Do not touch me!" she hissed.

Dan reached the pinnacle of his frustration. "We have not spoken in a hundred years, Cahira, how much longer do you propose we wait?"

"There are much more pressing matters to attend to," she said hotly, spinning around to resume her march.

"Cahira, please stop for a moment," he pleaded. "At least allow me to take you to town—we could arrive in minutes. On foot, it will be hours."

She spun back around, glaring up at him with eyes that blazed ochre even in the dark, rainy forest. "What would you say to me? That it was Angelique who seduced you, who tricked you into sleeping with her, disguised as me? I already know."

Dan was taken aback. "How long have you known?"

Cahira resumed her trek. "I figured it out not long after you left," she said over her shoulder.

"Then why…why are you so angry with me?"

Cahira froze in place but did not turn around. "Because I cannot give you what you want from me."

"What do you mean?" he asked, confused.

"You know what I mean," she said in a low voice. He couldn't see her face, but he could picture it, a round little face with wide eyes and heavy lashes, her small nose and full lips in a scowl. The sprinkle of freckles across the bridge of her nose. The tiny scar on her forehead.

"That has never mattered to me," he softly reminded her.

She turned to reveal tears welling up in her eyes. "But one day, it would matter. One day, you will try, and I won't be able to say no to you because I love you, and it would break me. You might be a grand mix of creatures, Dan, but you are still a man with desires. Desires I'm not certain I can ever fulfill."

Dan swallowed his own rising emotion. "When I say it does not matter to me, it isn't to trick you. It's because I know how you are and my love for you transcends human desires. I am bound to you forever, even without your magic."

She sniffed, one of the tears escaping down her cheek. "I'm not ready to believe you yet."

"You don't have to," he said gently, taking a step closer. "But please stop hating me until you get there."

"Fine," she grumbled, wiping her eyes with the back of her hand.

"Let me take us into town," he repeated. "It will save you energy."

She stepped forward towards him, her shoulders falling as if speaking the words she had been holding in for over a century finally allowed them to. He pulled her into his arms, and she closed her eyes, resting her head on his chest as she wrapped her arms around him. His entire body sighed with relief at her presence, his nose filling with the sweetness of spring. He put one hand on the back of her neck to tighten his hold, his heart giving a sharp thud when he felt the braid she still wore in her hair. "Hold on," he told her as he gathered up the energy around them to race through the forest.

They stopped at its edge, but he found himself unable to let her go. Remarkably, she didn't resist, briefly savoring their reconnection before pulling away. An icy blast of wind hit as they entered the city, bringing forward one of their last memories together.

It was the end of October, the heaviest the rainfall had ever been since they'd arrived in France, years ago. Cahira paced, frustrated to be stuck indoors for another evening, Geri's head moving back and forth as she watched her from her perch on Dan's bed.

"I haven't been able to get any new books," she answered his raised eyebrow. "My mind feels like it's growing stagnant."

"Why don't you teach me something?" he suggested, swallowing the last of his ale before rising to scoop up the dinner dishes.

She gave him a look. "I teach you everything I learn right when I read it."

"Just trying to come up with ideas."

"Why don't you tell me a story?"

Dan placed the cups and plates into the soapy dish bin. "I don't know any stories."

"Yes, you do," she argued. "You know the tales of the Norsemen."

Dan paused to think, watching the rain pour down the windows. "Have I ever told you about Ragnarok?"

Cahira lit up. "You have not," she said excitedly. "Is it another monster?"

"No, it is about the end of days."

"Even better." She grabbed a blanket off his bed and settled by the fireplace, Geri joining her.

Dan poured another cup of ale and followed suit. "At the end, there will be a Great Winter," he began, "and biting winds will blow in from every corner of the world and last for years. Mankind will grow weak trying to survive, but the gods will be unable to help them, for they will be waging their own battles. The two wolves who have hunted the sun and the moon through the skies since the beginning of time, Skoll and Hati, will finally catch their prey. The stars will also disappear, leaving nothing but a black void in the heavens, while Yggdrasil, the great tree that holds the cosmos together, will fall, taking all the trees and mountains of earth down with it. Fenrir will break free, while Jormungand, the mighty serpent who dwells at the bottom of the ocean will rise from its depths."

"Fenrir is the name of your wolf half," she interrupted.

Dan nodded. "Legend has it that he will run freely across the earth, devouring everything in his path, while Jormungand spits his venom over all the world, poisoning the land, the sea, and the air. Odin, the All-Father will try to fight Fenrir, but he will swallow him. Odin's son, Vidar, will avenge his father, stabbing his sword through the wolf's throat and killing him for good.

"Meanwhile, Thor, the god of thunder, and Jormungand will fight, and Thor will succeed in killing him with his hammer. But the serpent will have covered him in so much venom that he will die as well. Then the remains of the world will sink into the bottom of the sea, and nothing will be left but the great void. Creation and all that has occurred since will be completely undone, as if it had never happened." He took a swig of ale.

Cahira looked thoughtful. "Do you think that will really happen—that Odin will kill you?"

Dan chuckled. "Well, there is more to the story. After the end, a new world, lush and beautiful, will arise out of the waters. Odin's sons Vidar, Baldur, and Hodr and Thor's sons Modi and Magni will survive the downfall of the old world and live joyously in the next. A man and a woman named Lif and Lifthrasir, the only humans that successfully hid away will repopulate the earth, with the sons of the gods ruling over them."

"Apparently they didn't anticipate that Baldr and Fenrir would be fused together into one immortal creature," Cahira commented.

"No, I'm sure they did not."

She ran her fingers down the fur of her wolf, who was snoring steadily against her. "Do you think Odin is still alive, out there somewhere as a human?"

Dan shifted his weight. "I'm sure it is possible. But remember, I have no soul memories that I can recall. I honored the old gods so long ago that I'm not sure I would recognize him even if I did see him."

Thunder suddenly cracked above them. "It sounds like Thor is still around," she joked before she let out a yawn. "Perhaps it will be an early night for me after all."

Dan stifled his own yawn, his belly full and the ale creeping up on him. He started to rise when she shook her head. "Let's sleep by the fire tonight," she suggested.

He reached over to grab another blanket, stretching out on the rug by the hearth. Eventually her breathing turned to snores as he followed, dreaming of giant serpents and floods, Geri curled up between them.

"Come, there's work to be done," her voice broke through. He blinked, the cozy memory shattered by the harsh cityscape laid out before them.

Although a steady drizzle fell, it was business as usual on the docks, merchants and sailors in slick hooded cloaks as they transported their cargo and made their sales, the urchins tramping through the frothing river muck, searching for whatever treasures they could find. Dan kept his gaze averted as they walked, knowing his size alone was enough to draw stares, following closely behind Cahira as she wove them through carts, crates, and bustling. She ducked into a building where a very bored looking man with crooked teeth and spectacles sat behind a desk. "May I help you…miss?"

"I am here to retrieve my ship," she told him, pulling folded papers out of the pocket of her trousers

The man peered at them between the smudged lens of his glasses before signing them with a flick of his hand. "Travel is not recommended today on account of the rain."

"My husband and I are transporting a deceased body home to France," Cahira told him. "We will be leaving today."

The man looked from Dan to her with raised eyebrows. "You plan to dock at Calais?"

"Yes," Cahira nodded.

"Very well. I hope your husband is a seasoned sailor, the waters begin to get rough this time of year," the man said, continuing to shuffle, stamp, and mark the paperwork.

"Oh no, I will be the one sailing my ship. Thank you," she snatched the paper from him and hurried out the door before he could comment further.

Dan smiled to himself, jogging to keep up with her as she strode down a narrow bridge to where her boat was docked. It was a basic sailing ship with three masts and square sails, knocking gently against the dock in the sprinkling rain. It appeared ready for loading, the ropes untied, and the deck swept clean. He turned to question her, when he caught sight of a woman standing on the deck as if she waited for them.

Dan scowled when he recognized her, her bright hazel eyes glowing underneath her hood.

"Please forgive me for using my powers against you," Sandrine said immediately.

Dan did not reply, still not ready to trust any creature that had come out of Angelique's domain. His clenched jaw released, however, when Cahira rested her hand on his arm. "Sandrine accompanied me here from France," she explained. "Not long after you disappeared, she sailed to Africa with Lesplaies against Angelique's wishes. I went back to the Bohemian Forest, where I lived for years before she eventually found me. Not only did she successfully kill that rotten god, but she confirmed that my vision of Anubis was real. She wanted to join me in my search for the Ancient Ones, helping me kill Angelique's *daemons* in the process."

"You do not have to fear anything from me," Dan said. "But you make sure she keeps those angry eyes of hers far away from me."

Cahira nodded. "Thank you," she offered before she climbed aboard to greet Sandrine.

He let loose a large sigh, grateful at least to be with her as he climbed aboard to join them.

LIBRAEAN

THE JOURNEY TO THE DOCKS WAS NOT A PARTICULARLY LONG ONE, but Libraean still dozed off, the lull of the carriage proving irresistible to an aging creature who had barely slept in recent days. He knew they grew close when he heard seagulls, distant bells, and the low utterances of dockmen preparing for nightfall.

The docks themselves were relatively clear in the evening hours, most of the men who worked them retired to the pubs after an arduous day. A few remained, working under the yellow glow of gaslit lamps to unload the rest of their cargo, while pickpockets and river tramps haunted the shadows, and those who slept aboard their ships until daybreak snored. Libraean assumed the cold weather kept many away as sailing season edged closer to its yearly respite.

He took a deep breath when he saw Cahira's boat, a sturdy but simple merchant ship swaying gently in the dark water. For the first time in a very long time, he felt a twinge of fear. Sailing to an unknown land was not something new to him, but he had grown older since those days, becoming more set in his ways as the years passed on. He enjoyed stability and quiet, and he was unprepared for the turbulent seas. At least he had Jacob, his close proximity bringing him comfort now rather than provoking his fury. But David's state caused him trepidation, and he hoped he would wake by the time they reached their destination.

He watched Daniel and Lucius retrieve the coffin from the hearse, shaking his head at the irony. Lucius had come up with the idea, with the foresight to come up with a sound excuse for abrupt evening travel, such as transporting their dead brother for burial in his homeland, lest it raise unnecessary suspicion. Libraean had initially protested, but Lucius pointed out that it was not the first time David had slept in a crypt, and coffins had grown considerably more comfortable than in previous centuries. Reluctantly, Libraean agreed, revealing the unused coffins he once discovered in the vaults years ago.

Morrigan played the part of a grieving widow so masterfully that the shipping guards didn't press the issue, one even offering her his handkerchief and comforting hand. In her elegant mourning gown and black lace veil, she played the frail woman nicely against Cahira's exaggerated masculinity, the latter dressed entirely in a gentleman's attire, complete with sailor's cap and swagger. The neighboring sailors seemed to know her, calling her Captain Pelletier and throwing a few good-natured jokes her way as she finished her last-minute preparations.

Once the ship was packed with their trunks and David's coffin, Daniel helped Libraean board. His knees gave their telltale crack as he descended the narrow ladder into the cabins, letting him know he'd be stuck in the hold more often than he would be on deck. His thoughts floated to David's manor, hoping the packs of wolves Cahira brought along with her would prove reliable watching over the household in their absence. He had managed to bring along two trunks, one packed with books, the other filled with various swords and archaic weaponry, but there was still so much left behind in the Lardone vaults—including David's amassed fortune—that the loss would be devastating. He tried not to think about it, convincing himself their histories would stay safe.

The boat had five small rooms below deck, the captain's quarters, two smaller rooms for passengers, a galley with a sitting area, and a privy. Underneath them was the storage hold where David's coffin was stashed. As simple as the boat was, the accommodations were clean and well-kept, and Cahira flitted about to ensure everything was in order. The women had wordlessly agreed to share the Captain's quarters, while Libraean and Jacob took the room closest to them, leaving Lucius and Dan, who both looked annoyed at the arrangements, to take the one furthest of all.

Libraean hobbled into his room and immediately smiled when he saw Jacob. He'd already set out a few of his books and papers on the small desk bolted to the wall. Two single beds had been stacked on top of each other on the opposite side, with barely enough room to walk in between. "Your knees aren't going to be able to make it to the top," Jacob said in half-jest. "So I suppose we will sacrifice mine."

"You take good care of me." Libraean smiled before he inched down on the firm mattress with a groan.

From above, he heard Dan's baritone voice.

"I already thought of that," came Cahira's haughty reply as she descended the ladder.

Librean peeked his head out to see another woman coming in behind her, ducking to save her head from bumping the ceiling on her way down. She was also dressed in men's clothing, with wide, soulful green eyes, cool ebony skin, and hair that rose from her head in tightly wound curls. She had an intimidating presence, but her movements were graceful and poised, reminding Libraean of a cobra right before it struck.

"Forgive me, I forgot in all the commotion," Cahira explained. "This is Sandrine, my dear friend, one of the goddesses Angelique tried to recruit. She is the one who revealed Angelique's true nature to me so I could escape before it was too late. Africa is her homeland and on her most recent trip there, she met Anubis. He told her where I could find David, and after relaying the message, she agreed to accompany me on the journey."

"Anubis?" Morrigan surfaced from the back, Lucius trailing closely behind her.

Lucius and Sandrine caught eyes. "You," he said in surprise.

"Hello, Louis." She nodded her head once in his direction.

"Sandrine helped me see Angelique for what she was," Lucius explained in response to Morrigan's raised eyebrow. "She is trustworthy."

"Then we are honored to travel with you," Jacob said politely.

"How is my son?" Morrigan asked her quietly.

"Ah, so you are the Mother of Gods." Sandrine eyes swept across her in observation. "Unfortunately, I could not speak to him at length, for a war takes place where we are headed. He has seen better days, but he has one of the strongest temperaments I have ever witnessed."

Morrigan smiled sadly.

"Please get settled," Cahira told the group. "There are provisions in the galley—human food and bottles of blood. We set sail within the hour." With nothing more, she and Sandrine headed back up the ladder.

Libraean turned back to his room but felt Morrigan slide her hand around his arm. "May I talk to you?" she asked him gently. He nodded, welcoming her into the narrow quarters.

"Do you need privacy?" Jacob asked immediately. He had already prepared the room for comfort, folded blankets on each bed near several pillows.

"Not at all," Morrigan assured him. She smoothed her black skirts behind her as she sat on the tiny desk chair. "I have decided to continue the process of accessing my memories. Lucius seems to think this war goes beyond some rogue god destroying our world, that there are other motives at play. The medium who restored the first half of my memories told me in confidence that it is I who is being targeted in this war, since I am the remaining goddess who helped birth this world."

Libraean sank onto his bed, his mind beginning to spin. He slowed his thoughts down with a sigh, removing his glasses and wiping them with the corner of his shirt. "Morrigan, has Lucius fed in the last few hours?"

She blinked. "Yes, he ate before we left."

"Call him in here."

She was surprised but compliant, and soon Lucius's tall frame appeared in the doorway. He took one look at the tiny room and gestured them out into the galley's sitting room. "If we are going to converse, let us do so in some modicum of comfort."

As the creatures settled around the table, Jacob went down to retrieve two bottles of wine out of their trunks in the hold, one tainted and one plain, as well as a quartet of glasses.

Morrigan frowned, rising to her feet. "Jacob, please do not feel as though you must serve us."

"This is just as much for me, madame, as it is for you," Jacob explained, taking his seat and prying open the cork of a fresh bottle.

Lucius immediately helped himself, swirling the liquid in his glass as he waited patiently for them to speak.

Libraean was in no mood for wine, blood-infused or otherwise, and instead placed his hand supportively on Jacob's knee. His gray eyes offered a little sparkle back in Libraean's direction before he took a long, careful sip of his wine and cleared his throat to speak. "There is something I must tell you all about my time as an angel."

"An angel?" Lucius's handsome face wrinkled in confusion.

"Jacob is the reincarnation of the angel, Gabriel, who once served the God of man," Morrigan explained to him.

"Ah." Lucius still appeared bewildered, but was quiet, waiting for him to continue.

Jacob cleared his throat again. "We angels were taught that God was the Creator of the Heavens and the Earth, that it was He who was the only one true God. He kept us isolated from all other gods and creatures, keeping us in compliance with His laws. Whether that was His intention, or the intention of those who soon took control of the Heavenly realm, I am uncertain. Jesus was the only one I could communicate with towards the end of my tenure." His eyes fixated on his glass, briefly transfixed before he continued.

"God Himself had become a fragmented deity as so many different cultures and religions claimed to know Him—each proclaiming that their version was correct. Humans didn't realize that they were creating a contradicting deity that no one could access, something like tiny orbs fused together to create a larger one. I remember bits of my life as a young angel when we served Him directly, when he was known to us as Yahweh, but those memories have long since disappeared from my consciousness. I'm not sure if it was intentional, or if it was this human life that took them for good. What I can remember is a group of angels who call themselves the Holy Watchers became the ones who exclusively speak to God, and they are the ones who currently run the Kingdom of Heaven. All other angels must answer to them. Jesus has been relocated to his own heavenly realm on their orders, separated from his own Father." He took another sip of wine, visibly nervous.

"You are amongst family here," Morrigan reminded him in her soft, melodious voice.

Jacob gave her a small, shy smile. "Forgive me, it frightens me to speak so plainly about these things. I am embarrassed to admit I still fear repercussions."

"That is the very nature of modern religion, is it not?" Lucius commented scornfully.

Jacob sighed, neither agreeing nor disagreeing with his comment. "My brothers and I continued our work on earth regardless of how things were being run, hunting the occasional daemon, answering the petitions of our human following. Then one day, I overheard a conversation about a rogue god who was destroying the realms that existed outside of ours, including the Egyptian Underworld. Frantic, I tried to tell my brothers he must be stopped, but none wanted to intervene. Finally, it was Jesus who gave me his blessing to contact Ms. Cahira, who I hoped would be the one to find Mr. David and prevent the destruction of the realms. It was I who alerted her, but the price I had to pay for it was my wings—I was born again in this land with half of my memories wiped clean. They could not prevent me from remembering Libreaen, however, and I've started to remember more, the longer he is near me."

"I understand." Morrigan looked down at her folded hands.

"Well, that's it," Lucius interjected. "These Holy Watchers have recruited an agent of destruction to work on their behalf, to destroy the other gods and goddesses who threaten their power."

Libraean felt a wave of unease. "So we are not merely fighting one rogue individual, but an entire army of angels backed by the most popular God among us."

The room was quiet.

"What I cannot understand is why the hundreds of different religions that serve that God aren't going after each other, even though most of them exist in eternal conflict," he continued. "Why target us?"

"We all know why," Lucius said dryly. "Having different sects does not threaten the Watchers' power over man." He pointed a narrow finger in Morrigan's direction. "But she does."

"How can a goddess be the creator of all when it should be a man," Jacob murmured in agreement.

Libraean threw his glasses on the table in frustration. "Well, then how do we stop it?"

Morrigan sighed. "We will access my memories, join Anubis in Africa, and restore David back to health. As long as you all remain by my side, collectively, we are a powerful force against them."

"Yes, of course," Libraean reiterated his loyalty, Jacob echoing the sentiment.

He didn't expect Lucius to respond, but he watched him look down at his glass. He spoke in a tone a little above a whisper. "There is no me without you."

They were interrupted by Cahira at the door. "Drinking already? We have yet to set sail."

"Cahira, I must ask you a favor." Morrigan rose to her feet. "Daniel told us about your power long before we met. I am assuming David told you everything regarding me as well. I have full confidence in your abilities, yet the choice is ultimately yours—will you help me access my repressed memories, the ones that existed right before I was reborn in this life?"

Cahira looked taken aback, but she agreed. "Of course. Let us set sail, then I will be at your service. We will travel down the Thames and around the Dover Strait, where we will cross the English Channel. I'm confident I can step away for a few hours once we've reached the Atlantic. As long as the weather holds, of course."

"Thank you," Morrigan said softly, a faraway look settling in her eyes.

The ship began to sway as its anchors were lifted, shifting into position. "It is nightfall." Cahira looked to Morrigan. "Can we have clear skies?"

CHAPTER THIRTEEN

🕸 The Sacrifice 🕸

The Atlantic Ocean
Morrigan

ORRIGAN'S EYES SLOWLY OPENED.

It had been a few days since they reached the Atlantic Ocean, the weather clear but giving no sign of relenting on the cold. Sandrine and Cahira took shifts steering, letting Morrigan enjoy the sensation of solitude, for no matter who occupied the bed across from her, they slept while she was awake. It offered plenty of time to gather her thoughts, considering all that had been laid before her and what was to come. She also appreciated the break from Lucius, who was becoming increasingly more difficult for her to be around, the mere smell of him able to derail her at a moment's notice. She never would have imagined she'd be trapped in a similar predicament as before, this time favoring the man she'd spent lifetimes trying to escape from. But there was no running from it now, the three of them trapped together until the world was put back in order. She hoped it would be sooner than later; she assumed being immortal robbed a soul of its emotions, yet in her case, it seemed quite the opposite.

She sensed daylight, noticing Sandrine's long form stretched out beneath the blankets. Though they hadn't had much time to correspond, Morrigan felt she was an old, unthreatening soul, one with secrets as deep as hers and her presence brought her peace. She rose from the bed, careful not to wake her, slipping a robe over the thin chemise she'd slept in.

The cabins were quiet as the nocturnal creatures slept, even Dan who sat with his arms crossed on the ladder, his eyes drifting open and shut as he listened for Cahira as she steered the ship above. Morrigan gave him a soft, reassuring pat on his knee as she moved past him, heading down a shorter set of steps into the storage hold. The boat swayed gently as she maneuvered around the piles of trunks towards the coffin that rested against the back wall. She knelt down to pry open the clasps, the wooden lid creaking as she lifted it.

Although she braced herself, his appearance alarmed her each time she saw him. So deep was his slumber, that he looked truly dead, his skin drained of any color, his lips dry and cracked. The coffin they found for him in the Lardone vaults was lined with deep blue velvet, his rusted gold curls spread around him like a halo. Emotion caught in her throat as she stared at him, tracing the line of his nose and jaw with her eyes, longing to see his kind green eyes. No matter what Libraean said, she knew it was her fault he was gone.

She pulled herself as close as she could next to him, brushing his hair back from his forehead. His chest moved so slightly that only a vampyre could see it, a trickle of wind escaping underneath his nose. "Where are you?" she whispered.

She hadn't expected a reply, but the silence in the hold felt particularly painful. "I hope someday you'll forgive me for all of this," she added, "but understand if you don't. I just hope you'll come back from wherever you are soon... you are still needed here."

She heard shuffling above her and hurried to close the casket. She pulled herself out of the hold in time to see Lucius standing outside his cabin door. "Morrigan, come here," he whispered loudly, waving her into his room.

She pulled her robe tighter against the chill as she entered his unsettled room. There were pieces of parchment strewn across the floors, some nailed to the walls, and books opened up on every available surface. She realized Lucius was just as unkempt, his hair in complete disarray, dressed in nothing but a loose linen shirt and trousers. "You took Libraean's books?"

"I borrowed them," he told her. "Well, I took them—they were both sleeping. But that is not the point." He directed her to the wall where he had created a timeline out of chalk, his neat handwriting scrawled across the thick wooden planks. He'd sketched out their entire history in one long timeline from the beginning in Egypt, all the way to the present day, each one of them included. There was a big question mark that broke up the line labeled 'L', right between his time in Tartarus and his resurgence as Hades. Right above, she noticed that this was around the time that she and David ('M' and 'D') lived in the Otherrealms. She waited for him to explain.

"This is what I cannot seem to understand," he began. "According to Librean's texts, all of us died during the Bronze Age. Anubis dragged my soul to Tartarus while you and David went to the Upperrealms, where you lived until around seventeen hundred BC, when you became the Celtic deities Daghda and Morrigan. I rose around four hundred BC and of course, Librean reincarnated a handful of years before that. My point is, there is a lot of time that is unaccounted for."

Morrigan frowned. "You were in Tartarus during those years."

"Yes, but why can't I remember anything specific? I can recall being in Hades with Isis right before we returned, but Tartarus remains a mystery."

"We all lose our memories when we reincarnate, that is the law of the earth."

"Yes, but I still didn't remember them in the Underworld. My mind started to spin once I heard Jacob speak of angels and Watchers. I should know them—I have spent lifetimes studying history, philosophy, and the arts, yet for some reason, I cannot seem to recall exactly what the Watchers are—they are words without pictures, even thoughts of angels are hazy. And there is no logical reason for it."

Morrigan frowned. "Perhaps you just don't remember yet. You do have eons of memories to recover. It takes time."

"Oh, I remember everything now," he sighed, looking at the lines of chalk scrawled across the wall. "It has been a tumultuous whirlwind, like a nightmare I can't quite escape from. Memories of parched earth, cities carved out stone, open seas, castles, wars, other worlds. I'm sure some things have escaped me, including the same memories you are missing, but I should remember my first days in Tartarus."

"Do you think your memories were taken from you? Like a spell?"

"Exactly." He brightened, grateful she understood. "I think it's another piece of the puzzle. After Cahira pulls the memories from you, I think we should explore mine."

Morrigan nodded, though a dismal feeling settled over her.

They were interrupted by a knock at the door. Cahira apprehended the room in the same way Morrigan had, complete with raised eyebrow. "It is now twilight and Sandrine is at the wheel," she told her. "I can try to help you now, if you'd like."

Morrigan was hit with another wave of unease. Lucius instinctively gripped her hand to steady her. She tried to smile at him but found she could not, her nerves dominating her rational mind as they followed Cahira into the main sitting area. Dan was already in attendance, Libraean and Jacob groggily joining. Jacob attempted to stifle a yawn as he wrapped his blankets tightly around him, having difficulty adjusting both to the late hours and the freezing air that drifted down into the ship. Lucius chose not to sit, wearing a deep frown as he leaned against the wall directly across from her, as if prepared to strike when needed.

Cahira had already set up the table and dimmed the lamps around them before lighting the wide candle she'd placed between her and Morrigan. "Can you travel to the astral realm, or do you need aid?" she asked her as she sat down.

"I can," Morrigan replied.

"It will be like we are traveling there, but instead we will be traveling to the space around it, your unconscious mind. Your consciousness is not letting you find it, but I can push you there if you let me in."

Morrigan nodded.

Cahira pulled an old watch out of her pocket, setting it on the table in a bowl, which echoed its melodic tick throughout the hold. "Stare into the light and focus on the sound," she instructed in a low voice. "Return to the place you left."

Morrigan glanced up at Lucius, whose eyes seemed to glow in the dim light. "The Underworld," she whispered as she closed her eyes, pulling up the memory of her woods and his worried expression as he held her hands.

"Do you think it is David?" she heard him say.

"I do not believe so..." Morrigan murmured as the ship around her began to melt away.

The Underworld

LUCIUS GRABBED BOTH HER HANDS IN DESPERATION, her figure beginning to dissipate as it was pulled from the dark realm. "Please come back," he pleaded, worry in his eyes.

She cupped her hands around his face as she pushed her lips against his. "I will," she promised.

And then he was gone, her senses completely snuffed out only to assault her again at whirlwind speed. Her vision took a moment to focus on what stood immediately before her, a circle of ancient centaurs, peering down at her sternly.

"You summoned me?" she asked, trying to temper the surprise in her voice as her crows settled around her. A shiver ran across her barely clad skin, her eyes catching tattoos and war paint scrawled across an arm that held her spear, affirming they had called Morrigan, not Nephthys, to come forth.

She recognized the centaur standing in the middle as Sagittari, the alpha of the Carpathian Sagittaureans and the father of Chiron, the beloved teacher of the Ancient Greeks. She had not seen him for centuries, yet he still looked the same, his chest broad and carpeted by auburn hair, the same shade that covered his equine torso and limbs.

He wore a grimace as he peered down at her, crossing his thick arms. "We did not summon you. We do not need the help of any woman, even the great Morrigan. It was one of our outcasts, a fallen soldier, who you would do well to remember."

They parted like the sea, revealing the corpse of a young centaur crumpled across the forest floor amongst the pine needles. His freshly expired fire still billowed smoke, its crackling embers filling up the lack of sound the spring woods suffered at nightfall. His fist was still clenched around a bundle of crow feathers, his human skin and horsehair matted with dried blood. Morrigan observed a deep gash across one of his legs, the other cruelly severed at the knee. She could tell by the clotting of his wounds that they had begun to putrefy long before he had expired.

Morrigan approached cautiously, wondering why such a creature had called her in his final moments. The centaur was quite adolescent compared to the rest of his herd, perhaps only a few hundred years old. His skin was still smooth and unblemished, and if one did not see his mutilation, he could have easily been a young man who had simply fallen asleep in the leaves. She knelt down, brushing back a lock of black hair from his cheek. He had been dead for only minutes, his skin still exuding a faint equine musk with a curious twist of cardamom and clove.

"I am surprised you do not remember me."

She jumped back to see his spirit standing above his corpse. He was as handsome as she'd pictured in her mind, his eyes a fantastic shade of gold.

She froze in sudden recognition.

It was Hekate's child, the grown version of the baby she'd rescued centuries ago in Wallachia. Isis's child... Lucius's child.

"I hoped to survive long enough to tell you what has happened, but it took a lot to revive such an old war goddess," he said good-naturedly.

Morrigan had trouble steadying herself, unsettled she'd forgotten such an important event in her earthly life while simultaneously disarmed by the apparition of her current lover's son. He stood before her in a near identical rendition of him, despite his equine appendages.

"I suppose this means you are not calling me out of spite," she said. She noticed the rest of the centaurs had disappeared, leaving them alone in the quiet woods.

"Do not worry, I have long understood why you turned me into this creature and hid me away among the Sagittaureans. Your plan worked, I lived undisturbed and protected while enjoying a life of freedom for centuries. That is not why I summoned you." He began to pace in a manner similar to his father, his four legs moving in the elegant rhythm that only horses can manage. "When the leaves began to tarnish in the summer heat, I discovered a woman as I hunted alone in the woods. She appeared to be lost and frightened, and for reasons I cannot explain, I immediately went to her aid. I do not have to tell you about our traditions, nor the oath we take to live our lives free from the distraction of women, yet I was never a true Sagittaurean, after all. I fell helplessly in love with her, and eventually she convinced me to have a child with her. She informed me whilst pregnant that I was the last descendent of the most powerful family of witches that had ever existed and that our child would have unfathomable power. I did not believe her, but she was a witch herself and she showed me in visions the story of my bloodline, ending with how a dark goddess called the Morrigan brought me to the Sagittaureans to protect me. She had me so deeply in love with her that I broke my vows, fleeing the Carpathian Mountains and my brethren to start a new life with her and our child.

"We did not make it far before she gave birth. I was overjoyed at first, but as I held my daughter in my arms, her mother told me her plans to murder her, that she wanted us both to consume her power. Repulsed and horrified, I resisted, leading to a fight where she injured me and escaped. My herd found me here, and since I committed the most terrible sin amongst us, they took one of my legs."

Morrigan openly fumed. "Such archaic practice," she muttered.

The centaur smiled sadly. "My wounds were going to kill me regardless, for she slashed me with a silver blade. After the herd left me to die, I attempted to summon you. I do not know who that woman truly is, but I believe she is a wicked sorceress. I cannot bear it if she harms my child. Please, you rescued me once long ago, and I beg of you now, please save my daughter."

Emotion overcame Morrigan. She had assumed her sister's ancient bloodline would end with her last celibate son, but here, another Pădurii child lived, brimming with power, with no idea who or what she was, vulnerable to forces who would steal her power by any means necessary. "Of course I will protect her," she murmured.

The young centaur bowed to her gratefully as his ghost began to fade. "I thank you, Dark Goddess. Maybe one day we will cross paths again in the Eternal Forest of the Dead." And then she was alone in the frigid Carpathian woods, a dead centaur at her feet.

She looked around to see if the herd was near, but they had long deserted her and the young man. She knelt down where he lay, running her fingers over his eyes so that two gold coins appeared. "Safe passage across the River Styx, that Charon carries you to your heavenly realm unscathed," she whispered. Satisfied that Anubis would recognize the spell she left on his soul, she immediately shifted into a wolf.

She briefly savored one of her favorite forms as she took off into the woods at blinding speed. She searched the air for the scent of cardamom, picking it up easily in the seasonally barren woods. It called to her from a mile inwards, a place far away from even the most remote human villages and Sagittaurean Territory.

The crows that scoured the skies above the elderly trees called down to let her know her path was safe as she wove through the coniferous throng into the heart of the mountains. A ramshackle cabin finally surfaced, artfully hidden by pines but with telltale smoke escaping out of its fireplace. Her crows landed on the rooftop softly to conceal her arrival.

Morrigan saw no evidence of livestock nor gardens, the shack itself haphazardly built as if someone had thrown it together in neglectful haste. She crawled out of her wolf guise and into one of a cloaked old hag, scooping up a fallen branch to act as a cane as she hobbled towards the door.

It was covered only by a meager blanket, allowing the cold spring air to invade the room undeterred, as a baby cried softly from within.

"Hello?" Morrigan croaked, peering inside. She was accosted by the reek of spoiled meat, noticing heaps of raw flesh stacked near the pathetic fire. She realized they were once human.

A face suddenly popped into view, startling her enough to distract her from the repulsive revelation. The face itself was unrecognizable, but it housed a pair of eyes that Morrigan would never forget, no matter what host they took on. It was Delicia. "What do you want?" she snapped.

Her body was just as bony as the one they had once shared, petite, but with strong hands and arms. Her mouth was thin and her eyes, dark brown, both set deeply in a plain face surrounded by flaxen hair. Specks of crimson dotted her mouth and flecked her skin.

"I am lost and cannot find my way," Morrigan said in the shaky voice of an ancient woman.

"That is no issue of mine," Delicia growled in annoyance. Her eyes darted back and forth, searching behind where Morrigan stood.

"Is that a child I hear crying?" Morrigan croaked.

"That is not a human child, pay her no mind. How did you find me here?" she asked suspiciously. Up close, her skin seemed unnatural, as if someone had plastered another's flesh onto her bones.

"I do not know how I got here," Morrigan continued the ruse. "I have been lost in the forest for days. Please, let me warm myself by the fire."

Delicia frowned. "Wait—I know you…"

Morrigan tumbled through the doorway as she snapped back into her maiden warrior aspect. She flew towards the baby, whose weak cries had turned to hysterical, high-pitched wails, responding instinctively to the shift of energy in the room.

Delicia halted her process by grabbing the roots of her hair, throwing her into the wall with supernatural strength. Morrigan had managed to claw at her skin, tearing some of it away to reveal leathery black scales. It was as Morrigan suspected—she was actually a daemon.

Her crows flew down through the open chimney, paying the fire no mind, several scooping up the baby and her blankets, the others taking advantage of the rips in Delicia's fake flesh to tear it the rest of the way off. She tried to fight them off, but they worked quickly, setting to work on the exposed scales with their razor-sharp claws and beaks. She howled in pain, inhuman screeches piercing the air.

Morrigan grabbed the stick she had used as a cane and broke it in two, hurling the sharp end at Delicia. It punctured through her scales to her insides, impaling her against the wall. Her true form was repulsive, an aberrant reptile covered in viscous flakes. Putrid green oozed from the wound as she writhed, slowly losing consciousness.

"You think you are saving the child, but they will find it," she taunted weakly. "I am only one of many, Morrigan. Just wait until you see what's in store for you."

"I'll be waiting." Morrigan kicked the stake to drive it deeper, sufficiently snuffing out the life of the hideous creature.

She raced out of the cabin to find the baby nestled amongst the patiently waiting crows. She appeared calm, but dangerously malnourished. Morrigan scooped her into her arms. "We need shelter, well hidden," she told her flock. "This baby is brimming with power—they'll be after her soon."

The crows obediently took off into the skies. Morrigan cradled the baby against her chest, creating a sling with the blankets. Then she darted after them on foot, leaving the daemoness and her carnage behind.

The sun began to set, casting a frigid chill into the air. Morrigan remained in her semi-corporeal form, and she knew the child needed real warmth. Thankfully, the crows had discovered a small cave carved into the mountainside. She climbed up to it only to discover it was guarded by a pack of wolves.

They snarled, hackles raised for only a moment before realizing who she was. They backed away as the alpha approached her cautiously, sniffing the air around her.

"This child is under my protection now," Morrigan informed her. "We would like to rest here, if you wouldn't mind sharing your shelter. But no harm comes to her, not now and not ever."

The wolf bowed her head in accord, informing the rest of her pack, who parted to let them enter. Morrigan felt the baby stir against her chest as she nestled against the wall, the wolves remaining at the cave's entrance to provide them additional protection against the cold air. The baby still shivered, however, her little mouth rooting desperately for sustenance. Her skin had already started to mottle, barely able to make anything more than a faint squeaking. Morrigan panicked, searching the wolves for a recent mother, but all were either pregnant or beyond the age of nursing pups.

She pulled the baby close to her. "There is only one way I can help you, sweet *bairn*," she whispered. "And that requires your magic. You can petition me as your guardian goddess, and I will have a humanlike form until you no longer need me. If you will it, it can be so."

The baby could barely look at her, the light in her eyes growing dim.

Morrigan began to sing a Celtic song from long ago, the Ode to the Morrigan. The garbled crooning of crows soon filled the chamber, and the wolves that guarded them added their echoing howls. The baby stared at her with wide, adoring eyes, brought back to life by the songs of the wood. Soon her little hands reached out to graze Morrigan's hair, as if pulling her into the earthly realm.

Morrigan closed her eyes, knowing that if the child succeeded, she could save her, but she would be trapped on earth until she released her. She thought of Lucius, nervously waiting for her in the Underworld, and she felt heavy with grief. For a fleeting moment, she wondered if he could handle life on earth again. She imagined what it could be like to have him near, this child giving them a chance at what they'd always secretly wanted together. She knew he would follow her the moment she told him, but would it be the best for his mental state? His scrying pool, she remembered. The decision does not have to be mine. He will see us and then the choice will be his.

Her thoughts were interrupted by a sharp pain at her breast. She looked down to see the baby had latched, her breasts now swollen with milk like they were long ago when she birthed her twins. She recalled the painful regret at not being able to nurture them, leaving them behind with her sister and wet nurse as she went into hiding for their protection. She never realized how sweet the act of nourishing a young one could be, artfully masking the discomfort. She smiled, sweeping back the soft, fuzzy hairs on the top of her head. The child had done it—Morrigan was material in the physical realm.

She closed her eyes again, suddenly exhausted, imagining how Lucius's face would light up when she showed him his daughter. "I will call you Cahira," she decided. "My little warrior." And she lay back, letting the baby, her baby, bring itself back to health.

Morrigan wrenched herself back into consciousness with a gasp, immediately feeling as though she had been thrown into a fire. Scrambling to her feet, she realized it burned in patches all around her, contained in piles of crumbled stone and debris, its thick smoke overpowering the air. She looked up to see a cracked and oozing ceiling, as if lava pulsated above, waiting for the stone to collapse under its pressure so it could devour everything beneath.

Memories of the years raising Cahira into womanhood rushed into her mind, followed by the memory of her own death, torn to shreds by a direwolf. Yet this was unlike any realm of the Underworld she had ever seen. Had she been sent to Tartarus? She moved forward tentatively as clouds of ash squeezed her lungs. Her squinted eyes caught a sparkling heap of shattered stone, and as she moved closer, she realized they were shards of obsidian. The reality of her situation hit her. "Lucius?" she cried out, breaking into a sprint.

The world around her became clearer as she ran, Lucius's magnificent Underworld palace reduced to smoldering rubble. The smog thickened the deeper into the realm she ran, nearly sending her tumbling down into an open crevasse. She stopped herself just in time to avoid falling into the tumultuous waters below, their angry waves crashing against the rocks. The water was black and smelled of rot, as if her beloved death rivers had been polluted by the ruins of a hundred fallen realms. Panic clutched her chest, for she felt it in her bones—she no longer had any power here.

She forced herself to pause, shutting her eyes to collect herself. She had lived in a physical body on earth before; she was still strong even without supernatural aid. She exhaled with new resolve and leapt easily over the harrowing gorge.

As soon as she landed on the other side, she sensed him.

She burst into another destroyed realm, this one hers, the trees burnt to skeletons, inky tar bubbling down the trunks of those that survived. Then she saw him. His body slumped over a plank, his arms tied at each end with rope, his black dragon wings ripped violently out of his back and broken around him. The only thing holding them together was their thin, tattered skin. He looked emaciated, cuts and bruises cruelly interrupting his smooth, pale flesh.

Horrified, she ran to him, dropping to her knees to take his head in her hands. He appeared unconscious, one of his eyes bruised, his bottom lip split open and bleeding down his chin. "Lucius." Her voice did not sound like hers, trembling as her body had begun to. "What has happened?"

Miraculously, his eyes opened slowly and tried to focus on her face. The eye that had been blackened was filled with blood, gruesomely obscuring its golden iris. "Nephthys?" he croaked.

"Yes, I'm here," she said. "You must tell me who has done this to you. Who has destroyed the Underworld?"

He coughed, tossing blood to the ground. The sight of it fueled Morrigan's rage, anger replacing her fear. She grabbed a piece of jagged stone from the ground and tore through the ropes that held him. He crumpled to the floor, his broken skeletal wings folding helplessly around him.

"Lucius, who is doing this?" she repeated.

When she still received no answer, she swooped back down to the ground, gathering him in her arms. He laid in her lap, gazing up at her adoringly as she smoothed back his tousled hair. "You came back to me," he managed, attempting to smile.

"Of course, I did. Didn't you see me in your pool? When I didn't hear from you, I thought you decided not to join me, to wait here for me to return."

He coughed, settling back down with a wheeze. It sounded as though some of his ribs had been broken. "No," he said, in a rattling voice, "she came here not long after you left."

"She?" Morrigan scowled. "Lucius, the entire Underworld is ablaze. You must tell me who did this so I can stop her."

"Oh no, my dear, it is far too late for that," a voice interrupted.

Morrigan lunged, halted by the power of a woman standing before her, dressed in blinding red robes with icy blonde hair billowing around her. She smiled as she held her in the air, Morrigan hopelessly frozen.

"You have no power here anymore, Nephthys, or Morrigan, or whatever you're calling yourself these days," she said jovially. Her eyes matched the color of her dress, angry red orbs that burned like the fire roaring around her. "You do not know how long I have waited for you. Our Set refused to summon you here no matter how hard I tried to persuade him." She released her, and Morrigan fell to the ground with a thud.

She lifted herself up to her feet, but did not rush her again, deciding instead to calmly wait and plan her next move. "You are what Delicia promised would return for me."

The woman laughed. "Delicia, yes. One of my favorite daemons. The one who helped me birth our daughter. Which you stole."

Morrigan's eyes narrowed. "She is protected now."

"Oh, it is not time for her quite yet. But her power will be mine regardless, after I have put everything in place."

"Who are you?" Morrigan demanded.

"I am so happy you asked," the woman said, clasping her hands together with delight. She morphed into a woman with black hair and green eyes, a perfect replica of Isis. "We can take whatever form we want," she said in Isis's voice before switching to a young, curvaceous woman with freckled skin and rose gold hair. Morrigan's breath caught in her throat as she recognized David's former lover, Gaia. "We are Chaos," she said, pleased at Morrigan's reaction. "It is a shame that you never considered us, that you forgot all about the place from which you were born.

"At the beginning, heka grew out of chaos," she said in a singsong voice, "and as heka evolved into four gods who would create the earth and its humans, Chaos would quietly grow into its own palatable force. At first, we were just a breath of wind, watching as humanity blossomed, governed by the kings and queens who spoke into existence. But as one of the goddesses grew stronger, so did we—so did I."

She began to casually pace, unbothered by the destructive inferno raging around her. Morrigan noticed she was barefoot on the scorching ground. "The earth you created has its own set of laws, all contingent on balance. Without light there is no dark, without dark, there is no light. You have all spent so much time focused on the battle between brothers, the god of dark and the god of light, that no one ever stopped to consider the shadow of the goddess who started it all." She turned towards Morrigan as she shifted back into her twin. "I am your mirror in every aspect, except where your heart holds human emotion, mine holds nothing at all. I am completely unburdened by conscience, empathy, or love. I exist as your perfect opposition, causing strife and mayhem wherever I can because it brings me joy. While you feel and brood and serve, I am free to do as I please. In fact, it makes me laugh to think you were the one who was supposed to be a chaos goddess yourself, but you just surrendered that power to me."

"How?"

"Come now, Lilith. Why do you think you fell so easily for Osiris and he for you?"

Morrigan felt the blood drain from her face.

Isis's radiant green eyes sparkled. "Love is Chaos. It is the most destructive force in existence, and you were its first agent. The union between you and Osiris caused a rippling effect amongst you all, and yet, instead of that chaos staying inside you, it split away, creating me. I was finally a real goddess, the goddess Discordia, birthed out of your own heart. Your actions taught me that I could use love and seduction to my own advantage. In fact, that was my first victim, the poor goddess Aphrodite, who I murdered before I ate her flesh, infusing myself with her power. Then I realized your sister had been left unprotected and I killed her, too, taking her power and devouring her soul."

Morrigan shrieked with rage, but Discordia was prepared, freezing her once again and lifting her into the sky. With a wave of her hand, she broke all the bones in Morrigan's leg, the sound of shattering glass deafening in her ears. She bit her lip to withstand the pain, her entire being shaking to keep from crying out.

"Isn't it amazing how I can bend the realm to my will, including the deities that reside in it? I got that power from your husband as he made love to me on the volcanic shores of Tartarus. Now where was I?" Discordia paused, then smiled. She sat on one of the rocks, crossing a thin bronze leg over the other. "Oh yes, seducing your husband. Back in the ancient days, I pretended to be Isis, visiting him in Hades's palace and gaining his trust until he finally came up with the idea to bring us both back to earth and impregnate me. I think my favorite part of our Set is his ability to be manipulated—all he needs is a gentle push and his mind concocts all sorts of diabolical schemes. He was the one who came up with the idea of having children with me to protect me, but he didn't realize that combining his power with Isis's would make our own earthly goddesses, similar to how you and Osiris created Anubis and Horus.

"Anyway, I am the reason that Gaia girl came out of the tree powerless, for the heka was already mine and my daughters'. She was a tiny piece of Isis's soul that I accidentally left behind. Once I found out, I set her up to die—I couldn't risk any leftover part of Isis threatening my daughters' power. Though, in hindsight, I regret the whole daughter experience, since it failed me, but that is another story."

Morrigan tried to focus on her words, but both the implications of her words and the excruciating pain was making it difficult. Her lungs burned with each breath of smoky air.

"I did try to manipulate Set again after David sent him back to Tartarus, but unfortunately, he caught on. I took on your perfect likeness, making love to him exactly how you do, but he knew it wasn't you. His love for you is not chaotic like it is with Osiris and while I can use his broken heart to manipulate him, when he is confident in your love for him, it has the opposite effect." She sighed wistfully, staring at the unconscious Lucius crumpled on the ground.

Morrigan thought of her last words to Lucius in Wallachia, picturing herself in Delicia's body, her hands on his chest: I can never love you the way you need me to, but your fire will always burn in my veins…

"He was intended to be the greatest chaos god of all," Discordia interrupted in lamentation, "and he could have been such a powerful force in my army. Originally, I thought you being together was the key to provoking his destructiveness, yet you have somehow managed to domesticate him beyond reform. This is the reason I have to keep you apart—for without you, he is an unbridled force of calamitous energy that I eventually will succeed in exploiting."

"Why destroy our realms?" Morrigan managed to ask. "Why not live in your own?"

Discordia looked delighted by the question but snapped her arm bone for good measure. It took everything for Morrigan not to scream. "I was approached by those who speak for the God of men. They want to ensure His eternal power—in other words, their eternal power. They've witnessed how much havoc I can wreak over the years and asked me to rid the world of all outer realms except theirs, taking the pagan gods and goddesses along with them. I have agreed, and in return, I can live forever on earth with any chaos gods I chose. They like us, for these Holy Watchers realized that the more strife exists on the mortal plane, the more humans turn to their God for help, which fuels their power. I am a helpful, necessary being to them, therefore I will continue to live on."

"If you kill us, we will reincarnate," Morrigan struggled to speak. "That is the laws of the earth."

"Yes, but the laws also take your memories. You will not remember any of this when you return, and I will find your human self before you realize who you truly are. Then I will kill you and take your powers, just like I did your sister. You won't have a realm to return to, so you will simply cease to be."

She shifted her form again, this time into the witch Hekate, Isis's brilliant emerald eyes behind cascades of rich chestnut hair. Gold hoops hung from her ears, colored scarves around her waist. Again, she delighted in Morrigan's surprise. "Yes, you were right back then—I was not really your sister. After I brought Set into the world as Lucius the vampyre, I hid away with my daughters. The oldest eventually turned on me when she realized I planned to eat her to absorb the combination of Set and Isis's power. That meddlesome Council aided her, putting me back in that damned tree. When Lucius tried to pull me out the second time, thinking I was Isis, he accidentally split her in half, bringing forth the human Gaia and sending me to Tartarus. I reincarnated many years later as Hekate.

"When you threw me off the tower into the river, I wasn't really dead—I am far too powerful to die that easily. Instead, my soul found its way into a young nemorti whose body I used to collect the Wolf and the pieces of my brother, Ares. Then I hid, lying low until everything had settled. Though his body was badly mangled, I eventually resurrected him. That is my favorite power of your sister's, by the way," she added, "the power of resurrection." She blew along her palm, sealing the fractured pieces of Morrigan's arm bone for emphasis. Morrigan wouldn't let herself feel relief, assuming it was only a matter of moments before she broke it again.

"Ares is currently creating a slew of immortals on earth, many of whom I will use as my personal vessels," she continued. "It's remarkable—not only can I take the appearance of souls who have already died, but I can slip into any soulless body I choose. I also brought back the Wolf, who is restored to his mindless, controllable version without humanity, who hunts creatures for me. Soon I will have taken out every single god and goddess that man has ever created. Except the ones who will serve me, of course."

"Why are you telling me all of this if I will just forget?" Morrigan asked, her vision starting to waver.

Her sister's face smiled, the eyes of the wretched creature wearing it sparkling in its mask. "Because a part of me hopes I won't find you in time, that you will remember all of this and we can have ourselves a proper fight. Nothing excites me more than that." She winked at her before rising to her feet. She shifted into a new form, one Morrigan had never met before, with similar blue eyes to hers and cascades of dark hair. "Come find me if you'd like. I'm thinking of calling myself Angelique." She smiled sweetly as she raised her palms to unleash more torment.

Morrigan bore the onslaught of pain like a stone, grinding her teeth as the sensation of a thousand needles tore into her skin, the pressure breaking both her arms. The agony finally succeeded in blurring her eyesight, but she saw Lucius's figure from the corner of it, pulling himself forward and using every ounce of his strength to throw himself around her, stopping the flow of Discordia's power.

She could hear the creature chuckling as she readjusted, pooling more of it together, but Morrigan focused on him instead, the smell of his hair, the warmth of his skin as he cradled her, covering her with his body and broken wings. The woods he'd created for her blazed all around them, debris continuing to fall around them, their home destroyed. "Shhh," he whispered, pressing his lips on her forehead. "It will all be over soon."

There was blinding heat, and then, there was nothing.

THE ATLANTIC OCEAN

MORRIGAN'S EYES SNAPPED OPEN TO MEET CAHIRA'S. Tears poured out them, the formidable woman with a tight jaw and swagger melting away. Morrigan realized her own cheeks were wet, and without a second thought, she rushed to throw her arms around her.

"My daughter," she whispered incredulously. They trembled together in embrace before Morrigan's eyes caught Lucius's, his own expression trapped somewhere between sorrow and shock. But before anyone could speak, the ship lurched, sending them all crashing against the wall.

"Cahira!" Sandrine screamed from the dock.

The ship started to rock back and forth with violent force, pouring frigid ocean water into the hold. Dan and Cahira scrambled to climb the ladder, as Morrigan helped Libraean and Jacob to their room, bolting the door behind them. As soon as she succeeded, she was abruptly tossed the other way, her spine smacking the wood.

"Get the weapons!" Cahira's voice bellowed, an uncharacteristic twinge of terror tightening her words.

Lucius grabbed Morrigan's arm as they fought their way to the storage hold. Two of the trunks had already burst open and spilled out, their contents floating in the pool of seawater. He struggled to pry the weapons chest open as they battled against the lurching vessel, finally able to grab a pistol and as many swords and knives as they could muster. They made it back on deck, and Morrigan halted immediately in her tracks.

Although she was no stranger to daemons and had just torn her way through an army of rock creatures, nothing prepared her for the leviathan rising from the tempestuous sea. Snaking out of the frothy waters was a hideous creature so massive, it grazed the heavens. At first, she thought octopus-like tendrils lashed out at their paltry boat, but she gasped when she saw at least a dozen serpentine heads, each of their jaws unhinged to display rows of venomous fangs. Although they had no eyes to accompany their distorted mouths, they snapped at them with impeccable aim, ripping through the wood and sails in the process.

Sandrine had already wrapped herself around one, muscles taut as she squeezed the life out of it as it thrashed. Several other heads tried to tear her away, but Lucius tossed a sword at Cahira who skillfully caught the blade and beheaded them all with a warrior's cry.

Morrigan tossed another sword to Dan, who raced to the other side. Lucius took a few shots, rupturing their skulls in a spray of visceral slime, before tucking the gun in his waist and wielding his own sword. Morrigan pulled out her wings to reach the highest heads and soon the five creatures fell into a unified dance as severed heads fell down around them in gruesome chunks.

Morrigan quickly realized, however, that for each head they chopped, another grew back in its place. She slashed regardless, puncturing through the skulls that dove for her with the pointed edge of her narrow sword. It became a whirlwind of fruitless stabbing and screeching heads, acidic spit and blood flying across the poor ship that threatened to buckle under the stress, fighting to stay upright as the ocean waves crashed around them.

Morrigan dropped down to the deck, just as Lucius skidded across it, grabbing her around the waist and pulling her down into the hatch in one easy movement.

"What are you doing?" she cried.

"Morrigan, you have to listen to me. This is a hydra—the more we chop off its heads, the more they will grow. It is an unkillable *daemon*."

"Then what are we supposed to do?" she shouted over the noise.

"We have to send it back to Tartarus."

"How?"

Lucius smiled sadly, putting a hand on her face.

"Don't you dare," she hissed at him, throwing his hands off her as she started to pull herself back up.

He grabbed her by the arms before she could resist, talking calmly although calamity raged above them. "Anubis once opened the portal to take me down with it."

"Anubis is not here!"

"But your other son is. Both your sons have the power to open realms. All it takes is one of them and an abominable creature's death to open the mouth of Tartarus. We cannot kill the hydra, but you can kill me. I can take it along for the ride."

282

Flashes of David in Romania as she begged him to kill her on the castle floor. Flashes of them in the riotous Upperrealms, incensed as she sunk her knife into his chest. She was not going through that again. "No," she snapped at him.

Lucius smiled, water running down his face, his hair in his eyes. "I suppose you really do love me."

"There is no me without you!" she sputtered in exasperation, throwing his own words back at him as she physically shoved him away.

The ship suddenly lurched in the opposite direction, throwing him back to her. He steadied himself, grabbing her face in his hands. "We have to do this now."

But before Morrigan could argue further, a voice surfaced in her head. She gestured for Lucius to wait as she listened.

Morrigan, I need you to bind Cahira. Dan's voice echoed in her head.

"What do you mean?" she demanded, speaking the words aloud so that Lucius could hear.

We cannot kill this creature, but I can. It's not just a hydra, but the remnants of Jörmungandr, my brother. At its belly is an open mouth wide enough to swallow a creature whole. Once inside, I can turn into the wolf and tear it apart from the inside out, but it will kill me, and Cahira won't let it happen.

"No, she wouldn't," Morrigan murmured. "Daniel, there has to be another way."

There isn't. The wolf killed you long ago, and it's time for you to help me kill it for good. You must all be together to save the realms, but I am not one of you. My only job is to protect her—and I plan on doing just that.

Sorrow came over her, freezing her in place.

Bind her now or she will die too! Dan's voice roared in her head, shaking her back into action.

Lucius searched her eyes, waiting.

"Hold off the creature," she told him. "I must bind Cahira so Dan can end its life with his sacrifice. I must tell Libraean to open the portal."

Already on it, madame. Libraean's saddened voice drifted into her head. *Our Wolf speaks loud enough for me to hear.*

"Go!" she told Lucius.

He catapulted back onto the slick deck and slid across it, this time grabbing Cahira. She nearly sliced his head off in response, but he guided her towards Morrigan, who wrapped her arms around her from the back.

"What are you doing?" she screamed as her sword clattered to the ground, falling into the water as the boat gave another violent sway.

Morrigan took a deep breath, focusing on the water around them to steady its waves, creating a funnel that surrounded her and Cahira. Please forgive me.

"Let me go!" Cahira screeched as she fought her, digging her elbows into Morrigan's ribs.

Lucius and Sandrine continued to chop at the hundreds of loathsome, snapping heads. Morrigan watched Dan hoist himself onto the edge of the ship, searching for the creature's snapping belly. He threw his sword to Lucius before turning to look at Cahira. His voice was so loud and clear, Morrigan heard it in her own mind.

Cahira, as soon as I descend, turn me into the wolf.

Although Morrigan had immortal strength on her side, she struggled to hold Cahira, who now thrashed with her entire body to escape her grasp. "No!" she screamed.

With burning sapphire eyes, Dan gave her a wistful, I love you, and with nothing more, he jumped down into the belly of the beast.

The sound Cahira made jarred Morrigan to the core. "Cahira, turn him or it will be for nothing!" she cried.

"Veniunt ad me lupum!" she sobbed.

Morrigan watched as the hydra abandoned its ceaseless lunging, its heads twisting and tangling with each other as it let loose a screeching wail. A swirling tempest began to churn around it, the portal ready to open.

Lucius ran towards it to assist, throwing his arm over the edge and slicing across his flesh so that his black blood fell freely into the stormy waters. The struggling portal responded immediately, the hydra continuing to shriek and thrash as it sunk, as hundreds of skeletal hands reached out to drag it back to its home.

Cahira hung limply against Morrigan as she cried, Morrigan now holding her against her chest for comfort rather than bondage, the water she surrounded them with returning to the sea. The scent of Cahira's damp hair reminded her of when she was a child, filling her with such pain she trembled. She looked up to see Lucius pull back his bloody arm as the creature sank, the portal swallowing up its latest prize.

And then, the waters stilled.

Sandrine rushed over to them, her stoic face distorted by empathy, as Cahira's wails were the only sound left, echoing across the placid waters.

Morrigan felt heat suddenly radiating from Cahira's skin, forcing her to release her grasp. Yet Cahira did not move, shaking with sorrow and anger as the air around them grew hot and heavy.

"Morrigan." Lucius's voice reminded her that she was his granddaughter without saying so. She complied, stretching her arms up to the sky to blanket her daughter with cool rain, putting out the fires that raged within her...just as she'd done for him.

It was Sandrine's turn to embrace Cahira, lifting her up from where she sat and guiding her back down into the hold.

Once they descended, Morrigan released her own emotions, standing still on the deck as black tears added themselves to the water streaming down her face. She wept for it all—for Dan's death, for Cahira's heart, for knowing that Cahira would never forgive her, for David, for Lucius, for the creatures, the humans, the dying gods. She didn't even fight Lucius's embrace as he came up behind her, holding her firmly against him. He didn't speak, only kept her upright as she let herself fall apart.

Her eyes caught the threatening clouds accumulating above her, knowing the boat couldn't handle another storm. She calmed her breath, swallowing her emotions back down where they came from. Lucius released her, turning her gently around to kiss her forehead.

"It was his choice to make. She will understand one day."

"Since when did you become the one who calms me down?" she teased half-heartedly. She found herself enjoying his soothing warmth, suddenly wanting him to continue holding her until she fell asleep. But something in his face had changed, and he looked right past her as if he'd seen a ghost.

She turned around slowly to see David standing in the rain, staring at them in bewilderment.

He met her eyes. "What did I miss?"

PARIS, 1761
LOUIS

L OUIS STOOD AT THE WINDOW OF HIS OFFICE, staring out into the woods that lay beyond the chateau. Though it hung low, the sun was still in the sky, offering him precious moments of solitude before its descent would rouse Angelique and her motley crew of creatures from their chambers.

He pulled out his pocket watch to check the time. In less than an hour, he would no longer be human. He would never again sleep, nor eat, nor see again the light of day. He would be bound to the darkness, a slave to a thirst he could not understand. He had been preparing for it his entire life, yet now it seemed so frighteningly unknown.

He sighed, putting the watch back in the pocket of his breeches. It had once belonged to the Marquis, stolen after Angelique killed him as the final part of their plan to take over his name and his property. Louis had trusted her judgement for years, ever since she took care of the son he'd murdered, encouraging him to take his place. He had no reason not to believe her. She even looked like the woman he had dreamed about since he was old enough to remember, who brought him comfort as a motherless child.

He hadn't realized he was wrong until one day, around the age of fourteen. She stayed at his chateau more often than not, but would occasionally retreat back to her city home, which served as the headquarters to the Galère. He found ways to occupy his restless mind, amassing more books than could fit in his library, going for long rides on his horses or creating puzzles for his servants to solve. He especially had a fondness for animals, feeding the stray cats and dogs that wandered up to the house, sprinkling the garden with seeds for the birds. His favorites were the crows,

287

beautiful sleek creatures who waited patiently for whatever leftovers they could salvage after the strays had long retreated. Eventually, he started to feed them their own meal afterwards, setting out chicken eggs and the scraps of raw meat he snuck out of the kitchen when his servants weren't looking. It soon became a game to him, creeping around the watchful eye of his tempestuous bodyguard, Kali, who surely would have scorned such a thing. Soon the crows began to recognize him, several clustering on the ledge of his bedchamber's balcony around feeding time, squawking their reminder.

On that particular day, they'd arrived later than usual, just as the sun crept below the tree line. He opened his grand balcony windows to step out, happy to see that five had gathered in wait, admiring their shiny black feathers and their intelligent eyes as they studied him. They startled as he drew closer, and as they flew away, he heard a hiss coming from behind him.

Angelique stood in his room, both her clenched knuckles and face white with rage.

"What's wrong?" he asked her, both in confusion and alarm.

Angelique's teeth gritted as she spoke, "Why on earth are you feeding those horrible creatures?"

"Horrible?" Louis had never seen her so angry before. It twisted up her face, robbing it of its beauty. In his dreams, she had always been surrounded by crows, often with no distinction between where her raven hair ended and their feathers began. He couldn't imagine why the sight of them upset her so.

"This is all the more reason why I need to move in here with you full time. Kali has told me you've been sneaking out when you think no one is watching to feed the animals. You must cease this foolishness. You will one day be a vampire—a king! Animals and humans are our food source, not pets to play with!"

"Forgive me," he whispered, casting his eyes down to the floor with shame.

She sighed. "I came here to tell you that my spies at the palace have informed me the king's heir apparent has borne another son. This is wonderful news, since we will have full control over this child, unlike our struggles with the first. It will be a much easier swap after we kill the rest of them. That being said, I will be moving into the chateau this week. Although this new revelation has bought us time, we will be increasing your lessons or there will be no way we will be able to pass you off as king. As of this moment, you will no longer be permitted outdoors. Once you have turned, the sun will be your enemy, anyway, it's pointless to enjoy it now."

He didn't have an opportunity to reply, for she turned on her heel and flounced out. She whipped back around before reaching the door, however, throwing a bony finger his way. "And if I see one more damned crow on this balcony, I'll eat it myself." And with that, she left, leaving a trail of her rose perfume behind her.

Louis could almost smell the stifling concoction now as the memory faded. It had changed as of late, an earthy scent somewhere between the rainy woods and a freshly lit log on the fire as her manipulation tactics switched from matronly to seductive. She had yet to visit his bedroom since he'd grown into manhood, but he knew it was coming after his transition. He wondered if he'd still be able to maintain the ruse as artfully after he changed.

He blinked, realizing the sun had disappeared. "Tell me again about how this works," he asked the apparition seated on the leather chair nearest to the window as his eyes soaked up his very last sunset.

"It will be painful, but brief. But I believe it is the only way to ensure your strength and longevity in the years to come," Thoth explained in his gentle voice. "Do not be afraid, Louis. You have done this once before."

Louis turned to face him. He was a serene god with long tapered fingers and delicate features that once peeked out from behind a crown of ibis feathers. He'd removed it over time, exposing closely clipped curls and a narrow nose that held up glasses to aid his kind, but beady eyes. He'd also begun to mimic Louis's style of dress, as if he'd realized his godly visage was no longer needed the longer they were friends. "And you are sure that I will remember her once I see her?" he asked him.

"You once made Ares with your own blood," Thoth reminded him. "As it is returned to you, you will remember who you are. It may not be all at once, but hopefully I will still be able to reach you before I return to flesh. I have watched memories return to others as I guided them."

Louis sighed again, growing more anxious as the minutes ticked by. "My only worry is if I can keep up the charade until it is time to leave."

"You did end up rising up from an orphaned servant boy into a power-ful Marquis," Thoth pointed out with a smile. "And in your past life, you convinced an entire kingdom you were a prince. It is what you excel at. Besides, power hungry creatures are often blinded by their own agenda." He winked at him.

"Yes, yes, apparently I was quite the monster in my own time."

"Unfortunately, you were always wise beyond your years, making it difficult to best you. I do not believe Angelique is of the same temperament."

Louis was quiet. The last bit of color dropped from the sky, forcing the day into night. He swallowed. It was time.

Thoth rose from his chair. "I know this is a lot for a young man to bear," he offered gently. "I am sorry to be the perpetual harbinger of unpleasant news."

Louis gave him a small smile. "Even if you didn't contact me, I've long sensed that Angelique is not who she claims to be. I have also had the strange foreboding that I have lived other lives before this one, long before you visited my chambers."

Thoth nodded. "I must take my leave of you before they rise. Be well, young Louis. I hope to see you again soon."

Louis nodded, silently hoping he too would see his strange friend once again.

No sooner had the ancient god disappeared was there a knock at the door. "Louis," came Kali's graveled voice. "It is time for your transformation."

Louis looked out his window one last time, this time to see the silhouette of a giant crow against the sapphire sky. He was startled until he caught its eyes. "Tell her I'm going to find her," he whispered.

The bird let out a low roll from its throat, much like a deep purr, the sound immediately bringing him comfort.

"Master Louis." The voice behind the door grew sharper.

Louis adjusted his ascot and ran his fingers through his raven waves, before he withdrew from his room, never to be human again.

Revelations

❧

The Ancient Ones Trilogy
BOOK III
COMING 2022

H<small>E AWOKE WITH A START.</small>
  He immediately reached up to feel his face, his fingertips meeting a prickle of a beard spread along his cheeks. A breeze colder than he'd remembered from his last time on earth came through the opening of the shabby tent he found himself in. The sound of men conversing drifted in with it, along with the smell of freshly dampened earth and meat cooking over a campfire. He took a moment to let everything sink in. He'd finally done it—he had taken over the body of a human.

He lifted up his fur blanket to see pale muscular legs dusted with freckles, his shirt streaked with mud and grime. The clothes the man had fought in were hanging up to dry, a variety of weapons and boots laid sloppily underneath pacross the earth.

A soldier appeared at the opening of his tent, speaking to him in Gaelic. Lucius tried to focus on the language he'd thoroughly studied but never spoke, realizing the man was telling him there was food ready if he was hungry. He grunted his thanks, observing his voice was low and graveled.

He waited until the man disappeared before rising from his sleeping area and throwing on the clothes. He shivered, realizing the fur he was sleeping under doubled as a cloak. He grabbed it, as well as the man's sword, before strapping his boots to his feet and withdrawing from his tent.

Although the night was crisp, the many fires crackling around him brought warmth to the camp, some men with tents, some content to sleep under the stars. They seemed to be enjoying their moment of rest, letting him know the battle recently fought had been won. No one questioned him as he made his way past them, heading towards the black woods that hummed not far behind them. The moon was dark, but the sky was filled with stars, casting their glow onto the barren tree branches. This world was much different than he remembered, the wind robbed of heat, the incessant buzz of mosquitos replaced by the low, throaty hoot of owls, the ground soft and covered in green. He understood why she'd chosen to live there, it was magnificent.

It took a moment for his eyes to adjust to the total darkness as he entered the woods, finding a tree stump to sit on. He slowed down his thoughts, closing his eyes and imagining her, just like he'd summoned Cerberus so many eons ago, focusing on her eyes and the feel of her hair.

"I was wondering when you'd summon me."

Her voice was unmistakable, causing him to jump to his feet. But the woman standing behind him was not the lithe, almond skinned Nephthys he remembered, but a woman who was petite, but rippled with muscle, her pale skin interrupted by dark blue tattoos. Her jet-black hair was short and wild, contained only by the diadem of corvid bones that lay across her forehead. She was dressed in a tunic that had been split into two, revealing her ribs and hip bones, an angry spear in her fist and a black bird perched on her shoulder. She was scowling at him, but in that moment, all the anger he'd felt towards her melted away as he looked into her eyes, for they were the same radiant blue as his wife's.

"You'll be needing to do more than just stare, Cuhullin, if you want my help," she said coldly, reminding Lucius that she was seeing a Celtic warrior, not him.

"Forgive me," Lucius stammered, hoping he wasn't stumbling over the language. "What must I do to earn your favor?"

She snorted. "You do not need my favor. You were so confident in your own strength before, why petition me now? Have you lost faith in yourself?"

"Perhaps," Lucius said carefully. He hadn't realized the body he'd chosen to invade would be a warrior that she disliked, and he deeply regretted the oversight. "I had a vision that I should summon you and ask for your forgiveness," he lied.

"I will bestow my blessings as I see fit," she told him. "Not because you suddenly want to repent for the slight made against me."

Lucius tried another avenue. "Where is Daghda, your husband?"

Her face darkened. "Daghda no longer has interest in war."

"Ah, well your blessing means more to me than any other god," he said quickly.

Morrigan narrowed her eyes. "You are a vile human," she chastised him with her finger. "Any human that mocks a crone does not deserve my blessing."

Lucius sighed, realizing he'd need to take a completely different approach. "I have a confession I must make."

Morrigan raised a dark eyebrow, the movement rattling her crown of bones.

"I am actually a god trapped in this human's body," he told her. "The human summoned me here to help him win his war, but when I arrived, he used Druid magic to entrap me."

"I thought your eyes looked peculiar," she murmured as she came up closer to him, searching his face.

"Forgive me for the deception, I was not sure if you would be a friend or a foe," Lucius explained, trying not to lose focus as her scent drifted into his nose, a richer, smokier version of what he'd breathed in during their days together. His rational mind scolded him, furious at how weak he'd suddenly become in her presence, their tumultuous past gradually fading away the more they spoke.

"Aye, it makes sense that you did," she nodded. "Unfortunately, you are in a detestable body. It belongs to Cuhullin, a hero to the humans. He is Lugh's son, so I cannot be rid of him, but he's offended me many times. I long for the day I can watch him die."

"Then I regret being trapped in such a vessel."

She studied him for a moment, her hand settled on her hip bone. "I will help you," she decided.

"What about the other gods?" he asked.

"I work alone."

He had trouble containing his surprise. "Even without your husband?"

Anger suddenly lit up her eyes. "Somehow you surmised that I am the strongest god nearby, and you summoned me accordingly. I am making the decision to help you, but if you speak any more about the husband I left far behind me, I will gut you like a fish."

Lucius blinked, thoroughly taken aback. Not only had she become more deliciously combative than when he'd known her, but she had left Osiris. His mind spun at the possibilities. Perhaps he could remain in this human's body and be with her again. It wasn't a desirable shell by any means, but he could work around it. He thought about Isis waiting in the Underworld for him to return—perhaps she could figure out a way to bring them back to earth, as Osiris and Nephthys had done. She would chastise him for even considering being with Nephthys again after how much pain she'd caused him, but she'd eventually come around. It's not like he could blame her if she did protest—logically he knew he was a damned fool, but at the moment, he did not care.

"Are you alright?" Morrigan asked.

"Yes," he mumbled. "It just feels strange to be here."

She laughed. "Yes, but it is a wonderful realm, is it not? Do you feel the cold breeze on your skin, the fresh air in your lungs? 'Tis perfect. Come, I will take you to a friend who can help you. You can tell me about yourself as we walk."

"Oh, forgive me, I am Hades, King of the Underworld."

She stopped in her tracks, and he watched a shadow cross over her face, as if his words reminded her of something. He held his breath, hoping she wouldn't realize who he really was. Not yet, he thought, just give me a bit more time.

"You are the second creature I have met who spoke to me of this Underworld," she told him. "On the battlefield, after the fight had ended and only the crows were left to feast, I saw the ghost of a man who wanted to know why I had abandoned the Underworld. He was greatly upset, telling me I was supposed to take care of the souls there. I never heard of such a place before, and now in two separate instances, it has been mentioned."

Lucius hoped his face didn't betray his confusion. "I am surprised you are not familiar with the Underworld. I thought all gods have knowledge of the realms."

"No," she admitted as she resumed her pace. "My first memory is when I woke up on earth, covered in mud."

"You have no memories of your lives before?"

"I was told it was the Druids who brought us to life," she explained.

"It is said that all of us have souls from different realms, and that Daghda and I once lived in one together, centuries ago. Yet I cannot recall any of it."

"Strange," Lucius commented as they moved deeper into the woods, crunching through sticks and fallen leaves. "Well, the Underworld is quite beautiful in its own right. The work serves me well, but I do miss the feeling of sun on my face."

"You were on earth before?" she looked up at him.

"Long ago," he admitted. "But only the desert where there is parched earth and dusty air."

Suddenly she grabbed his arm. It took everything in him not to scoop her up in response. He couldn't believe he'd spent such a long time away from her and still the incessant desire remained. He tried to replace it with memories of his death in Egypt, recalling his hatred, but it was fruitless, the pain diminished over time.

"I remember the desert," she whispered, her eyes wide. "I remember leafy palms and falcons soaring through the clear skies. How can I remember that which I have never seen?"

"Perhaps once you have taken me to see your friend, you could ask one of your Druids for help?" he gently suggested. "They seem to be the ones who have the magic in this realm."

"Aye…" she murmured, letting go of his arm as she walked ahead of him.

"So, you knew the man whose body I am in?" he asked, trailing after her.

"Yes, he was a detestable man," she told him with a sneer. "I am a shapeshifter, which is what I use when I need to work amongst the humans. An old woman had her farm ransacked, one of her cows stolen. So I took on her form and stole the cow back from those who snatched her. Apparently, I was on Cuhullin's land, and he chased after her, threatening her life. When I shifted into a raven, he let me go and begged for forgiveness."

"Which you did not give him," Lucius smiled.

"Of course not," Morrigan huffed. "How despicable to steal an old woman's cow, then threaten her when she takes back what is rightfully hers?"

"Well, I would never want to be on your bad side," he remarked. Then he added before he could help himself, "One would think the humans would be falling over themselves to win the favor of such a beautiful goddess, especially one so deadly."

She stopped dead in her tracks. "You should not play with me," she warned him. "I have not felt the touch of a man in a very long time."

Lucius met her eyes, his resolve instantly gone, his blood screaming to touch her, but before he could step forward to obey, they were interrupted by a loud rustling in the bushes. He turned to see a giant sartyr with a long, scraggly beard and a pair of antlers that arched up out of his skull. The creature grinned as soon as his eyes fell on Morrigan, and the old familiar pang of jealousy promptly lit a fire in Lucius's stomach.

"The Phantom Queen," the creature greeted her. "What brings you into my woods?"

"I am in need of your skills," Morrigan gestured towards Lucius. "My friend is a Greek god, trapped inside the body of the human who summoned him. Can you help him be free of it?"

The woodland god crossed his arms as he looked him over. "Yes, I can help you, Hades of the Underworld," he addressed him. "I am Cernunnos."

"Cernunnos does not hail from these lands," Morrigan explained, "but he travels through all the woods in the North, keeping watch on what transpires in the wooded realm."

Lucius kept quiet. He was certain the creature knew who he really was, but for whatever reason, he was not betraying his identity. He knew that meant one of two things—that he was afraid of upsetting Morrigan, or he wanted a favor in return for his silence.

Suddenly her gaze was pulled up to the sky, her crows accumulating vociferously above her. "The battle has begun, and I am late," she realized.

"I can take things from here," Cernunnos assured her as he took a seat on a nearby boulder, his massive weight sending up a cloud of dust and dried leaves.

Morrigan drew in towards Lucius, so she was standing mere inches apart. "You can find me before you go back, if you'd like," she said with a salacious glint in her eye, before she abruptly transformed into a crow, departing in a flurry of black feathers. He stared wistfully after her as she disappeared, almost forgetting there was an oversized satyr seated nearby.

"Does she know who you really are?" the god interrupted his thoughts.

Lucius frowned. "If you know who I really am, why did you tell her I was something different?"

Cernunnos gave him a shrug. "I want no godly discord in my woods. There is enough of that between the humans. I know all about you, that you are a dark god banished to Tartarus by his own wife and brother. I wondered when you would discover there was a tear in the realms and come back. They created it when the Druids brought them here."

"How do you know?"

"I am Lord of the Forest. I see all that transpires on the earth."

Lucius crossed his arms. "Well, you may have figured out my identity, but I am only here because I found a way to possess a human."

"Ah," Cernunnos smiled under his bristly beard. "But now you know how to rise up properly."

Lucius was mystified. "Why do you help me?"

Cernunnos shrugged again. "I do not like her husband."

Lucius grinned. "Then I appreciate your aid."

The woodland god rose from where he sat, the effort filling the forest with the sound of creaking trees. "I assume you know how to get back to your realm," he stated, rather than asked, as he headed back into the darkness from where he'd emerged. Lucius watched him go, his antlers disturbing the skeletal branches as he lumbered beneath the treetops. He sighed, resting his hands on his hips. He longed to go after her, but he knew that although he'd find temporary solace and release in her arms, he would be deceiving her by using another man's body, something she would never forgive him for. He wanted to make love to her because she wanted him, not because she was tricked into it, and definitely not with the cumbersome body of some red-haired oaf that stunk of aging dirt with too large of feet. Besides, now there was another way. "I will come back to find you," he whispered up into the night sky. Then before he could talk himself out of it, he released the human from his clutches, his soul diving back down to the Underworld.

Discover more from this author at
www.quillandcrowpublishinghouse.com

CPSIA information can be obtained
at www.ICGtesting.com
Printed in the USA
BVHW070931291021
620251BV00005B/121